TORNGAT

A novel

By

J. Richard Wright

Torngat is a work of fiction. Names, characters, places and incidents are the products of the author's imagination or are used fictitiously. Any resemblance to actual events, locales or persons living or dead is entirely coincidental.

However, having said that, in this work and some other works by this author, there may be a one or more precipitating events which happened personally to the author but did not involve other individuals.

ISBN Number: 978-1535362023
EAN Number: 1535362022

All rights reserved - Publisher: Createspace

Visit **www.jrichardwright.com** for author info and ordering hard or soft copies.

Book cover creation and design by: Sherron Moorhead – www.motivationgraphics.com

Other books by the author:

- *The Plan* (Now available on Amazon.com & Amazon.ca)

Note to Readers: Thank you for reading my second novel **Torngat**. In the ever-changing world of moving books to readers, an author figuratively lives or dies by Reader Reviews. By writing an Amazon book review you help me gather readers so I can keep writing. If you buy my book and write an Amazon review, contact me with your <u>address</u> via my web site: **www.jrichardwright.com** I will then mail you a personalized bookmark for each book you purchase and review. A caution: One star selected means poor and five stars means good. Offer ends July 31, 2017.

Canada Printing

For Sue and Heinz Rautenberg,
Whose caring, compassion and generosity
Has made life so much better
On the home front.

ACKNOWLEDGEMENTS:

==

First and foremost I wish to thank my dear friend, Sherron Moorhead, artist, graphic designer, and worker of virtual magic for the creation of a striking cover for *Torngat*. In doing so, Sherron not only brings her technical skills into play, she also draws on her artistic soul to find, select and blend just the right elements to deliver an intriguing representation of my novel. The result is that she has served readers: a generous helping of mood, a strategic serving of information, and a subliminal but healthy dose of curiosity and anticipation for what lies beneath. While some say you can't judge a book by its cover, Sherron's work makes us take a fresh look at that adage.

And thank you to the real Robert D. Moorhead who did a beta read of *Torngat* four times and aggressively stomped out those typos and non-sequiturs, questioned anything that did not seem factually accurate, and made suggestions, gratefully received. Bob is either a closet masochist or my best friend to take on this task. Indubitably, it must be the latter.

In addition, I wish to thank Captain Gordon A. A. Wilson, 414 Squadron (Electronic Warfare/Retired), Canadian Forces Base, North Bay, Ontario, who provided invaluable aviation and military info, graciously reviewed the in-flight intercept protocols, and helped render an accurate account of how a supersonic engagement would occur between friend and foe in the Labrador night sky. After six years as an RCAF fighter pilot, Gordon flew commercial airliners until 2000. He then embarked on authoring three books of his own: *NORAD and the Soviet Nuclear threat*, *Lancaster Manual 1943*, and *The Lancaster*, all available on Amazon.

In Northern Canada, Nunatsiavut to be precise, help in making *Torngat* accurate came from the kind and patient Janice Goudie, Customer Experiences Manager, working out of Goose Bay Labrador, and Gary Baikie, Parks Canada Superintendent for the Torngat Mountains National Park. Both generously answered questions regarding weather, seasons, and Torngat Mountains. Of course, the writer took artistic license with *Castle Peak* and the *Plains of Pharsalus*. The former location exists under a different name on Baffin Island, Canada, and the latter location resides solely in my imagination.

While many people provided much-needed information for *Torngat*, all errors and omissions are strictly mine.

And a posthumous thank you to my amazing parents, Harry and Olive Wright, who moved our family to Menihek, Labrador, in the early 50s where I embarked on the great adventure of growing up in a five-family settlement. From age six, my father, an adventurer in his own right, taught me to safely hunt, fish and survive in the drizzle and black flies of summer, and the -60°F temperatures and blizzards of winter. In addition to delivering much love and life lessons, my mother ensured I never forgot my manners despite our remote setting. Thank you both for your faith and courage in letting me shoulder my Mossberg rifle and explore the rivers, lakes and forests of the Labrador wilderness. In doing so, I had the privilege of often walking where no other human being had ever set foot before. However, as long as I was back in time for supper, all was right with our world.

To Jerome St. Onge & family from Schefferville, Quebec, where, as a young man, I read hydro meters on the Reservation for the Iron Ore Company of Canada: Thanks for the hot tea, the stories and the friendship on those sub-zero, winter days. And, also, thank you for the many moccasins which you sourced for me; one set hangs with my snowshoes on my wall today.

And, finally, a big thank you to my other beta readers in order of literary consumption, and who also made valuable suggestions regarding the manuscript: Lorna Stone (always my first and most loyal reader); Sue and Heinz Rautenberg; Diane Underwood; and, of course, the person who always reminds me I'm no smarter than anyone else, and yet *still* gives me tons of love, ideas and support – my precious and much loved Sandi.

Thank you all.

Prologue

December 26, 1981
2200 Hours
Torngat Mountains, Labrador, Canada
Canadian Air Defence Command CF-101 at 20,000 Feet

Canadian Forces Air Defence Command Squadron Leader David Corrigan pulls his CF-101 Voodoo all-weather interceptor in a tight 180-degree turn and heads southwest again, his wingman following him through the blackness of the subarctic night sky. Through the intercom he hears his Airborne Intercept (AI) Navigator, nicknamed SO, lament in the rear position: "Dave, it's gone again!"

"Half-pint Control, Delta Lima zero two missed intercept, request new vector heading, over." Corrigan speaks slowly and deliberately into his radio mic, despite his frustration about being jerked all over the night sky looking for the bogie. In all likelihood, it's simply ice crystals or the Aurora Borealis playing tricks on Canadian Forces Station Saglek Control, and the North American Air Defense Command's (NORAD) radar.

The controller responds: "Delta Lima zero two, continue turn heading zero four five, target fifty miles at angels three five, speed 2,500 knots!" Suddenly the controller yells: "My God! It stopped dead."

Corrigan calmly acknowledges the transmission: "Wilco, target heading zero four five, climbing angels three five, out." He eases the control column to the right, applies pressure to start turning, and rolls out on heading zero four five maintaining a steady climb of 6,000 feet-per-minute to angels three five. This proves they are chasing the Northern Lights. Speed of 2,500 knots? Not bloody likely, he thinks. Stopped dead? Impossible!

SO radios from the back seat: "This will take us right over the Torngat Mountains, Dave. Might even be a little bumpy at angels three five. Hell of a winter storm forming down there." He ceases transmitting for a few seconds and when he resumes, his voice shakes with excitement. "I have it on radar again, we're heading right for it…closing fast…it should be on our starboard side, one o'clock high in about twenty seconds." There is a momentary pause and then: "Bloody hell!"

Corrigan throttles back to 300 knots in amazement at what they are both seeing; the jet reluctantly slows in its climb. As they approach their target, now almost at stall speed, he sees a spinning, circular craft easily 300 feet in diameter and at least 60 feet thick. It floats in the air, lit with a blue light from inside; the light somehow penetrates a metal-looking hull giving it an incandescence unlike anything he's ever seen in his ten-year military career.

"That's no Bear," his AI Nav says confirming the obvious. What they are seeing isn't what they expected: a Soviet TU-95 Bear bomber.

The radio crackles to life. "Delta Lima zero two, do you see what we see, over?" Captain Michael Boyd inquires. Boyd is Corrigan's wingman flying in loose deuce formation with him. He is also in a Voodoo fighter.

"Roger, Delta Lima zero five…. arm weapon systems and let's overfly it for a couple of miles and then return, circle it to starboard and see if it displays its intentions, over."

"Roger, out."

"Delta Lima zero two, half-pint control, have you identified the bogie, over?"

Corrigan thinks long and hard before he answers. It's been clocked at 2,500 knots, is stationery in the air with no visible support, and has stopped on a dime whereas the resultant G-forces would kill any normal *human* pilot. Despite the only conclusion he can draw, he decides against editorializing; instead he offers a description. Trying not to sound overly dramatic, he laconically drawls: "I have a disc in sight, over."

His radio remains silent for a full minute. Finally the controller responds carefully: "Delta Lima zero two, please confirm. Did you say you have a *Santa Claus* in sight over?" Corrigan doesn't reply for a full 30 seconds, busy circling the craft. Yes, it is what the military and NASA term a "*Santa Claus*" – or an extreme unknown. It spins silently at 35,000 feet without benefit of jet propulsion or rotors to keep it aloft. Nothing in the military or commercial field can do that, he knows. And if the military had something as sophisticated as this craft under wraps, it certainly wouldn't bother spending billions of dollars to keep thousands of bombers and jet aircraft war-ready as a defensive deterrent. Finally, he clicks his radio button: "Roger, Half-pint Control. Bogie is stationery. But, now that we've caught it, what the hell do we do with it, over?"

Squadron Leader Corrigan's CF-101, accompanied by his wingman, continues in an elliptical orbit around the stationary craft hovering in the night sky.

"Delta Lima zero two, Senior Director requests visual description, over."

"Roger…we have a stationary, metallic-looking disc about 60 feet thick and 300 feet in diameter. It appears to be seamless and lit from within by some form of blue light, over."

"Standby, Delta Lima zero two…Deputy Commander NORAD on the phone."

"Roger," Corrigan replies, with a calmness he isn't really feeling. He can hear the tenseness in the controller's voice.

They are past the disc again and he moves the stick to the right, rolls the jet on its side and pulls to tighten the turn for another pass. He has to be careful in high-G turns since the tail can be "blanked out" by turbulence from his wings causing the nose of his fighter to pitch up resulting in loss of control. In a few seconds they come streaking back, and again whip past the huge, blue metallic craft sitting in the empty air as though suspended from a skyhook. Corrigan eyes his instruments, checking his six pack including the heading indicator, airspeed indicator, attitude indicator, altimeter, vertical speed indicator, and turn & bank indicator. He continues his scan taking in his oil pressure and fuel gauge. All are behaving normally. And he still has more than 7,000 pounds of fuel aboard. The world is as it should be. Except for the weird sci-fi scenario outside his cockpit. Time for another turn.

The craft neither attempts to move away nor react in any way to their presence as they approach again. On closer inspection, Corrigan sees that it is actually spinning and yet the light surrounding it seems to remain motionless, like a blue gauze covering. What the hell is it and where did it come from, he asks himself? Every *Strange Tales* comic book he's ever read is coming to life before his very eyes. Is this intercept the vanguard of contact with beings from other planets? Is this a historical event that will catapult mankind a thousand years into the future with new technologies and knowledge that might even bring peace to mother earth? After all, when aerial phenomena are usually chased by North American forces they generally zip away or simply disappear. This one is sitting there as though waiting for a signal from the jet.

He and his wingman continue to orbit about the craft shooting by at 300 knots and then turning as swiftly as possible for a return pass. Corrigan feels the G forces in the tight turns. To prevent blood fleeing from his brain and blacking out from lack of oxygen, he holds his breath and bears down. This maneuver forces blood from his lower extremities back into his head. The turn complete, they roar through the night sky back towards the disc. Each time they complete a 180 degree turn, he fears the craft won't be there on their return. However, the blue light continues to pulse and then grows in size as they fly towards it.

The full moon is off to their starboard side as he rolls into another tight turn. The jet heels over once more coming round in a heavy G-force turn. With the aircraft standing on one wing he looks down and sees the Torngat Mountains far below; the greyness of the Labrador Sea borders the rough topography gouged out to form an insane maze awash in moonlight. The valleys are deep, black and almost non-existent, while the snowy peaks of the mountains shine blue-white in the pale light of the moon. His gaze drifts back to the visible coast and the moonlit sea. Next stop, Greenland, he thinks. Looking northeast he sees a heavy mass of clouds forming. SO is right; major winter storm action down there.

This could very well be his last flight in the Voodoo, Corrigan further muses. The veteran CF-101, nicknamed the *One-oh-Wonder*, is on the chopping block, giving way to the newer McDonnell Douglas CF-18 Hornet. He and his navigator are scheduled for Hornet flight training the following month.

Corrigan and his wingman continue to circle the craft that remains motionless except for spinning inside the light. This is a historic event, he reasons. Here for the first time, they may be about to communicate with some form of extraterrestrial beings and offer understanding and camaraderie. This could be a unique opportunity to unite the world. Indeed, earth's political differences would seem puny compared to whatever is in that saucer-shaped craft. Finally, he thinks, the Cold War will never have a chance to heat up. Countries will gather together to present a united and friendly front to these new entities. The mere fact they have made it to earth shows they are, at least, technically superior. He is excited by the possibilities.

His radio crackles again. "Delta Lima zero two, Half-pint Control. NORAD has confirmed its initial orders: Engage target immediately and confirm, over!"

Squadron Leader Corrigan can scarcely believe his ears: "Control, say again, over."

"Delta Lima zero two, you are to destroy the target immediately, please confirm, over."

My God, he thinks. Are they insane? Shoot it down without attempting to signal or contact it in any way? The craft hasn't displayed any hostile intentions. It's just *there*! But he has little choice. "Roger, Delta Lima zero two engaging, out."

The two fighter interceptors head back towards the craft again; it's a sitting duck a few miles away. He looks back at his barely visible wingman. "Delta Lima zero five, remain clear, I am going to engage target, over."

Corrigan's wingman radios his affirmative, and quickly peels off to circle back and still be in a position a few degrees off Corrigan's six to back him up if needed. Corrigan does a wide 360 degree turn to gain another minute to plan his attack. Approaching within a few miles of the spinning craft, Corrigan is waging an inner battle with himself over his orders. He doesn't want to shoot it down when it hasn't done anything to warrant an attack, but orders are orders. Now he wishes the damn thing would just disappear. "C'mon, c'mon…" he mouths aloud. "Take off, eh!"

The craft sits silently, innocently spinning in its blue light.

Corrigan flashes his landing lights on and off, hoping it will notice him and get the hell out of there. Nothing happens. He flicks the fire selector switch to guns on the Hughes M-13 integrated fire control system. Target dead ahead. He brings his four 20 mm M39 single-barrel revolver cannons to bear, ready to send the disc plunging into the mountains below. His choice of machine guns over the more lethal Falcon AIM-4D heat-seeking missiles to mitigate damage is a certainly a passive-aggressive approach to his orders. Still, it's one within his choice. Deep down, despite his in-grained military discipline, Corrigan has always been an independent thinker. Right now, his gut tells him this is all terribly wrong. For the first time in his military career he knows he is going to do something totally out of character. From the back seat he hears SO switch on his mic and say nothing; he merely clears his throat. As longtime partners, they can practically read each other's minds. There is agreement in the cockpit.

With his speed throttled back to 285 knots, he lines up for his run. He hears the cheeping in his earphones: Target acquired. He only has to press the firing button and it will all be over. Or, maybe just beginning if that thing takes offense at him trying to shoot it down. Only God knows the reaction they might engender from the craft. Visions of *Star Trek* space battles pop into his mind way too quickly.

From the rear position, SO has nothing to do at this point since the guns will be fired by Corrigan visually in a curved pursuit attack.

Still, Corrigan has no choice. He has to fire. But, in the last instant before he hits the firing button, he realizes he doesn't have to *hit* the target. Abruptly he pulls the jet slightly upward and fires a quick burst over the top of the saucer. The staccato of his machine guns rumbles through the jet. The tracer shells cast a path of gold, liquid fire reaching into the ink-colored night sky over the saucer.

Almost immediately a beam of sparkling red light shoots out from the craft and envelopes the entire jet. Amazingly the CF-101's speed drops off as though it has ploughed into a huge mound of Jell-O. Thrown against their restraining straps for almost ten seconds, the pilot and navigator experience the jaw-clenching G forces of an abrupt de-acceleration. Finally they slap back deep into their seats. Their cockpit instrumentation lighting has begun to wink off at the same time the Voodoo's Pratt & Whitney J57 turbojet engines spool down to silence.

Bathed in the sparkling, fire-red light emanating from the cobalt blue disc, the sudden quiet is the loudest stillness Corrigan has ever heard. Momentarily he seems to exist in a frozen vacuum, a bizarre contortion of existence somewhere between a dream state and reality. The pilot has less than three seconds to realize his jet aircraft is now stationary in midair and he is losing all his systems. He stares uncomprehendingly at the alien craft as SO yells a confused epitaph from the navigator's position. Then the blue spinning craft, and the jet attached to it by the red beam, drop like a stone towards the mountains below. They disappear from their altitude in less than a second. The last thing Corrigan ever hears from his crackling and dying radio is his wingman desperately yelling at him: "Dave…SO…for God's sake…where are you…where did you go? Mayday, Mayday, Mayday!"

PART ONE

DIAMONDS IN THE SKY

*Like buried treasures, the outposts of the universe
Have beckoned to the adventurous from immemorial times.*
George Ellery Hale 1868-1938

~1~

50 Miles southeast of George River, Nunavik Territory
The Present

The Bell Huey helicopter appeared as just another mosquito in the sky. It slipped over the distant ridge of the almost treeless terrain stretching for miles, and dropped abruptly into a valley painted gold and black by the yellow rays and dark shadows cast by the setting sun.

The pilot flew low more out of boredom than anything else. He certainly didn't have to worry about obstacles in the Ungava hinterland. Stunted spruce trees, areas of arctic lichen, caribou moss, arctic lupine, Labrador tea, tufted saxifrage, and nests of stubborn buttercups dotted the tundra; nothing grew over a few feet in height. Northern Ungava and Labrador was like that as you left the tree line behind in favor of the great rock sheets of the Canadian Shield. Some plants had taken more than a quarter of a century to grow to their present height of a few inches. October's end now signaled that the vegetation would soon hibernate under a deep blanket of snow.

Geologist Matthew Corrigan stepped out of a once-white canvas tent now mottled and stained with grime and mildew. A square aluminum plate was stitched to its roof through which a round, tin, stove chimney poked spouting blue wood smoke. Beside the tent was a muddy ATV, a lineup of white-tagged, two-foot high canvas sacks, and a woodpile covered with a plastic sheet held down by rocks.

Outside the front flap of the tent stood a much-used fire pit under a triangle of iron stays from which a soot-covered copper kettle dangled. On a flat rock nearby sat a grease-stained Coleman stove. He swatted at an ensemble of thirsty mosquitoes that immediately swarmed him; ducking away he managed to elude them for a few seconds.

But the bugs seemed to have temporarily vanished merely to seek reinforcements; they returned with a bloodthirsty vengeance diving into his eyes and buzzing in his ears. He sincerely regretted stepping outside the tent to finish his meal.

Just a shade over six feet, Matthew had blue eyes that seemed bluer because of his deep tan, and a mop of brown hair that now badly needed cutting. His reprieve from the insects didn't last and he soon resumed swatting them as they attacked his half-finished plate of spaghetti and wieners. He stared up the valley as the distinctive sounds of the copter became audible. The tent flap opened again and his partner Stan Peck joined him. Peck had dark hair and eyes, and a five-o'clock shadow that refused to disperse no matter how hard he shaved. They stared off towards the copter as its faint stutter grew louder.

Both men were dressed in heavy twill trousers, wool shirts and had kerchiefs tied tightly around their necks to help reduce the number of mosquitoes and black flies getting under their garments. Each also sported an ex-army issue .45 caliber pistol in a formed leather holster hanging from a heavy leather belt. Prospecting in wilderness terrain yielded many surprises such as curious wolf packs, and hungry and unpredictable bears.

The difference between the wolves and the bears was that the wolves would assess their potential as victims and generally wind up choosing to avoid humans. A hungry bear just considered people one more menu item.

So there was little to worry about with the wolves. However, Peck had emptied his pistol into a Barren-Ground Black Bear the previous spring when it turned aggressive and got between him and his .303 Lee Enfield rifle; an attack was imminent so he'd had no choice. Fortunately, he'd hit a vital organ and narrowly avoided injury or death. The bear wasn't so lucky.

While both men liked exploration, they were getting tired after two weeks of conducting ground studies to follow up on the results of an airborne geophysical survey that indicated the presence of kimberlites; kimberlites signified the possibility of diamonds. Lined up beside their tent were rows of samples in heavy canvas bags that they would bring back to George River for testing. If successful, the next stage would be to proceed to core drilling with the results tested for the presence of micro or macro diamonds. More positives would lead to mini-bulk sampling and even bulk sampling, all of which involved the very expensive importation of drilling and earth moving equipment. But that was getting way out in front of where they were presently. So far, despite many positive signs, nobody had found diamonds in Labrador.

"What the hell?" Stan asked, gazing at the copter. "Our ride isn't supposed to be here for another day at least."

"Maybe it's a Leap Year," Matthew replied. He stretched an arm back in an effort to remove a kink from his shoulder.

"It's October."

"So sue me…it's a theory… like evolution."

"Oh man, don't start that again," Stan groaned. Two men living in an exploration tent in the wilderness for weeks at a time yielded ample opportunity for debate on many subjects.

"Well, we haven't finished taking samples from the north ridge," Matthew said, helping himself to another fork full of spaghetti. "Wonder what's up?"

Stan ducked back into the tent as the Bell Huey helicopter thundered over their camp and paused, its rotors sending air curls downward causing the tent to flap madly and strain against its ground spikes. Matthew ignored the wind and waited as the pilot spiraled down the last thirty feet and bumped his steel skids firmly onto the tundra, barely 100 feet away. The engine wound down and he jumped out of the cockpit. Ducking his head low, and holding his ball cap secure, he trotted over to where Matthew was standing. The geologist nodded, lifting his plate slightly; he didn't recognize the pilot.

From the tent, a falsetto voice: "Tell him I'm never leaving this paradise. Never, I say!"

Matthew grinned at the pilot, "Poor fellow is bushed."

The pilot nodded, returning the grin. "Matthew Corrigan, right?"

Matthew nodded, they shook hands and the pilot dragged out a letter from his pocket. "I think you're going back with me."

Setting the tin plate down on a nearby flat piece of shale, Matthew tore open the envelope. It was from Andre Jacquard, the President of *Labrador & Ungava Diamond Explorations.* It was an invitation to meet with him at the company's head office in Montreal in two days – barely enough time to get there even if he left immediately.

Stan exited the tent and shook hands with the pilot. "Allan Way, new guy, long-time-no-see," he said, with a smile. "Last time you were working out of Wabush."

The copter pilot nodded.

Wabush and its close-by settlement, Labrador City, featured iron ore mines off a spur line halfway up the QNS&L rail line between Sept-

Iles and Knob Lake.

"Hi Stan," he responded. "Labrador & Ungava Diamonds made me an offer I couldn't refuse. Guess you heard they finally mothballed Wabush?"

Peck nodded. "China and India steel consumption slows down and the price of ore drops like a stone. Not sure relying on this globalization crap has been good for us. Someone half a world away sneezes and we get pneumonia."

"True enough," Matthew agreed. "Guess we have to find markets on other worlds. He waved the letter. "Stan, I've received a royal summons to Montreal. El Presidente."

"For when?"

"Now," the pilot interrupted.

Stan lifted his eyebrows at Matthew: "So what's up?"

"No idea," Matthew replied, shrugging. "I only met the man once when he cut the ribbon on our office."

Their office was essentially a large plywood 40 x 40-foot shack with foot-thick insulation back in George River. Perusing the letter, Matthew mused: "You'd better come back with us, Stan. They don't like singles out here alone."

Stan waved a hand dismissing the company rule. "What they don't know won't hurt them. I'll finish over there tomorrow morning. Al here can pick me up around 1400 hours if that's okay with him. Besides, without you aboard tomorrow, we can take all the samples back in a single flight." He looked to the pilot who peered at the rows of canvas bags beside the tent and nodded. "We'll take half of them back now."

"Okay," Matthew said. "Put the gravel and rock sample bag I brought back last Sunday aside. I want to have it tested later. Really. I'm serious."

Stan looked at the bag Matthew indicated. It was different from the others as it had a red tag attached. He grinned: "Your personal rock collection, is it?"

"Just don't lose it."

Matthew had taken the ATV some days ago and travelled to an area he'd spotted on one of their flights in. He'd been curious to explore what he believed to be an ancient, dried-up creek bed and had brought back some quartz and other gravel samples for his own satisfaction. He wanted to personally have a better look at his material back at the company ore testing lab. Accordingly, Stan had carefully labeled the bag: *Matthew's Rock Collection.*

The two men shook hands. Matthew packed his personal gear and within an hour the helicopter landed in a vacant lot in George River. It was about one hundred and fifty feet from the *Labrador & Ungava Diamond Explorations'* headquarters. Matthew leaped out with his duffle bag and thanked the pilot. He made his way over to the office as the noise of the rotors increased and the copter took off again to land at the nearby airstrip. A rough, hand-painted sign over the entrance shortened the name to *Labrador & Ungava Diamonds*, an abbreviation that worked far better for its people.

The plywood and shingled building was composed of an ante room crammed with tents, poles, sleeping bags, Coleman lanterns and stoves, boxes of dehydrated food (preconfigured by a nutritionist to satisfy the requirements for a hungry two-man crew for a week's outing) and other assorted camping and mining gear.

Cases of Deet and OFF mosquito repellent were piled against the wall along with bags of mosquito netting. Old butter boxes were stacked like a giant bookcase against another wall and contained pointed-tip, chisel-tip and other rock hammers, hardness picks, chisels, compact shovels, leather toolkits, geo-rock bags and regular canvas knapsacks. A dozen rain ponchos and down parkas hung on nails over lines of both rubber and work boots. Stacks of leather gloves and paper-banded wool socks were stacked in one corner. Finally, in another corner stood a rack containing an assortment of high powered rifles and boxes of ammunition acknowledging that this was, indeed, a wild and dangerous land.

Standing in the doorway, Matthew stamped his feet on a mud-encrusted matt to remove any loose sediment from his boots, a salute to the janitor who swept the floor at night with a broom and a shovel.

The office itself offered five desks, two drafting boards, numerous chairs and stools, and assorted tables piled with instruments and stacks of papers. Some smaller tables against the wall supported an array of short-wave radio gear, two personal computers and two large microscopes. Transits standing in various corners and a row of metal filing cabinets completed the furnishings. Surveying and color-coded surficial geologic maps, interspersed with *Playboy* fold-outs of golden, airbrushed-to-perfection girls, covered almost every inch of the walls. The radio crackled with cross-talk as two helicopters and a de Havilland Norseman ferried men, supplies and samples back and forth onto the tundra. Not a hint of lace or chintz anywhere; this was, without doubt, a man's world.

In the office, five of these men hustled about trading papers and sticking colored pins in wall maps. They examined data from air surveys on their computers and, with the touch of a button turned the data into colored graphical representations integrated with area maps. The company was already drilling core samples at two sites and they were hoping for a third.

As Matthew entered the office, the men all took the time to pause in their duties, look up and wave. He waved back at them and shrugged out of his jacket.

"Hey, Mr. VIP, you got the soil and stream samplings with you?" Chief Geologist Brian Hawkins called to Matthew, getting right down to business. Hawkins was a fit looking mid-forties man of six-foot, three-inches clad in dusty tan chinos, a red tartan wool shirt and scuffed engineer boots. The getup, immensely practical in the north, was almost uniformly adopted by the other man except for shirt colors.

"Half of them. Stan will bring the rest tomorrow when he comes in," Matthew answered.

"Tomorrow? He should have come back in with you. I told Al two trips if necessary."

"It's one night, Brian. We still had a section along the north ridge to finish. Besides, Stan says bringing me back early means he'll bring the rest of the samples and the gear in one more trip. No half loads."

"Yeah…okay," Hawkins answered, grudgingly." He moved to a drafting board and used a T-Square to connect some lines. "What's up with you and the boss?"

"No idea," Matthew said, with a shrug. "Did he say anything?"

"No, we never talked to him or anyone else from head office. Letter came in on the sched flight." The sched flight was a weekly DC-3 flight that brought supplies from Sept-Iles. Mail usually consisted of personal letters, magazines and newspapers since most company communications were conducted by satellite-supported email. The appearance of a letter from head office marked *Personal & Confidential* had caused much speculation amongst the crew.

"Then how do you know there's anything up with me and the boss?"

Hawkins gave him a look as though he'd just failed kindergarten. "Cause we steamed open your letter, Einstein. For Christ's sake, do you think we're mind readers here?" The ghost of a grin lit up his usually somber face as a chorus of guffaws came from the rest of the exploration crew.

Matthew merely smiled. "Children!" he said. "I'm working with children."

<h2 style="text-align:center">~2~</h2>

The Air Canada 737 touched down at Montreal's Trudeau International Airport at precisely 7:10 PM in the evening, bounced twice and then settled into a smooth roll on the tarmac as the two jet engines went into reverse thrust with a roar; passengers felt their seat belts cut into their midriffs. The aircraft hadn't stopped taxing when, against the instructions of the flight attendants, passengers leapt to their feet and began opening overhead baggage compartments.

Matthew looked at his thirty-something travelling companion and smiled. His seatmate, Monique Boivin, a pretty blond with a Crest-strip smile, also kept her seat. They had shared conversation during the flight, taken several politicians to task and even did some mild flirting, mostly on her end. Now their short-term relationship was about to end.

"I bet the herd will grab all the limos and we'll have to take the shuttle into Montreal," she said.

"Better than being caught in a stampede," Matthew answered. "Perhaps we could share a taxi; if we can find one?"

"But of course." Shyly she looked away. "I am staying at La Hotel Bonaventure."

"Well, I'm not sure where I'm staying yet," Matthew said. It was true. He hadn't booked a hotel. Likely his company had already done him the honor.

Monique was suppressing a grin. "One hopes you can find a room?"

"If not, I'll have to rely on the kindness of strangers," he replied automatically, and immediately chastised himself.

What the hell am I saying?

"I'm sure some stranger will be kind to you," she replied, a tiny smile on her lips. "A drink later, perhaps?"

With her invitation on the table, Matthew suddenly felt deep regret. He wasn't in any shape to start a relationship, however brief. And yet, here he was, out of the North for a few days and this beautiful stranger was already hinting she'd like to know him better. He felt his stomach sinking and wondered if he had unconsciously led her on.

Matthew had always been fortunate with the ladies with his rugged good looks coupled with a quiet strength that manifested itself in a presence few could ignore. When his wife Helene had first told him how attractive he truly was, even to strangers, he had blushed modestly and told her she was full of blarney. Blissfully unaware, he ignored the obvious realities of his good fortune and stated that a human being's worth couldn't be measured by an accident of birth; it was what was inside a person that counted.

"Excuse me, Mr. Corrigan?" He looked up to see a flight attendant leaning over him with a small piece of paper in hand. She smiled. "This was just delivered when we opened our doors. I doubt you'll decipher the writing but it's from a Mr. Andre Jacquard." Hesitantly she straightened up and read from the paper. "He's sent a car and has booked you into the Château Champlain. It's imperative he see you in his office as soon as you…we…land. Which we have," she finished lamely."

The flight attendant handed him the note with a flourish. She was right. It wasn't exactly calligraphy; more like a doctor's scrawl. Smoothing her navy blue uniform, she half turned on her heel then rotated back. "Air Canada hopes you had a pleasant flight" she said, with a grin. "If there's anything further I can do…?" Catching a glare from Monique, the flight attendant quickly drew her professional shroud about her and began squeezing her way back to the front of the plane.

"Monique…." He began.

"Duty calls?"

"Yes." He sighed, actually much relieved. "Sorry."

"Perhaps we will meet some other time," she ventured tentatively, now seemingly unsure of how interested he really was.

"That would be very nice," he lied, now sorry he had given the wrong impression.

"I'm sure it would be," she said. They scrawled email addresses on scraps of paper.

Parting at the baggage carousel, Matthew received an impulsive but perfunctory kiss on the cheek. He sighed. Surely she sensed his insincerity and any potential ardor was already on life support. Oh well, in his world, there never was hope of anything developing beyond the aircraft cabin. At that moment, he noticed a driver holding up a sign reading *Corrigan*. He looked for Monique to offer her a ride but she had already disappeared. I'm getting the royal treatment, he thought as the driver took his bags. Something is up for sure.

The drive into the heart of downtown Montreal was uneventful except for the French driver actively listening to *Hockey Night in Canada* on Radio-Canada. Well-lit expressways surrendered to city streets and skyscrapers peppered with lights, both which seemed almost surreal thanks to his recent time in the darkness of the North. The cabbie let off a tirade after every goal scored by a Bruins' player against the Canadiens. He then seemed to feel some angry compulsion to pass every other car on the road.

"Hey Dale Earnhardt …slow down!" Matthew said in annoyance. At first he always felt nervous at the seemingly excessive speed on freeways when he rejoined urban civilization. Twenty miles an hour in the North was perfectly acceptable on pothole-cratered gravel roads.

"My name is Mario," the driver replied.

"Well I'll bet your last name isn't Andretti, so cool it."

"Sorry, Monsieur."

"That's okay…I'm a Montreal Canadiens' fan too."

Arriving at a converted historical building in Old Montreal, Mario shook his head when Matthew asked for the fare amount. "We are on contract with Labrador & Ungava Diamonds."

Matthew peeled off a ten dollar bill and passed it to him anyway. "Vivre les Canadiens de Montréal," he said, and with a smile, grabbed his flight bag from the seat beside him, crossed the small sidewalk and entered the building. A security guard consulted a list and checked him through in the deserted lobby where he took an elevator to the third floor. Pushing through glass doors gauchely emblazoned with a picture of a large diamond ring, he was surprised to see a receptionist sitting at a desk in the waiting room. She was grey-haired, early 60s he guessed, and obviously impatient to get home. It was well past normal office hours.

She looked up at him, sighed in relief and grabbed her coat and purse. "I'm Mary and I'm off," she said. "Mister Jacquard will see you in the inner sanctum and I get to go home to a cold dinner, a pissed off cat and TV reruns. Why he insisted I stay, I'll never know. Like he can't answer a phone himself?" She fled through the open office door, and Matthew could have sworn he heard the words: "Rat bastard..." murmured on her way out.

"Mary, you ole witch, you gone yet?" boomed a deep voice from within. "Corrigan? You out there?"

Matthew entered Jacquard's cavernous office. After the sparseness of the subarctic and his own plywood playground, he was slightly taken aback by the rich walnut paneling, the brass fittings and the oversized cherry wood desk nestled in a beige carpet so plush that it desperately needed a good mowing. One wall offered a bookcase with multiple glass doors behind which sat hundreds of leather volumes, most with gold embossed titles suggesting a single set. The opposing wall featured a backlit bar with an Olympic-size selection of liquor bottles.

"Sit down, sit down," Jacquard said, not bothering to rise to meet him but waving towards a pair of leather chairs in front of his desk.

He leaned across and shook Matthew's hand. His grip was surprisingly strong as was his liquor-tinged breath. Matthew sat back and took a moment to appraise the president of Labrador & Ungava Diamonds. Meanwhile the man patted his pockets and looked about as though he had lost something. Realizing he was ignoring his guest, he shrugged and smiled at Matthew.

Jacquard was a small man with close-cropped grey hair and a bulbous, spider-veined nose suggesting the spirits lining the wall were there for more than show. He wore a worsted brown jacket, blue shirt and a wool tie loosened at the collar. Each hand sported two gold rings inset with what Matthew supposed were real diamonds of various colors from sapphire blue to yellow to pure white. He had a reputation as a self-made man with sharp elbows who fought his way up from a very modest existence, and generally got what he wanted by hook and sometimes crook.

Early in his life, some smart real estate investments had made him a multi-millionaire. After that he'd entered the mining industry doing very well through purchasing and re-opening a supposedly defunct gold mine in Val D'Or, Quebec; he moved on from there.

Unfortunately, he had left a trail of broken partnerships and severed alliances along his career path but always seemed to come out on top himself. His latest venture, however, had eaten up substantial capital which he had hoped to recoup through an IPO supposed to have taken place the previous week. Being on exploration on the tundra, and not having time to catch up on the news, Matthew didn't know if he had successfully taken his company public or not.

Right now the man was preoccupied as he leafed through a personnel jacket on his desk, grunting every few seconds. He stopped at one page and stayed there for a moment. "Royal Canadian Air Force?"

"For a time," Matthew admitted.

"Why'd you leave?"

"Started with irregular T-waves on an ECG. I was flying CC-130 Hercules. They grounded me for medical reasons."

"Too bad," Jacquard said. Both knew he couldn't have cared less. "So you went back to school again and got a Masters in Earth and Planetary Science majoring in Geology...blah, blah, and blah...also mineralogy. Let's see, you worked for the Ministry of Lands and Forests before you came here. Your heart bother you now?"

"No, it straightened itself out while I was still in the RCAF. I was reactivated to flying status but it was time to leave the service anyhow."

"I never have to worry about heart trouble," Jacquard declared.

"No?" Matthew inquired politely.

"Naw, you got to have one to have trouble."

Jacquard guffawed to himself and then yanked a desk drawer open and withdrew a small object which he slapped down on his desk with a sharp rap and pushed it forward. Matthew was relieved to see the desk sported a thin sheet of translucent plastic over the polished wood as protection. "Ever see a baby like this?" the CEO inquired, gruffly. He pulled out a well-cured meerschaum pipe from the same open drawer and began stuffing it with Erin Moor mixture from a small, rectangular yellow can. He lit it and studied Matthew's reaction. "I'm no expert but this could cut up to, maybe an eight-carat gem, barring unforeseen surprises. A diamantaire can give us a better idea of its potential."

Matthew turned the rough diamond over in his hands and whistled in appreciation. It was almost pure white on one side, an octahedral shape with rounded points and ribs. A small feather inclusion extended a few millimeters into the body, but that could be trimmed yielding an impressive amount of gemstone to work with. He guessed at what was surrounding it; probably an iron or iron-nickel alloy in which the diamond was stuck. Matthew whistled. "Where did it come from?"

"From up where I'm spending a lot of dollars having you fellows scratch around in the dirt and find nothing," Jacquard said. "An old Indian guy, a Montagnais named Jerome St. Onge, walked in here, and plopped it down on my desk. He said I should send Matthew Corrigan up to Nain, Labrador, to see him if I wanted to know where this originated. He refused to say any more. Just looked me in the eye and said: 'Matthew Corrigan, no other man'."

"Why me?" Matthew asked in surprise. He searched his memory for the name and drew a blank.

"That's what he said," Jacquard answered. And then in a more suspicious tone: "How do you know this St. Onge fellow?"

"Know him? I've never met him."

"Really?" Jacquard asked. His tone was calculating, almost oily. Clearly he didn't believe his employee.

Matthew shook his head. If Jacquard had a mustache he'd be twirling it now, he thought.

The man picked up the rough diamond. "Look, this thing is certainly worth at least five figures, if not six. If it's cut properly, that is. And he just leaves it with me? How did he know I wouldn't keep it?"

"Perhaps he knows you," Matthew said honestly.

"What do you mean?"

"Well, you're a businessman. He figures you'll comply with his request since he's the only one who knows where he found this gem."

"You mean I'm too greedy to settle for one diamond?" He was puffing furiously on his pipe now to keep it going.

Matthew couldn't help smiling. He shrugged: "That's your interpretation."

"He also said that if you're willing to come to Nain, to accept this as his gift."

"What do you mean, gift?"

"He said *you* could keep the diamond."

"Why?"

"I don't know. You're the guy who doesn't know him. At least you claim not to know him."

"I'm not acquainted with Mr. St. Onge and I've never been to Nain."

Jacquard grunted and settled back in his chair. He didn't say anything for a moment, letting everything percolate as he thumbed a gold butane lighter again and began sucking on his pipe. Clouds of blue smoke circled his head. "So...when can you leave?"

"Back to George River?" Matthew asked.

"Hell, no!" Jacquard exclaimed. "Haven't you been listening?"

"You want me to go after some old gentleman in Labrador, someone I've never met? Someone who shows up in your office with a diamond that could have come from anywhere? Does he even know what he's found? It's value?"

"I don't know," Jacquard said, waving his hand around to take in his office. "I think I'd better enlighten you on a few realities of this business. Despite these trappings of wealth, unless you find some evidence of diamonds in Labrador, my next office is likely to be in a Porta-Potty. Not even a *new* Porta-Potty. We cancelled an IPO this week, and two of our largest backers have given me until the end of the year to show results or they're pulling out."

"I didn't know Labrador & Ungava Diamonds was in trouble," Matthew admitted, surprised and even a little shaken by the revelation.

"Of course not. You guys up there just go about your work and collect your big salaries from *Labrador & Ungava Diamonds'* money tree." His pipe had gone out. He lit it again and threw both feet onto his desk. "Look, it's not your fault we haven't located kimberlitic pipes on our acres so far...but we've have found indicator minerals for the region. It's only a matter of time until we get a positive yield. Unfortunately our time to find them is finite. We'll crash and burn on January 1st of next year. That's about 60 days."

"So you really want me to meet with Mr. St. Onge?"

"Yeah. And find out where this beauty came from so we can do an online claim stake and tie up the rights."

"Does he know that's what you intend to do?"

"I don't really care. He didn't look stupid. He comes to a mining company and tells them he knows where there's a huge diamond find. What does he expect I'll do? Stay home and knit?"

"But you intend to offer him a share?"

"Sure, but look at it from my side of the desk," Jacquard said patiently. "I'm sitting here looking at a shutdown and possible bankruptcy and suddenly this old medicine man –."

"Medicine man?" Matthew interrupted.

"Yeah, he said something about that – medicine man, shaman, or spirit man – whatever the hell he called himself. Anyhow, suddenly Tonto rides up and throws a big, bad-ass diamond at me and says he needs to see Matthew Corrigan up there in Labrador. Now what do you think I should do? Say, no thanks and move into the Porta-Potty? Or send my man out to have a look-see? Hmmm…let me cogitate on that for a bit." Again he puffed aggressively on his pipe, glaring at Matthew all the while.

"Alright," Matthew said. "You're the boss. So, he asked specifically for me." He picked up the diamond to examine it again.

Jacquard quickly stretched across the desk to take the rough stone from Matthew and then abruptly withdrew his hand. "That's worth a small fortune. But, apparently it's yours."

Matthew shook his head. "We'll see about that. Meanwhile you keep it safe."

Jacquard paused, looked longingly at the diamond and then at Matthew. "You know how to make a small fortune in the diamond business?" he asked.

"No," Matthew answered.

"Start with a *large* one," Jacquard said.

Amused, Matthew handed the diamond back. "You're the boss."

Jacquard carefully placed the gem back in his drawer. He sighed and said: "Thanks. Just go meet the bloody guy. But keep it quiet. And get some results. I'm not enamored with the aroma of crap in my office, eh?"

~3~

Matthew called back to head office the next morning to ask Jacquard if they were providing him with travel services or should he make his own arrangements. Mary, the receptionist, told him Jacquard was out catching a last round of golf with some investors and city officials but would be back after lunch. However, she had put together an itinerary and purchased tickets and accommodations. She booked him in Nain for three nights.

"You'll be staying at the Menihek Lodge," she said. "Lucky for you they have space because they only have 25 rooms. But understand, these are northern accommodation, nice, clean and friendly but don't go expecting the Queen Elizabeth Hotel."

"You forget I work in the North," Matthew answered. "What about the flight?"

Mary laughed. "Flights, you mean. I'll fax your itinerary to Château Champlain, care of Room 1010…or do you have a laptop with you?"

"Yes, email it. When do I leave?"

"Tomorrow morning," she said. "You'll take Air Canada from Montreal to Sept-Iles and pick up a *Labrador Adventure Air Services* cargo and mail flight the next day. They run along the Quebec North Shore and up the Labrador coast to Nain. You'll fly in the right seat of a de Havilland Beaver but you're going to be landing at every little piss-ant settlement all the way up the coast."

"C'est la vie," Matthew sighed. "What about the return?"

"We've no idea how long you'll be there, so Mr. Jacquard said to grab whatever return flight you can find and report back here. If you need to spend more than three days, he'll cover it of course. Oh, he also wants to hear from you right after you've met with Mr. St. Onge."

Matthew thanked Mary, hung up, sat back on the bed and opened his laptop to check his mail. Within a few minutes he had his itinerary from her. He would pick up his tickets at the airport the next morning. The rest of the day was his, although he sort of wished it wasn't.

After a breakfast at the coffee shop, he took a cab to the familiar suburb of Verdun. He paid the fare, tipped the driver five dollars and disembarked on Melrose Avenue. It was a typical older Montreal suburban street with rows of almost century-old flats running up and down on both sides. Many had been converted into condos. Standing in front of his former home, he felt a familiar depression returning. He was under no illusions. This was the reason he stayed in the North as much as possible. Still, it would be cowardly not to return and see how Helene was faring.

He mounted the porch and rang the bell for the upper flat. Footsteps quickly descended a flight of stairs and the door opened. Helene stared at him.

"Oh, it's you," his wife said quietly and without surprise. She hadn't seen him in eighteen months.

"Hello Helene, I'm down for a day or two and thought I'd see how you're doing," he explained.

She was as pretty as she'd ever been. Chestnut hair trimmed short, figure still without an ounce of fat, and beautiful olive skin derived from her Italian heritage. The only thing missing was the light of life in her hazel eyes. It had been cruelly extinguished almost three years before on a lovely spring afternoon.

They'd both tried to keep going after the accident but it soon became apparent they'd be better off if they went their separate ways. He'd resisted the breakup but she persisted. In the end he reluctantly agreed to the path she had chosen.

"Where are you staying?" she inquired. Her voice was distant and disinterested.

"Château Champlain."

"Have you been up to the cabin?"

Helene was talking about the family cabin they had purchased in the Laurentian Mountains five years before. The family had spent summers there hiking, and swimming in a nearby lake. And, winter had been especially fun with them all snow-shoeing, tobogganing and skiing together.

"Not this trip," he replied. "At least, so far."

"I received the papers in September, thank you. I signed them and sent them back. We should be officially divorced in a matter of weeks I think."

"Okay," he responded heavily. "May I come in?"

"I suppose." Without another word she started back up the stairs. He followed her up into the flat, down the center hall and into the familiar living room. The furniture hadn't changed. The TV set was on in the corner near the window, the volume low. It was tuned to Sesame Street, their daughter Chantal's favorite program. A book was open on the arm of an overstuffed chair they'd bought at the Hudson's Bay Company. It was a weekday so Helene likely had never returned to her law practice. Not that she needed the money now.

He looked about foolishly hoping their daughter would round the corner at full tilt as usual and rush into his arms. Instead, the quiet of the apartment was broken only by the shrill, far away laughter of joyful children responding to a treatise on a letter of the alphabet. A grandfather clock ticked in the corner. Matthew swallowed; he turned to find Helene watching him.

"I hope you aren't here to ask me to reconsider," she said softly, even kindly.

"No," he said. "I gave up on that a long time ago."

"So why are you here?"

"I don't know...." His voice broke and he used every ounce of his inner strength to keep his emotions in check. "I just wanted to see how you are." He paused. "Money?"

"Not an issue." She said it bitterly. "You know the amount we settled for. Have you accessed it?"

Matthew shook his head. The settlement with the amusement park had been well into the low seven figures. Half had been deposited in an account for him. "I don't want money. I want my daughter back."

"You think I don't?"

"I never meant it that way. I wanted to tell you that..." his voice trailed off. "I mean, I'm sorry. I'm so sorry."

"You weren't responsible, Matthew. I'm trying to heal. Unless you forgive yourself, you'll never heal."

"I shouldn't have taken her. You wanted us to wait for a week or so. That damned park should have tested those new bolts *before* they put people on that bloody ride!" His hurt was replaced by anger. He forced himself to calm down. "This isn't helping anyone. I'm sorry I came. Didn't mean to reopen the wound."

"I'm seeing someone." She said it flatly, without enthusiasm.

He was surprised. "Who?"

"Nobody you know. He's a physician. He understands and accepts me for who I am now and what I've gone through."

He couldn't help but feel irritation. "My God, I accepted you. As my wife! I tried to help you. I tried to help us both."

"You couldn't help anyone, Matthew. You were broken too."

Helene was right. The worst period of his life came rushing back.

Chantal had been four years old when overseas industrial counterfeit bolts, used on an amusement park ride, snapped resulting in her death. A later investigation showed they weren't up to standard; their tensile strength couldn't withstand the torque placed on them. Shoddy workmanship and steel that hadn't been fired properly to guarantee its integrity meant the centrifugal force of the amusement park ride caused them to fail. In the ensuing violent reaction, Chantal had been torn from her harness and flung from the ride. Matthew, screaming in terror, vainly tried to adjust his grasp on her hand before she vanished from their seat. Now, three years after the accident, it was as fresh in his mind as though it happened yesterday.

Whirling, whirling...snap!

Hanging on for them both at the time, he could still feel his tenuous grasp on the tips of her fingers slipping before she plummeted to the ground. The torture and guilt ate at him like a cancer, fed by a question he asked himself a million times: If he'd let go his grasp on the harness immediately, could he have saved her? Or would they both have flown out of the spinning car? And, wouldn't that have been better? Though he knew the answer to that one, it provided little solace.

So here he was trying to give comfort to Helene. Instead, as his emotions ramped up, it seemed a counterfeit attempt at best. He was the one in need of comfort.

"I'll leave," he offered.

She placed a hand on his arm. "We had a good marriage, Matthew. But nothing could survive what we went through. And a marriage, at best, is always a fragile thing. Thank you for filing the papers. Very soon it'll be final. Please go on and make a life for yourself. Find someone else, someone who can help you." She led him down the hall and opened the door.

He descended the apartment stairs towards the front door, Helene following. With a huge lump in his throat, he stepped out on the porch and turned towards her. She remained halfway hidden behind the door, clutching it close, almost using it as a shield. "Please don't doubt that I love you any less," she said. "But we have no future together. The guilt, the regrets and our sorrow were destroying us. Chantal wouldn't have wanted that to happen."

"Chantal would have wanted her mother and father to be together, to remember her and find a way out of the hurt."

Helene shook her head sadly. "We tried for more than a year. We couldn't do it. For God sakes, you have to let it go. I'm sorry but that's all I can tell you. Now please, Matthew, don't come back here again." Softly she closed the door on their life together.

Realizing he hadn't called a taxi, he sat on the front steps to regain control of his emotions. He could imagine the neighbors speculating on what he was doing back home, but he really didn't care.

Within a few minutes, a cab pulled up. Helene must have seen he didn't have a car and called the cab, he guessed. The passenger window came down as he approached the cab. "Monsieur Corrigan?" the driver questioned. Matthew nodded and opened the rear door, turning as he did so. He saw her watching him with curtains pulled apart. He started to lift a hand to wave but she didn't seem to notice him. She looked off in the distance as though lost in thought. Then she turned away. The curtains closed. Not even a backward glance.

He tried to swallow his disappointment. He had come here for her not for him, he reminded himself. Time to realize that his life in Montreal was no more. In essence, there was no more Helene. There certainly was no more Chantal. And, finally, there was no more family.

He had the cab take him to a Metro store for flowers and then to Notre-Dame-des-Neiges Catholic Cemetery where he quickly found Chantal's grave and stood mutely before it looking at the metal plaque set flush in the neatly trimmed grass. He felt sick. This was all that was left of his beautiful, energetic and loving little girl. The priest's words that everything happened for a reason did scant to salve his anger or mitigate his sorrow. The giant crater in his heart had mended somewhat over the years, of course. But if visualized, he was sure it would have been bloodless, black and scarred. And the ache in his gut remained, as always, pink and throbbing.

He thought of the funeral where the priest had urged everyone to celebrate Chantal's life rather than mourn her loss. The memory was tinged with bitterness. He really couldn't blame the man for trying to help ease the pain but it was like applying a Band-Aid to a major arterial wound. The hemorrhaging wasn't going to stop any time soon. Celebrate her life? She was four years old.

He said three Hail Marys and three Our Fathers as was his custom, and asked God to make her happy and to tell her how sorry he was for failing her. Then he returned to the waiting taxi.

Back at the Château Champlain hotel he took a high-backed, red leather stool at the bar and ordered a Screwdriver. He wasn't much of a drinker but felt a need to deaden himself slightly. Obviously he had blundered again by going to see Helene. She'd made it plain before that it was over between them. And despite her assurances that she didn't blame him for the accident, he knew that deep down, buried somewhere in her subconscious, she blamed him.

Though she had insisted they separate, whenever he returned to Montreal he always felt tremendous guilt for having done so. By fleeing to work in the North, he felt he had abandoned his wife to an unquenchable sadness. Maybe this visit to her would finally allow the message to sink in; she was surviving fine without him. In fact, she had a boyfriend and was moving on. There was no place left for him in her life and all he did was remind her of their loss.

Now, please don't come back here again.

But, if she was doing so well in adjusting, what the hell was Chantal's favorite program, *Sesame Street,* doing on their TV, he asked himself. He hoped she really was seeing someone. At least he'd know she was being looked after. Sadly, he had surrendered that right when he lost their daughter.

"The papers are signed."

"What did you say, Monsieur?" the young bartender asked.

"Sorry," Matthew said. "Just talking to myself." He dropped a ten dollar bill on the counter and went up to his room. His 10th floor view was towards the inner city rather than the St. Lawrence River and he watched traffic flowing smoothly on Rue Peel to intersect with Boulevard René Lévesque. The sun was setting on downtown Montreal casting deep shadows on a small park several blocks up from the hotel. It was painting swatches of gold on the sides of surrounding limestone and brick buildings while illuminating the fall spectacle of almost bare trees and blowing leaves. The red and orange splash of colors in the nearby Laurentian Mountains would be gone by now, he thought. All that would be left would be the bare starkness of deciduous tree skeletons, and the ample spruce trees waiting to be made beautiful again by the first winter snows.

He turned from the window, lay down on the bed and stared at the ceiling. The phone rang. It was Helene. His heart began to pound. Was she calling to say she'd reconsidered? He could tell immediately from her tone that something was wrong.

"I'm sorry to bother you, Matthew. You said you were at Château Champlain."

"No problem," he said, keeping his voice even, not allowing hope to stray into his tone.

"A-After you left something strange happened. Two men came to the door. They said they were from the insurance company."

"What insurance company?"

"The one we settled with."

He was surprised to say the least. "What did they want?"

"They said they wanted to ensure their service was satisfactory."

"What?" he said. "Their service? We nailed their hide to the wall. Why should they care about their service?"

"I don't know," Helene answered. "Actually I asked them the same thing. They said it was a follow-up quality survey. New parameters and processes within their company meant they had to assess their dealings with all their clients."

"We never were their *clients*." Matthew felt his temper rising.

"I'm a lawyer, Matthew. I know all that."

"So who the hell were they? What did they look like?"

"Typical businessmen: dark suits, white shirts and ties. One was a giant of a man, must have been over six-foot-six-inches. They really made me nervous."

"Go on."

"The taller one asked a few questions about us. For background, he said. I answered them. Then he started asking all sorts of questions about you. Were you intending to stay up in the North? How often did you come out of there? Were you doing any flying? They knew you were an air force pilot. In fact, from their questions they seemed to already know a great deal about you."

"What does all this have to do with client satisfaction?"

"Absolutely nothing and I told them so."

"So what happened? What else did they ask?"

"One was looking at a picture of us on the mantle; you know the one, the three of us at Knott's Berry Farm?"

Matthew did and was somehow pleased it was still there; she hadn't cut him out of it or shoved it in a drawer. "What about it?"

"He asked if they could have it for their files. Then he asked me if I knew someone named St. Onge?"

"How did they –? Never mind, what happened next?"

"I said that if they weren't out of here in five seconds, they'd be dealing with the police."

"Did they leave?"

"Yes. But before they went, one guy took out his cell phone and snapped a picture of our photo. At the same time – I think to distract me – the other man got all huffy and said that if I wasn't interested in cooperating I was merely hurting future clients. They got out pretty quick when I picked up the phone."

"Did you call Jean?" Jean Fissette was the lead lawyer in their lawsuit.

"Yes. He said not to worry and he'd call them up and find out what was going on. And he'd tell them if there was any more contact with us, he'd file a harassment suit. He said he'd get back to me after he talked to them."

"Alright, Helene." He read her his itinerary, gave her the number for the Menihek Lodge and asked her to call him when it was sorted out. She agreed to do so, the coolness back in her voice.

"What's going on, Matthew?"

"I don't know," he replied.

"They didn't seem like insurance people. More like police or something."

"When I know, Helene, I'll let you know. For sure. Sorry about this."

After he hung up he lay back down on the bed and pondered what she'd said. Ultimately he decided it had to be a mix-up. Still, they had no right to ask personal questions. In fact, they had no right to contact Helene at all. And, what was that about St. Onge? Where the hell did that come from? At least Fissette wouldn't let it rest. He'd go after them like a hungry pit bull.

Eventually he shrugged off any concern. He also decided he'd better understand what Helene was trying to tell him in plain English. It was over between them. Plain and simple. Time to get it through his head. Time to shelve hope. Time to move on.

Though more restless than hungry, he decided to dine at Montreal's favorite deli, Schwartz's on St-Laurent Boulevard, also known in Montreal as *The Main*. At least there he would be surrounded by sound and laughter and conversation. Perhaps he could lose himself and his lingering sadness in the crowd.

Exiting the lobby, the doorman whistled him up a cab. Arriving at Schwartz's he was happy to find the inevitable lineup only had about eight people in front of him. He hunched his shoulders in his Navy surplus pea coat against the cold wind, and settled himself to wait. As he watched his companions he was reminded again that Montreal truly was a city of love. Young couples held hands, snuggled, kissed briefly and giggled as they waited. The air was alive with the French language and it began to reawaken his limited but valued vocabulary.

When his order came, his smoked meat sandwich was predictably delicious and for a few minutes he did lose himself in the taste and the restaurant's clatter and cacophony. How many times had they come here as a family? How many times had he watched Chantal's eyes widen as he pretended he was about to put hot mustard on her smoked meat? And, she never ate the rye bread, only the meat and the kosher dills, just like her mother. "I have to watch my figure, Daddy," she'd say, mimicking Helene's oft repeated refrain.

His glance wandered to his dining companions, sitting almost exclusively in pairs or with their families. It had always been a happy place. It still was for the other patrons. Suddenly he lost his taste for his sandwich.

He couldn't wait to fly back to the North.

~4~

The Air Canada jet blasted its way into the sky, looped out over the St. Lawrence River and then set a course for Sept-Iles, 475 miles to the northeast.

Matthew grabbed an in-flight magazine which featured several articles about the North. He read as the flight droned on. It lasted slightly more than an hour due to a brief stop-over in Quebec City. Now, as they dropped through three thousand feet, Matthew looked over to his right at the grey waters of the mouth of the mighty St. Lawrence River. It had widened dramatically on its way to the Atlantic Ocean. Mentally he waited for the aircraft to turn from its downwind leg onto its base leg. The turn began a little wide of where he would have made it with his Hercules but his former aircraft had STOL capabilities – Short-Take-Off-Landing – and the Boeing 737 did not. Within a few minutes, the pilot brought them from their base leg onto their final approach, and the airliner soon bumped its tires on the asphalt. Matthew noted they were on Sept-Iles' Runway 24, a 5900-foot-long strip where he'd landed his Canadian air force Hercules many times. Bordering the asphalt, tufts of scrub grass, sand and the occasional patch of snow swept by as the pilot braked and the roar of reverse thrust on the engines shuddered through the cabin.

He had just started reading an interesting article on Sept-Iles itself as they landed at the city airport. The pilot announced their gate was not ready to receive them so they would hold for a short period on a taxiway. This gave him time to finish the article.

It explored the relationship between Sept-Iles' success and how it was linked to the discovery of iron ore in the North. Pertinent since he was staying there that evening. He hurried to get through it.

Sept-Iles now boasted a population of almost 25,000 people. Originally a small fishing village, the rich iron ore deposits found in the Labrador Trough had changed everything in the 1950s. Sept-Iles had become the jump off point for geologists, engineers, drillers, blasters, carpenters, pipe fitters, truckers, heavy equipment operators, and other mining and construction workers travelling the 359 miles north via the Quebec, North Shore & Labrador (QNS&L) Railway up to the mining settlement named Burnt Creek.

The name was soon changed to Knob Lake after a knob of iron ore sitting on a nearby mountain. In turn, Knob Lake was renamed Schefferville, after Roman Catholic Bishop Lionel Scheffer who served as Vicar Apostolic of Labrador until his death in 1966. Though effectively owned by the Iron Ore Company of Canada, the town was incorporated as a separate civil entity for tax and grant reasons.

Everywhere, "Ore by 54" had been the rallying cry as the railway, the Menihek Dam, the town and the mines' infrastructures were built by legions of men working under the worst climatic conditions possible. More freight was transported by Hollinger Ungava Transport, an airline created and owned by the Iron Ore Company of Canada, than had been carried by the famed Belin Airlift of World War II. Up to eight DC-3s, one Lockheed Lodestar, a Canso and a Lancaster bomber, converted to carry fuel, were involved.

The Canadians, supplemented with a post war contingent of immigrants from the United Kingdom, Italy, Portugal, Germany, Greece, and other European countries devastated by WW II, slogged through muskeg bogs, around hundreds of lakes and across treacherous mountains to build the railroad some experts maintained "couldn't be built."

And, certainly the experts said, it was also impossible to build it on budget or on time. This was an era before satellite mapping and parts of Labrador were marked *Unexplored* on maps.

Later acknowledged as pioneer heroes who didn't know they were doing the impossible, the builders of the railroad simply did it. Further, those who opened and worked the mines for the next 25 years were immortalized as men of steel stubbornly tearing iron from the death grip of Canada's subarctic permafrost.

For more than 30 years afterwards, the Iron Ore Company of Canada leveraged the work and sacrifices of the thousands of men who risked their lives to build the railroad, the Menihek Dam, the town and the entire mining infrastructure. In effect, the entire operation had one goal: Dig as much iron out of the ground as possible in the shortest amount of time. Markets were fickle and you had to make hay while the sun shined. The Schefferville iron mines shipped ore south to the newly constructed Sept-Iles' deep water port and ore transit docks. The 125-ore-car trains, fronted by up to four diesel engines and trailing two cabooses, were on the move 24-hours-a-day during production with every other type of train – passenger, freight, ballast and supply – sent off on sidings to give the ore trains priority. Legions of speeders carrying maintenance gangs plied the tracks from Sept-Iles to Schefferville repairing rail line faults wherever detected.

While the many railroad camps along the line had names such as

Seahorse, Waco, Oreway, and Menihek, most were better known by their "mile" designations: Seahorse was Mile 155; Oreway was Mile 186; and, Menihek, featuring a three-generator powerhouse and a hydroelectric dam spanning the Ashuanipi River, was known as Mile 330.

During the 1960s and 1970s Sept-Iles was second only to the western Port of Vancouver in terms of yearly tonnage shipped. While men and equipment flowed north through the port, iron ore ran south to where huge ships moved the ore to smelters in Philadelphia, Baltimore and Rotterdam. After the Iron Ore Company decided to close Schefferville in 1982, only mines in Wabush and Labrador City continued to ship ore via a spur line from Emeril to the QNS&L and then to Sept-Iles. The result was Sept-Iles quieted somewhat.

With the industrialization of China and India, however, and a fresh world need for iron, a new company, Labrador Iron Mines began working the old Schefferville claim area in 2011. The QNS&L, which had been sold for a single dollar to three First Nations' bands, and renamed the Tshiuetin (North Wind) Railway, was again pressed into service. Sept-Iles boomed again in its role as a valuable waypoint.

But no longer was iron the only mineral sought in Ungava and Labrador. Now experts were certain a treasure trove of diamonds, gold and other precious metals were also waiting to be discovered. And there were spin-off benefits to the search for diamonds. While drilling for diamonds in Voisey Bay area of Labrador in 1993, Diamond Fields Resources Inc. had discovered a significant nickel deposit estimated to be 141 million tons at 1.6 percent nickel. Labrador, part of the Precambrian shield, was once again a hot spot for geological exploration.

Matthew closed the magazine as the captain announced that their aircraft had received clearance to proceed to their gate.

After a harrowing ride from another of La Belle Province's cabbies, Matthew checked into Château Sept-Iles, found his room, opened his flight bag and hung it in the closet. He examined himself in the mirror. Knowing he was headed back to the North was almost an elixir.

He washed his face, gargled with Listerine, finished his ablutions and exited the bathroom.

Indeed, he looked better after a good night's rest. His gaze was clear, he had regained some color in his face and his posture no longer portrayed him as having the weight of the world on his shoulders.

He donned kaki chinos, a blue cotton shirt, a beige wool sweater and a brown suede jacket, and headed downstairs and out onto the rather desolate looking street. Anything was preferable to staying in his room where his mind would conjure up images he desperately wanted to avoid. Though he knew it would be a formidable hike, he set off for the beach.

A brisk, early November breeze from the shoreline stirred the sand sprinkling the pavement as he welcomed the fresh salt air of the Gulf of St. Lawrence River in his lungs.

Not a diesel bus fume, nor the ozone-like smell of a streetcar sparking its way along squeaking steel tracks, marred the atmosphere. He breathed deeply as he made his way along deserted streets down to the Sept-Iles' boardwalk and strode along the well-weathered planks. He watched the waves from the gulf break on the rocks and run out on the intermittent stretches of sand. Gulls chased the retreating surf and picked at a bounty of dead, silver-sided capelin washing up on the beaches.

These seven-to-ten inch fish spawned on the sandy bottoms of the estuary. But once they had done the deed, they had a high mortality rate, almost 100 percent for males.

Their corpses invariably washed up on gulf beaches to rot in the sun or provide fodder for other creatures of nature. In particular, sea gulls enthusiastically reaped the rewards of this annual reality and fattened themselves up for the rigors of the usual harsh winter in the offing.

Here and there patches of snow sat in the shadows of sand dunes and rocks as Matthew walked. The wind whipped his pants around his legs and he squinted against the air-born sand granule stinging his face. He spent a half-hour on a boardwalk bench going over his visit to Helene while gazing at a pewter sky.

In retrospect, it had been a mistake. And while he had rationalized the need to check up on her, in some far off corner of his mind, he'd hoped she had reevaluated their relationship and saw what they were losing.

Wrong.

All he'd done was stir up sadness for them both. And she'd made it plain: She had no desire for further contact. For her, relief lay in the reality their divorce would soon be final.

He sighed and walked up to Au P'tit Snack on Rue Napoleon, got a bag of French fries and headed back to the shore where he found a bench and slowly ate.

He waited till he was nearly finished before surrendering his remaining food to the sea gulls. They quickly formed a shrieking, darting, weaving mass overhead; they'd abandoned their work on the beaches for the efficiency of handouts from boardwalk strollers. Depositing the empty bag in a refuse container, he escaped the gulls.

The breeze coming off the grey and choppy waters had become more chilling, an unmistakable message that the big snows of winter were on their way. As the waves and white caps increased in number and size, he began to shiver.

Now flecks of snow were appearing on the wind. Within minutes they grew into big fluffy flakes; time to head back to the hotel.

From his room he called *Labrador Adventure Air Services* and confirmed he'd be a passenger on their coastal mail flight in the morning. He was advised he was the *only* passenger and to be at the airport by 7:30 AM. It would be still dark, the clerk informed him, but they could take off before daybreak even though it would be VFR all the way. Minister of Transport rules only forbade them from landing in the dark. Since daylight was imminent, they were permitted to take off.

Matthew thanked the voice on the other end of the phone and the man said: See you when you get here."

He was about to take an afternoon snooze when there was a knock on his door. A bell hop handed him an envelope. He gave the man a five-dollar bill and closed the door. The envelope had no return address. It was simply marked *Monsieur Corrigan*. He tore it open; a folded sheet of squared paper revealed a brief handwritten note. It was an invitation to have a drink at 9 PM that evening in the lounge downstairs. It was simply signed: "M."

He thought long and hard. The only M who came to mind was Jacquard's secretary Mary. What was she doing here? Had their boss sent her on an errand with some catch-up info critical to his Nain meeting with St. Onge? Why didn't he call? Mary knew where he was; she'd made all his reservations. The whole meeting over the diamond was already strange enough but perhaps Mary had information Jacquard wouldn't trust over a telephone line.

He chastised himself; he was beginning to sound more than a little melodramatic. Nevertheless, if the Innu medicine man was going to take him to the source of the diamond, the information could be worth hundreds of millions – possibly even billions – of dollars. Staking a claim first would mean his company would be able to buy up leases and capitalize on exclusivity prior to anyone else discovering the location.

He found himself yawning and decided on a nap. He'd meet Mary later and get the scoop.

When he awoke, Matthew jumped up in alarm. It was dark outside. Snapping on the bedside light he was relieved to see it was only 8:30 PM. He lifted the telephone and the operator came on: "Oui, Monsieur?

"I'd like to check if a certain guest is registered here," he said, sleepily. "Do you have a Mary–?" Matthew stopped. He didn't know her last name. "Je m'excuse. J'ai fait une erreur."

Quietly he hung up the phone and tried to figure out a plausible reason, one obviously very important, for Jacquard to send Mary all the way to Sept-Iles to intercept him. Surely a telephone call would have been enough? Unless there was more happening behind the scenes than he knew. He began to wonder if Jacquard's story about a mysterious Indian dropping that sizeable diamond on his desk was even true.

He thought about placing a call to Jacquard in Montreal but realized the office would be closed. Quickly he washed his face, brushed his teeth and extracted his navy blue blazer which suited his slightly wrinkled chinos. He hurriedly fashioned a Windsor knot in a red tartan tie. The tie and his blue, button-down shirt made him look presentable. After dark, Quebecers preferred some formality. It wouldn't be the first lounge where he'd been refused entry because he wasn't wearing a jacket. It was an effective strategy to keep a certain ruffian element out of the finer hotels. Finer, of course, was a relative term. Still, miners, explorers and construction workers, travelling to and from the North, had a tendency to over-celebrate when they hit "civilization" or when they were about to leave it. Better dress seemed to remind them to behave.

Matthew stepped into the dimly lit lounge. It offered a 16-foot, classical vaulted ceiling supported by pale yellow walls boasting a plethora of trim, and decorative baroque moldings. Gold leaf framed paintings, dangling cut-glass chandeliers and a woven, rose-colored French Fleur de Lys patterned carpet gave the room a Louie XIV look. Unfortunately, cocktail tables and modern stuffed lounge chairs did little to support the historical theme. Also, to one side were coffee urns and silver serving ware on long tables. Obviously the room was set up for flexibility. It could serve drinks in the evening and a continental breakfast in the morning.

A piano was tinkling off in the corner. A busy waitress, in a skirt with a length designed to maximize tips from northern male workers, glided between the bar and customers delivering an assortment of beers and liquor while taking new orders. Matthew scanned the room for Mary. He immediately tuned out the couples and searched for loners. There were only two that he could see; judging from their heavy beards, neither of them was Jacquard's secretary.

Suddenly he focused on a lone female sitting near the back of the room watching him, a half smile on her lips. He approached her and stood over the table. She sat back comfortably sideways in the lounge chair, a martini of some sort before her. Her well-tanned and attractive legs were crossed strategically and the only evidence of nervousness was manifested in the constant motion of her foot.

"Hello Mr. Corrigan," she said, cocking her head to one side. "Small world, isn't it?"

"Monique," he said, "from the plane." They shook hands. Or rather she presented her hand and he gripped it for a moment.

"The same," she laughed, gesturing for him to sit, as she swept back her blond hair. "At least you remember my name so I assume I made some sort of impression."

"What are you doing here? How did you know I'd be here?"

"I saw you in the airport," she said. "But you were too quick for me. You grabbed a taxi and were gone. Finding you, however, wasn't hard in this town."

He sat down and ordered a coke with lime. "Well, this is certainly serendipitous."

"Not as much as you might think," she replied, mischievously. "I wasn't at the airport by chance."

"Okay, I'll bite. Why were you at the airport?"

"To meet you."

"Really?" Matthew looked at her, trying to gauge what she meant. Her foot kept moving up and down. He tried not to look at her legs which were beautiful in the extreme. Instead he concentrated on her green eyes and a pixie face framed by her blond tresses.

She continued to smile at him. "I have a proposition for you."

"What sort of proposition?"

"My organization would like to hire you."

"Doing what?"

"Doing exactly what you are doing now. But you'll be reporting to us."

"Who is *us*?"

"We are a diamond exploration company anxious to make inroads in Labrador. We're the competition, so to speak."

"Specifically who?"

"I'm not at liberty to say." She paused, and then added: "Until you accept our offer, of course. Then I can answer all your questions."

"Monique, I'm confused. You say you're an agent for my company's competition and you suddenly want to hire me. Why the sudden interest? You don't know anything about me."

"Actually we do. We've done our homework. We know you graduated top of your class from McGill University, majoring in Geology. You worked for Canada's Natural Resources for two years, then quit and travelled in Europe for a year before returning to Canada and joining the air force. You were selected for flight school and achieved the rank of Captain flying transport and other non-combat aircraft. During your hitch you dated longtime girlfriend Helene Gervais, a Montreal lawyer, and got married. You continued flying until you failed a flight medical. They grounded you. Your medical problems disappeared, you were re-certified. You got out as soon as your hitch was up.

"On leaving the air force you went back to McGill to complete a Masters and secured a job with Labrador & Ungava Diamond Explorations. You worked in exploration for them in various communities across the North and spend considerable time away from home. Still your wife's busy law practice kept her occupied. You and your wife eventually had a little girl. And you purchased a flat in Verdun." Seeing the sudden pain on his face, she stopped abruptly. "I'm sorry," she whispered.

"Aren't we all?" he answered, bitterly.

"We are puzzled by one thing."

"One thing?" he shot back, somehow resenting this intrusion into his private life.

"We understand there was a substantial settlement with the amusement park. And yet you returned to your job and the North."

"This is very personal, Monique. You're crossing the line a bit, wouldn't you say?"

"Of course. Again, I apologize."

Matthew sighed. What did it matter? He said: "My wife knew some excellent litigators. I signed on for the suit. I guess it was to punish them and provide a bloody good financial incentive for this never to happen again. To anyone else, I mean. Our lawyers negotiated with their insurance company and we settled. I've never touched a cent of the settlement. And, I doubt I ever will."

"I understand perfectly." She said it smoothly. In fact, too smoothly.

"Oh, you've also lost a child?" He stared at her.

Monique flushed with embarrassment. He felt bad for being so sarcastic. Even in the reduced lighting of the cocktail lounge, he could see how red her face had become. She uncrossed her legs and leaned forward. "I never meant to offend you nor hurt you. I can't really imagine what it would be like." She sipped her drink and sat back.

As his resentment faded he couldn't help noticing her full, red lips. He caught a scent of her perfume as the pink tip of her tongue emerged briefly and swirled a drop of amber liquor away from the rim of her glass. She was gorgeous for sure but, as usual, he forced any thoughts of romance out of his mind. Even after a prolonged separation from Helene, he wasn't quite ready to deal with the complications and vulnerability associated with any sort of romance. In fact, he didn't know if he would ever share his life with another person again. Presently he doubted the rewards were worth the pain he felt over the impending divorce.

"Well, unfortunately it's about to be two-for-two. I not only lost my daughter, but my wife and I are also in the process of divorcing. Long time in coming, but inevitable. According to her anyway. And legions of social studies. That's my pathetic tale, what's yours?"

She took another sip of her drink to cover her awkwardness. "Oh, I want to make something clear. On our flight to Montreal where you and I met, I didn't know anything about you. I didn't even know my organization was thinking about recruiting you. And, you *weren't* wearing a wedding ring."

"Fair enough," he answered, somehow relieved that their brief flirtation hadn't been business based.

"I fly the Sept-Iles to Montreal route quite often for my company," she continued. "We might have accidentally met a dozen times."

She seemed overly anxious he understand she wasn't in recruitment mode before.

"Okay, I believe you," he said, with a smile. Still, there must be dozens of unemployed geologists out there eager to be taken on by your company. Why me?"

She looked directly at him. "Okay. I'm going to be completely candid, Matthew. We're interested because of the St. Onge diamond."

~5~

Sky St. Onge was no stranger to death. In fact she knew it intimately. It had visited her many times in its varied forms: as a bold, frontal assault manifested via violent, overt tearing and ripping of flesh; as an insidious cancerous beast stealing and shutting down bodily processes one after the other; and, as a silent killer waiting for the opportune moment, and then striking swiftly and silently through an organ arrest or an unseen hemorrhage.

She had courageously faced and defeated death time and again, gaining precious years for some, and months or days for others. But fallout from death could not be defeated forever; for each defeat, she grieved more than the last time. Her final bow to the master of inevitability was lost to a gushing river of red where, despite her training, despite her experience, and despite the valiant and heroic attempts by her and the team to mitigate or forestall the end, death won out. The horror echoed in her thoughts.

"Doctor, we have to call it."

"Sky, stop...stop, it's no use...she's gone."

"She's eight years old for God's sake...."

"Sweet Jesus, somebody get her out of here."

The eternal stillness that death suddenly brought, the shock and the tears of so many, not to mention the unbearable guilt she wrongly accepted and even embraced, proved to be beyond her coping mechanisms. No matter what her peers and team members said, no matter what forgiveness was offered by the family, no matter that the coroner's report had found the team blameless, for Sky St. Onge there was no redemption. In the end she discovered a hard truth: she could be strong for others but not for herself. She left her hard-won life in the South for the safety of the North. And despite repeated calls from the hospital for her to return, she refused to even respond.

Now she found herself facing the *enemy* once again in the Montreal hospital. She closed her eyes, and held the hand of the old man in the bed. In her mind she whispered: *Grandfather, are you there?*

Only silence came back to her.

Grandfather I need you, don't go. Please…stay with me.

It was all so familiar: the antiseptic smell; the gentle and regular tones of the heart monitor; and, the sound of the rubber soles of the nurses efficiently breezing down the corridor, or in and out of the room for a quick assessment, a comforting smile and a sympathetic nod. At least she could be thankful for small mercies. His kidneys were producing output, his heart rhythm was strong and his blood pressure was only slightly elevated. She sighed heavily.

The reality was that the jury was still out on a final prognosis. They would have to wait until his body brought him back to the land of the conscious to judge residual damage. If he didn't awaken, the ultimate cruelty for this vigorous elder would be to lie in a vegetative state for the rest of his earthly existence. Still she tried to be positive. With luck the clot busting drugs administered in Nain had mitigated the damage. Now they had to wait and see.

As a little girl living with her grandfather, they had grown so close they often seemed to know what each other was thinking. Sky had actually conducted small experiments where she talked in her mind to her grandfather. Once he had been standing at the wood stove in their kitchen, busily mixing porridge, and she said a quiet hello to him. Then she asked him to turn. To her great surprise he had turned from the stove, a wide smile on his face. He had looked at her and asked: "Good morning to you too my little one; why did you ask me to turn?"

He had actually laughed out loud at how wide her eyes had grown and he had held a finger to his lips, raised his eyebrows and said: "Our secret." Though she tried many times after that (and she knew he heard her), he would never answer. Nor would he explain why he refused to answer. Now, standing in his hospital room, Sky tried again:

Grandfather, are you there?

Yes, my dear, I am here...for now.

You can hear me?

Of course my child. But there is darkness where I dwell.

You can be healed?

Perhaps.

Will they come?

That is not their mission, to save an old man.

You told me they did so before.

An accident of kindness. Besides, they leave very soon.

Where do they go?

Home.

Grandfather, all is being done that can be done for you. What can I do?

You must take the man to the other people. Before they leave. That is their request.

You mean the white man you asked to come to our home?

Yes. They have only asked one thing of me since that night on the ice so long ago.

You know they frighten me, Grandfather? Actually, they terrify me! I can't help it.

That is not their intent. They are righteous and I am in their debt. Please do what I ask.

I will try.

You are the only other person in the world who knows exactly where they dwell, my girl.

Yes Grandfather. I know.

It is the right thing to do. They leave at the Winter Solstice. But you will need the ice.

It should be good enough by then, Grandfather.

You are a fine person, Sky. I am so proud of you.

I love you, Grandfather.

And I love you, Princess.

Sky couldn't help smiling. It had been years since her Grandfather had called her by that name. She sighed, dreading what he was requesting she do.

I ask you one thing, Grandfather: Why is this man so important? Why?

And so he told her. She swallowed hard and nodded, finally understanding the significance and importance of the task. She had been thinking hard of ways to avoid it, but now she knew there was no way she could refuse her grandfather.

Only for you would I do this.

I know. And you are the only one I would ever trust to do so.

I will bring him to the other people.

Thank you…now I must rest.

Sky sat back and waited for a few moments to see if there was going to be any further communication. Did he mean he was simply taking a breather, or did he need to take a long rest? She had so many questions.

Though Sky tried to continue the conversation, there was no response. Indeed, their talk must have taxed him dearly. She resolved to come back the next day and pulled the thin white blanket up to his chin. Looking lovingly at the well-lined and weathered face of the man who had raised her, she saw that his breathing was regular. She checked other vitals on the monitor.

Blood pressure an acceptable 130/90...

Respiratory rate 16…

Oximetry 94 percent…

Finally, his rhythm was a controlled atrial fib. All-in-all, his stats were acceptable for a man who had thrown a clot. The hope was he would regain consciousness with only minor impairments. And, these could be overcome with rehabilitation. But first he had to wake up.

From around her neck Sky removed a tiny wolf head carefully carved from a brilliant blue and green piece of Labradorite. She looped the caribou hide thong behind his head and placed the family totem on his chest. She then kissed his forehead and left the room. Stopping briefly at the nurse's station, she told Sandi, the blond Charge Nurse, to call her at any time of the day or night if her grandfather's condition changed. As she talked she became aware of a number of nurses in the background whispering among themselves while casting veiled glances her way. She recognized an imaging technologist talking to the group and looked her straight in the eye. "Nancy, how are you?"

Nancy Denise blushed and smiled. "Just fine, Doctor St. Onge. And, how are you?"

"Never better," Sky returned her gaze, unwavering. "Never better."

The Charge Nurse at the desk looked at her in surprise, now willing to extend any professional courtesy requested. "You're a physician?"

"Yes," she answered. "I'll be on my cell. I know he's in good hands. Thank you."

The other nurses resumed their duties and were bustling about as she left the station. While waiting for the elevator, Nancy walked by. In a tone that was direct but still tinged with sympathy and kindness she said: "We miss you so much, Sky."

Sky nodded by way of acknowledgement but said nothing. She didn't trust her voice at that moment.

~6~

Matthew arrived at the Sept-Iles Airport by 7:00 AM and the cab dropped him off in front of a half-round, steel Quonset hut with a *Labrador Adventure Air Services* sign mounted over the door. Directly under the larger sign was a smaller white one with painted black letters. It read:

Aviation in itself is not inherently dangerous but, like the sea, it is unremittingly unforgiving of carelessness. So pay attention, dumb ass!

Beside the half-round, steel Quonset hut was a large hangar with doors wide open. It was still dark but it would be light soon. Inside, in the dead white fluorescent lights, he could see a Cessna 180 perched high on its float/wheel amphibious package and an old twin-engine Beech-18 sitting on its tail. The engine cowlings on both of the Beechcraft power plants were off and two mechanics were working on the starboard engine.

A wrench clattered to the concrete floor followed by a hearty bout of cursing. One of the men retrieved it and the tirade abruptly ceased.

On the ramp outside, in front of the hut, sat a yellow de Havilland Beaver, also a tail dragger and sporting a set of seemingly oversized "tundra" tires. The large, low-pressure balloon tires were favored by many northern wilderness pilots since they enabled them to more easily land on rough terrain, cushioning the shock and impact of the landing. When there were no landing strips in sight for hundreds of miles, they could be, literally, a life saver in the event of an emergency.

The smell of Avgas 80-87 was heavy in the biting cold morning air and Matthew guessed a sample had been drawn during the preflight inspection to check for water in the gas. Likely it had been thrown in the gravel bordering the tarmac rather than disposed of in a green-friendly manner. Expediency was, more often than not, employed by those who worked in the North. After all, time was money.

Matthew glanced again at the two mechanics working on the Beech-18 in the hangar. He heard an industrial heater start up in the back of the hangar just as one the men came over, nodded politely at him and began to roll the door closed to preserve their heat. Matthew started for the door of the Quonset hut.

A tall, harried-looking 40-something man in a war surplus flight jacket festooned with pens and pencils in sleeve pockets, and carrying a metal clipboard, banged through the outer storm door of the hut. Backlit by the yellow interior light streaming from the office, he paused on the dark stained plywood step outside when he spotted Matthew. A ball cap with a *Labrador Adventure Air Services* badge on it was slapped on his head and unruly prematurely grey curls spilled out from its perimeter. He looked down at the clipboard. "Matthew Corrigan?"

"Right here," Matthew responded picking up his flight bag and moving closer. They shook hands and the pilot introduced himself as Buzz Neal. "Call me Buzz."

"That's a new one, a pilot named Buzz," Matthew joked.

"Ain't it though," Buzz answered, with a grin. He took the flight bag, opened the door of the airplane and slid it inside into an aft storage space. "Your company runs a tab with us so you're good to go. Last chance for the can. Cause once we reach altitude, we're staying there until we reach our destination."

"I'm okay," Matthew replied.

"Weather is a little uncertain so we may have a bumpy ride," he said. "Nothing to worry about though; we have lots of alternates and our tires enable us to put down almost anywhere reasonably flat. We're loaded, fueled and I opened our flight plan. Nothing left to do other than make like the hockey players and get the puck out of here." He grinned and motioned towards the craft.

They pulled themselves into the cockpit, Matthew occupying the right seat. As is typical in tail draggers, there was virtually no visibility forward until the tail lifted so both men stared through the windscreen at the purple and gold glow of the early morning sky; the light expanded, slowly banishing the darkness.

The pilot reached down with his left hand and pumped the floor-mounted primer near the doorway five times. He set the mixture lever on the pedestal to rich. Next he advanced the throttle a few times, and brought it back to idle. "Okay, pray this baby starts," he said. "I had a minor on the engine and sometimes those clowns wind up with a few pieces left over."

"I hate that when it happens," Matthew replied, doing his best to look serious.

The pilot nodded: "Me too. Course they only had a dozen extra pieces this time."

Matthew smiled at the pilot. Typical black humor from a northerner. He knew that this bush pilot, like so many others, often risked his life flying across the world's roughest terrain in schizophrenic weather to do an emergency medivac or deliver dangerous cargoes such as fuel or explosives. Necessity meant they sometimes bent the rules with overloaded aircraft, by flying in weather below minimums, or by dragging their carcasses into the cockpit when they should have been crawling into a bed. For some, their luck eventually ran out. Then the blame invariably landed on the dead pilot for breaking the rules. Of course, though the bush airlines claimed to always stress safety, privately it was an entirely different matter. Those pilots who refused to push the envelope a little to fill a need or protect a contract soon found themselves unemployed and living back in the South.

Actually, I'm kidding," Buzz said. "Our lead mechanic is a guy called Scott Ruttan. He's a legend up here. If he can't find a part, he'll make one out of anything that is handy. And, most times, even the manufacturer will admit that the part that Scott makes, has well exceeded the tolerance levels and minimum specs of an original."

Buzz clicked the green master switch on and flipped and held a toggle switch to engage the starter. After a few revolutions of the propeller blades, the engine coughed to life. Standing on the brakes, he ran it up to 1750 RPM before turning the magnetos from left to both, to right and back to both, watching the drop in RPM as the engine ran. It didn't exceed 100. He then pulled on the red cockpit lights and watched the instrument panel light up as well. Standing on the brakes, he advanced the throttle slightly watching his oil pressure and temperature. The engine wound up and the airframe shuddered, anxious to move forward. The needle moved up into the green at 40 degrees and he transferred his gaze to the temperature gauge for the cylinder head. The noise was deafening inside the cockpit.

Matthew knew they needed at least 100 degrees on the cylinder head before they could take off. It would take a few minutes in the frigid morning air.

The pilot brought the throttle back to 1,000 RPM. As they waited for the engine to warm up, he ducked outside and pulled the chocks from the wheels.

Back inside he donned a Velcro-secured kneeboard to his thigh – checklist attached – and flipped through some pages including a folded map. Working diligently from a list taped to the instrument panel, he did his pre-takeoff check.

With permission to taxi, and an immediate take-off clearance secured, they accelerated down the runway. Buzz watched the edge of the tarmac, steering with his brakes until their speed was such that the rudder took hold. The tail lifted and the pilot and Matthew could see out the front. The landing lights on the strip's border passed faster and faster. "Let's see if she flies," Buzz pilot yelled and eased back on the yoke. They lifted into the air towards the promise of a rising sun. "I'll be damned," he continued with a grin. At 500 feet he set his flaps to "climb" and trimmed the airplane again.

Matthew had heard enough. "I flew Hercules in the air force," he responded with a smile.

"Oh!" Buzz said. "Rats! Guess I can't make you all nervous, eh?"

"Maybe if you were at the end of the runway with an RPG or a shoulder-borne missile launcher."

"You flew in Sandland?"

"Afghanistan. Troops, equipment, supplies. Flying doesn't scare me; ground fire does."

"Jeez." He picked up his manifest and checked it as he prepared to bank left and head overland. "Our first stop is Black Tickle, then Rigolet, Hopedale, inland to Voisey Bay, and finally over to Nain back on the coast. Full day for us."

A blue-white covering of snow blanketed the entire town of Sept-Iles this morning. The temperature had plunged overnight and Matthew had awoken to the first of many fresh snowfalls to come. In fact, the snow was late for this year.

As they gained altitude, he looked down at round, yellow, lamplight pools far below illuminating a series of rail yard tracks and equipment lined up with military precision. They funneled down in number and exited the yard past cranes and loaders and large, snow-covered buildings. Over to the left he glimpsed a system of docks, one with a large ore ship beside it sitting in its cold, watery slip. Away from the docks, he could make out shore ice forming along the edges of the black, unfriendly-looking waters of the St. Lawrence River.

They banked, turned and swept over residential streets where houses were paired with cars on driveways. Most featured orange parking lights and spouted plumes of vapor as drivers sipped their coffee inside and waited for their automobiles to warm up.

They flew in silence for some time. Buzz occasionally adjusted his instruments or checked his GPS stuck over the instrument panel.

Though they flew VFR, he was now employing his GPS to navigate in the early morning.

Occasionally he'd check a map to compare and confirm their location with some way point now becoming visible. "Love this technology but GPS is an *aid* to navigation, not an *end* to navigation," he shouted over the racket of the radial engine. He gestured at the GPS screen and then tapped the map and grinned.

Matthew nodded. He was well aware that while technology was invaluable when navigating, you'd better have a back-up plan if the technology crapped out. Which it seemed it was wont to do when things were getting hairy in the cockpit.

Under a grey sky they made a smooth landing and take-off at Black Tickle leaving a padlocked bag of mail behind. Later they landed at Rigolet where they ate a lunch of egg salad sandwiches and cokes from *The Grub Box*. With his feet dangling out the aircraft door, he looked over at Buzz sitting on the gravel on an overturned wooden orange crate. The pilot scrounged it from beside the terminal which was essentially an aluminum boxlike building with a stone Inuksuk out front. More than eight inches of snow covered the ground.

Like most of the settlements along the Labrador coast, Rigolet was a cluster of dozens of plywood-sided homes and some larger public buildings serving, in this case, a population of 300-plus people. Gravel streets with twin black tire tracks running through the snow wandered in front or behind the wooden houses, wherever a road was needed. He knew most of the structures would feature a large fuel oil tank for heating; no natural gas up here. Beside or behind every house was a tarped snowmobile awaiting deeper snow.

Another distinguishing reality in the town was an absence of air conditioners in their windows. Since summers very rarely hit 75 degrees, there was no need for artificial cooling in Labrador. And the pollution count up here, even on hot summer days, was nil. Matthew found himself enjoying the crisp, clean air even though he'd only been in the city for a few days. He inhaled again; a pungent smell of spruce drifted over on a light breeze.

"I spent some time as a youngster up in Goose," Matthew said by way of making conversation.

Goose Bay, previously a strategic Cold War military base, was a hundred miles away.

"Really? What did your father do?" the pilot asked.

"Air Defence Command," Matthew answered. "He flew the old CF-101 Voodoo Interceptors. Lots of business during the Cold War."

"Yeah, I heard Goose Bay was one of the busiest airports in the world during the 60s and 70s in terms of landings and take-offs. Because of the military. Did your Dad retire from the air force or did he get out before retirement?"

Matthew hesitated. "He went missing on a mission. They never found him."

"Wow! Soviets shoot him down?"

"I don't think so," Matthew answered, with a smile. "Air force was long on apologies and misgivings, short on explanations. Course it was different then; everything was hush-hush. They said he died a hero, whatever that meant. Mom qualified for a survivor's pension, we got a medal, posthumously, and then they threw us off the base. We couldn't live there anymore with Dad gone. So we moved to Montreal, and Mom went back to teaching. When I joined the RCAF, I tried to find out what happened to him. Hit a stone wall. Top Secret."

"Is your Mom still in Montreal?"

"No, she died a few years ago. Still wondering what happened to my father."

"Brothers? Sisters?"

"Nope. Only child."

"Tough."

"Others have it tougher."

"Yeah, I bitched about no shoes till I met a man with no feet."

"Up here it's more likely he'd have no toes," Matthew commented.

They both laughed. But not too hard. Frostbitten toes weren't overly funny in the North.

They finished eating, crushed and disposed of the cans and wax paper in a bin, and took off. As they climbed to 5,000 feet en route to Hopedale, Matthew looked down at hundreds of lakes, their waters mostly frozen into opaque glacial surfaces not yet fully covered with snow. While the cabin of the Beaver was toasty warm, he knew that outside, water would freeze within a minute.

On the land, the bare, grey rock of the Precambrian Shield poked through the snow in places, and thin layers of soil and moss lurked in other spots for as far as his eye could see. He recalled a story his father told him as a child, one his mother repeated as he got older. "My boy, God made the world in six days," his father had said. "When he saw what a mess He'd made of Labrador, He spent the seventh day throwing rocks at it." The evidentiary truth of the story was once again laid out in rock-solid detail below him. But as they flew farther north, the patches of rock and gleam of dull silvery lakes surrendered to an unbroken carpet of white. In addition, the forests of spruce trees gradually surrendered to the harshness of the North and grew lean and sparse.

Though, currently Labrador was proving its inherent worth to the civilized world through its value in metals and minerals resources, it was still a rough and unpredictable wilderness with unforgiving outcomes for those who underestimated it.

Southern fishermen and hunters in their Eddie Bauer outfits, had boldly invaded it in summer for its unique sportsman opportunities; those who failed to engage local guides occasionally got lost. Their fates were often determined only years later: some had been killed and eaten by bears; others had gone septic from infected insect bites; and, still others appeared to have simply died from starvation and exposure.

Nor was winter, with temperatures plunging as low as -60 degrees Fahrenheit, a time for fun and games.

Magnum blizzards with blinding whiteouts and winds so fierce a man couldn't stand upright, bedeviled and froze people to death mere yards from shelters they could no longer see. Many a man had needlessly died simply because he didn't understand and respect Labrador. It was a deceptively challenging land for clueless novices to survive unscathed. Those who ventured deep into its remoteness had to be savvy, tough and lucky.

After two more deliveries, the light was waning when Buzz stood the Beaver on its wing and banked over Nain.

He lined up for his final approach onto a somewhat level, snow-covered, 2,000 foot runway on the edge of town near the water. It had obviously been plowed recently since Matthew could see gravel poking through the snow as they let down and the strip grew larger in the windscreen. "Tomorrow, the skis go on this baby," the pilot shouted. "At least then I'll have options if things go south. So to speak," he added with a grin.

The town itself was boxed in by the Labrador Sea to the east and low rolling mountains to the west. The inlet beside the airstrip was already frozen solid. A nest of a few hundred white and battleship grey buildings meandered up a valley till settlers appeared to have lost interest and the buildings petered out. Unlike in the South, this wasn't an area where land developers were eager to exploit it for personal gain.

He gazed through his side window on final approach. The plane dropped lower and lower and he could make out a hockey-stick shaped government wharf and snowy streets that appeared to have been built as the need for more houses happened. It was a community planned by necessity. In fact, he liked the eclectic design of most northern communities since they seemed to serve the needs of their residents as opposed to the abstract and esoteric postulates of a remote planner who thought he or she knew what was best for everyone else. Everywhere in the town below, lights were snapping on in a vain attempt to keep the gathering darkness at bay.

"Oldest and northernmost settlement in Labrador," Buzz yelled, over the noise of the engine. "Settled in 1771 by Moravian Missionaries gonna convert the Eskimos. Around eleven hundred people call Nain home now. Inuit, Innu and whites. "

They swept in, felt a sudden wind gust pick them up and then drop them. They bounced twice on their balloon tires, and then he managed to stick the landing. "Third times the charm," Buzz said unconcernedly, a grin on his face as they taxied to the ramp.

Matthew thanked the pilot and hauled his flight bag over to where a Dodge Ram pickup was idling. Though the wind was light, the bitter cold seemed to intensify for every second he was exposed. On their final approach, he had seen the ice was already well entrenched on the bay beside the town; the snow banks were also much higher here. Old Man Winter had settled in for his almost nine month sojourn.

A single, large, red corrugated metal shed with a "NAIN" sign on it, and a red and white drooping windsock were the main features of the airport. A few 50-gallon fuel drums stood near the shed as well as some parked equipment tarped over as protection from the elements. A bearded man of around 65, with ample girth and wearing a parka and knee-high rubber boots with the tops of multiple woolen socks spilling out of them, stared at him as he approached. "Looking for a ride, buddy?" he called, sticking out his gloved hand. "Bob Crummy."

Matthew shook his hand. "Matthew Corrigan. Matter of fact, I am looking for a ride. Just over to the Menihek Lodge." He shook Crummy's hand.

"Today, I'm the stand-in for the lodge shuttle, which is in the shop," Crummy said, patting his Ram pickup. "Sarah said she had a customer coming in on the mail plane." The man looked around and whistled shrilly: "Solomon! Here boy!" A particularly large white King German Shepherd bounded in from somewhere on the sidelines and scrambled over the truck's tailgate to settle in for the short ride to town.

"You here on some sort of business?" Crummy inquired politely, taking Matthew's bag and putting it in the truck bed beside the dog.

"Actually I'm here to meet a fellow named Jerome St. Onge," Matthew answered, as the truck began to bump its way over the road into the settlement. On all sides house lights were popping on even faster in the gathering gloom. The heater blasted away on maximum and he held his hands over a vent. The frozen springs and shock absorbers on the truck creaked and groaned as they drove.

"Seeing him about his diamond?"

Surprised by the man's knowledge, Matthew tried to bluff: "What diamond?"

Crummy looked at him, smiled and shook his head. "Have it your way. Anyhow, don't think you're gonna be meeting him any time soon."

Matthew looked over at him. "Why not?"

"He's not here."

"Not here? You sure? You know him?"

"Jerome? Known him all my life; ever since the search."

"What search?"

"Beginning of the 80s, I think. We had a beauty of a winter storm with an offshore wind and Jerome got caught way the hell up north on an ice flow. It broke from the shore ice off the Torngat Mountains somewhere. Heading out into the Labrador Sea like Old Captain High-Liner, he was. Cagey old coot had a small shortwave and a battery he always carried wrapped up on his towing sled. Anyhow, he radioed for help. Some freak atmospheric conditions bounced the signal to a ham operator in Greenland. In turn, the Greenland feller managed to relay the SOS back to Canada. Got picked up by a Pinetree Line Radar Station at Saglek Harbour, also farther north on the coast."

Crummy paused to miss a snowmobiler who suddenly appeared over a small snow bank and darted onto the road. The rider's headlight gyrated wildly as the snowmobiler swerved and accelerated aggressively ahead of their truck spitting up chunks of snow that smacked their windshield. Abruptly the machine plunged over a snow bank lining the road and disappeared between some dimly lit houses.

"Shit," Crummy growled, hitting the wipers to clear the snow. "That's Bart, my son. Probably full of beer. He's 30 years-old, going on about nine."

"So what happened with this search?" Matthew pressed, now curious. The truck bumped over more hard-packed ice and snow. Trying to salt the roads in the North would be like sweeping sand out of a tent in the Sahara desert. Instead, people simply drove on successive layers of plowed and well-packed snow and ice.

"Well, as I was saying, the Saglek base was part of the Pinetree Radar Line but it was considered Canadian *and* U.S. territory even though it was in Canada. The line, you remember, was to warn us if the Soviets were coming over the pole with their bombers or missiles during the Cold War. The Northeast Air Command, the 924th Aircraft Control and Radar Squadron, was there functioning as a Ground Control Interceptor station. They were supposed to guide interceptor aircraft towards unidentified intruders. The interceptors were usually scrambled from Goose Bay.

"Anyhow, when the call for help came, Saglek didn't have any aircraft available. All they had were some Trackmasters, so they radioed Goose Bay. RCAF Air Search & Rescue scrambled a Twin Otter and a CH-113 Labrador helicopter. The Otter finally spotted Jerome huddled on an ice flow beside his broken down snowmobile. It was getting dark. They lost him again as the blizzard hit. They couldn't get the rescue helicopter to his position in time. Friggen temperature went down to -40 degrees that night. And we never knew shit about *wind chill* back then. Storm and the wind never stopped. We knew he'd been carried well out onto the Labrador Sea. Even if they found him next day, he would have been a friggen Popsicle. Fact is they couldn't even begin searching for three more days because of the storm."

"Well, he must have survived."

"That was the strange thing about it. Three days later, when the storm died down, and they were sending out more planes to see if they could spot his body, he comes into town. No snowmobile, no rifle, no gear and no frost bite. Just him, hale and hearty. Somehow he got off the ice flow and walked hundreds of miles south to Nain. Strange, eh?"

"Alright, I'll bite," Matthew said. "How did he do it?"

"Don't know," Crummy said. "Wouldn't talk about it to any of us. In fact, the air force even came and talked to him the day after he got back. Saw them here in their uniforms. Whatever they said seemed to hit him pretty hard. Jerome changed. Kept to himself, never smiled, and really pounded back the Moosehead. Then more air force officers came to see him. Twice. No…three more times. Wanted to know how he got off the ice, I guess. We heard he wouldn't say a word. In town, we figured he got some Eskimo help. We called 'em Eskimos back then…Inuit today."

"Lucky guy," Matthew said.

"Not lucky. A month later, when he had a few more brews than he should, we found out he was hitting the bottle cause he'd lost his son. Never said how. Then, his daughter-in-law, an Irish lass, came to live with him with her baby. When they came, Jerome stopped the brews and devoted himself to his granddaughter. Took her everywhere. Taught her the ways of the Innu, how to shoot, hunt and survive off the land. Then his daughter-in-law had a heart attack. Sky was five years old when she lost her mother. So Jerome raised her."

"Sky?" Matthew asked.

"Jerome's granddaughter."

"I see," Matthew said, thinking he'd learned all he could about Jerome St. Onge.

"After a while, it seemed they were looking after each other. But he'd still take off on these hunts every few months or so. Neighbors would take care of Sky. Seems he was obsessed with the Torngat Mountains for years. Be gone for two weeks or more. He'd use his Ski-doo in winter and his boat in summer. Never came back with any ptarmigan or caribou or even fish. Don't know what the hell he was hunting." Crummy stopped talking for a moment and then seemed to remember something. "One other strange thing happened with Jerome."

They had pulled up to a one-storey, white aluminum-slatted building with a blue wooden sign featuring flat gold letters announcing the *Menihek Lodge*. Snow half-covered ten vertical windows on one side of the building.

"What other strange thing happened to him?" Matthew inquired politely.

"Well, we had this geology student up here working with a prospecting company for the summer. They were looking for uranium. Anyhow, Duane Van Horne – the student – he's in the restaurant here in the lodge showing some folks how his Geiger counter works, eh? Jerome comes in and the machine goes crazy. Duane tries to talk to the old man but he won't hear of it. Naturally the kid was concerned the old guy had somehow been exposed to dangerous radiation. Plus, I'm sure he wanted to know where Jerome had been since he might have found a uranium deposit. Duane even went to his home. Old man threw him off his property. Not before he met Sky though." He winked at Matthew and raised his eyebrows meaningfully.

Their truck was now parked and idling at the wooden steps leading to the lodge front door. They were immersed in a white mist of condensation from the exhaust drifting forward over the cab.

"Once he met her, he was smitten. You see, Sky had grown up to be a real looker. Van Horne was a geology student out of Carleton University in Ottawa and he was up here for the next three summers doing prospecting work. He and Sky were pretty much an item. We all thought they'd get married. Then, the year the kid graduated from Carleton and stopped coming up here, it seems they broke up."

"I see," Matthew said, no longer really interested. "You said Jerome St. Onge isn't here. Did you mean he's out hunting or something?"

"No. I heard they took him to the outside yesterday via an emergency flight; straight to a Montreal hospital, he went."

The "outside" was a term often used by people in Labrador to indicate the South, traditionally viewed by Northerners as one huge urban center.

"Hospital? What happened?" Matthew asked.

"Something in his head went wrong."

"What do you mean, went wrong?"

"One of those brain things."

"An aneurism?" Matthew felt his heart sinking.

Crummy thought hard. "No, they called it something else."

"Stroke?"

"That's it. I heard he was in a coma in Montreal. They aren't sure if he's gonna wake up. Finds a diamond and then craps out. Poor ole bugger don't have no luck. Not good luck, leastwise."

Realizing his trip was now for nothing, Matthew tried to remain gracious as he thanked Crummy for the ride, retrieved his flight bag from the truck bed under the watchful gaze of Solomon the Shepherd, and signed the register in the lodge foyer.

Matthew's room was clean and comfortable consisting of a queen bed, dresser, mirror and a small desk. Newly installed Berber carpet helped insulate the cool floor. He unpacked and then ate a hot chicken sandwich and coffee in the restaurant/lounge. He wasn't surprised to find out that the modest surroundings were costing his company $175 a night. After all, this was the North where everything was imported and so everything came at a premium.

It was too late to call Jacquard and he wouldn't have anything definite to tell him anyway. He'd have to verify if St. Onge had truly been stricken and left Nain. But he'd do that before he called his boss. Sometimes things got blown out of proportion.

Later he lay on his bed and absentmindedly gazed at a satellite TV channel with the sound off. His mind drifted back to his chat with Monique in Sept-Iles. After she'd dropped her bombshell about the diamond, he began to suspect it wasn't much of a secret. Small wonder Crummy concluded he was up in Nain about the gem. But what puzzled him was how Monique and her mysterious company knew he was involved so quickly. He'd only found out about the diamond himself less than 72 hours prior.

Of course he'd politely declined Monique's invitation for employment. Matthew was a loyal type of guy and he wasn't about to betray a company that had been good to him for years. Monique good naturedly even quoted a ridiculous figure as a salary which confirmed his belief that it wasn't his skills being sought, as much as his pseudo relationship to Jerome St. Onge and his diamond find.

If there was a kimberlite pipe that had spit diamonds to the earth's surface, companies would almost kill to find the location and buy up the leases.

One thing for sure: If he ever ran into Monique again, he'd certainly press her more firmly for the name of the company employing her. He didn't know why, but he sensed there was more going on than was evident on the surface. Somehow, the whole exercise felt increasingly like a legion of suitors eagerly gathering to compete for the hand of a princess without knowing anything about her. In the morning he would check and see if he could find the status of Mr. St. Onge, and verify that the man was, indeed, in a Montreal hospital.

~7~

Morning came early in the North though the same couldn't be said about daylight this time of the year. Matthew woke to the sounds of showers running, toilets flushing, thumping boots, throat clearing and curses emanating through the walls from rooms on either side as his lodge mates rolled out of the sack and completed their early morning ablutions. Out his window he could see it was still pitch black. He looked at his travel alarm beside him: 6:30 AM. It wouldn't be light for another two hours at this time of the year. He decided to get another hour of sleep but the smell of bacon frying reached his nose. He groaned; the kitchen was in another wing entirely but he still smelled bacon. It had to be one of the most powerful aromas in the world. It could penetrate virtually anything, even quarter-inch steel plate as he found out when he worked on board ship for a summer. He pulled his pillow over his head but he was fighting a losing battle. He finally surrendered and rolled out of his bunk to satisfy his need: Bacon, bacon, bacon!

After a generous breakfast of eggs, bacon, pancakes and home fries, he summoned his waitress, a slender girl of First Nations' origin. He stuck out his hand: "Hi, I'm Matthew Corrigan."

For a moment the girl hesitated, obviously puzzled, but then grasped his hand and gave it too good a squeeze. "I'm Normand Fortier, please to meet you Mr. Corrigan. What else would you like?" She readied her pad.

"Normand, I'm here to meet Jerome St. Onge and I need to know where he lives. I understand most people know each other in town. Can you possibly direct me to his residence?"

The girl's mouth formed a perfect O. "You haven't heard? Jerome was taken to hospital on the outside."

Matthew gently pressed. "Do you know where exactly?"

"No," the waitress said. "But you could check with our Outpost Nurse at the Health Clinic, or Constable Andre Davignon over at the RCMP Detachment. Diane and Andre helped load him on the plane. His granddaughter travelled out with him on the medivac."

Matthew thanked her, got directions to the clinic and retired to his room where he donned a heavy wool sweater and his Sears parka. Then he set off on foot to find the clinic.

The air was clean, clear and nippy again. The sky showed a golden ball debuting on a silver streaked horizon graduating to deep blue directly overhead. He could see a fresh mantle of snow had fallen the previous night since, for the time being, there was an absence of truck tracks on the road. They had gotten about ten inches, virtually a free pass in the North, yet the cause for panic in southern cities.

Barking dogs sounded from different points of the compass in town and he spied two Husky's rough housing with each other in a fenced off yard. Snow banks on either side of the roads were already plowed six feet high from prior storms. Off in the distance, he could hear the throaty roar of a tractor plowing, retreating and then gearing up for another push at a stubborn snowbank somewhere.

Arriving at the clinic, he found Outpost Nurse Diane Underwood in her office. She was a petite, pretty woman, with dark hair and blue eyes, likely in her 50s, he guessed. Her desk was littered with papers. She stood up and he saw she was wearing standard green scrubs topped with a wrinkled white lab coat with a stethoscope looped around her neck. He explained who he was and that he worked for *Labrador & Ungava Diamond Explorations* out of Montreal. He was looking for information on Jerome St. Onge.

Diane sat back down behind the desk and toyed with a pencil. At first she was a little reluctant to release any details on St. Onge but, after explaining why he needed the information, she relented. She seemed to be more comfortable after learning he was there by invitation. Still, her words were chosen carefully.

"We needed to transfer him to a major facility," she said slowly. "The clinic isn't equipped to handle his type of injury. The Royal Victoria Hospital in Montreal accepts our patients. Any further inquiries will have to be directed to Doctor Tabah, his attending physician at the Royal Vic. His granddaughter concurred with my diagnosis so we readied him for transfer. Naturally she accompanied him on the medivac. I'm afraid I can't tell you any more since you aren't a family member."

"His granddaughter's name is Sky St. Onge?"

"That's right. She's still in Montreal with him as far as I know. I did inquire re his status, of course. He's stable. But that's as much as I know for now."

"That's all I need, Diane. Thank you very much." He rose to leave.

"I'm assuming you're also here about the 'secret' diamond he found?"

Matthew stopped and smiled. Obviously, in such a close-knit community, information was an enduring form of currency. He decided the cat was not only out of the bag, but the feline was taking out advertisements in every medium available to it: "*Jerome St. Onge found a diamond*" must be the prevailing headline. He decided there was nothing to gain by hiding his interest. Diane looked expectantly at him. She had been forthright and one good turn deserved something in return.

"Mr. St. Onge came to my boss in Montreal and asked specifically to meet with me about a diamond he'd unearthed somewhere. Why? I have no idea since we've never met. I was instructed to come to Nain to see him, which I've done. Unfortunately, the poor man appears to be gravely ill; that's all I know."

"I see," Diane said, rising from behind her desk to walk him to the door. "Well, I imagine there'll be a lot of competition to find out where he found it. Too bad he showed it to the wrong person. Since then, we've had a parade of strangers coming into Nain looking for Jerome. To get away from them, he took off with his snowmobile and stayed away until two days ago. Came back into town, maybe for your meeting. Sadly he collapsed and fell off his Ski-Doo before he got home. He was found up on Sand Banks Road. We stabilized him and got him on an aircraft out. Sky was with him so I didn't have to send a nurse."

Matthew put the information together in his head. It seemed St. Onge had taken steps *not* to give the location of the diamond find away. And he'd come back into Nain the day before Matthew was to arrive. But why had he picked Matthew Corrigan? Why did the man want to meet with someone he'd never met before? The answer, it appeared, was now locked in the brain of the comatose patient in a Montreal hospital. Matthew extended his hand. "Thanks again, Diane. I can find my way out."

He went to leave and then turned back. "You said he told the wrong person about the diamond. Do you know who that was, per chance?"

She smiled. "Bob Crummy, biggest gossip this side of the Torngat Mountains. And I'm including the British Isles and most of Europe in my assessment. Also Crummy does some guiding for company geologists when they happen through. Bet he was on the horn within the hour selling the info to whoever would buy." She shook her head and laughed. "At least it got Sarah some business over at the Lodge."

"I suppose," Matthew said. "Who does the booking for *Labrador Adventure Air Services?* I have to get back to Montreal."

"Check with Vern at the fuel depot. He usually takes reservations and will tell you if the return flight is booked or not. It will be in by noon since it isn't a mail flight today. He'll probably do a turnaround and head right back to Sept-Iles."

"Thank you. Gives me a few hours. I'll check with him and tour the town till then."

"Won't take you long," Diane said, with a smile.

Coming out of the building, Matthew was surprised to see Crummy's truck slide to a stop in front of him. The man buzzed down the window: "Give you a lift?"

Matthew shrugged, knocked snow from his boots and got in. They started off with a jerk.

"Back to the Lodge, I take it, Matt?" Crummy grinned at him, two incisor teeth gleaning gold in the sunlight filtering in through the truck window.

"Sure…Bob," Matthew said with a smile. "Although, I hoped to look around town first."

"We can do that," he answered. "Hang on and I'll give you the grand tour of Nain, Labrador."

He turned left, shifted into a higher gear and drove to the wharf while explaining how the supply ships had stopped because of ice and wouldn't resume till April or May. Groceries and the like would be brought in by air until spring. Next he pointed with pride at the Nain Husky Centre, the town's arena, then steered by the Jens Haven Memorial School where 340 students attended. Next he and pulled up to the large white church visible from most points in the community. He told Matthew it was established by the Moravian Missionaries and services were conducted in English and Inuktitut.

He put the truck back in gear again and drove by the RCMP Detachment where he said they had one corporal and two constables holding down the fort. Most of the problems in Nain, like many other northern communities, centered on domestic disputes, the occasional minor theft and assaults. Generally they were fueled by alcohol.

"Mounties tell me if someone dropped all the alcohol in Nain into a hole, they could close the detachment," Crummy said. "Lots of northerners have alcohol problems. Did you know that legally the Innu weren't allowed to drink or have alcohol in their possession under the Federal 'Indian Act' until 1963? Mounties used to spend most of their time chasing white bootleggers or trying to find and destroy the Indian stills." He grinned. "They used to make their own moonshine; they called it Moose Milk."

Crummy pulled the truck down a side road and they were suddenly in front of the clinic again. He braked and shifted into neutral. "And you already saw the clinic. So that ends the tour." He looked at the clinic. "Guess you were in there checking out what happened to Jerome?"

Matthew wasn't overly surprised the ride wasn't as much of a friendly gesture as it was to solicit information. "As you said, I'm not going to meet him here."

Crummy nodded. "Any news on his condition?"

"Just that he's stable. That's all I was told"

"Of course, you not being family and all."

"That's right. If you wouldn't mind, Bob, I will take a ride back to the lodge. Got to pack and settle up."

"Crummy looked at him in surprise. "No reason to stay, eh? You don't know where that diamond came from?" He squinted at Matthew. "Do you?"

"No I don't, Bob. And we may never find out."

"But it confirms there's diamonds in Labrador."

"I guess. Maybe."

Crummy gave him a look. "Are you saying it came from somewhere else? This is a scam?"

"I'm not saying anything. I don't know anything. Now I'm supposed to see a Mr. Collenette at the fuel depot to see if I can get on the return flight."

"Don't worry. There'll be room. You're as good as out of here."

He put the truck back in gear and hit the accelerator.

True to Crummy's prediction, there was room available on the aircraft. Matthew's new friend drove him back to the lodge and, an hour later, over to the airstrip. Matthew insisted he accept a 50-dollar bill for gas. There was no argument; gas cost $1.80 a liter in Nain.

Back in Sept-Iles that night, he accessed the hotel's Wi-Fi system, and sent an email to Jacquard telling him what he'd discovered in Nain. The next morning, Air Canada took him back to Montreal.

Landing at Trudeau International airport, he was planning to go back to his company's main office, but changed his mind at the last moment. "Take me to the Royal Victoria Hospital," he told the driver. No use putting off the inevitable; Jacquard would want a full report on St. Onge's condition.

The Royal Victoria Hospital in Montreal was a major trauma and research center. If anything was going to help St. Onge, the Royal Vic would provide it. The cab pulled up at the main entrance and dropped him off. Though Matthew grew up in Montreal, he knew the hospital by reputation only. Now he found himself standing in front of a neo-gothic looking grey stone building of Scottish baronial architecture complete with crenelated structures and the romantic turrets of a fairy tale castle.

Since he couldn't leave his flight bag in the cab, he carried it in hand. He entered and found the information desk inside the door. After giving St. Onge's name he was directed to a busy nursing station on the neurological floor. After a few moments, a harried looking nurse put down a sheaf of papers and came over to the counter. Despite the fact she was obviously tired and stressed, she put on her best smile and asked how she could help him. He gave St. Onge's name.

The nurse gave him St. Onge's room number from memory and went back to her papers. A moment later he cautiously entered a room containing two single beds. The first was empty. The farthest bed, the one by the window, was obviously occupied as he could see the bottom half of a patient protruding under white covers. From behind a partially pulled privacy curtain a young woman clad in jeans and a royal blue cowboy shirt with silver buttons stepped into view, a plastic glass and a sponge swab in hand. She looked at him curiously and then spoke softly but firmly: "Yes? Can I help you?"

All Matthew could do was stare. The woman was either in her late 20s or very early 30s with shoulder-length black hair curling inward around an oval face dominated by startling dark eyes flecked with gold amidst long dark lashes. In fact, her eyes seemed to sparkle as she looked at him. Her full lips framed a wide handsome mouth with a natural upward curve at its ends; this graced her with a pleasant built-in smile even when her features were at rest. Much like a dolphin, he thought. He noted her tapered eyebrows were almost straight, certainly natural, no plucking here, and her complexion could only be categorized as a beautiful light gold. Matthew saw she was a native Canadian, and one of extraordinary beauty. She raised her eyebrows when he didn't answer and tried again. "Excuse me, are you assigned to this room?" She looked at the first bed which was stripped down and devoid of sheets or blankets.

Realizing he was standing in the doorway with his flight bag in hand, he put down the bag, feeling slightly foolish. It was only natural for her to assume he was a new patient. He shook his head: "No, I'm looking for someone." He continued to stare.

"Yes…?" she finally prompted, as though speaking to a child.

"Jerome St. Onge?"

Now a guarded look crossed her features and the smile in her eyes disappeared. She seemed to instinctively move sideways to get between Matthew and the patient's bed. Though her posture was ramrod straight, she moved with an easy grace and he couldn't help noticing a lithe figure that was more gamine than full, featuring pert breasts and slightly curved hips. Indeed, this girl was fashion model material.

"Who are you?" Her tone was more confrontational than curious.

"Matthew Corrigan," he said gently, realizing a certain tension had sifted into the room. Wisely he realized that what he said was as important as how he said it.

"Oh, I see," she breathed out, perhaps a shade more friendly. "The diamond."

Feeling totally mercenary, he tried to cover. "I-I just wanted to see how he's doing." The moment it was out of his mouth he knew how lame it sounded.

"Of course you did."

No mistaking the sarcasm now.

"I mean, he asked me to come to Nain to meet with him."

"Well as you can see, he isn't receiving visitors today," she said, gesturing for him to step closer. She sighed, now seeming tired, defeated.

Matthew left his flight bag and stepped to the side of the bed. An elderly gentleman lay motionless, hands at his sides outside the blanket.

He noted an ancient but proud, squared face with a weathered complexion and deep character lines etched into his skin around a formidable, hawk-like nose. His long grey and white hair had been carefully braided and curled around the back of his head to lie beside him on the pillow. His lips were shiny with a moisturizer to prevent them from drying out. Various plastic bags hung from a stand beside the man with tubes running under the covers. A monitoring station emitted a soft regular beep in time with several diagnostic lines running across its screen. The lines translated into bold digital readouts on the side of the screen.

Standing beside the girl now, Matthew could smell a hint of lavender wafting over from her. He sneaked another glance; she was amazingly beautiful. Angry with himself, he pushed the thought aside. What was the matter with him? This poor old fellow could be on his deathbed and here he was finding it hard to take his eyes off this girl who was obviously the man's granddaughter. He took refuge in the belief that years in the North and a lack of female companionship were subverting his natural empathy.

"See what I mean, Mr. Corrigan?" she murmured.

"I'm sorry," Matthew said and stepped back so he wasn't crowding her. She didn't look like someone you should crowd. "I take it, you're Sky, Jerome's granddaughter?"

"My grandfather has never met you and yet you are so familiar with him?" It was a direct challenge to his use of the first name and he realized how disrespectful it must seem. He felt himself flushing red; little prickles of sweat invaded his hairline. "I'm sorry," he stammered, again. "I didn't mean any disrespect."

"No, of course not. He's merely a means to an end."

Her verbal assault made him step backwards. He held up both hands. He didn't deserve her attack. "Miss, I am trying to do my job and it was your grandfather who asked to meet with me. You're right, I've never met him before and I have no idea what sort of agenda he has with this diamond. All I did was get my sorry tail up to Nain as he requested through my boss. Then I found out he was down here in Montreal. I'm sorry this happened but it wasn't my fault."

She let go the anger and sighed, gesturing with one hand. "It's me that should apologize. I'm angry at what's happened and you're just a convenient target. So I'm sorry. And yes, I'm Sky St. Onge."

Matthew nodded and straightened in relief, realizing he'd been slightly crouched as though to ward off further attacks.

"Perhaps you'd join me for a coffee?" she asked. She extended her hand and he shook it.

"I think a coffee is an excellent idea," he answered. "Is there a machine around here?"

"Let's go to the cafeteria," she returned. "At least it's brewed there."

He left his bag and Sky led the way as they traversed from one wing to another. She cut through a supply room with two doors as a shortcut, and bypassed elevators which surprised Matthew since he assumed the cafeteria would be in the basement like most other older hospitals.

"I hope it's still up here," she said, continuing to lead the way.

"You've gotten to know your way around this hospital," he commented as they walked, trying to break an uncomfortable silence.

In fact, the cafeteria turned out to be on the third floor of the surgical pavilion.

"I seem to, don't I?" she returned, without pausing.

It was mid-afternoon but the room was very busy. They took their coffee, each with a dab of cream, and located an empty table near a wall. A tall man in surgical scrubs immediately sat down at a table next to them. He had an impressive scar on his cheek. He opened a newspaper and settled in behind it.

"How is your grandfather?" Matthew asked, this time with evident sincerity. "And what exactly happened? Medically, I mean."

"Cerebral event, threw a clot. We have no idea how bad it is until he regains consciousness which could be in an hour, a week, a month. Or never. Clot busters were administered in Nain. Now we wait."

"I'm sorry," he said again. "Really."

She nodded. "Mr. Corrigan, I asked you for a coffee for a reason. My grandfather asked me to guide you to where he found the diamond."

"He was awake?" Matthew asked in surprise.

"Oh no," she said hastily. "This was after the stroke." She seemed to catch herself but then shrugged and continued. "Let's say we have a strange connection, a link that transcends how you and I communicate. Anyhow, it is very important to him that I take you to where the diamond originated."

She looked down at her coffee, failing to meet his eyes. He couldn't help feeling that there was more going on here than he was privy to; essentially she'd told him she had a conversation with her grandfather, in her *mind*.

Matthew looked at her closely. "I guess I have to ask: Why? Why did he choose me out of dozens of prospecting companies that would have paid him a fortune if he led them to a viable diamond find? As you know, I've never met your grandfather."

Sky shook her head ever so slightly and then shrugged again. "I can't tell you why. He must have his reasons."

"Miss St. Onge –," he began, but she held up a hand.

"Is it important *why*? My grandfather is offering you something some people would kill to know. His motives are known only to him. Are you saying you aren't interested?"

Here was another direct challenge. Her voice definitely conveyed impatience.

Realizing she could very well decide to step away from the whole affair and also that she wasn't far from doing so, Matthew backtracked as gracefully as he could. "Please don't misunderstand, I'm not looking a gift horse in the mouth," he explained. "I'm just curious where he got my name. But you're right. It doesn't matter. My company is depending on me to find this site and I'd be lying if I didn't tell you it's my CEO's top priority. Unless I bring back some proof of diamonds in Labrador, his whole operation might shut down."

Sky appeared to look uneasy for a moment but quickly regained her composure. "I'm not sure this is about your boss or his company."

"He wants me to stake a claim, you know." He had to be honest with her.

"That's not my concern," she said. "My job is to get you there. That's it."

"Fair enough."

She raised her head and stared him in the eye. "There is a condition."

"Name it." He wasn't about to bargain.

"Where we will go is an extremely dangerous journey. It doesn't take much to get injured or killed out there. So I'm in charge of this trek and you will do everything I tell you to do without fail and without hesitation. Even though you may not understand my reasoning at the moment. Do you agree?"

"You won't make me quack like a duck, will you?" he asked, trying to lighten the mood. She stared at him.

"And…she never even quacked a smile," he murmured and sighed. "Alright, you have my word."

"Yes…I suppose I do…as long as it suits you," she finished. "That's the way it's always been. Right, Kemo Sabe?"

It didn't take a genius to see where she was going with her comment. "What is it with you?" he asked in annoyance. "Don't you trust anyone who isn't Indian?"

She laughed openly at this. "Can't think why an 'Indian' wouldn't trust a white man, do you? Anyhow, we're called Innu now. And, in case you're wondering, Innu means human being. And, there isn't one Labrador Innu I know who has been to India, wears a sari or even likes curry. Chris Columbus got it all wrong. In addition to him not even landing in North America."

Matthew swallowed and tried a weak defense. "In the United States I think they still refer to themselves as Indians."

"Good for them." She finished her coffee. "As long as the weather holds, we'll leave from Nain, December 9th."

"Meaning …?" he asked.

"Meaning as long as it doesn't warm up. Greenhouse gases are impacting the Arctic, and we never know conditions for certain. To make this trip, we need the ice."

He nodded and tried for additional clarification: "So you were with your grandfather when he found the diamond?"

"I know where we have to go," she said, not directly answering the question. There was an undercurrent of tension coming through again so he didn't press it.

"Got it. Nain. Need ice. For more than drinks."

She ignored his second attempt at humor and pulled a small calendar card from her breast pocket and looked at it. "That means you should be in Nain On December 7th to prepare. It will allow us time to get there before the Winter Solstice. I'll arrange all supplies and our transportation. And please dress appropriately for arctic weather."

"So we'll be gone all day?"

Slowly she raised her gaze from the calendar card understanding for the first time how little he understood about their proposed journey. "A week in and a week out; if we're lucky."

"What? We're going to be out there for two weeks?"

"That's right. We'll be going into the Torngat Mountains. It will be deadly cold and desolate. And no food available since I don't fancy killing anything unless we're critical. So we carry everything in. If we get hit with blizzards, we hunker down until they pass."

"Can't we fly in?" he asked, trying not to sound like he was whining.

"And land where? On the side of a mountain?"

"They make these new things called helicopters."

"So you don't care if the pilot flies back and tells everyone where he dropped us and we soon see a fleet of other helicopters arriving carrying prospectors and mining company execs from as far away as Tiera Del Fuego?"

"Oh, of course. We need to keep the location confidential."

"Advisable. For your purpose anyhow, wouldn't you say?"

"Wait a minute..." he said, alarmed. "You said the Torngat Mountains?"

"Correct."

"Declared a National Park in 2005. The 1930s National Park Act forbids mining activities." Matthew felt his heart sink, more for his boss than himself.

Sky was ready with the lie she knew she would have to tell eventually even though she hated doing it. But she would do anything for her grandfather. "We travel to the northern end of the Torngats. The site is outside park boundaries. It's in the Nunavik region of the mountains."

"Are you sure?"

"Reasonably sure," she said. "But again, I'm supposed to take you to a certain destination defined by GPS coordinates from my grandfather. I'm not there to facilitate staking a claim, tying up mineral rights or making your boss a billionaire."

"That's okay," Matthew replied. "If you get me to where the gem came from, I'll take care of the rest."

"So we agree, Mr. Corrigan. You'll be in Nain on December 7th."

"Am I going to like this trip," he asked, again trying not to sound like he was whining.

"You?" she quipped, with the barest smile. "I seriously doubt it. But if you listen to me and do everything I tell you, *when* I tell you, we should get back okay. If you don't listen, expect a whole other outcome."

"Such as?" he asked naively.

She shrugged: "Without being overly dramatic? I suppose someone will eventually find our remains and bring back a pile of bleached bones."

~8~

United States Air Force Major Paul G. Stone didn't like the dark. In particular, he didn't like the dark when he didn't know who was keeping him in the dark. And right now, as he boarded an elevator in Montreal's Place Ville Marie's downtown office complex, and rode upward, he felt more like a cloak and dagger operative than a major in the USAF.

Stone disembarked on the 20th floor. Two doors down the corridor, he opened one labelled *Universal Exports*. In days gone by he had smiled at the idea of naming their front company after the corporation British Secret Service Agent James Bond often represented as a cover during clandestine missions abroad. But the joke wore thin with his inability to learn why he, an American military officer, had been charged with setting up a base in Canada and covertly importing an armada of weaponized drones into northern Labrador.

He knew, there were only two prominent Unmanned Combat Aerial Vehicle (UCAV) programs within the United States: that of the military, and that of the Central Intelligence Agency (CIA). The military's UCAV program was overt, meaning it was recognized by the public and only operated where US troops were stationed. On the other hand, the CIA's program, which had been formed after the September 11th terrorist attacks, was clandestine and operated unfettered by any public knowledge or oversight other than special congressional committees. To him, what he was doing smelled to high Heaven like CIA.

Working in the National Air and Space Intelligence Division of the Wright Patterson Air Force base in Dayton, Ohio, evolved from the old Foreign Technology Division, Major Paul Stone had been coordinating analysis of new Russian and Chinese air weaponry in relation to performance, strategic capabilities and vulnerabilities. His work was both challenging and interesting.

Stone's dear wife Janet, had died the year before and his son, also in the Air Force, was an F-16 pilot on assignment in Kuwait. In other words Stone had no firm attachments in Ohio other than a few cousins he saw on holidays. He wondered if this was why he had been chosen for his current assignment.

Almost one year ago, he'd been approached by the Wright Patterson Base Commanding Officer (CO) saying he was being seconded to a highly classified military operation based out of Canada. They told him his past experience setting up, organizing, supplying and maintaining support facilities in foreign countries, as well as his logistics and fulfillment roles during his career, made him an ideal candidate.

When he inquired if he would be working with the Canadian military, his CO finally admitted that this operation – code named *Operation Flashbang* – wasn't so much *Top Secret* as *Ultra-Top Secret* and the Canadians were not participating. He further confessed to Stone that even he didn't know the whole picture. All he knew was that *Operation Flashbang* was sanctioned by the US Joint Chiefs of Staff and that, somehow, all reporting was done to a civilian authority, both covert and unnamed. Possibly CIA. He would, in effect, be the in-situ liaison officer in Montreal with orders not to liaise with anyone.

It turned out to be the strangest mission Stone had ever been assigned. Though he had served in hostile locations, Canada, of course, was one of the USA's staunchest allies. And yet, the level of security and secrecy seemed to be even greater than operating on unfriendly soil.

Major Stone was first tasked with setting up a covert front in Montreal. He arranged a five-office suite in the heart of the city's business district and incorporated the name. Next he contracted to have the offices painted, carpeted and furnished as well as electronically swept for listening devices. He then contacted Bell Canada, Cogeco Cable and Hydro Quebec for telephone, internet and power needs which included a 220 volt services.

Once the civilian organizations had completed installation of a phone system, a closed loop Local Area Network (LAN), and various plugs and outlets, a team of US military technicians, dressed in civvies, invaded the offices and rewired everything while installing encryption devices and heavy shielding protection for all routers and cables. Next they installed new hardened computers, Fax machines, telephones, and wall-mounted monitors.

The walls, floor and ceiling of their main, windowless communications room were seamlessly covered with Monsanto's Flectron metalized fabric, a Radio Frequency Identification and electromagnetic shielding material that covered every inch of the room's interior. It featured zero openings once the door was closed and Velcro-sealed from the inside. In keeping with the secret agent theme, this room soon came to be affectionately known by staff as the *Cone of Silence*, a prop from the *Maxwell Smart* TV series. In effect, the room thwarted eavesdropping or electronic monitoring of any of their communications equipment or confidential meetings.

In addition, it featured a 2,000 pound safe installed on metal stringers the width of the room to spread the weight. Only he, Stone, had access to it. He was charged with personally ensuring all staff confidential papers were stored in it every night. The civilian-dressed US Army installer told him that each day he would receive a new electronic combination via an encrypted email. Said daily combinations would be automatically downloaded to the safe.

"What if I blow it entering the combination?" Stone had asked.

"The third time you do it, or if you try to move it, the safe will kill you," the technician cautioned. Stone began to smile but the technician did not. Nor did he reveal how it would happen. Instead he merely nodded towards a heavy black cable leading from the safe to a custom uninterruptible power supply which, in turn, led to a hardwired power source with a 220 volt tag attached to it. "It's all in the guidelines," he said, handing Stone a manual stamped **Top Secret**. "Read it carefully. This is not a joke, sir."

During the office setup, Stone's masters had pretty much remained out of sight. With the office front in place, he received one visit from a short, rotund man in a dark business suit who dropped in and introduced himself as *Mr. Black*. He laid out the ground rules and procedures for communicating with himself and his people, and told Stone this assignment was super critical. In fact, the continued dominance of the USA as the premier world power likely depended on their mission.

More details followed: the entire operation had been highly

compartmentalized with information shared on a time-sensitive, need-to-know basis. And, the Canadians had approved the US use of a defunct Cold War military base named CFS Saglek Harbour in Labrador. Its purpose: US military training exercises.

Black added that an agreement had been reached with the Canadian Government to declare the base US territory as during the Cold War, so no customs/immigration steps would be needed. The Canadians had generously ceded the decommissioned CFS Saglek Harbour base for a single dollar for two years. Stone's job was to rebuild and reactivate it for subarctic training exercises.

"Though you're supposed to be a liaison officer, if you get a phone call, email, text or smoke signal from the media or anyone in the Canadian military, you are to immediately refer it to me," Black had said.

Then he had removed a heavy sheaf of papers from his briefcase. They spelled out the major's orders in more detail. In addition, a section on protocols and procedures pretty much explained how he would conduct all activities other than use of the washroom. Black cautioned him not to deviate in any way from those orders or procedures unless given special permission by himself or his people. The back page of the binder listed the code names of three people, including Mr. Black, who could be contacted.

On closer examination, Stone discovered that the Saglek Harbour base was situated 300 miles northeast of Goose Bay in northern Labrador. It lay just south of the Torngat Mountains and its National Park Preserve. The base needed to serve 200 personnel and a variety of military aircraft. Once it was operational, he was to facilitate the covert movement of a series of UCAVs and other military aircraft onto Canadian soil.

Stone's orders also showed an extensive list of personnel and co-team members including procurement and construction personnel who would facilitate the first phase of *Operation Flashbang*. Most, it turned out, were from the US Army Corp of Engineers. But there was also a civilian contingent supplied for building the early phases of the base.

Among the staffing sub-teams teams named, two puzzled him. *Tactical Air Control Team*, and *Mission Recovery Team*. These were asterisked and were explained in a foot-note simply: *As needed*. So, while everyone else from cooks to weapons specialists had a timeline for their arrival on base, these groups did not.

As he worked with the engineering corps to rebuild Saglek, Mr. Black regularly phoned him, read out a 15 digit alpha-numeric code as identification on his fully encrypted telephone, or emailed requests encrypted at both ends for progress reports on the set-up of the new base. Occasionally the orders changed with the addition or subtraction of facilities or equipment.

In the last year Stone and his staff had managed to: open the base and fully equip it so it now sheltered and fed up to 200 US military personnel; set up multiple UCAV ground control stations and satellite-based control or data links enabling remote pilotage of the UCAVs; and, receive military stores and "assets" on a weekly basis.

Indeed, redundancy seemed to be deemed critical since he'd been ordered to install three "shielded" Caterpillar 2000KW diesel electric industrial generators – one operating and two on standby to power the base. Each generator operated on its own independent circuit system and was primed to cut in with the loss of either of the other two. Chances of the base experiencing a total power failure had been reduced to almost nil.

A series of new hangars had also been constructed at Saglek for storing, assembling and maintaining all their unmanned and manned aircraft. The hangars had been built, Stone learned, because the Canadians had no idea these UCAVs were present, operational and armed to the teeth. They would usually fly in under cover of darkness, in the radar "shadow" of USAF supply aircraft, and also in pieces in C-17 Globemaster III cargo planes from the Heavy Airlift Wing. In keeping with their military exercise routines, five brand new Lockheed F-35 Lightning all-weather, stealth aircraft, had been deployed to Saglek as well as 12 F-16s, two Bell Huey helicopters and several reconnaissance aircraft that turned out to be modified Cessna's.

Their arsenal now contained a wide variety of armaments such as the General Atomics MQ-1 Avenger with AGM-114 Hellfire air-to-ground missiles, the Global Hawk retrofitted to carry conventional laser-guided bombs, MQ-1 Predators carrying Hellfires, Stingers or Griffin missiles, and the top secret, massive Super Eagle Drone capable of carrying 30,000-pound Bunker Buster bombs with a penetrating power of a dozen feet of solid concrete before exploding. All were fitted with multispectral targeting systems allowing them to paint the target with a laser or infrared beam and seal the target's fate once launch took place.

Also, the existing 4,700-foot runway had been salvaged from the ravages of time and weather, and had been repaired, widened and then lengthened to 6,500 feet.

In conjunction with on-site flight leaders and tactical personnel, Stone designed a "cover" program whereas the flights in and out of the base were presented as benign military exercises such as patrols, mock combat, and air search & rescue. In reality, performances were strictly theatre for the array of foreign spy satellites doubtlessly tuned to their location.

The base was also protected from inadvertent fly-bys compliments of Boeing E-3 Sentry planes known as AWACS, or Airborne Early Warning and Control Aircraft, deployed as needed.

On his frequent visits to the base Stone ensured security was tight. Movement was facilitated through a regimented system of electronic badges in various colors containing customized access codes, and a comprehensive system of retinal and fingerprint scan stations. He'd also interacted with the base's new CO, Colonel Robert D. Moorhead, a square-head type, tight-lipped, grim looking man who had been living on base since its inception and spent half his time in his office and the other half in his quarters. He had never been sighted at the commissary or the *Palm Tree Club* where officers and enlisted personnel could consume a strictly regulated amount of spirits. Moorhead even took a tray from the base cafeteria and ate in his room. Probably wouldn't be attending the Spring Prom neither, Stone mused.

For their stated purpose of war games, the major felt they were amalgamating one hell of a large collection of things that went 'bang!' And for him to be kept out of the inner loop for so long, the stakes must be extremely high.

Stone was also sure that agreement or no agreement, if the Canadians found out they were bringing in so many live fire weapons, there would be questions, lots of questions, notwithstanding the Canadian military's desire to play ball with their closest friends. As North American Aerospace Defense (NORAD) allies, leasing land for training was one thing. Using Canada as a base to mass an attack on *someone* crossed from strategic to political.

Stone had two offices, one in Saglek Harbour in Labrador, and one in Montreal. With the completion of the construction of the base, his core staff in Montreal had shrunk. Most had moved north already. His immediate Montreal staff now consisted only of Sally Taylor, his attractive administration secretary, whose true occupation was Staff Sargent in the USAF. Lieutenant Gilles Doyon, Logistics Officer in charge of USAF Standard Base Supply System adherence had moved north a few days ago leaving he and Sally as the proverbial Last of the Mohicans. He knew that soon he would lose her too; she wasn't slated to go north. Her time on the project had drawn to a close. Apparently she was shipping out for Guam the day they closed the office. That would certainly keep her out of circulation.

With an empty office this morning, only Sally greeted him as he entered. Not in a good mood, he merely nodded at the redhead and thumbed through some mail. It was the usual conglomeration of ads for enhanced business services and offers of ever faster internet connections. He threw them into the basket beside Sally's desk and began to move towards his own sparsely furnished office.

"Oh, Major Stone...?"

"Mr. Stone," Stone corrected her.

"Sorry, there's a man waiting in your office."

"Damnit all, Sally, why didn't you say so? Who is he?"

"Mr. Black," Sally said, "He was here before."

Stone opened the door to see Black sitting in one of two visitor chairs in front of his desk. The man didn't bother turning as he said: "Good morning Mr. Stone."

"Good morning, sir," Stone returned, taking his seat behind his desk and striving to keep any tone of annoyance out of his voice. It would have been nice to have a little notice of the man's impending visit. "To what do I owe this pleasure?"

"Merely checking in to thank you for a job well done," Black said, a slight smile on his lips. "Saglek Harbour is now operating and fully staffed, and I believe you have made an excellent start on receiving the assets."

Stone nodded politely while examining his guest more fully. The man was about 45 years of age with thinning dark hair; and he looked somewhat soft in the paunch. Though far from being a fashion consultant, Stone could see that his navy blue suit was custom-fitted; his white shirt and dark paisley tie would allow him to easily blend into a crowd of bankers or businessman. When Black threw one knee over the other, Stone noticed his highly polished black, wing-tip shoes and his first thought was: the man looks like an IBM salesman. Over the years he'd dealt with enough of them in his on-again, off-again roles as defense procurement and acquisition officer.

"You will close out the lease on this office and your condo, pay any penalties and move to Saglek where you will continue to receive and store the assets until we need them," Black said, flicking a piece of lint off his tie.

"Yes, sir," he answered. "Am I to assume that I will not be coordinating the removal of the equipment and the rest of the furniture, sir?

"One of our teams will dispose of the furniture here and remove all signs this was a well-secured site. It'll look exactly like when you moved in, except for a fresh coat of paint. You will leave absolutely nothing behind. Not even a coat rack. And no forwarding address. Once you've closed out the leases, no good-byes, thanks-for-the-memories, or mention of ever returning to Montreal. We know you have not formed any attachments here so there's no problem there. However, we also know you sometimes spend a few moments joking with your condo doorman, so no good-byes there neither. All other team members received the same instructions. You will all simply vanish."

Though used to the chain of command, Stone was becoming increasingly impatient with the cloak and dagger game. Obviously someone had been keeping an eye on him, even at his Montreal home. He decided to it was time to push back. "So, Mr. Black, you now have a fully functional base with our *assets* coming in daily. May I ask: To what end?"

Black smiled again. "You may ask but no answers yet, Major." Then he seemed to reconsider. "Still, perhaps some background is in order."

Stone nodded, willing to accept anything that would lead him farther down the murky road towards enlightenment.

"The United States has become used to being the sole superpower of the world," Black said. "Now, however, with unstable oil prices the Russian economy is in disarray, and Mr. Russian President is becoming even more aggressive than usual. China is in the process of building up its strategic and conventional military which worries us greatly. And, the Middle East continues to be one giant fuck-up as usual with a few wealthy countries like Saudi, UAE, Oman and Dubai buying gold-plated Cadillacs while their Muslim Taliban and ISIS protesters blow up their cities and citizens, and blame us for their problems. We are worried that the feeling of power we've enjoyed for more than 25 years is slipping, as is our ability to shape world events.

"Well, to be perfectly frank," he continued with a smile, "to allow the uber-rich to further prosper and the proletariat to, at least, keep their bellies full." He leaned back in his chair and grinned. Rather than being in a hurry he seemed intent on relaxing a little.

Stone leaned forward. "If you say so, sir."

Black shrugged and made himself more comfortable. "Well I'm taking away all the God, community, country and patriotic horse shit that we shovel out to get the citizens to do what the gentry want them to do. It's the same in every country, just a matter of manner and degree.

"But I digress. I head an organization of which you have never heard, nor will you," Black answered. "Essentially we have provided governments with counsel and even direction in certain specific and strategic areas for more than 50 years now. Over this last half-century we have cultivated favor, dependence and even fear with the decision makers. We work with local, state and federal organizations. And liaison with elite members of groups such as Bilderberg and the Bohemian Group. Essentially what the conspiracy theorists call the Illuminati. We work hard to keep the masses in check and convince them to embrace the ideology of corporatism as being necessary and desirable in our world. When we run into anyone – the government, military, NGOs, corps or individuals – who fail to realize the value of our counsel, we show them how much we know about them, their families and their businesses. Including their private lives. Everybody has something to hide."

Stone sat back in his chair: "Are you telling me you blackmail people?"

"Blackmail is such a harsh word," Black said, again with an enigmatic smile. "Let's say we strongly encourage them to consider our case favorably. But rest assured, this mostly happens at the lower levels of organizations. We have little trouble influencing the leaders of said organizations with their penchant for peccadillos whether they be off-shore accounts, a pretty skirt set up in a hidden apartment, or perhaps a walk on the wild side in lady's underwear. Whatever. It's the lower levels who cause us the most headaches."

"I see," Stone said.

"Some theorists say we are a shadow government. I prefer to say we are an adjunct government. Or even a sub rosa advisory board."

"Unelected," Stone pointed out. "And operating outside the strains of democratic and civilized behavior."

Black smiled again. "We are here to serve. Just like you are. To achieve your objective in the military, you use bombs, bullets and bayonets that rip, tear, and shred human flesh. We use information as an incentive. Who would *you* say is the more civilized?"

Stone sighed. "So why are you telling me this? If your organization is so secret?"

"Doesn't matter, Major," Black shot back. "Any right thinking person would know we exist in some form. Besides, most people like to think their destiny is in their own hands through freedom of choice and the democratic process. They're way more comfortable with self-deception, which works well for us. After all, why have the harshness of reality when you can have the comfort of illusion?"

Stone stared at him.

"We aren't a malicious organization, Major. We simply provide advice to maintain balance, stability and the status quo. Surely that isn't bad."

Though a well-informed and educated man, Paul Stone now had confirmation about the hidden realities of politics and power.

Black's cell phone rang and he dug it out of his pocket.

"Go ahead," he said without preamble. He listened intently for a moment. "How do you know? Alright, if you are sure. Proceed." There was more information imparted by the caller and Black's features clouded and he flushed beet red: "I don't fucking care!" he grunted. "Find out!" He pressed end on his phone. "Now, where the hell were we?"

Stone was decidedly uncomfortable and wanted this man out of his office as soon as possible. "So what's next?" he asked, lamely.

"You mean after you get to Saglek?"

"Yes."

"You'll be given certain duties necessary to the operation by Colonel Moorhead the base CO. If everything goes as planned, you should be home within a few more months. Probably doing what you were doing at Wright-Patterson before you left."

"Aren't we bringing in a hell of a lot of UCAVs, sir?" Stone pressed, gently. "And munitions. Including some major amounts. If these are for war games, I'd say we are going to lose a hell of a lot of personnel. So, again, to what end?"

Black smiled, tolerantly. "As you know, Major, the next war will be mainly fought with missiles, and UCAVs for mop up. Canadian Defense Research and Development has been testing their drones for functionality in the extreme conditions of the High Arctic out of Canadian Forces Station Alert. We needed an arctic-like location to do the same. Hence Saglek."

"What about Alaska?"

"We like Canada," Black replied, the falsehood rolling smoothly off his tongue. "Look, it costs five or six million dollars to train an F-18 pilot and almost $30 million to buy one. If they go down, we lose that investment. Drones are far cheaper. But they need testing under all weather conditions."

Somehow Stone knew he was lying. Test flying drones in varying weather conditions didn't require 50 fully armed vehicles.

Black took his briefcase, rose and paused at the closed door, hand on the knob. "What do you think is America's greatest weapon, Major?"

Stone took a moment to think. "Information?" he ventured, seizing on Black's theme.

"True to a degree," Black said, again with the patronizing smile. "Information is very important for decision making. But when it comes to taking down those who would attempt to thwart our goals or mean us harm, the answer is *technology*. Technology that we can weaponize will determine whether we live or die in the future. And that's what we have to concentrate on getting. The best technology on earth. Or, from anywhere else, for that matter."

He smiled, yanked the office door open and breezed through it as though he remembered an important meeting. Stone stared after him as he waved at Sally and slammed the outer office door.

~ 9 ~

Thousands of miles away from Montreal, there were other forces at work that would probably not been a surprise to Black. No longer did any world military force operate in a silo where it could keep its secrets from the rest of the world. There were always eyes-in-the-sky watching and electronic ears listening. Even the most secure internet connections were always deemed to be vulnerable.

In a wintry Moscow suburb, Major Oleg Serdyukov sighed and drank from his cup of sweetened tea that had already gone cold. He set it down on his large mahogany desk and looked around the dark, oak-paneled office. For his level, he was lucky to have such an office as this. In reality, it was offered to him as part of a perceived incentive to move to glass-sided GRU Headquarters and away from the halls of power in the Kremlin. A booby prize, so to speak. Now, though he intensely disliked the traffic-ridden drive to "The Aquarium," as the GRU headquarters at the Khodinka Airfield had been nicknamed, he wouldn't trade the inconvenience for the opportunity to sit back in the Kremlin in central Moscow any day of the week.

The major already had the "pleasure" of serving there for a few years and he likened it to a beehive filled with nervous worker bees maneuvering through a poisoned web of intrigue employing lies, double dealings, spying and betrayals to survive. The goal was to climb the ladder of importance at all costs. Indeed, those tip toeing down the corridors of power spent a minor portion of their days dealing with governing challenges, and a major portion seeking to upgrade their power and influence through fostering alliances, initiating deals, practicing sycophancy and looking over their shoulders.

After all, it was only through power and influence could one guarantee one's personal security and privilege. And, as he'd soon found out, Russia's current President wasn't above pitting his executives in both the Politburo and the Central Committee, and on down the line, against each other. Those who pleased him most, advanced. Those who didn't, were either demoted or simply vanished. Whether they wound up in non-descript jobs out of the limelight, or in concrete footers for new buildings was anyone's guess. The President, if asked, would only laugh and say they were contributing to the foundation of the Federation.

No, Serdyukov hoped he would remain in GRU headquarters until he retired in a few years. His duties here were simple: Acting Commander of a special group of *Spetsnaz* units returned to GRU from the *General Staff of the Armed Forces of the Russian Federation*. Most of these units had remained part of the wider *Special Operations Forces of the Russian Federation* during the latest reorganization, but a few specialized units were segregated and moved to new training facilities at the airport.

Traditionally the Spetsnaz were composed of elite groups of GRU operatives skilled in the art of weapons handling, rappelling, explosives training, marksmanship, counter-terrorism, parachute training, hand-to-hand combat, alpine climbing and demolition. In other words, if an operation was top secret or required an array of military cross-training, these were your boys. Serdyukov's units, however, were selected for their smarts as well as their military prowess.

All could flawlessly speak multiple languages, including English, French, Spanish and German. In English, for example, they learned dialects and accents ranging from stuffy Great Britain to the US Deep South. Acting and deception training lessons were also given for work behind enemy lines. Finally, each man had also been required to obtain advanced degrees in areas such as chemistry, biology, nuclear physics, and computer sciences. In effect, his men were the cream.

To be certain Serdyukov had administrative duties as well involving training schedules, payroll, supply chain management and budgets, all requiring reports in triplicate. But his main focus was and would remain the on-going training and readiness of his units.

The major picked up his daily edition of *Pravda*, shook out the folds and then abruptly set it down again. The newspaper was a shadow of its former self. It now had a print run of a mere one hundred thousand copies rather than the millions it printed during the hay days of communism.

With the dissolution of the USSR, President Boris Yeltzin had sold the newspaper off to a Greek business family in 1991, likely to show the

West that the days of propaganda and lies were over in Russia. The Communist Party of the Russian Federation had bought it back in 1997 and re-established it as the official mouthpiece of the Federation. Unfortunately, the Internet now gave citizens the real scoop on what was happening in the world, and so *Pravda's* popularity had declined drastically. Still, Serdyukov knew it was politically astute to have a copy folded on one's desk to show you were still a good Party member and, if nothing else, that you were up to speed on the current bullshit the Party was slavishly shoveling out to its members.

He reached over and roughly fingered his copy, tearing a page or two in the process. Now it looked like it had been thoroughly read.

And, as a loyal Party member, whether you believed the garbage being printed or not, you *believed* the garbage being printed. He gazed absentmindedly out the window. Though the weather was dull and dreary, there was another, larger shadow hanging over the day; Serdyukov was dreading his next appointment. Largely, he assumed, his dread came out of the fact he was ignorant of the subject of the meeting. In fact, so much so, it was causing him consternation and heartburn. In vain, he had tried to convince himself it could be nothing. He should be so lucky. On the other hand, it could mean that everything was about to change. After all, how often did a Major General visit a lowly major such as himself unless there was something of significance in the works? Even if they had been allies, maybe even friends, during his days in the Kremlin. Perhaps it was Ukraine again, he reasoned. Perhaps his boys were to be deployed to the border to create more hell for those poor misguided nationalistic bastards on the other side. They couldn't seem to get it in their heads that Ukraine was endemic to Russia's core, its heart so to speak. Though achieving independence in 1991 with the end of the USSR, Ukraine was squarely in the Bear's sights. Russia had already annexed Crimea, and was working with pro-Russian rebels in Ukraine to weaken its borders and its misguided concept of independence. So maybe the rebels needed some unofficial help once again. Hopefully it wouldn't mean downing another civilian airliner.

The knock came abruptly and without warning. Where the hell was his secretary, Kalina? That wasn't her knock.

Without further preamble the door opened and Major General Sergei Topkolov entered and slapped his top heavy hat down on

Serdyukov's desk, the oversized crown providing a perfect landing pad. He grunted a greeting and plopped down in the guest chair without invitation. Serdyukov leaped to his feet and saluted.

"Oh, sit down, Oleg," Topkolov said, tiredly. "Jesus Christ, we're beyond that."

"So wonderful to see you again, General," Serdyukov lied, smoothly.

His visitor gave him an enigmatic look, shaking his head at the same time.

Serdyukov swallowed hard wondering just how serious this visit would be.

"Now there's a pile of shit if I've ever heard one," Topkolov said with a grin. "Who the hell wants a visit from anyone in the Kremlin? Out here you're away from all the political nonsense and can wait for retirement and maybe a small dacha on the Black Sea? If Ukraine permits it, of course." The last sentence came out in a bitter aside.

"General, I –," Serdyukov began.

"Sergei…." Topkolov interrupted, with a smile.

Serdyukov hesitated and then smiled. "Tell me this isn't bad news, Sergei." Though they had known each other for more than two decades, Serdyukov had learned long ago not to be presumptuous unless invited to do so by a superior.

"No, Comrade. It's merely another operation."

"Ukraine?"

"No. This involves Canada."

"Canada!? What did they do?"

"Other than they keep questionable company, very little. I must now put you on notice. This comes from the highest level of command, Oleg. Top Secret. Marshal Titov is in the loop."

Serdyukov felt his heart beginning to pound. Damn, he thought. Just when everything seemed to be going smoothly. If it was Top Secret, that meant a mission with risk involved. And, if things went bad on the mission, he'd be the one who got screwed. So who wanted *risk* at this stage of his career? Certainly not him. "Whatever, I can do, I'll do for Mother Russia," he said sweetly, trying to force a smile.

"Sure you will, Oleg. Anyhow, listen carefully. No notes. The Canadians have allowed the Americans to reactivate and arm a base in northern Labrador. An old radar base named Saglek Harbour. From the cold war. It was part of the Pinetree Radar Defense line back in the 60s and 70s. They mothballed it decades ago but now our recon satellites show major activity there for the last year."

"A new defence base?"

"No, this isn't for defence, we are sure. They've been bringing in military drones by the dozens and hiding them."

"Are they nuclear?"

"We don't think so. Which, in turn, makes no sense."

"Alright...?" Serdyukov said, hesitantly. "What they do on their own soil, or NORAD's controlled soil, is their own business, isn't it?"

Yes, but we like to know *what* they are doing, *when* they are doing it and, mostly, *why* they are doing it. It's the last part that scares us. They are bringing in Avengers, Reapers, Predators and some we don't recognize."

"How can I help?"

"You know our interest in the Arctic has increased of late. We feel the only way to find out for sure what is going on, is to put boots on the ground."

"Send in a unit?" Serdyukov was shocked.

"A small team. Not a full unit. And not right now. But I want to give you a heads up. We would send in no more than five, maybe even three. They will be facing Arctic conditions and will have to use extreme stealth. They must speak Canadian English. Those new suits we have, they work well against infrared detection?"

"Dyflon IR coatings are excellent but not 100 percent," Serdyukov said and hurriedly added, "Sergei, imagine the consequences if they are caught?"

"Our mission planners are working to ensure that doesn't happen. They'll need the suits for some reconnaissance work. But they'll be disguised as Canadian Innu and hunters so they can travel openly to get near the base and observe."

"We'll need Canadian equipment and clothes and identities for them."

"Yes, so you can source that now. It may not happen but I am preparing you. Select your best team. Accelerate training with an Arctic component and have them start using Canadian English right now, eh?"

He grinned. Then, as an afterthought, "Oh, they will carry a special *99-Rasplavleniye* to be used in the event of imminent capture. Or, at the end of the mission."

The *99-Rasplavleniye*, which translated into 99-Meltdown, was a new, Russian-developed, phosphorous-based incendiary device that also used magnesium and thermite to enhance its effects. Once lit, it would reduce 99 percent of its immediate surroundings to cinders within 15 to 20 meters. That included flesh, bones and even hardened steel. It was so devastating, that within 30 seconds, even the rocks and earth beneath it would begin to melt. Not a scrap of hair, bone or DNA would survive.

"This is a suicide mission?" Serdyukov asked, in disbelief. "What if they succeed and are undetected? Will there be an attempt to retrieve them? Any attempt?"

He knew most of these men and wasn't about to abandon them without at least a modicum of resistance.

The general stood up and crossed to Serdyukov's single office window. He looked out the 15-story glass building at the thin lane leading through the 10-meter high cement wall behind the Institute for Cosmic Biology; it provided one of two access routes to GRU headquarters. A guard stood outside a small, lighted guardhouse at the lane entrance and paced up and down in front of the red-striped gate as he covertly smoked.

A light snow had begun falling and droves of grey mist were blowing over from the airfield. A man wearing a brown Russian wool military great coat, fronted by two rows of brass buttons, and a badged Ushanka on his head, hurried across the slush of the half-full parking lot within the wall. He clutched his briefcase tightly, and headed for his small car. There was little doubt he was anxious to escape the office. Maybe he was looking forward to a nice hot bowl of borscht at home. All in all, a typical dreary winter day, Topkolov thought. He could feel Sergei's eyes drilling into his back but he wasn't ready to answer yet.

In the gathering twilight he could make out the yellow lights of the Institute for Biology winking on, one-by-one as darkness began smothering the gloom. He knew they did a lot more than dissect frogs over there. After all, you don't need hazmat suits and auxiliary air supplies for cutting up a reptile.

Finally he turned and faced Oleg Serdyukov with a look of pity.

After all, Oleg would be the one who had to break the news to the team.

"No," the general answered bluntly. "They won't be extracted. This is a one-way mission. Once they transmit what they've found and carried out further orders, they will become Federation heroes. Unsung of course, but nevertheless, heroes. Ensuring a 100 percent absence of risk, means they have to be dispatched on site and leave no trace of their presence. *No trace!* That is why those you select must be our most dedicated. Our most loyal. Our most committed. Of course their families, parents, wives, children will be well cared for, so assure them of that fact."

"Yes sir. But –?"

Topkolov interrupted him. "They may not have to go, Oleg. But if they do, they won't be coming back."

~10~

After exiting the Montreal hospital, Matthew decided to head straight for Labrador and Ungava Diamonds' headquarters and bring Jacquard up to date. He called Mary and 30 minutes later, as he pushed through the open door, he encountered the secretary hard at work typing frantically on her keyboard.

"He's expecting you," Mary said, and motioned Matthew towards the president's open door. Jacquard was at his desk. He put the phone down as Matthew tapped on the doorframe.

"C'mon in, Matthew," Jacquard called. "More bad luck, eh?"

"Sort of bad," Matthew agreed.

"Sort of bad?" Jacquard queried. "Bloody awful is more like it. Our friend is comatose, you say. He's not talking and he's not walking, so how the hell will we find the source of his diamond?"

"His granddaughter will take me there."

Jacquard stared at him, hope shining in his eyes. "His granddaughter? She knows where the diamond came from?" he asked.

"That's what she says. Claims her grandfather asked her to take me."

"So he had a contingency plan in case something happened to him," Jacquard said, much relieved. "What a guy!"

Matthew hesitated remembering what Sky had said during their coffee time; her and her grandfather had a special "connection." He decided to be straightforward with his boss. If things didn't work out, at least he would realize beforehand there were some anomalies in the situation.

"Actually she says it was *after* he stroked out. She talked to him…in her mind."

"God almighty," Jacquard whispered in despair, dropping his head into his hands. "We're dealing with a family of Looney Tunes."

"The diamond is real," Matthew reminded him.

Jacquard's head snapped up. "That's true. The diamond is real and it came from somewhere. If she knows where, that's all we need. Does she want us to fly you guys there?"

"No. She said that if we wanted things to remain confidential, she'd have to guide me by land. One week in and one week out."

"No brass monkeys need apply," Jacquard said, hunching his shoulders against the imagined cold. "When?"

"I have to be in Nain by December 7th which, she said, should get us there in time."

"In time for what?"

"I've no idea…though she did mention something about the Winter Solstice."

"Stranger and stranger," Jacquard mused. "Maybe it's a medicine man thing."

Matthew cocked his head. "So, do you want me to go?"

"Does a Polar Bear shit on the ice?"

"Alright, I've got almost five weeks left. Should I head back to George River?"

"Hell no," Jacquard answered, expansively. "Take a vacation. Stay drunk for a week. Take your kids to visit Disney World."

Matthew stared at him. "You know we lost our daughter," he said, simply.

Jacquard held up his hands, chastened.

"I'm sorry, Matthew. I forgot. Didn't mean anything by it. Hasn't been that long, has it? How is your wife making out?"

"We'll be divorced in a few weeks I imagine."

"Oh boy…I can't say anything right today." He got up, crossed to his extensive bar and took out two glasses which he filled with a healthy dose of Canadian Club. He handed one to Matthew and held his own glass up in a toast.

"Stand down until you go. Full salary, of course. And a bonus if we pull this off. I'll tell the George River office you're on a special assignment for me." He shook his head. "I'm just relieved the company may *not* be going tits up. That's all. Here's to success." He downed his drink in one swallow.

Matthew did the same. Than he dropped his bombshell.

"She says we'll be going into the Torngat Mountains."

Jacquard's head came up. "Holy Mary Mother of God! Doesn't she know that's now a National Park? If the diamonds are in there, we won't be able to buy up leases and mine them."

"She claims the site is just outside the park boundaries, near the Nunavik side."

"Well I hope she knows what she's talking about," Jacquard said. "Otherwise we're going to be in deep trouble."

* * *

Sky stepped out of the Royal Vic's main entrance. The sky was blue, the newly fallen snow blindingly white, and the temperature hovered around -5 C. Absolutely no change in her grandfather's condition made her more and more upset. They had scheduled an MRI to see if they could spot the clot though the damage was likely permanent by now. What she needed to know was the extent of the damage.

Usually there was a line-up of cabs waiting to pounce on hospital visitors but there was none in sight at the moment.

She paused on the steps and was about to go back inside to call one when a Diamond Taxi car pulled up and disembarked an elderly passenger. The old man staggered around to the back to meet the driver who removed a walker from the trunk, made sure the elderly gent was stable, and then prepared to leave.

"Excuse me, are you available?" Sky called.

The driver nodded as the old man proceeded to limp past Sky on the sidewalk. He gave her an appraising glance, raised an eyebrow and asked: "Where you been all my life, beautiful?"

Sky couldn't help laughing and quickly answered: "Waiting for you, oh wise one."

"Well you just made an old guy's day, gorgeous!" He grinned and shuffled off towards the main entrance ramp.

"And it didn't take much," Sky muttered to herself feeling an empathy for the fellow who probably felt as young as a twenty-year-old in his mind, but was now saddled with an aged and ailing body. Like her grandfather who lay still and silent three floors up.

"You must not leave me, grandfather."

"Château Champlain, s'il vous plait?" Sky called as she entered the cab.

She checked her purse to ensure she had enough money on hand to pay the driver. Some were still pretty traditional and didn't carry a debit machine. It was cash or nothing. After a brief search she was successful. She figured that the thirty dollars she found would cover the fare.

In fact, it felt strange to actually be carrying a purse rather than a carbine after more than a year of living up in Labrador. She had carefully chosen one that looked more like a small valise rather than a woman's purse design. As far as Sky was concerned, the stores could keep their obscenely priced Gucci and Coach hand-bags, products manufactured in low wage countries, just like the more modestly priced.

She settled back in her seat as the driver accelerated away. As they headed south, Sky allowed herself to enjoy the parade of French and British architecture that had wisely been protected by Montreal's city fathers. Despite the constant and savage pressure of developers and profiteers to rip down and replace, Montreal was still an impressive mixture of old and new buildings. Its rich architectural legacy was the result of two successive colonizations by the French and British beginning in the early 1500s. A violent history of successive wars with the Iroquois Nation eventually gave way to time and progress, and modern Montreal became the financial and industrial capital of Canada for almost a century and a half. Every major bank had its 19-Century-built headquarters on St. James Street.

Then the 1976 provincial election of the Francophone Parti Québécois brought the specter of separation from Canada front and center. An attempted genocide of the English language in the province, through Bill 101, also meant Saint James Street was renamed Saint

Jacques Street and almost every other named feature in the province from lakes to mountains to city parks were all given new francophone names. If separation did occur, the corporations and banks with headquarters in Quebec would be vulnerable.

Nationalization of these banks or businesses would be entirely possible as a fledgling nationalistic-centric government attempted to mitigate political damage and control its finances.

Therefore, in the 1970s and 1980s, banks, insurance companies and hundreds of other sizeable retail and industrial businesses fled their long established homes in Montreal to re-establish their headquarters in Toronto, Ontario. And, Toronto and the rest of the province welcomed them with open arms. Toronto quickly assumed its new title of 'largest city in Canada.' It didn't seem to faze the Parti Québécois who were more concerned with culture than business and finances.

While this exodus may have been responsible for keeping much of the legacy architecture of Montreal from being built over, the City of Toronto only too willingly caved in to the pressures of greedy developers and big money. And as development ran rampant in the province, more than a few town councilors found new ways to fund their retirements.

Without a single thought given to preserving its 19th Century architecture, it happily razed most of its significant downtown stone buildings and replaced them with towering monoliths of steel and glass with all the architectural attractiveness of giant shiny cereal boxes. It was determined to become a 21st Century city even at the price of losing what was irreplaceable.

Seeing what was happening in Toronto, Montreal made sure to protect its history. For instance, it brought in severe height restrictions of a maximum of 223 meters above sea level for buildings thus assuring no structure would ever exceed the height of Mount Royal, the much beloved, inner-city mountain. For Old Montreal, with street widths and architecture more resembling Paris than North America, height restrictions and building codes were even more severe in their limitations. They wisely preserved and protected. The result was a beautiful city featuring world famous cathedrals, basilicas and other historical buildings and monuments dating back to the 16th century.

The cab dropped Sky off at Château Champlain and she entered the rich, wood-paneled lobby. Having left her key card at the front desk, she approached it just as another person walked up to her right. He gallantly waved her ahead and she smiled. And then stared at Matthew Corrigan. The look on his face was as shocked as that on her own.

"Sky…Miss St. Onge!" he said, in surprise. "Are you staying here?"

For a moment she was too surprised to answer. This quickly changed to resentment. Was he spying on her? Playing games to ensure he didn't lose contact with his guide to the diamonds?

"When did you book in here?" she asked, her voice tight but controlled.

"T-Today," he stammered, puzzled at what looked like thunderclouds gathering in her eyes.

"Today?" she asked. "Why today?"

"I just came in this morning after I met you at the hospital."

"How did you know where I was staying?"

"I didn't," he said, defensively. "I always stay here. This is my preferred hotel in Montreal." Now he could feel his own hackles rising at her tone. Enough was enough. "Why? Would you like me to stay somewhere else?"

"That's really not my business," she said, somewhat dismissively.

"You could have fooled me."

Matthew was already wishing he hadn't pushed back. Usually he managed his emotions and kept them on an even keel. Indeed, there was likely a substantial amount of transference involved on both their parts: his from his visit to the Helene, and hers from her grandfather's illness.

Indeed, Sky was also wondering at her own abrasiveness. This wasn't like her. She didn't know why she felt the way she did since he seemed to be a nice enough guy, and, like her, was caught up in circumstances not of his own making. She decided she was letting her personal history and current issues control her feelings way too much. Time to calm down and not see conspiracies around every corner.

"Look, I'm sorry," she said, hating the fact she was apologizing to him for her behavior for the second time that day. "I'm just a little surprised to find you here. Please enjoy your stay." She turned to the desk clerk to ask for her room card but Matthew wasn't finished.

"If you're really sorry, you'll have dinner with me tonight."

She stared at him. "Are you asking me out on a date?" she inquired.

"Hell, no!" Matthew asserted in haste. "It's just I'm uncomfortable eating alone in public. I do all sorts of odd things, like turn my head at the wrong moment and stick food in my ear."

He thought he saw the ghost of a smile touch her lips so he continued. "Eat together. That's all. We don't even have to talk."

She considered his offer for a moment. "I'll see you down here at eight," she said, without looking at him. Then she took her card key and headed for the elevator.

"Well, I'll be damned," he said to himself as he faced the pretty, dark-haired desk clerk. "Any messages for me?"

"Did you have a red light on your phone, Monsieur?" she inquired politely.

"No idea. I haven't been upstairs since I registered."

She consulted her computer. "Rien, monsieur."

"Merci," he answered, and also headed for the elevators.

That evening he arrived down in the lobby at precisely eight o'clock since she might interpret being early as being too eager, and being late as showing some sort of disrespect for her. She definitely had a bee in her bonnet about something and he wished he knew what it was. He was still wondering why he had bothered to ask her to have dinner with him. It had just burst out without any forethought. Right now, he decided, she was a beautiful girl with a personality that fell far short of her looks.

Sky rounded a corner in the lobby. He noticed she was wearing chinos, a navy & brown knit ski sweater over a white blouse, and carried a light blue down coat and a small leather purse without buttons or bows or any other sign it was a female accouterment. Nor was she wearing jewelry of any kind.

"You're right on time," she said brightly.

"I thought it might be important that I was," Matthew answered cautiously.

Sky chuckled. "I'm not apologizing to you for the third time today even though I've been acting like a first-class hissy bitch. But let me assure you, it's nothing you've done."

Matthew answered: "I'm sure you have a lot on your mind and I can understand your anger over what happened to your grandfather."

'Stage three alright," she confirmed. "Anger and bargaining."

"Any word?"

"He's still the same. I feel guilty going out tonight when he's alone there in the hospital."

"There really isn't much you can do, is there?"

She sighed. "No there isn't. I've tried talking to him again but I'm getting nothing back."

Matthew really wasn't sure how to respond but decided to act like it was completely natural. "You mean speak to him…in your mind?"

She nodded slowly. "That's right." Her tone crisped up a shade; Matthew knew enough to let sleeping dogs lie.

He quickly changed the subject by clapping his hands together and saying: "So, is there any particular type of food you'd like tonight? Greek, German, Swahili…?"

She smiled. "I like that in a man."

"What?" he asked.

"An uncanny ability to know when to duck and weave."

"Yeah, well life has slapped me around enough for a while. I don't go looking for trouble." He realized how pathetic he sounded and tried to cover. "Poor me, eh?"

Sky gave him a questioning look and he immediately regretted his outburst; if anyone had issues at the moment, it was Sky and her grandfather.

They grabbed a cab and Sky allowed him to select a restaurant in the city's history-rich section called Old Montreal. He chose Vieux-Port Steakhouse. Later, seated in a slight alcove with a nearby fireplace, they dined by firelight on rib steaks with a fine, wine-based, demi-glace sauce and a nice bottle of Beaujolais. After finishing they declined dessert and ordered two Café au lait. Though they hadn't spoken much over dinner, Sky felt very comfortable with Matthew. Now the chewing was over, each felt a social obligation to say something.

"Good steak," Matthew commented, looking at his plate.

"Very good," Sky agreed.

"Love that demi-glace."

"Me too," she said.

He glanced up and she saw amusement in his glance.

"Come here often?" he asked.

"Not often enough."

"Is Nain your permanent home?"

"While grandfather is there, it will be my home." She hesitated as she realized her words might be too prophetic.

"Do you visit the South often?"

"I studied and lived here in Montreal for nine years."

"Really?" he exclaimed. "What did you study?"

Sky toyed with her coffee cup. This is what she had feared might happen. As usual, one question inevitably led to another, which would lead to another and another until her personal history was laid bare before this relative stranger. She didn't know Matthew Corrigan well enough to allow this. In fact she didn't like to confide in anyone other than her grandfather. At 33 years of age, Sky felt she had experienced more than enough loss, hurt and disappointment in her life.

"Are you still with me there, Sky?" Matthew prompted, with a gentle smile.

"Sorry," she said, quickly. "It's getting late. Would you mind terribly if we stopped by the hospital on our way back to the hotel?"

"Of course not," Matthew answered, though he knew it would add quite a few kilometers to their ride.

He summoned the waiter, ordered a cab and paid the bill, leaving a generous tip. Sky tried to pay her share but he wouldn't hear of it.

"I put you through this evening so it's only fair I pay the penalty," he said, lightly.

"It was a nice evening," she mused, though obviously distracted by something.

"Well, maybe we can do it again sometime," he ventured casually.

She didn't reply.

They pushed through the brown wooden doors onto Rue Saint-Gabriel and the waiter quickly locked the doors behind them. Matthew glanced at his watch. It was near 11 PM. He should have realized they were past closing time as there wasn't another soul in the place.

A light mist was blowing off the St. Lawrence River into Old Montreal. While not overly freezing, the dampness still seemed to penetrate his bones and nestle stubbornly in the marrow. He shivered. Must be getting old, he thought. Sky seemed impervious to the evening's coolness.

Hoping the cab would be along soon, he helped her into her jacket and wished he had worn more than a corduroy sports coat. He looked up and down the street at the 17th and 18th century buildings. North of them, the more modern section, bordered by Rue Notre Dame, had the occasional car going by. Down where they were in Old Montreal, at the corner of Saint Gabriel and Saint Paul, it was deserted. He looked northward again and saw a long, black limo cruising purposely southward towards them. The taxi company must have been out of regular cabs, he thought.

"Perfect timing," he said, as the limo approached.

And then it hit him: Saint Gabriel was a one-way street going north; the limo was coming south. Surely a Montreal driver would know that. Also, the fact that the Metro Police were notorious for their ticketing campaigns meant most drivers wouldn't risk such a move, even at night. Something wasn't right.

Matthew might have flown Hercules in the RCAF, but he had gone through basic military training like any soldier; this training helped make him constantly aware of his surroundings and to note anything odd or out of place. He had flown in many danger zones and often avoided disaster by following his instincts. Therefore he never dismissed bad feelings. And, he had a bad feeling now.

The limo was slowing and he saw two bulky men in the front seats. He couldn't be sure due to the darkness of the back windows, but he thought he saw movement between the front seats. That meant there was a third party riding in back. Matthew's hair was standing up on the back of his neck, definitely not good sign.

"Sky, get back –!" he managed to get out before the car jerked to a stop. The front and back doors of the limo burst open and two men dressed in black pants and sweaters jumped out. They each wore a ski mask, but Matthew sensed they didn't plan to hit the slopes that night. A huge man from the front seat went straight for Matthew while a slightly smaller fellow jumped from the back door and ran towards Sky.

She screamed and threw herself backwards toward the wooden restaurant doors.

"Shit," the shorter man cursed, grabbing her left arm with his left hand and pulling hard. Caught off guard she spun about until her back was to him. In his other hand he held a black, cloth sack which he pulled over her head. He yanked her backwards into a bear hug.

Matthew was backing up to get some space between himself and the giant who refused to allow him any room to maneuver. The man hit him twice in the chest and ribs with sledge-hammer blows, and then barreled forward and flattened him against the brick side of the building. Matthew stripped him of the ski mask which didn't seem to bother his assailant.

"Stay outta it!" the big man warned ominously, pinning Matthew's shoulders against the wall with two meat-pie-sized hands. Unblinking black eyes bored into his. Matthew noticed a thin, red half-moon scar on the man's left cheek. He heard Sky cry out and sought to push his attacker aside. He might as well have tried to move a half-ton boulder. The man clubbed him in the side of the head and pinned his shoulders again; the punch was so powerful he saw stars.

He tried to push forward but the giant held him in an iron grip. In fact, he seemed to be enjoying the combat and Matthew felt that he was probably disappointed that there wasn't more resistance involved. Matthew realized he didn't have the brute strength to win the battle, but he did have the smarts. One order of 'resistance' coming up.

In shock and trying to breathe with the man crushing him, Matthew nodded, forced himself to relax, and leaned his head back against the wall in defeat. Suddenly he snapped it forward driving his forehead into the middle of the big man's nose. Wetness exploded into his face as his opponent screamed and raised both hands to his face. Matthew drove his knee into his attacker's groin. The man twisted away in pain. With his arms now freed, Matthew's training decreed he seize the split-second advantage he'd gained and finish the fight. Using his weight, he delivered an elbow strike to the man's exposed neck. He collapsed face down on the sidewalk.

Stepping over his prone assailant, he saw the shorter man had his arms around Sky. She struggled gamely, but her feet were off the ground and she was being carried towards the limo's open back door. Matthew quickly kicked the door closed. Shorty wouldn't be able to open it again unless he released Sky.

"Alright, asshole," thundered the big guy from behind him. Against all odds, the giant was rising. His face was red and the scar on his cheek even more pronounced.

Matthew spun to face him. He blocked a blow aimed at his face but the man's reach was so long he was able to reach around with his other arm and club him hard in the kidney. Matthew gasped and dropped to one knee in pain. Rather than pressing his advantage, the man stepped back a few paces and then charged him like a locomotive bent on crushing its victim. He was coming fast, in fact, way too fast. Matthew didn't dodge or try to move out of the way. Instead he braced himself, bent down and then thrust his head between the man's legs. He drove himself to his feet, pinioning the man's legs and carrying him upward into the air. His momentum sent his foe sailing backwards over Matthew's head and towards the limo. His attacker smashed onto the roof, skidded off, and landed on the pavement on the other side of the car with a thud. The sound was followed by a groan of anguish. The limo roof would need body work.

Matthew then turned his attention back to Sky. The short man was holding her with one arm around her neck and in the process of yanking open the limo door again with the other. He got it open, got in himself and was trying to drag a fiercely resisting Sky inside. He was halfway in, his arm extended out the door holding her when Matthew slammed the limo door on it with all his might. The crunch of bone was loud, but not as loud as the shrill scream from inside.

A third voice, likely the driver, was yelling: "Abort, abort!"

The injured arm was yanked inside, the door hastily pulled closed and Matthew heard the lock being hammered shut. He kicked the back door window with all his might. No spider vein of cracks radiated outward from where his heel made contact. Bullet-proof, he decided as he pulled Sky to safety back on the sidewalk. Almost simultaneously he heard the back door on the other side slamming shut. The limo squealed off down the street, its tires spinning on the damp pavement, its rear end fishtailing as it accelerated. It pulled right onto a street south of Rue Saint Paul and vanished from sight.

Matthew sank to his knees on the sidewalk, gasping for breath.

"Are you alright, Matthew?" Sky panted, also dropping to her knees beside him. "Answer me! Oh damn it, you're bleeding."

He laughed and coughed, still too winded to talk. She frantically checked his face, body and limbs.

"Not...my...blood," he managed to get out.

"Are you okay?" she demanded, her hands cupping his face.

"I...I think I broke a nail," he gasped.

"Cut the comedy," she admonished, angrily. "Are you hurt?

He was now shaking so hard he thought his teeth would chatter. Pulling himself to his feet, he bent over, placed his hands on his knees and tried to concentrate on breathing.

"Hurts everywhere," he finally answered. His chest felt as though he'd been run over by a truck and his lower back was on fire every time he moved or breathed. "I-I can't stop shaking."

"Adrenalin," Sky said. "Fight or flight. It'll wear off. We have to get you to a hospital."

"Friends of yours?" he asked.

"Dear God, no! Were they trying to mug us?"

"No, I think they were trying to kidnap you."

"Kidnap me?" she exclaimed. "Why? Why would anyone want to kidnap me?"

"I don't know. Have you annoyed anybody? Of late, I mean?"

"Annoy who?" she asked, her tone betraying confusion. They'd barely escaped a violent attack; God only knew where it might have ended.

"Are you rich?" he asked.

"Hardly," she said, picking up her small purse from the sidewalk.

"But you could be."

"What are you talking about?" she asked.

"The diamond," he said flatly, and winched in pain as he moved.

"That's what this was about?"

"Unless you know something and aren't telling me."

A cab with a Hochelaga Taxi sign atop it came around the corner and pulled to a stop beside them. Obviously the one they ordered.

"Let's take this cab…instead," he quipped, again. "The other guy's customer service sucks." He tried to sound nonchalant but it was getting harder to do as the shock wore off and his pain grew.

She helped him into the back of the taxi while telling the driver to take them to the Royal Victoria Hospital, emergency entrance. "And hurry!" she added.

Matthew groaned as he sat in the back seat. Every time he took a deep breath it hurt.

"Try not to move," she said. "You could have broken ribs." She opened his coat and scanned his body. "Did he use a weapon? Were you stabbed or cut anywhere?"

"Don't think so." He tried to smile at her as she felt his pulse, looked in his eyes and turned his head left and right; her fingers expertly probed his neck as she did so. He realized from the professional way she examined him that she had medical training. "You're a nurse, right?"

She didn't reply. Again.

"We have to report this to the police," he continued.

She shook her head. "And say what? We were attacked by two men for no reason. Not a good idea, particularly at this time."

In fact, there was no way Sky wanted the police or any other authorities involved in their business. In particular if it involved the diamond. If that subject came up it could compromise everything. If she was to honor her grandfather's wish, she had to keep their journey as low key as possible.

"It should be reported," Matthew groaned.

"So what if it was about the diamond? Would you like that plastered on the front page of the Montreal Gazette? 'Exploration team embarking on major diamond expedition attacked'." She paused and then continued. "At least we'll have lots of company on our journey."

He realized she was right. Some minutes later they arrived at the hospital ER entrance. Sky threw a twenty dollar bill at the cabbie. As they disembarked he found he was very dizzy. She helped him through the emergency entrance just as a pretty blond girl in scrubs happened by. Spotting his bloodied face she ran over and helped Sky support him. "I'm doing triage tonight," she said. "What happened?"

"Assault, trouble breathing, contusions, possible broken ribs and I don't know if he's been cut or stabbed," Sky said. "I need to get him into an examination room."

"Sky! What the hell?" came a voice from the side and a young, brown-haired doctor carrying a metal clipboard appeared. "Where did you come from?"

"Francois, thank God. Can I get an exam room...I need to check him out."

"I'll take him, Sky," Doctor Francois Vivier said kindly, but she shook her head.

"Just an examination room, my friend...please!?"

"Sure, number four is empty. Do you want some help?"

"I'll probably need some pain meds, but for now I'll examine him."

"Call out if you need anything. I'm in number seven."

"You're a dear," she said. "Like always."

"Oh Sky…we must talk….I tried to call you," Francois said hurriedly.

"I know," she called back to him as she maneuvered Matthew into the examining room. "Everybody did…but I simply wasn't ready to talk. My apologies, my friend."

"You worked here?" Matthew asked, his teeth clenched from the pain of moving.

"One time," she muttered, throwing her purse on a table in the corner of the examination room. She whipped the privacy curtains closed.

Before he knew it, she had eased off his sports coat and his shirt. She turned him around, snatched an instrument off the wall, popped a piece of plastic on the lens and snapped on a light. "Are you still dizzy? Nauseous?"

"Not as much as I was," he replied. "At least, not now."

"Look at the light," she ordered, moving it from one eye to the other, and watching his pupils contract and dilate. "Count backwards from ten."

Matthew did so.

"How many fingers am I holding up?"

"Four," he said.

"Five," she corrected, a tinge of worry in her voice.

"The other is a thumb," he asserted.

"Mr. Corrigan, if you weren't already bruised, you soon would be," she said, not bothering to hide her annoyance. "Lie down."

He lay down on the gurney.

"Lift up," she commanded as she opened his belt and pants.

"Whoa nurse, this is our first date–!"

Before he could protest further she ripped his pants and underwear down over his buttocks in one fluid motion leaving him naked before her, his pants around his ankles only held there by his shoes and socks.

"For God's sake!" he said in shock.

"Stay still," she ordered, pulling on a lamp cord near the head of the gurney and increasing the intensity of the light. He moaned and closed his eyes as he felt her fingers probing his body. She did her ABC assessment – airway, breathing and circulation. Next she checked his throat and neck, walked her fingers over his ribs, and palpated his stomach, liver and spleen. Finally she inspected his legs and arms.

"Look nurse...."

"Stop calling me *nurse*. Nurses are God's gift to humanity but I'm a physician, a surgeon."

"You're a what?"

"Stow it for a minute," she snapped. "Nurse? Please!"

A nurse appeared within a few seconds. Surprisingly it was the triage nurse. "Slow night," she said.

Matthew opened his eyes and realized she was seeing him. *All of him*. He hastily dragged his hands up to cover his groin. The nurse couldn't help smiling. "It's quite okay sir, I've seen one before," she said. "In a magazine." Her grin widened.

"Where did he hit you?" Sky asked, all business.

"Not down there for sure," Matthew answered, still concerned about his nakedness.

She reached to a shelf under a table and dropped a towel over his lap which he grabbed like a life preserver.

"Be straight for a minute. Please!"

"Alright. Chest and ribs twice, side of the head once and for the icing on the cake, once in the left kidney."

"What about your forehead?"

"I hit him in the nose with it; it's his blood."

"May I borrow your stethoscope?" Sky asked, and the nurse handed her scope over. Sky thanked her, tore open an alcohol wipe and swabbed the ear pieces. Then she listened to Matthew's heart. Next she instructed him to breathe deeply and listened to his lung sounds. He took deep breaths as instructed, awakening considerable pain. His forehead was becoming more discolored now and an impressive hematoma was present and rapidly increasing in size.

Sky passed the scope back to the nurse. Her main concern was that he might have a pericardial tamponade. She explored his sternum and he groaned. If the blows had been hard enough they could have ruptured some internal vessels. If so, fluid, most likely blood, could invade the sac around the heart and interfere with its function.

"Okay, I was worried about a possible fluid leak into your

pericardial sac but it's been a while and so far, so good. Your blood pressure seems fine, and your heart sounds strong. I think you've got bruised ribs at least. But, just in case they're broken, we'll get you X-Rayed. And, you should be monitored overnight."

"Oh no…" he began. She ignored his protest and rolled him onto his side so she could check his lower back.

"Pretty red over your kidney so there might be some blood in your urine for a few days as well," she said, gently easing him onto his back again.

"Great!" he muttered, feeling less of an inclination towards humor as the pain continued to grow."

"As far as your discomfort," Sky said, "just wait until tomorrow."

"You've got a lousy bedside manner, Doc."

"I'll get Doctor Vivier to order you some codeine now and I'll write you a script later." She snapped off her gloves and discarded them in a bin. "I'll also get him to admit you."

"No, I'm okay," he said, trying to sit up. "Really, I'm not staying, so don't bother."

She spun around and put her finger on his chest exactly where he'd been struck. It wasn't difficult to make him lie back down.

"Owww!" he exclaimed.

"You took hard shots to the chest and ribs from a very big man so you're staying here," she said. "Accept it. They'll check your vitals throughout the night and make sure everything is okay."

With that she stripped his underwear and pants over his shoes, and bundled them under her arm, Next she threw him a wrinkled but fresh gown from a pile on the second shelf of the table from which she had retrieved the towel. "Put this on, Matthew; whether you know it or not, you're here for the night."

Sky and the triage nurse swept the curtain aside to exit.

"My wallet," he called.

"I need it for your health card. I'll return everything tomorrow. Dr. Vivier will get you a room. Good night." She slipped out.

Without Sky, Matthew suddenly felt uniquely alone. Why, he wondered? He spent lots of time alone. Puzzled over his feelings he tried to reason why he felt this way. Could it be that he was actually missing *her*? Hardly, he decided. He barely knew her. Still….

~11~

True to her word, Sky returned with his clothes the next morning. She must have taken note of his size since she'd purchased a new, blue Hugo Boss shirt for him. His old one was bloodied with several buttons torn off.

"How do you feel?" she asked.

"Like a giant bruise," he replied with a groan.

Sky told him the X-Rays didn't show any fractures. "You'll be discharged by the staff man later," she added. "Under my supervision, of course. Meanwhile I'll check on my grandfather. Meet you in the cafeteria for lunch at noon."

She left and he went about gingerly getting dressed. Every time he lifted his arm or tried to twist, his body protested. A very pretty brunette nurse came in and told him he was free to go. She handed him a bottle of pills, said he should take one every four hours for pain, and not to operate any heavy equipment.

"So you're telling me no sex for a while?" he inquired.

She gave him a wide smile and then broke into a giggle. He felt much better after that.

It was 10:30 AM so he cooled his heels in a waiting area since Sky wouldn't be available until noon, at least. When lunchtime rolled around he entered the cafeteria, spotted her at a table near the far wall and gingerly sat down.

"Sore!" he exclaimed.

"Not surprised. It will take time."

"How's your grandfather? Any change?"

"None," she sighed. "The specialist says it isn't unusual. He needs time to heal and rest."

Matthew started to say he personally identified with that need very well. Instead he decided she might think he was undermining the seriousness of her grandfather's condition by equating it to his own. He kept silent. Though they had been through a pleasant dinner and a not so pleasant attack together afterwards, he still felt he should tread lightly around her. She seemed too quick to take offense at even the most innocent remark. Likely because of the stress she was under. She'd set up certain boundaries and he decided to respect them. The wisest course was to let her establish the tone and level of their relationship.

Quickly they filled two trays with soup, sandwiches and coffee, and sat back down.

"We've got some time before we leave on our journey from Nain," she said. "Part of it will be on snowmobiles. Then we'll be on foot and it will be quite strenuous. You should feel much better by that time, but for now, I want you to rest and heal, Mr. Corrigan."

So, we're back to Mr. Corrigan.

"I'll be ready," he answered.

"We have to be at the site before the Winter Solstice which is December 23rd this year," she said. "That's non-negotiable."

"Why?" he asked. "Why at that time?"

She hesitated and then said simply: "That's the deal. The Torngat Mountains do not forgive fools or amateurs. So we travel there when we should."

Matthew took a bite out of his sandwich, giving himself time to think. "I read the name of the range comes from the Inuktitut word *Torngait* meaning *Place of Spirits*. And some people even call them the *Devil Mountains*. I also read they're revered by our native peoples and not too many venture into them. So I'm guessing this is a superstitious-type thing."

Sky sighed and shook her head slightly. "Alright. First of all, there is no *our* native people. We don't belong to anybody."

"I'm sorry," he said, quickly. "I really don't mean to offend. I was trying to be inclusive."

"Relax," she replied, softening. Then she added: "By the time we get back I'll have you so politically correct, you'll be afraid to open your mouth."

He looked up cautiously and realized with much relief that he was seeing the natural dolphin-like smile in evidence again. He nodded gratefully. At the same time he realized he was actually a little scared of her; in fact, he was tip-toeing around her like he did around the boxes of blasting caps and high explosives at the George River warehouse.

"And, second, we don't revere the mountains as much as we respect them," she said. Then Sky continued with the lie she knew she'd have to maintain: "Around the time of the Winter Solstice, we usually have all the ice we need to travel to our destination. That's critical. After that, we'll make the return journey and hope to heck we can beat out any January thaw and any ice breakup. It seems to be happening more frequently in the North these days because of global warning. So my Winter Solstice timeline is more about safety than Voodoo."

She felt bad fibbing and consoled herself with the fact that what she said was partly true. While the Solstice timeline had been imposed on her and her grandfather by the agenda of the others, there could be a January thaw. And they did need ice thick enough on which to travel.

Matthew watched her and detected a concealed uneasiness with her explanation. He shrugged it aside.

She busied herself with taking a sip of coffee and he couldn't help noting her full lips once again. God she was pretty. But, he asked himself: Why was he so nervous around her? Though he had never been totally at ease around women, especially the beautiful ones, he thought he had mostly conquered his phobia after nine years of marriage. Obviously that was no longer the case. Or, was it the fact his company was relying on him to come through with a diamond find or it would cease to exist? Perhaps the stakes were so high he was becoming paranoid about offending Sky and losing what seemed the only path to success for Labrador & Ungava Diamonds. He decided to change the subject.

"Now I'm wondering if we did the right thing by not reporting what happened last night?" he said, putting down his cup.

"I don't know," she answered. "But if they're a competing prospecting company, what did they expect to do? Make me tell them where the diamond originated? And then, how would they keep me quiet? The whole thing is ludicrous. This is Canada."

Matthew noticed, however, that Sky's eyes had grown wary.

"Look," he said. "I think we have to be a little more careful now. No more going out alone at night. Don't answer the door unless you know who's behind it. Stuff like that."

"They might try again?"

"I don't know. But it was obviously you they were after. The big guy told me to stay out of it when he slammed me against the wall. And, they were dragging *you* into the car."

"I never thought I'd need my Winchester in Montreal."

"Yes, that would be all we need; you shooting up the streets. Instead, let's keep a low profile. If we see anything suspicious again, all bets are off. The hell with the diamond and secrecy. We go to the police. And we do so publicly. That will take care of them."

"Agreed."

"One other thing," Matthew said, not hiding his respect. "You worked here at the Royal Victoria? As a surgeon?"

Sky began gathering up her napkins and plates and putting them back on her tray. "That slipped out, Mr. Corrigan."

"For God's sake, Sky, please call me Matthew. After inspecting every inch of me, I think it's okay to be on a first name basis, don't you?"

She stood but stopped her preparations to leave. "Okay Matthew, You seem to be a very nice man and I haven't tried to pry into who you are, or what you are about. Without meaning to offend you in any way, I'm asking you to extend the same courtesy to me."

"Fair enough," he said, feeling his face turning red.

Instead of leaving, she sat back down. Surprisingly, she took his hand in hers and looked earnestly into his eyes. "I'd rather keep this whole affair on a business footing. For your sake as well as mine. I'm not someone you want to befriend, or try to get close to, Matthew. I have many issues in my life. And more than one oddity. So anything other than a business relationship would be a very bad idea.

"I don't need to know your history and you don't need to know anything about me for this whole arrangement to work. We'll meet in Nain, and I'll get you up to the diamond site. From there you can make your own decisions about what you wish to do. And I'll get you safely back to Nain. After that, you go about your life and I'll go about mine."

Matthew sat stunned. Don't try to get close to her? Did she think he was hitting on her? Was he? After all, this girl was visually striking, well-educated and had more than a dash of mystery thrown in. If she had a personality transplant, she'd be almost perfect, he thought. And there was no Helene in his life any more. His ex-wife had made that abundantly clear.

Sky let go of his hand, and he was surprised to see a sheen in her eyes. Her speech had obviously touched a nerve or stirred up old memories that weren't quite so pleasant. This was one complicated young lady, he decided. So he'd aim for guarded civility from now on.

She was looking straight at him. Likely waiting for some sign he got the picture.

"I-I'm in the process of getting a divorce," he heard himself say, almost simultaneously wishing he could slam his head against the table. What the hell was he doing? Why had he chosen to reveal a highly personal detail seconds after she told him to get lost? With his mouth as dry as the Gobi Desert he took a drink of cold coffee, mind whirling. Time to face facts. Time to admit truths. Yes, she was attractive. Yes, he was attracted to her. No, he wasn't going to screw up their arrangement. So cool your jets, he told himself angrily.

"I'm sorry to hear that," she was saying.

He gave her a blank look.

"Your divorce?" she reminded him.

"Of course," he managed to stutter out.

It's true. I am a certified idiot. But, in my favor, I only drool in private.

He could still feel her touch where she had held his hand moments before.

"So we're good?" she pressed.

"Yes, we're good." He sighed. He'd keep his distance. But there was still the matter of who had attempted to kidnap her. He couldn't simply walk away from that. "We still have to take precautions," he said, changing the subject, trying to recapture some dignity.

"I'll do that and you do it as well," she replied, nodding. "My priority right now is my grandfather. I intend to make sure he is as comfortable as possible and knows he is much loved. Hopefully there'll be some signs of improvement soon."

"I hope so," he said sincerely. He didn't ask her the question that was likely on both their minds: What if her grandfather failed to regain consciousness by the time they were ready to leave? Would that scrub the trip? He decided not to ask it. After all, he might not like the answer.

* * *

Jacquard leaned back in his leather office chair, sipped on a glass of Canadian Club and gestured towards Matthew's bruised forehead. "So, what's the other guy look like?"

"Worse," Matthew replied.

"So Pocahontas is going take you to where her grandfather found the diamond and it's not in the park boundaries? We dodged another bloody bullet."

"Her name is Sky," Matthew said, realizing that the man's cultural sensitivities were almost non-existent.

"Yeah, yeah…okay…Sky. Sorry. Guess I'm going to have to buck up on my political correctness."

"Political correctness or not, sir," Matthew replied, irritated, "I wouldn't push it if you meet her. She's the type that can smell hypocrisy from a mile away."

"Whoa! Forgive me, Your Highness."

"Mr. Jacquard, this family is doing you one heck of a favor. If you called Sky 'Pocahontas' to her face, she'd walk out the door and that would be the end of it. Totally and irrevocably finished. Perhaps you should accord her and her grandfather the respect you would any other person. Just a suggestion."

"Okay, I'll watch it," he said automatically, his mind obviously elsewhere. "Now do you need anything from me? Do you need our boys up north to help in any way?"

"Not at the moment but I may have to call on them later. Right now that's the least of my concerns. The fact Mr. St. Onge found an eight-carat diamond in Labrador isn't the secret we thought it was. It's common knowledge in Nain. And elsewhere, it seems."

"Bloody hell!" Jacquard said, taking another sip of his whiskey.

"There's more. I've been approached by a rival prospecting company looking to hire me away. And they've admitted it's because of the St. Onge diamond."

"Bastards! Who are they? What company?"

"She wouldn't say unless I accepted her offer."

"She?"

"A lady I met on Air Canada who has been looking at me pretty closely. Apparently Mr. St. Onge revealed the fact he'd found a diamond to a fellow named Bob Crummy in Nain. And the Outpost Nurse up there told me Crummy sells info to prospectors, mining companies and anyone else with a buck to donate to his favorite charity. That, by the way, just happens to be himself."

"What's the name of this women who tried to hire you?"

"Monique Boivin. She caught up with me in Sept-Iles and made me a salary offer way out of line for a geologist. When I pressed her, she said that, aside from my credentials, my appeal was this connection I had with the St. Onge Diamond."

"How did they know about any connection?" Jacquard asked. "Particularly if you don't know this guy. Or, at least, *say* you don't." He scrawled something on a small yellow scrap of paper and pressed a button on his phone."

"I'd imagine they got their info from Crummy. St. Onge must have mentioned me to him. Why, I still don't know. And, again, I've never met the man before."

Jacquard's looked at his doorway in annoyance and yelled: Mary!"

Mary appeared at the door. "You bellowed," she said.

"Why don't you answer the buzzer?" he asked.

"Because it's broken as I tell you every day and yet you won't let me get a man up here to fix it."

"Yeah, they'll solder a wire or something and charge me $150 for nothing." He handed her the piece of paper. "Google this woman. Check her out on LinkedIn, Facebook, Twitter, Tweet and other bird places. Get info on her. What company she works for, their HQ, net worth, specialty. Seems they're a mining company with at least one office in Sept-Iles."

"Jawohl, Commandant," she said and left.

"See? I don't get any respect either," Jacquard explained. "Maybe that's why I don't show other people more respect."

Matthew smiled: "I left my violin at home today, Rodney."

"Were you born a smart ass, or was it an elective for your major?" Jacquard asked.

"Never mind about that, there's more," Matthew said.

"More what?"

"More to this story. This bruise happened when Sky and I were jumped coming out of a restaurant in Old Montreal last night. Someone tried to kidnap her."

"Kidnap her? What the hell is going on, Matthew?"

"I don't know but I'll bet it has something to do with the diamond."

"What did the police say?"

"We didn't go to the police. I managed to discourage them and they jumped back in their car and took off. Sky felt publicity wouldn't be desirable at this time."

Jacquard got up, crossed to his bar and poured another drink. He motioned with the bottle towards Matthew who shook his head.

"Maybe it was a mugging attempt?"

'Muggers don't travel in limos," Matthew countered. "And they don't shout: 'Abort!' when things go wrong."

"Abort what?"

"Exactly. It's more a military term. Abort the mission."

"Any idea who they were?"

"Maybe they were sent by the company trying to hire me."

"To pry the location of the diamond site out of the girl?"

"What else could it be?"

"Alright," Jacquard said. "I really need the info on where he found it but I don't want anyone hurt. I mean it, Matthew. If those numbskulls want to play hardball, I can play hardball. But it'll be with the cops on our side. If you get even a sniff of anything going on, you call me. I golf with the Montreal Director of Police, and Marc will kick some ass if the competition is resorting to assaults to win. Meanwhile, I'll fill him in on what's going on. If they try anything else, you let me know right away. Okay?"

Matthew agreed and returned to his hotel room where he lay on his bed and thought over everything that happened in less than a week. He soon realized there were more than a few oddities: Jerome St. Onge showing up with a diamond find as Labrador and Ungava Diamonds was about to go under; the old man stroking out but his granddaughter being able to step in for him; the bizarre offer of a job from Monique Boivin because of the diamond; and, the attempted kidnapping of Sky. *And one of the men just happened to be a giant of a man.* He sat bolt upright on the bed.

He grabbed the telephone and dialed Helene's number. It was answered on the third ring.

"Helene Gervais…"

Matthew paused; his wife had used her maiden name.

"Oui, âllo?" she said again.

"Helene, it's me."

"Oh!" She seemed on edge. "Are you calling about the insurance men?"

"Yes, how did you know?"

"I just got off the phone with Jean. Whoever they were, they weren't from the insurance company."

"Listen, you said one of them was abnormally large."

"Yes, at least 6'5"…maybe more."

"Describe him."

"Well, dark suit, white shirt–!"

"No, describe *him*…blond, dark hair?"

"Black hair, prominent jaw, dark eyes…from what I remember."

"Did he have a scar on his left cheek?"

"I don't think so."

"You're sure?

"I didn't notice one," she said. Then she added: "You know, I did notice something strange about the tall man. I'd swear he was wearing makeup."

"Makeup?"

"Yes, makeup. I smelled it. Like they put on me when I appeared on that legal reality TV show. They called it something strange. I know…pancake makeup. They said it covered pimples, blemishes and even *scars*! That's what they said: *scars*!"

"Damn!" he said, before he could catch himself.

"What? What's going on Matthew? Tell me."

"I don't know exactly, Helene but I want you to do what I tell you. Please."

"What?"

"Don't let anyone in you don't know. Particularly those two guys. If you see them again, call the police immediately."

"You're scaring me, Matthew."

"Helene, you said they were asking you questions mostly about me? Correct?"

"Yes." Her voice had a definite quiver.

"Alright. This doesn't concern you. They're interested in me and what I'm doing."

"What *are* you doing?"

"Being a geologist. But we think we have a lead on a possible diamond site and the competition is playing dirty to try to find it before we do."

"Have you called the police?"

Matthew hesitated but then remembered what Jacquard had said. "My boss has notified the police. He knows the Director of Police Services personally, so I don't think they'll keep up their shenanigans. If they do they'll wind up in jail."

"Okay. I trust you."

"Thanks."

"One more thing, Matthew."

"Go ahead."

There was silence for a moment on the phone as though Helene was trying to find the right words. "I got our divorce decree in the mail today. You should have yours as well."

He felt a weird sickness spread through his body. His heart raced. It was over. They were divorced. Though it'd been over for years, his mind still reeled at the finality of it all.

"Now I understand why you answered: 'Helene Gervais'."

"I'm sorry. Maybe somewhat premature but I will probably revert to my maiden name."

"Right. Maybe you shouldn't have changed it when we got married. Save you some trouble." He regretted the sarcasm the moment it was out of his mouth.

"Don't be like that, Matthew."

He sighed. "I'm sorry Helene. I know we agreed…the whole thing. But it's still a shock."

"For me too. When I opened the envelope, I thought I would feel nothing. But then I cried for hours. For what we lost."

"Yes," Matthew agreed. "We lost our daughter first…and then each other."

He felt a lump in his throat. There was nothing more he wanted at that moment than to get off the phone.

"We can still be friends."

"Of course," he replied automatically. "Well don't forget what I said. If you have any problems or see those men again, call the police. And me. Okay?"

"Okay," she answered.

"Take care of yourself."

"Of course. And you too. I'm sorry it had to be this way, Matthew."

"Me too," he said with a heavy sigh. "And I wish we'd been able to find a way to deal with it much better than we did."

"I don't know if that was even possible," Helene replied.

"Statistically we fit right in with couples who lose a child."

"We have to put it all behind us. The bad…and the good."

"Whatever you want," he said. "Goodbye, Helene."

"Good-bye Matthew."

He waited till she hung up and then quietly did the same. He sighed and inevitably tried to think again about ways he might have saved their marriage. Unfortunately, from the outset, it seemed all his efforts had been in vain. Maybe there had never been any real hope after the accident. It takes *two* to create a marriage, he thought, but only *one* to end it. And the one that ended it was him. When he failed to save their daughter's life.

* * *

The next weeks passed with Matthew spending time at the snowed-in log cabin he and Helene had purchased in the Laurentians. It was a mere 50 miles northwest of Montreal and if you didn't have to travel near the weekend, traffic was generally pretty good. Driving north of the city he had marveled at how much snow had fallen in the mountains. They were virtually buried, snow topping the mountain peaks. Sort of like mini Rockies, he thought. If you squinted.

In their separation agreement, Helene had gladly ceded the cabin to him. She took the condo. She also ensured that a clause stipulated half of the settlement they received after Chantal's death would be set aside for him in a savings account to access when he chose to do so. He hadn't touched a penny.

When he arrived at the cabin, Matthew spent the first full day cleaning snow off the roof and shoveling it from around the windows and doors. He then cleaned the cabin and one of the two bedrooms. It had sat empty for more than six months. The next day was spent splitting a load of wood he had ordered for the fireplace and wood stove, replacing what he had used the first two days, and giving him enough of an over-pile to see him through the following few weeks. He always tried to keep at least two full cords of 16-inch logs split and ageing under a tarp beside the south wall. He was glad he did so since, for the remainder of his time there, it snowed every day until the accumulation was measured in feet.

Almost every *other* day, he found something to repair or improve around the cabin. He also restocked it with groceries, bought kerosene oil for a few lamps they kept in case the power went out, and spent time snowshoeing by himself in the woods.

One day he even drove over to Mont Tremblant and skied for a few hours. On the slopes he felt fine; when he ambled through the European-style village at the base of the mountain that evening, he felt terribly alone as couples and families around him laughed and rejoiced after a great ski day. The famous Quebec *joie de vivre* was present around every corner and in every restaurant and bar. He had planned to eat at Restaurant Patrick Bernard in the village but changed his mind.

Once he'd dried his skis and poles, and stowed them in his rented SUV, he got the hell out of there.

His evenings in the cabin were spent reading detective novels and hypnotically gazing into a crackling log fire where memories of happier times seemed to reside. Eventually he tried to enjoy them rather than repress them.

And the days flew by.

He'd had two visits within a day of smoke rising out of his fieldstone chimney. The first one was from Jacques Villeneuve who owned the local dépanneur down the road. The convenience store was generally where he and Helene had done all their grocery shopping for the cabin. While the prices were higher than in the nearby village of Sainte-Adèle, they had both agreed to patronize his store since it simply didn't have the numbers to keep it open without local patronage. If we don't support him, he won't be there for us, Helene had wisely stated. And Jacques had recognized what they were doing and was grateful for it.

On his visit, the elderly storeowner clad in a down parka, yellow plaid shirt and tattered coveralls, had expressed his heartfelt condolences for the loss of their child whom he used to playfully tease. He had always insisted on giving a free *Sweet Marie* chocolate bar to Chantal on every visit. Now, he asked how Helene was since he'd seen neither of them since Chantal's death. He explained that by the time he found out about the accident, it was too late for him to go to Montreal for the funeral. Matthew assured him they'd received the card and flowers. And, though Matthew himself had been up at the cabin once since the tragedy, Jacques and his wife had been away visiting cousins in New Brunswick at the time.

They chatted for a while over coffee. As he was leaving, Jacques had tramped back from his vehicle to the door with a fresh apple pie his wife had baked for Matthew. Though he and Helene had never met Josette, Jacques' wife had often sent delicious home baking their way.

The second visit came from a neighbor up the road who also kept a winter home there for skiing. Marie Charbonneau was a thirty-something divorcee who had openly and harmlessly flirted with Matthew from the first day they met. She had Matthew and his family over for dinner several times, and they had reciprocated. Marie liked her wine and was always telling Helene how lucky she was to have such a dedicated husband and father in her life. When she attended Chantal's funeral, however, she had been appropriately and genuinely quiet and distressed.

Matthew used to think of her as irrepressibly flighty but fun. Her behavior at the funeral, however, had shown another side of her that was both serious and sensitive. Also, surprisingly, after the funeral, she had visited Helene many times in Montreal when he was working up north. With both Matthew and Helene's parents deceased and Helene's sole sibling, her brother, in Denmark, more than once Marie had provided a shoulder on which to cry. In fact, she had been overwhelming in her support of his wife.

Former wife, he reminded himself.

When Marie showed up at the cabin this time, she had obviously heard about the divorce and again was seriously concerned. Over a cup of coffee they had talked about old times. She told him how she had seen Helene as often as she could. As a result the girls had gone out to dinner and shopping a number of times. Matthew thanked her for that. She shrugged and then she confessed they hadn't made contact in six months but it was likely because of...! She had hesitated, obviously embarrassed. Matthew put her out of her misery by assuring her he was aware Helene had a boyfriend and he wished her well.

He noted Marie didn't flirt with him this time, even a little. Perhaps it was out of respect for Chantal or even loyalty to Helene. However, at the door on the way out, she had turned to him and said her standing offer to help included him, of course. If he ever needed to talk, her door was open. Then she pecked him on the cheek and said she wanted him to know she would continue to be his friend. And not to worry. Contrary to her local reputation she was *not* a vamp; they could be friends. They both laughed, understanding each other perfectly.

Every three days Matthew called Sky in Montreal to check on Jerome St. Onge's progress. There was no appreciable change. Also, there had been no further problems regarding the assault. She had never caught sight of the two men again. And, she'd been watching very closely for them to make an encore appearance. Why someone tried to kidnap her that evening continued to be a mystery.

Sky promised to call him if there was any change in her grandfather's condition. When he apologized for bothering her, she hastened to add that she wasn't suggesting that he *not* call, simply that she would let him know if things improved. Not that it would make any difference to their travel plans since once the man woke up, he had a long road to rehabilitation ahead of him.

On his last call, a week before he was scheduled to leave for Nain, Sky told him the trip was still on. She was trying to make arrangements for her grandfather to be moved to a convalescence home if he didn't improve before she left. When Matthew had tentatively asked her if she was sure she still wanted to go, she assured him she did and for him to be in Nain on December 7th as per their agreement. Then she added: "After all, this is important."

He'd later puzzled over that comment. Important to her? Hardly. So she must have meant important to him? If so, it was more than magnanimous of her to have assumed a vested interest in guiding him. She had every right to put it off, in light of her grandfather's medical condition. Whatever her motivations, Matthew intended to let Jacquard know in no uncertain terms of her ongoing kindness.

On his last day at the cabin, he geared up by packing his heavy wool ski sweaters, his warmest wool socks, insulated underwear, woolen liners and leather mitts, and finally, his Baffin Endurance Winter boots. Quebec winters in the Laurentian Mountains could be every bit as bitingly cold as normal arctic temperatures. Accordingly, over time, he and his family had gathered an assortment of winter clothing to keep them warm for extended hikes or ski trips.

The only thing he hadn't done, in making the cabin ship-shape, was to enter Chantal's room where her mittens, parkas and other winter clothes waited to cruelly remind him of his loss. Not that he needed reminding. He had decided he'd leave it for a future visit. Then he would find out from Jacques if there were village children nearby who needed her clothes.

Chantal would like that, he knew. She had always been a kind child, happily sharing her toys and time with playmates. She seemed most pleased when Helene or Matthew smiled at her in approval of some kind action she'd taken such as offering a boot or dropped mitten up to her parents because – as she would patiently explain – she was the closest one to the floor.

Since he was booked on Air Canada, Montreal-to-Sept-Iles for the following morning, he intended to get to bed early. He fixed himself a steak, potatoes and peas for supper, and then elected to take a walk partway down the mountain; the fresh air would help him sleep much better.

After eating, he bundled up and set out down the plowed road. It was necessary to stick to it religiously since the unpacked, virgin snow on the off-road trails was quite deep in the mountains. He used a 3-D LED Maglite to illuminate his way. Five-foot-high snowbanks, topped by watermelon-sized chunks of ice and snow lined the road and he kept to the side in case a car or truck came around a curve. He was fully prepared to leap onto a snowbank if they were driving with the usual abandon rural drivers embraced. Many thought of it as payback for the inconveniences they faced being away from urban centers.

For the first fifteen minutes the only sound was the crunch of his boots interspersed with the hiss of his breath in the frosty air. Overhead, a silvery full moon cast a bluish white light on the snowy slopes turning the spruce trees at the base of the hills into dark sentinels bordering the road.

He walked a mile and a half and was about to turn back when he heard a lone wolf baying mournfully in the distance. He stopped to listen. The sound had barely echoed away in the mountains when other wolves replied in a wilderness cacophony dating back millions of years. Abruptly, after a particularly frantic chorus, they all ceased their calling and became still.

There was absolutely no sound now and Matthew felt an electric thrill as he looked up at the thousands of stars in the night sky. He could immediately make out the Big Dipper, the Small Dipper and Orion's belt. The night was Christmas-card beautiful. All it needed to make it complete was the sound of sleigh bells jingling in the distance.

He continued to look skyward for some reason and then swung his gaze towards the moon. As he looked at the brilliant white orb almost directly overhead he realized something was very wrong. Then it came to him: There were no shadows on the moon's face, no seas or plains or even tiny white dots signifying major craters. It appeared to be thoroughly whitewashed in some fashion, a blank, white disk devoid of character hanging in the sky. The only term that came to mind was "somber."

After staring at it for a minute, he thought it was actually spinning in place; goose bumps rose on his neck and arms. This was impossible.

There must be some sort of mist in front of it, he reasoned. But, upon further examination, he saw the sharp edges of the moon were clearly delineated. And, other than a slight wash from the moon's corona, the stars were as sharp and clear as tiny diamonds. He discounted the idea of a mist. After all, the moon was hundreds of thousands of miles away. What could hang in the air directly in front of it, in earth's atmosphere, and be precise enough to mask *only* the surface of the moon? Nothing, came the reply in his head. And why was he feeling spooked by it? There had to be a rational, scientific explanation for what he was observing.

He continued staring at the absence of a lunar landscape and had the eerie feeling something was staring right back at him, watching, measuring, calculating and evaluating. Get a grip, he told himself. There are no boogey men.

The sound of a splitting branch cracked off to his left side and he jumped and swung his head round. He stared intently at the line of black spruce trees. The sound had come from there. Could be a coyote, or even a wolf, he thought. He swung the Maglite towards where he heard the branch crack. A brilliant cone of light turned the ominous-looking shadows into normal spruce trees. He explored the tree bases to see if a breaking branch had betrayed itself by dumping a pile of snow beneath it. What he was able to illuminate, however, was smooth and unblemished.

For a moment he thought he saw a shadow, just outside his light field. It moved swiftly amongst the tree branches. He heart beat faster as he swung the light trying to track and pinpoint it. The shadow stayed a few degrees ahead of his light. He swung the beam hard to the right to get ahead of its path. Whatever *it* was, its speed was faster than any human or animal could muster through what must be deep powdery snow. It didn't tramp or run; rather it glided from left to right.

And then, it was gone!

Suddenly a blinding flash lit everything up as bright as day. Instinctively Matthew squeezed his eyes shut and dropped to one knee. Frozen chunks of road ice dug into his kneecap and shin.

What the hell –?

He stood back up quickly in case the flash had been the advent of headlights coming down the road.

Nothing. The light was gone.

He listened intently but failed to pick up any motor sounds, near or far. The night was back now, still, silent and maybe even a little threatening. Was someone playing games with him amongst the trees? He swung his flashlight left and right and slowly spun in a circle examining both sides of the road and his surroundings. All was as it should be. Off in the distance a wolf began to bay again, long, mournful, lonesome sounding notes.

He sighed and shook his head; his heartbeat returned to normal. Turning back towards the cabin, he gazed at the full moon again. He stopped in shock. Staring upwards he could scarcely believing what he was seeing. Now he could easily make out the lunar seas, the craters and the basaltic plains as well as most of the other moon shadows visible to the naked eye. He continued to stare at it for a full minute waiting for something to happen, perhaps for the mist to return. The moon simply hung overhead, no longer a cause for question or concern. Its face was as natural as at any other time.

As he trudged back to the cabin he decided to look up lunar anomalies and find one what could make the shadows on the face of the moon magically disappear and reappear in a relatively short time.

Matthew reached the cabin, entered and did something he had

seldom done before in the relative safety of the Laurentian Mountains; he locked the door. Next, he took off his heavy clothes, climbed into bed and was asleep moments after his head hit the pillow.

PART TWO

TORNGAT TREK

*At the northern extremity of the Labrador Coast, a range of high,
barren mountains with sharp precipices extending inward from
the sea (is) known to traditional Inuit as the abode of the master
spirit in their mythology.*
  Ernest W. Hawkes 1914

~1~

The following morning Matthew's flight to Sept-Iles was uneventful as was his flight up the coast on the mail plane with Buzz Neil again. This time there had been no mysterious meeting with Monique Boivin at his hotel, though he did find himself keeping an eye out for her.

Buzz was captaining a Twin Otter this morning with five aboriginal passengers accompanying them. Knowing he was also a pilot, he made sure Matthew sat in the right seat and even turned over the controls to him for a short time. When he saw how easily Matthew handled the aircraft, making the occasional course and altitude correction, and instinctively using the trim wheel to keep the nose even with the horizon, he relaxed. He even went back to fetch a band aid from the First Aid kit for a small Inuit boy who somehow cut his finger on a sharp aluminum edge near the door. An hour later, after doing paperwork in the cockpit for most of the time, he relieved Matthew at the controls and thanked him.

They hopped their way up the coast, from settlement to settlement, dropping mail, some freight and the occasional passenger. The ground was now firmly covered in deep snow with only clumps of spruce trees and the occasional rocky outcropping marring the white expanse three thousand feet below. Barren, rolling mountains lined the Labrador Sea shoreline which featured a thin strip of ice along its edge. The bays they passed over were mostly frozen.

The sun had set and they had only one passenger left by the time they landed in Nain. Darkness was already settling over the village. The pilot would stay overnight and take the aircraft back to Sept-Iles the following morning.

Matthew thanked Buzz for an interesting trip. He found himself shivering in the biting cold again as he pulled his two bulging and very heavy suitcases towards the airport shed. Ahead he spotted a Chrysler van parked with its engine running. He assumed this was the shuttle Bob Crummy had mentioned the last time he was in Nain. He made his way forward, dragging his cases through the thick snow.

A short, very thick First Nations young man in a sealskin anorak hopped out of the van and helped Matthew put his suitcases in the back. Meanwhile, a Land Rover pulled up and took the remaining passenger and Buzz away. Matthew's driver introduced himself as Joe Lightfoot and informed him of a change of plans.

"You aren't staying at the lodge," he pronounced. "Sky cancelled your reservations."

"Where am I staying?" Matthew inquired politely.

"At Jerome's house," Lightfoot answered, his tone matter-of-fact. "With her."

"Then lead on Macduff," Matthew said, not quite sure if this was a good idea.

"The name's Joe Lightfoot, not Macduff," the driver insisted, deadpan.

Okay, not an English scholar....

They arrived at St. Onge's bungalow and the driver hopped out, grabbed a suitcase in each hand and lifted them up the steps to the porch as though they weighed nothing. He opened the front door, deposited them inside, and followed the cases.

"Come in," he said. "Sky isn't here now but she'll be back soon."

They both entered the house. It was typical of a northern bungalow with an open living room/dining room combination and the kitchen divided by an eating bar. He could see four doors branching off the living room which was stuffed with cozy looking Roxborough colonial furniture perched on a large, oval braided rug. A wall of framed black & white photographs depicting fishing and hunting trips on one side faced another wall offering brilliantly colored Inuit art on different sized canvases. The couch, end tables, a sideboard and a coffee table all featured soapstone carvings of various traditional Arctic animals and hunters, some with ivory harpoons or arrows included.

Suddenly one of the doors was pawed open and a large, three-toned, white, grey and black Husky came bounding into the room happily twisting and turning and jumping up as he tried to lick Lightfoot's face. His tail wagged excitedly and his nails did an Astaire-Rogers number on the tile.

"Atemu, down boy, down," Lightfoot cried, staggering back and ruffling the dog's head while trying to calm him. "Good boy, good boy!"

The dog stopped, looked at Matthew and approached him

cautiously, tail down. He held out his hand and Atemu sniffed it and then moved closer. Matthew put both hands out and scratched his ears. The tail lifted and he barked once at him and then pushed into his knees. Matthew kept petting him.

"Atemu...good dog. Go lay down...go!" Lightfoot ordered. "He can be a nuisance."

The dog shuffled off, banished back to the room.

"Anyhow, thanks," Matthew said to the driver, handing him a twenty dollar bill. The man looked at it but didn't make any move to accept it.

"Behave yourself," Lightfoot said, a frown on his face.

"Of course," Matthew assured him and smiled.

"I'm serious," he said. "You stay in your room tonight."

"Whoa," Matthew said, backing up a step. "Look, I don't know what I'm getting into here but maybe I'd better stay at the Lodge."

"No way. And don't tell her I said anything." His tone changed: "Please?"

"She's your girlfriend?"

Lightfoot sighed and shook his head in exasperation.

"Okay," Matthew said. "How about telling me what's going on between you and Sky?

"Nothing is going on," he answered. "I don't want her hurt. Ever again. Certainly not by another white man."

Matthew surmised Lightfoot had a major crush on Sky. It appeared she didn't know about it and he wasn't planning on enlightening her.

"I think Doctor St. Onge can take care of herself," he said, now becoming irritated. In fact, he was becoming seriously irritated. "She's a grown woman, Joe."

"I know that! If it wasn't for her, I wouldn't be alive now. So, I protect her."

"I don't intend to hurt her or anyone," Matthew said, more and more irritated.

"Then make sure you don't," said Lightfoot placing his hands on his hips. "I have a black belt in Karate and can bench press 250 pounds."

"I'm deliriously happy for you," Matthew retorted, feeling more like a juvenile facing a bully rather than a mature man. "But understand something: Sky and I have a business arrangement. That's all. But if something were to…develop, I don't think it would need your permission."

Lightfoot stood there, his face flushed, his muscles bunching. Matthew wasn't sure if he was going to come at him or not.

"Matthew, I see you made it," Sky said brightly, breezing through the front door followed by a pile of cold air flooding into the entranceway. She pulled the door shut with a solid thud and turned to face him. Her face was ruddy from the outdoors, and her dark eyes were smiling. She immediately sensed something was going on and looked from Lightfoot to him and back again.

Matthew tried to return her smile and relax.

"Did Joe read you the riot act?" she asked, taking off her royal blue parka, unwinding a red scarf and hanging both in a hall closet.

Matthew didn't know quite what to say. Lightfoot was now staring at him with a pleading expression. He decided it was better to have allies than enemies in the North.

"Riot act?" he said, feigning puzzlement. "My friend Joe? Why would he do that?"

"He did," she pronounced, without hesitation.

She turned to Lightfoot.

"Thank you, Joe, but Mr. Corrigan is a perfect gentleman. I got to know him very well in Montreal and there is nothing to worry about."

Lightfoot nodded, avoiding her gaze. "I just want to be sure everything is okay."

"It's very okay, Joe. Thank you so much for picking him up. You're a dear."

She opened the door, pecked him on his cheek and sent him on his way. When the door closed, Matthew let out a breath. "That was weird. I think he's more than a little interested in you, Sky."

"Why would you say that?" she asked, hanging up his coat in the closet as well and entering the kitchen where she opened the refrigerator.

"He seemed to feel I have designs on you and he was pretty much acting like a jealous teenager."

"He *is* a teenager."

"What?" Matthew exclaimed.

"He's fifteen and he's my cousin."

Well he's certainly well built for a fifteen-year-old," Matthew said.

She laughed. "If you saw him with his shirt off you'd think he could give Mike Tyson a run for his money. My aunt thinks he's getting steroids smuggled up here. She searches his room almost every day. I told him that if I find out he's screwing up his body, I'd never speak to him again."

"If he's dedicated and can bench press 250 pounds, it might be all hard work."

Sky smiled at him, cracking the tops of two Molson Canadian beers and handing him a bottle. "He told you that, eh? The 250 pounds? Two roosters posturing?" She moved into the kitchen.

"And, the Black Belt," Matthew added.

"Well he doesn't exaggerate, I'll give him that. I've only got a brown belt."

She put her beer down on the 1960's era chrome kitchen table. Likely it was original, he thought. The furniture was from an era when products were almost bullet-proof.

"Study, discipline, effort and time. He wouldn't need drugs. He said you saved his life?"

"He went through some spring ice. I got him breathing again after I pulled him out. He was more upset over losing his snowmobile than the fact he almost died." She moved in the kitchen, opening cupboards and drawers. Silverware clattered as she hurriedly set the table.

Matthew watched her and thought: She's a totally different person up here; perhaps it's because she's in her element.

"I wanted you to stay here so we could spend some time discussing our little picnic," she continued. "I have some gear to show you later but first we'll eat."

She busied herself taking plates out of the refrigerator and placing Saran wrap over completed meals she must have cooked earlier. Thanks to a double rack, they both went into a microwave oven together and began heating. She stood beside the small oven, not saying a word. To cover the obvious awkwardness, she periodically peered through the small window to check on the progress of the two plates.

As she placed condiments on the table, Matthew was again intrigued by the way she moved. Whether she was walking, bending or turning to seize something, her lithe figure seemed to glide. And her erect posture and bearing never varied. It could almost be termed regal, he thought. Then he revised his original assessment and replaced it with the word: proud. Once or twice she caught him watching her and cocked her head to the side as though questioning what he was thinking. Still, she never spoke, just continued the tasks at hand.

"How is your grandfather?" he asked, finally. While she seemed content with the silence, he found it awkward.

"Same. At least I don't need to have him moved."

"They're keeping him?"

"Yes. When I worked there I did something for one of our neurologists and he thinks he owes me. So Grandfather can stay until we come back. They're also bringing in a physical therapist who will work on him while he's unconscious. Keep his muscles from atrophying and his ligaments and tendons stretched and supple for when he wakes up."

"I see," Matthew said. "What did you do? For the neurologist, I mean."

Sky looked at him for a moment debating if she wanted to answer. Matthew noticed she became evasive every time he asked a question about her or her medical career. Finally she answered.

"I caught a potential aneurism on a film on a light box I was about to use. It happened to belong to Dr. Boyer's mother. The attending physician couldn't understand how he missed it. He told Dr. Boyer about what I saw and a fellow surgeon operated and repaired it before it became a much bigger problem than it was. The surgeon said it was set to blow, and Dr. Boyer – the neurologist – thinks I saved his mother's life."

"Sound like maybe you did."

"Whatever. At least it bought me time for grandfather; he's in the best hands possible."

Sky opened the microwave and removed two large plates of roast beef, potatoes, turnips and asparagus covered with copious amounts of home-made gravy. As they ate, Matthew told her it matched any gourmet meal he'd ever eaten. She deflected the praise with an observation that he'd missed lunch and it was long past supper time. That might have influenced his glowing review.

Atemu tried to join them at the table but Sky quickly pulled out a can of Science Diet and filled his dog food dish in the corner. When he finished, Sky sternly suggested he forget the idea of begging at the table.

As he slunk away, Matthew managed to covertly slip him a piece of roast beef. Sky seemed not to notice but said: "He likes you. He's normally reserved for weeks with strangers, but he likes you already."

"Good judge of character," Matthew replied.

"And roast beef," she added, without looking up.

Afterwards Sky had him deposit his luggage in a small bedroom at the end of the living room and then led him into a second one. It was full of gear for their trek. She pointed out a yellow Arctic Oven 12 Extreme tent and an 18-ounce vinyl ground sheet good to -67 F. Two sets of caribou-hide Ojibway snowshoes stood in a corner. Piled against a wall were two North 49 Arctic Lite sleeping bags. Fold up cots would keep them off the ice and two Coleman catalytic heaters would keep them from freezing to death, she said. Against another wall were two *North 49 Catalyst 75* back packs.

On the bed was an assortment of gun-metal grey steel pitons, two hammers, numerous carabineers, two 60-meter coils of Maxim Glider climbing rope and two climbing safety helmets. Two short, large-scoop aluminum shovels were propped against the bed.

"We also have a second tent and inflatable mattresses," she said.

"His and hers tents," Matthew joked.

"Not quite," she said. "Number two is a smaller tent that we'll use on the second half of our trek, once we make it into the mountains. In it, to stay comfortable, I'll need your body heat and you'll need mine."

Really?

She picked up one of dozens and dozens of Expedition Foods' pouches on the bed and showed him what they'd be eating during their trip.

"Expedition Foods are really quite good," she explained "These will furnish our breakfast, lunch and dinner. Of course they're dehydrated but they're also light weight and calorie dense. Our energy requirements will increase by about 50 percent when we're out there. So we just add water boiled on our Coleman stove, let it stew for a time, and serve."

Matthew picked up a couple of the dehydrated food pouches; one was labeled chili and the second Chicken Tikka with rice. Others included: porridge with strawberries; egg, potato and mixed peppers; and, an assortment of desserts. Also on the bed and floor were PowerMonkey Extreme solar chargers, short-wave hand radios, a flare gun and flares, a GPS unit, Maglites, an Iridium satellite phone, a large and smaller first aid kit, and various other packs and cases of supplies. Placed across the top of a dresser in the corner were a Winchester lever-action .30-30 caliber carbine, a .22 semi-automatic Mossberg rifle, and several boxes of ammunition of varying sizes. A second, scoped, high-powered rifle of some sort stood in the corner.

She noticed him staring at all the weapons. "As an Innu guide, by law, I can legally carry weapons in Torngat National Park," she said. "White people cannot."

Hung on hangers on the wall were two dark, head-to-toe, zippered one-piece suits unlike anything he'd ever seen.

"What the heck are those?" he asked.

"They come from Tekplorer in Germany," she replied. "Grandfather and I have had them for a while. They have a thermal IR coating that reduces heat signatures."

"And you use them for…?" he asked, puzzled.

"In case we need them," she murmured, and abruptly flipped the light switch off on her way out of the room.

Matthew stood there in the dark. "Guess the tours over," he mused to himself. He had no choice other than to follow her into the living room where she sat down on a well-stuffed sofa and motioned him to a matching chair.

"We'll travel on two Renegade snowmobiles with each of us pulling a six-foot Hunter tow sled carrying our equipment and extra gasoline," she said. "We're talking almost 500 miles to a spot north of Eclipse Bay and near Cape Territok. It will take about three or four days to get there barring bad ice or storms."

"And then?" he inquired politely.

"And then we go inland for a time and finally have to leave our snowmobiles and travel on snowshoes. I'm guessing a week in total travel time."

"Couldn't we take the snowmobiles in with us?" Matthew asked.

"Only if you're prepared to carry them over rocks and up a mountain," she returned, without pause.

"I saw ropes and pitons," he said. "Doesn't give me a warm feeling."

She smiled: "Nor will you have any form of warm feeling again, until we get back."

Matthew nodded and she continued. "I'm not being sarcastic, Matthew. I know you have no idea where we're going or what we have to do to get there. But I want you to know that, despite the equipment and the technology we have, it's not an easy journey."

"But you've been there?"

"Twice with grandfather. Once when I was twenty-one and then about five years ago. We had a lot less gear than you and I have now. But, using the old ways, grandfather could live off the land. I'm good but I'm not as proficient as my grandfather."

"Has he known about the diamonds a long time?"

Sky hesitated again and then carefully chose her words. "He's been going there for many years but the diamonds were a relatively new…discovery."

"Okay," Matthew said. "But I'm going to get my boss to pay for all of this gear." He gestured towards the bedroom.

Sky held up her hand. "Don't worry about it. Most of that stuff is borrowed. Even the snowmobiles. The only other thing left to do is examine your clothes to make sure you're ready for some extreme cold."

Matthew unpacked and Sky was happy with everything except his choice of parka. She showed him her own North Face Mchaven Parka featuring 550-fill down insulation with an oversized military snorkel hood with a wire brim. The hood was trimmed with fur.

"These hoods allow you close them tight in a heavy wind but leave enough of an opening for you to see and breathe," she said, showing how she could squeeze the hood opening closed in various ways and the wire brim enabled it to retain the shape she chose. "I had one of the ladies here sew this wolverine fur on mine. It's the only fur that never frosts up."

Then, out of the parka pocket, she pulled a pair of glacier glasses with leather side panels for UV protection and the prevention of snow blindness. Finally she retrieved some dark plastic ski goggles from the bedroom and explained they would need to wear them on the snowmobiles to prevent frozen eyeballs and snow blindness.

"I have ski goggles at home but never thought of them," Matthew said.

"That's okay," Sky replied. "We're going over to the Northern Store tomorrow to get you a North Face Mchaven parka like mine. We'll pick you up glasses and goggles at the same time. Then we'll pack the sleds and leave the next day. Are you good with this?"

"Sure, it'll be a breeze," Matthew answered, trying to be upbeat.

"I'm not being picky about the parka," she said. "It's important that your clothing, your parka, undergarments, sweaters and such, breathe properly. If you sweat, it will cool off and eventually freeze. Cold water or ice removes heat from the body 25 times faster than cold air will."

"No problem," he assured her.

"Matthew, there is one other thing you have to know. There is no turning back. I intend to get us to our destination. I made a promise to my grandfather and it may be the last promise I ever make to him." Her eyes were shining now, her emotions running high.

Matthew nodded hastily. "I won't quit, Sky. I won't quit on you."

~2~

The next morning Sky took the tarps off two Renegade snowmobiles she had parked around the side of the bungalow. Attached to them were individual sleds ready to be loaded. Tucked inside each sled was a fiberglass pull-toboggan with a long tumpline attached.

She started one machine easily and gave it some gas, keeping it in neutral. She listened intently to the sound of the engine. Finally, satisfied, she gave it more throttle and slowly and carefully brought it around to the front door of the house. She disembarked and then asked Matthew to do the same with the other snowmobile. She watched him closely. There was no doubt in his mind; this was a test to see how well he could handle the machine. Fortunately he'd ridden many times, both in the Laurentians and in Ungava.

Without hesitation, he straddled the seat. He made sure the parking brake was engaged, pulled the *kill switch* to on, engaged the choke and twisted the key in the ignition to start. The engine caught immediately and he released the brake and gave it enough throttle to move it slowly until it was parked alongside Sky's machine. He turned it off and took out the key.

"Oh, leave it in, Matthew," Sky laughed. "Nobody is going to steal it up here."

"I guess the RCMP would deal with them?"

"They should be so lucky. If anyone interferes with our journey into the Torngats, the Great Spirit *Torngarsuk* will haunt them to their death and then strip the fresh meat from their bloody bones," she said earnestly. Then she smiled. "Or not."

Atemu suddenly dashed up, tail wagging. He let Matthew rub his ears and then scurried off over a snow bank to play with several other dogs running about. Sky watched the dog curiously and shook her head as though she couldn't comprehend his immediate acceptance of Matthew.

Sky pointed to the left handlebar of her Renegade. Attached to it was a GPS unit in a heavy, plastic, see-through case. "I had Joe put on an add-a-circuit and a separate power supply so we can keep it on when we switch the snowmobile off," she said. "There are waypoints programmed in which I hope we can make. Open water means we scrub them. And as you can see we have a compass installed on each sled for backup."

Next Sky took him to the Northern Store where he was outfitted with a new parka, minus the wolverine fur. Snow glasses followed and goggles were requested. He was surprised to be served by Joe Lightfoot who slapped the goggles down on the counter joining the parka and glasses.

"Is that everything?" Lightfoot asked, slightly sullen.

"Yes that will do," Sky said, smiling at him, but not in a patronizing way. "We'll be out there at least two weeks, Joe. And I checked this morning; Grandfather is still the same."

"Is he going to be alright?" Joe asked worriedly, his youth and vulnerability showing.

"I don't know but we'll pray for him, eh?"

"I do. Every night."

"Good man. Now I think we'll take another two dozen ER Survival Bars, just in case." She pointed towards a box of granola looking bars behind him.

"Did you let the Mounties know where you're going?" Joe asked, handing them to her.

"Yes…to a point. I left them 80 percent of our route but the final destination is not shown for obvious reasons. And we may have to deviate. They weren't happy. But we have the satellite phone as well."

"Be careful. You don't have grandfather with you. If you aren't back in two weeks, and we haven't heard from you, I'll come looking. You know that, right?"

"Listen to me carefully, Joe. If you do have to come looking, you bring Guy or one of the other Mounties with you. In winter you need a companion for backup, right? Promise?"

"Yeah Sky, I promise," he said, resolutely.

While they were talking Matthew looked around the Northern Store. It was typical of stores in remote locations stocking everything from eggs to ammo. The difference between a store in northern Labrador and one in the South was defined by price. In the North, a watermelon could be priced anywhere from $38 to $55, and a small loaf of white bread ran upwards of seven dollars.

He continued scanning the store and noticed his new friend from Nain, Bob Crummy. He was talking to two people in parkas. One, a large fellow, had a bushy black beard. The other person was much slighter. Crummy laughed and then looked directly at Matthew. He quickly turned away without a sign of recognition. He then said something and the small figure in the parka started to turn, and then abruptly stopped. This was followed by a hurried exit from the store. The man with the beard followed. Crummy looked at Matthew, pretended to notice him for the first time, grinned and waved. Then he followed the other two out.

Matthew paid for the purchases and he and Sky returned to the house. They spent the rest of the day packing gear and supplies on the sleds from a meticulously prepared list. Sky checked off each item and directed it to either Sled 1 or Sled 2. Matthew noticed that the food had been evenly divided, as were the two tents (one on each sled) the sleeping bags, the heaters, ammunition and four 10-gallon Jerry cans of gasoline each. "In case one sled goes through the ice we don't lose everything," she explained. "We can still get by."

The last two items were the rifles with the .30-30 going into a leather scabbard on the right side her snowmobile, and the .22 packed on Matthew's sled. Sky's sled got a third gun case, likely the high-powered rifle.

"Now we'll take the rifles and ammo back inside for tonight," she said. "There are lots of kids here and we don't want any accidents. Everything else is status quo under the tarps."

She turned to head into the house and then remembered something. "One more thing." Sky dug down into her packsack on the sled and pulled out what looked like a hardened telephone with a swing-up aerial. It was a satellite phone. She opened it and removed the battery, retrieved two other spare batteries from the knapsack, closed it and returned it to a case on the sled. She carried all three batteries inside with her for final charging.

Sky made supper that evening, spaghetti with rich meat sauce. The meat she explained was caribou but most of the taste was negated by the tomato, peppers and onions in the sauce. Matthew had caribou before and found it a coarse and tough meat so he wasn't necessarily disappointed it had been marinated and ground up.

Later they sat in the living room, the lights on low, and finished off a large bottle of wine. He noted it was a cabernet sauvignon from *Chateau des Charmes Estate Wines* in Niagara-on-the-Lake, Ontario.

"Sort of far from home, isn't it," he asked her, setting the empty bottle back on the coffee table.

"One of my favorites," she answered. "Discovered it during a trip to Ontario when I was doing my surgical residency. I've ordered it by the case ever since. Not that I drink much. A case will generally last me three months." She hopped off the couch and pulled out a second liter and a half bottle of the same brand from a kitchen cupboard. Though not quite as steady on her feet as she might have liked, she opened it and refilled both their empty glasses.

"I don't drink much neither," he said, feeling the effects of so much wine in such a short time. He took another healthy sip.

Obviously Sky was also feeling more relaxed as she lounged on the couch, her two feet up and resting on the back, wine in hand. Matthew was feeling similarly at ease in the overstuffed chair. Atemu lay curled on the rug next to the couch.

With the wine making him a little braver, he decided to see if she felt like sharing a bit of her history with him. "Last night, Joe gave me a pretty hard time before you arrived," he said, swallowing what started as a burp. "When I tried to find out why, he said he didn't want you hurt by another white man?"

He let the obvious question hang in the air and waited to see if she'd expand on what Joe meant. She didn't say anything for almost a full minute. It seemed like an eternity and had him squirming and wishing he hadn't brought up the subject. Finally she looked over at him.

"It was a long time ago," she said slowly and then seemed to warm to the subject. "I was a star-struck teen-ager. A guy from Ottawa came up here one summer when I was sixteen. He was a student studying geology at Carlton University with a summer job prospecting for uranium deposits. We fell in love and started seeing each other whenever he was in town. Every winter was torture when he went back to classes. Every summer was heaven when he came back to work in Nain."

"What's his name?"

"Duane Van Horne. His family is quite wealthy, majority shareholders in a number of mining companies, I think. Big mansion in Ottawa but Daddy was determined Duane would make his own way in their companies. At least, initially. He was three years older than me. Still, when he was here during the summer, we spent every second we could together. I was so flattered that this blond-haired, blue-eyed handsome guy from the nation's capital would fall for me, a simple Innu who had been south only once in her life."

"So you two were an item," Matthew said, taking another mouthful of wine. By this time his tongue was so numb he couldn't even taste what he was drinking.

"That's right, for three summers. He kept telling me he was going to take me away from Nain to this fairy tale existence on the outside. And he promised undying love as he tried to get into my panties." Sky hiccupped and also took a healthy guzzle of wine.

Matthew was about to ask if Van Horne had succeeded when some primal survival instinct spawned from the hypothalamus portion of his brain told him to keep his mouth shut. He did and Sky continued.

"He always professed to love me most when I was dressed in traditional Innu garb, in my moccasins and furs. Said I was *cute as a button*. Son of a bitch."

"Oh!" Matthew exclaimed, taken aback by her swearing. He slumped back in his chair. "So what happened?"

"He returned to university for his final year and I'd get the occasional email. But I felt things weren't quite right. He sounded different in his notes, if you know what I mean. I called him at the end of May and asked if he'd be coming to Nain in early June as usual. You see,

I thought he'd be working up here for the prospecting company that gave him the summer jobs. Anyhow, he was really vague at first, and then said he couldn't come at the usual time because his parents were throwing him a fancy graduation party at the Château Laurier Hotel. Apparently it was going to be a big Ottawa deal. After that, he didn't know where he'd be working. So I came up with a grand plan." She stared off into nothing.

"Okay, I'll bite. What plan?"

"I'd surprise him at his graduation party. Then he'd have someone to dance with. Get it? Me." She giggled, her words fuzzy with wine.

"That was nice," Matthew replied, his head swimming. Time to slow down on the vino. "Go on with this fairy trail…I mean *tale*…of intrigue." Clearly he wasn't feeling any pain neither.

Sky laughed and laughed some more. Finally she stopped laughing all together and became serious again. She took a deep breath and continued.

"I figured if this hotel was such a big deal, you must have to book a graduation party well in advance. So I called the Château Laurier, pretended to be a decorator and said I lost the paper telling me when the Van Horne party was scheduled. They told me June 10th in the Main Ballroom. They even gave me the time: 8:30 PM!"

"Did you go?" Matthew asked, now more awake as he sensed a change in Sky's tone.

"Damn right I went. Unfortunately, an eighteen-year-old from up here isn't quite as clued in as those on the outside. You might say I was innocent. Or naive. Or even stupid" She started to giggle again but it soon ceased. "Against his better judgement, Grandfather paid my fare."

"So you flew to Ottawa?"

"Well, I sure didn't walk." Again the brief laugh, but this time with a tremor in her voice. "I flew in complete with the furs and mukluks just like he liked. I checked into this 'palace' called the Lord Elgin Hotel. Never stayed in a place like that before. Then at nine o'clock I showed up at the Château Laurier in my furs looking for the Main Ballroom. As luck would have it, outside the door I ran into a nice young man in a tuxedo who asked if he could help me. I told him I was looking for Duane Van Horne's graduation party and he told me he was Duane's brother, Bradley."

"Was Duane glad to see you?"

"Hold your horses there, Red Ryder...I'm getting to it. Where was I? Oh right, Bradley. I remembered Duane saying he never got along with his brother Bradley but he seemed very nice to me. When he found out who I was, his face lit up ever so nicely. He shook my hand and said he was so *glad* to finally meet me. So *glad*. And he was so *glad* I'd made the effort to come all the way down from Labrador to Duane's party to surprise him.

"Anyhow, we were standing at the big glass doors into the Grand Ballroom when two white-haired men in tuxedos came out, stared at me for a minute, raised their eye brows and went about their business. Bradley told me to ignore them. Then he said that, to really surprise Duane, I should run through the doors and up the aisle where Duane was sitting on a small raised stage beyond the dance floor. That way he'd see me before anyone said anything. Be surprised."

"And you were dressed in your furs?"

"Yes, the way he liked. Cute as a button." She chuckled again. This time it came out sounding even more tenuous.

"So you ran into the ballroom," Matthew said, not liking where this was going.

"I did. I ran past all these silver-laden dining tables on either side where men in tuxedos and women in ball gowns were sipping from crystal goblets and speaking in hushed tones. The room was pretty dark except for a spotlight on the small stage where Duane was making a speech into a microphone. He was standing beside this stunning blond in a white evening gown. She had sparkles in her hair; sparkles on her eye lids; sparkles on her dress; and, probably sparkles up her ass, if she'd been checked.

"I skidded to a stop on the dance floor and looked up at Duane with a big grin and threw out my arms. Sort of 'Surprise...I'm here!' Then I saw it. Behind him and Miss Sparkles was a big, white banner reading: CONGRATULATIONS CANDICE AND DUANE.

"First I thought, *two* graduates. Anyhow, you talk about your skunk at a garden party! There were exclamations. There were gasps. There were gulps. There were all kinds of utterances of surprise. And dismay. The dismay came from Duane who recoiled knocking over his and her drinks on the table. He cried out: 'Sky! What the hell are you doing here'?"

"Son of a bitch," Matthew said, taking another mouthful of wine.

"Yep. Then I heard this loud laughter at the back of the room and turned to see Bradley braying like a mule and slapping his thigh at his joke on his brother. Meanwhile, Sparkles jumped to her feet and grabbed Duane's arm, rather possessively, I thought. And, the spotlight caught the stone on her left hand glittering like a super nova. I think it was about that time I figured out in my pea-sized brain that this wasn't a graduation party. It was an *engagement* party."

"Oh boy," Matthew said, watching Sky flush crimson at the memory.

"Wait, it gets better," she said, her voice shaking. "As the shock wore off a bit I could hear everyone around me commenting. Phrases like: 'Must be his Indian lover. Who let *her* in? It's got to be his little squaw girl from Labrador.' And finally: 'Must be a joke on *him*!' But you see, Matthew, the joke was on *me*."

By now Matthew felt utterly sober. He could only imagine adrenaline had counteracted the effects of the wine. He felt a mixture of anger and sadness as he watched several tears wind their way down Sky's face. Atemu sat up and forced his head onto her lap looking up at her with his soft brown eyes. He whined gently giving a hopeful wag of his tail as he tried to bring comfort.

"Sky, I don't know what to say," Matthew said, softly.

She looked over, her cheeks glistening and then she looked at her glass. "Damn wine makes me maudlin." She tried to smile, wiping away the tears.

"What did you do?" Matthew asked, unable to let it go.

"Oh I looked around at all those grand people in their evening clothes and jewelry, probably the pillars of Ottawa's society, and realized I was suddenly sweating like a hen hauling logs. Probably from embarrassment. So I called up to Duane: 'Sorry for crashing your party…!' and I started peeling off my fur mitts, fur anorak, fur mukluks and fur pants, dropping them one-by-one on the dance floor. More shrieks of horror; they thought I was stripping totally bare buff. Meanwhile, I said quite loudly I hoped the penicillin had worked for his syphilis, and his herpes had gone dormant again. About this time, Sparkles dropped his arm like he was radioactive."

The humor was like a pin prick in a balloon of tension and Matthew burst out laughing. But she wasn't finished.

"Next I assured him that since he'd been two-timing me, he'd never see little Duane Junior again. But someday there'd be an heir contesting the Van Horne fortune. Lot of stirring in the peanut gallery over that one. Finally, to show what a *classy* girl I was, I lifted my head high and marched back towards Bradley who was bent over in glee. A lot of people were snickering at me. I tried to be cool, you know, but inside, I was devastated. I faced Bradley who was still laughing so hard he had tears streaming down his puss."

"And?"

"Well, first I thanked him for helping me understand what was going on. Then I slapped him so hard he fell on his ass. After all, *classy* only goes so far."

"Good for you," Matthew said.

"Do you know the one thing what makes me feel okay about the whole, sordid affair, Matthew?"

"What, Sky?"

"I never did let the bastard into my panties."

* * *

By six the following morning, Sky and Matthew had dressed, finished breakfast and were loading the rifles and ammo onto the sleds. Her .30-30 went into the scabbard near her right knee on the snowmobile. It was still pitch dark and had hit -20 below Fahrenheit. Neither had mentioned the revelations of the night before and Matthew sensed he should leave the subject alone. She had shared something very personal and he respected her enough not to mention it further. Both of them, however, admitted to major headaches.

They went back inside and called the Royal Vic Hospital; there was no change in her grandfather's condition. Still, she left her satellite phone number with the nurses for any emergency. Matthew had called Andre Jacquard's office. He wasn't in so he left a message with Mary saying they were about to embark on their search for the diamond site. He also left the satellite phone number.

This morning, Sky was all business again.

"Weather is a little uncertain but we have to get on the trail," she said, busily securing her rifle tight in the scabbard with a leather cinch.

Atemu bounded around the snowmobiles in the dark, sure he was going with them on their trip. Sky finally called him over but he ran to Matthew instead.

"What's with my dog?" she asked, though her tone wasn't entirely displeased. "You have bacon in your pockets?"

Matthew smiled and shook his head as he played with the dog, picking up and throwing a black rubber ball that had seen better days. He was careful to make sure he threw it on the road so it didn't get lost in the snow. Atemu scrambled to retrieve it. Finally, he led the dog over to the front door where the dog smelled a rat and was reluctant to enter. Sky got him in, gave him a big hug, boxed his ears and closed the door. She said her cousin would be over later to take him to his own house. Matthew found he still had the rubber ball in hand so, rather than open the door again and give the dog the false hope that he might accompany them after all, he slipped it in under the tarp of his sled. It would be safe there till they returned.

Sky handed Matthew a silver HJC helmet. She explained that it was fitted with a Chatterbox XBi2-H-Plus Bluetooth communication system so they could talk en route.

"How far are we going with the snowmobiles?" Matthew asked.

"About 500 kilometers north as the crow flies before we head inland," she replied.

"Then we'll be there tomorrow or the next day?"

"We aren't crows," she pointed out. "Mostly we'll have to follow the shoreline so it's probably more than 1,000 kilometers in and out of the bays and going around obstacles. Your neighborhood fractal geometry at work."

"Oh...."

"We also won't be going 50 mph with these." She gestured at the Renegades and their American speedometers. "By the way, to avoid confusion, we'll use the Imperial system for this trip if that's okay."

"No problem," he said, slapping one of the red plastic Jerry cans. "How many miles per gallon will we get?"

"We'll be lucky to get 15 to 20 towing these sleds."

"We won't have enough fuel, will we?"

"No," she returned. "Grandfather and I have two fuel caches in the

Torngats. We'll fill up there, leave our empties and pick them up on the way back for refilling. Joe likes to shoot photos in the mountains and he transports full ones back to the caches for us."

"You said four days on the snowmobiles and maybe three on foot."

"Yes, but the foot part includes some climbing. Take about a day and a half. And for the trip I'm including fuel stops, bathroom breaks, meals and a possible brief storm or two. We'll probably average 15 to 25 mph on the snowmobiles. By the way, we'll use bicycle hand signals. And when we hit the shore ice, stay a hundred feet behind and ten or fifteen windward to avoid my "snow dust." That way, if the ice gives way and I go swimming, you have time to stop and pull me out. We never know with the ice these days." She pointed to a coiled rope on his sled.

Matthew got on his snowmobile, holding his helmet.

"Okay, time to get moving," she said, donning a balaclava followed by her helmet. Matthew did likewise. He saw she was talking so he keyed the system on the side of his helmet and waved. Her voice crackled in his ears. "Mathew, are you receiving?"

"Roger, I read you 5-by-5, over."

"Were you in the military?" she asked.

"Yes, I captained a Hercules in the RCAF."

"Okay that explains it. We can use this system like a walkie-talkie if you'd like. Don't have to do all the Roger-Roger stuff…Captain."

"Wilco," he answered.

She gave him a look and circled her finger in the air motioning him to start up.

All business again….

Within a few minutes they were purring down a street bordered by six-foot high snowbanks towards Unity Bay with Sky leading.

Here and there lights were snapping on in the houses, spilling their warm, yellow glow onto the snow as they passed by. His snowmobile bucked as it hit chunks of ice on the road and he flicked on his headlight. Through a mist of churned up snow in front, he could barely see the red tail light of Sky's machine.

They reached the bay and carefully travelled down onto the snowy beach and then onto the open ice. Her voice suddenly erupted in his earphones again and he reached up and reduced the volume. "Okay,

Captain, time to blast off," she said, amusement in her voice.

Sky opened up her throttle with a roar and her Renegade took off. Matthew did the same and they began racing across a seemingly unending white expanse, the sun merely a hint of gold on the eastern horizon. Within fifteen minutes they had crossed Unity Bay and rounded a point of land where they carefully skirted Akpiksai Bay close to shore, and then headed north. The freezing wind tugged at his clothes and he was grateful for the new parka.

Matthew felt many things as they began their journey: freedom, excitement and perhaps a little trepidation. After all, they were heading into an extremely hostile northern wilderness which had stolen the lives of many others who went before them. The only thing standing between Matthew and a similar fate was a single girl into whose hands he had placed his trust.

And also, he thought…his life.

~3~

Major Paul Stone stood in his parka on the Saglek airport ramp watching two F-35 Lightning jets roar down the runway side-by-side and lift smoothly into the cold Labrador air.

The aircraft peeled off to the north, climbed swiftly and were soon out of sight in the low clouds, their rolling thunder gradually muted by distance. Around him, enlisted men moved in and out of buildings. Doors slammed, machinery sounded and airmen called to each other. It was a busy base, no doubt of that. Personally he couldn't wait to find out the end game.

He'd been in Saglek Harbour for a full week now and was finding the base pretty much operated smoothly without any interference from him, thank you very much. But there had been surprises in store when he arrived. Three, in fact.

The first was that after being so busy for the last year, he suddenly had time on his hands. Colonel Robert D. Moorhead was very much a squared-away, take-charge person and assigned Stone to coordinating base maintenance and resupply. Moorhead soon showed he was a hard-bitten warrior with a chest full of ribbons, zero humor and even less tolerance for discussion. So, after setting up the entire base infrastructure, Stone now felt more than a little used up and discarded.

The second surprise was when he arrived via Hercules transport at the base and didn't see any base military personnel heading out on leave. When he had expressed his curiosity to the Technical Sergeant who supervised the unloading, the man had simply said: "Sorry sir, but there are no leaves permitted from this base. Those of us assigned here are not permitted leave for any reason, even family emergencies. At least for the duration."

He didn't explain what the "duration" meant. Duration of what? The day? The mission? Their lives?

When he checked into his new office and received his first visit from the base CO, Moorhead delivered the third and final surprise. His lackluster duties at Saglek.

"Have you reviewed your orders, Major?" Moorhead asked, sitting in the only chair in the sparse office that didn't have a box planted on it.

"Briefly sir," Stone replied, unloading a desk stapler from a box of office supplies shipped from Montreal. "Coordinate base infrastructure maintenance, and oversee resupply operations."

"Correct," Moorhead said. His tone was hushed; he bit off his words less they echo in the office and maybe betray some perceived confidentiality.

Moorhead stared at him, waiting for some form of protest. On Stone's part, he felt that the Colonel probably had a comeback already planned and was merely waiting to use it. Internally he debated whether or not to give him the satisfaction. He decided not to bother. As in any military force, you followed orders believing that the chain of command had wisdom beyond your own limited vision.

Stone studied the man some more. He had a well-weathered but unlined complexion topped by a severe crewcut. His obviously premature white hair resembled short porcupine quills. With grey, watery eyes that seldom blinked, and, instead remained fixed on his subject, he looked somewhat reptilian. Stone wondered why he felt so exposed in front of Moorhead. Perhaps it was because he had the unsettled feeling the man could read his thoughts. His brief inspection assured him of one thing: This was one tough hombre and if you ever wronged him in your career, you'd be sentenced to a life of looking over your shoulder knowing that, one day, payback would arrive and bite you real good.

"No offense to anyone Colonel, but I'm wondering if that's the best use of my skill set."

"No it isn't, Major," Moorhead said. "It's vastly underutilizing your experience and your skills. You know it and I know it."

Stone looked in surprise at the Colonel. "Well, why am I here–?" he left the question hanging.

"Two reasons. The first is because we can't have you and your knowledge about this base out in the great beyond. Every pilot, technician, mechanic, engineer, MP, cook, and bottle-washer is up here until we complete our mission. Every man who worked beyond the initial construction of the building on this base has remained here. Remember how careful you had to be to use only military personnel once we finished the building shells and the runway paving? And, how you had to immediately ship out the civilian contractors before anything strategic was received or installed? That was because we didn't want to detain civilian personnel. Now people and supplies flow in; nothing flows out. Even the transport pilots who fly up here almost daily aren't allowed off their airplanes to pee. They see nothing and they know nothing."

"You're saying I'm here in *cold* storage to maintain confidentiality, pardon the pun?"

The colonel didn't bothered to acknowledge his attempt at humor. "Not quite," he said.

Then came details of the third surprise.

"The second reason is that when we begin the operational phase Major, you'll be leading the Mission Recovery Team."

"Mission Recovery Team? Recovering what, sir?"

"Foreign technology. That is your specialty, correct?"

"Yes, my last assignment at Wright-Patterson. Evaluating, anyhow. Not recovering."

"Well, this time you'll be doing both: Evaluating for selection, and also recovering."

Stone sat down in his own chair as he digested this newest information. His CO said nothing further, waiting for his questions.

"Where the heck is the foreign technology up here, Colonel? Or are we expecting the Russians or Chinese to start pranging into the tundra?"

Moorhead stared at him for a moment trying to decide what he could reveal and what he could not at this time. He finally decided to start with broad strokes and whittle it down to a few specifics but being careful not to reveal the end game.

"As you know, Major, we have ears on all global communications. The NSA and the Canadian's Communication Security Establishment, among others, share their Intel with us. In the Torngat Mountains, some remarkable occurrences have been taking place."

"What sort of occurrences, sir?" Stone asked, dutifully.

"First we've been intercepting indecipherable UHF chatter. For decades. And, for decades we officially listed it as freak radio waves. As our technology improved, we realized these were actual transmissions between parties. Occasionally our cryptologists would haul out the captured intercepts and try to decipher them. Never succeeded. Until recently we assumed it was because they were all gibberish. However, two years ago, using an IBM Deep Blue-type custom program, our analysts came to a startling conclusion: What we were hearing was a language. A language between technologies. Machines talking."

"Machine?" Stone said, now interested. "What machines?"

"I can't tell you that right now, Major, but I can tell you we did break down some of it. And because of the intercepted chatter, its frequency and the length of the messages, it pointed to an upcoming event. And, from some of our other Intel, we know that event is taking place during the Winter solstice. Up here. Further, we tied those messages to some strange vehicular traffic we were seeing."

"Ground?"

"No, air. The chatter always matched an increase in bogie traffic in the area. Our conclusion: A covert operation was in progress but it was winding down."

"Perhaps the chatter was in an old Russian or Chinese dialect, sir?"

"No," Moorhead replied. "Deep Blue analyzed morphology, syntax and a bunch of other things I don't understand. It concluded this was technology chatting with other technology, making instant decisions, and then relaying and acting on those decisions."

"Then, do we have any idea of what the operation or event is?" Stone knew there were limits to what he was being told but he began to add up some of the numbers. The secrecy, the hurried preparations, the large number of UCAVs and the promise of foreign technology. Were they planning on taking down some new and very secret Russian or Chinese drones?

Moorhead shook his head. "We have a suspicion as to the origin of the activity. Based on that suspicion, we initiated this mission; we had to act before it was too late."

"Am I allowed to know the origin? If it's merely a suspicion, I mean."

"Not yet. But here's the big picture, Major. If the US wants to remain a world power, we need to stay ahead of the curve. These days the technology gap between what we have and what our competitors has is shrinking rapidly. Mostly, it's because the bastards steal stuff from us, but the end result is the same. So we need to find a great leap forward."

It sounded like Mr. Black's refrain, he thought. "And that would be how, Colonel?"

"Before we get into that let me set the stage for you. As you know, back in the 1970s and 1980s, during the Cold War, Saglek Harbour was an active, US-staffed, radar base on the Pinetree Radar Line. One night, December 26, 1981 to be exact, two things occurred: First, the Canadians were alerted by NORAD of an intruder entering ADIZ and refusing to identify itself. They dispatched two CF-101 Voodoos to intercept the bogie over northern Labrador. Saglek was vectoring the Voodoos to the target when one jet went down in the Torngat Mountains."

"Shot down, Colonel?" Stone asked.

The colonel hesitated but then said: "We aren't exactly sure what happened."

"Was the crew lost?" Stone asked.

Moorhead nodded. "Nor did we find the wreckage," he added. "Despite an exhaustive search."

"Okay. You mentioned two things happened."

"Yes. The second was that Saglek picked up a distress call from a civilian ham operator out of Sisimiut, Greenland. On the same night. It seems the ham operator had picked up an SOS from a Canadian Indian trapped on an ice flow. He was being swept out into the Labrador Sea. A freak radio bounce, it seems. He relayed the SOS to here, Saglek Harbour. The base didn't have the assets to help; they were between flights. So they radioed Goose Bay. Unfortunately our US Military Airlift Command assets were useless for this type of rescue.

"But Canadian Air Command, 5 Wing at Goose, was able to send out a fixed wing and a Labrador helicopter to try to find and rescue the man. The Air Search & Rescue aircraft located the fellow on an ice flow but couldn't vector the bird to him in time; a major blizzard had set in and visibility had dropped to zero. Temperatures were approaching -50 degrees that night and there was an off-shore wind gusting to 60 mph which was had sent the ice flow out into the Labrador Sea. The poor bugger was doomed."

Moorhead paused, lit a cigarette in defiance of regulations and continued. "At this time, Goose got a *Mayday* call from an interceptor tracking a bogie within the zone. This was from one of the two Voodoo interceptors over the Torngat Mountains. Since helping the Indian was now out of the question, they redirected Air Search & Rescue to the Voodoo's location."

"How far away were they?" Stone asked.

"About 150 nautical miles, if I remember correctly," Moorhead replied. "Not that it did much good. Ground visibility was zero there too. That's when everything went to hell."

"How so?" Stone asked, sitting forward on his chair.

"While Air Search & Rescue was headed towards the remaining Voodoo, guess what they picked up on radar? A blip right over the ice flow where they figured the Indian was situated. Based on estimates of wind speed and drift, of course. And the blip wasn't one of ours."

"Soviet?"

Moorhead stared off into the distance as though he could see through walls. He shifted uncomfortably in his chair. "At the time they didn't know who it was, but they knew it wasn't ours. The Canucks were already returning to Goose. NORAD thought it had to be a copter since it was stationary. Then, after 15 minutes of hover, it took off and accelerated to about 900 knots on its way deep into the Torngat Mountain where it disappeared. No copter hit those speeds in 1981."

With his in-depth knowledge of foreign technology and weaponry, this was an area of expertise where Stone felt he could add value. "The Russian Yak-38 Forger VTOL aircraft supposedly had its maiden flight in 1971 and entered active service about five years later," Stone said. "They were used almost exclusively on the Soviet Navy's Kiev-class aircraft carriers. As you know, they could hover and do vertical take-offs and landings."

"We don't think it was any Yak-38," Moorhead answered: "I know the Yak intimately."

Stone pressed on. "There could have been a Soviet aircraft carrier in international waters off Labrador that night. Heard the chatter and sent up a Yak."

"Okay, when it entered service, how many crew members?"

"Crew of one until they developed the YAK-38UV later. Then two crew members. As for speed, the initial Forger had a top speed of 723 knots. Close to what radar picked up."

"Yes, but obviously there is no room for a passenger."

"No," Stone agreed, politely. "But what does that have to do with the blip?"

"The Yak couldn't land and rescue anyone, even if it could fly in that weather."

"How would that make a difference?" Stone repeated. He eyed the colonel who was definitely showing signs of uneasiness. Obviously he was choosing his words very carefully.

"Because, seven days later, the Indian, the one they couldn't save, the one under that radar blip that night, walked back into his home in Nain, Labrador. No frostbite, no gear and as healthy as you or I. So something else picked him up, Major. And that's why we're up here."

"We're here because of what happened in *1981*?" Stone said, shocked *and* awed.

"There's a little more to the story," Moorhead conceded. "The Indian refused a debriefing. And, though there continued to be all kinds of radar alerts around the Torngats, we could never successfully intercept anything. Whatever was flying in and out was simply too fast. We figured the Soviets had some new fighters. And so we started paying attention. And we noticed this Indian...Innu, I think they're called up here? Anyhow, the same guy, Jerome St. Onge, began to regularly travel up to the area near where he was rescued. It was in the general vicinity of where the radar returns were centered. In addition, we intercepted a report to Health Canada, from some geology student, saying the old man had set off his Geiger counter in Nain. That really piqued our curiosity."

"Did you think he was meeting with some foreign powers up here with a covert agenda?" Stone was now intensely interested.

"We didn't know, but it was enough for us to put up some "eyes in the sky" and watch him on his trips into the Torngats.""

"What happened?" Stone pressed.

"He would make Cape Territok, head into the interior from the coast into the Torngat mountain range…and vanish."

"Vanish? What do you mean?"

"He'd vanish, he'd disappear, or he'd disintegrate for all the hell I know."

"Maybe he was hiding."

"Look, when we became aware he was returning to an area close to where he'd been rescued, we followed him with civilian looking aircraft to find out what he was doing," Moorhead said. "He'd go up there once or twice a year. In fact, we employed a fellow in Nain, guy named Crummy, to let us know when St. Onge was heading out. We'd have a pilot fly out of Goose with a Cessna or Piper, intercept him en route and track him. Invariably he'd lose him. But when we picked up more radar intrusions in later years, we employed drone technology to watch him 24/7 on his treks. Eyes during daylight and infrared at night. He'd make camp on this crazy mountaintop plateau, at 3,000 feet plus. Then, sometime during the night, he'd vanish from his tent. And he'd be gone for three or four days. Then he'd suddenly reappear in his tent, pack up and head back home."

"So he'd go up there and hunt," Stone said. "What was so important about an Indian going hunting in Labrador?"

"It wasn't just him. We were looking at the big picture. Weird radar returns of solid targets we could never intercept. This fellow setting off a radiation detector. Machine-to-machine chatter. And no visible reason for his trips north. Never came back with game or anything. Nothing made sense. We asked: Were the Soviets setting up some sort of base up here and St. Onge was helping them? So we started searching all 3,745 square miles of the Torngat Mountains. We flew up every fiord, down into every canyon and searched every valley and plain. Nothing. Zero. Nada. And no radar activity during our search. So we thought, if there is a base, only St. Onge knows where it is."

Stone stared at the Colonel, unable to mask his doubt. "A hostile base in Labrador?"

"Remember, in '43, during the Second World War, the Germans

sent U-537 to northern Labrador where they set up an automatic weather station code named Kurt. They built it in Martin Bay near Cape Chidley at the northeastern tip of Labrador. It broadcast weather readings every three hours in two-minute bursts. And to hide its true purpose and identity, they labeled it *Canadian Meteor Service* and left all sorts of empty American cigarette packages scattered around the site so everyone would think it was a joint US-Canada station. So, because of the remoteness up here, a covert base isn't as far-fetched as you'd think.

"Anyhow, we were convinced St. Onge had something to do with what was going on. So, one year, we readied a Marine Commando Away Team, training at Goose Bay. We followed him in...white cammo gear, and the lot. We temporarily lost him but then our UAV showed him safely camped on this weird looking mountain top as usual. He went to sleep in his tent. We were watching him 24/7 and there was no way out. No way out of that tent without us seeing him. At that point, the agency decided they could no longer allow him to operate unfettered and in such a strange fashion."

"And...?"

Moorhead looked perplexed.

"Sir...?" Stone prompted.

"After he hadn't come out of the tent for a full day, we used a stealth whirly bird and had our men engage; they landed up there to see what the hell he was doing," Moorhead said.

"What did he say when *American* soldiers barged in?" Stone asked with a slight smile.

"Nothing," Moorhead replied. "He'd vanished."

<h1 style="text-align:center">~4~</h1>

Matthew and Sky had been travelling for approximately four hours over rough ice when she held up her hand. He brought his snowmobile to a stop about 40 feet behind her. They were crossing another bay and had found it was wiser to keep their speed around 20 mph after Matthew ran up on an ice pressure ridge before he saw it. The Renegade had almost overturned, taking him and the sled with it. Whenever they stopped, both walked for a few minutes to reinvigorate their bodies and warm up, trading calories for body heat.

For hours now they had been weaving around islands and more islands with Sky checking her GSP time and again.

She had explained their course as: 'Follow the shoreline where necessary and cut directly across the bays when we can get away with it.' More than once she had signaled a stop, disembarked from her snowmobile and walked ahead carrying a steel pole with a chisel at the end.

She used this to chip at the ice and test its depth before proceeding. At one point she almost lost her pole when it abruptly plummeted through rotten ice. She waved him back, turned them around and retraced their route, hugging the shoreline for more miles.

This day featured heavy overcast with low clouds being bullied about by a steady wind as Matthew dismounted, removed his helmet and tramped towards his companion. Sky had taken off her own helmet and was pulling up her balaclava. The wool was covered with a layer of white ice where she breathed.

He kept walking forward trying not to exert himself any more than necessary. Replacing depleted oxygen in his body meant he would have to take another deep breath. In turn that meant he had to suffer the painful intake of the freezing air that hurt like hell as it knifed its way down his throat and cut into his lungs. He lowered his chin in an attempt to avoid the freezing air by straining, and therefore filtering it, through his collar. It still felt like he was breathing razor blades.

She straddled her snowmobile without saying anything. Looking far off towards the horizon, she sniffed the air. Then she took off her mitts, pulled out a brass compass and stuck her finger in her mouth and held it up. She checked which side of her finger had dried first from the light wind, looked at the compass and then spoke without looking up. "You know, when I was young, grandfather taught me how to anticipate weather. It was based on how quickly a wind would scatter a cloud, or from the strength of gusts, how birds of animals were behaving, or even what we could smell in the air: earth, ice or salt water," she said. "As a hunter, he had to know the weather and if it was safe to hunt. Mostly, he got it right, like the majority of our people. But these days our weather signals don't mean anything. A cloud scattering could signal a storm that comes in an hour or a day; nothing is predictable or dependable. Even walruses, seals and polar bears are confused by strange temperature changes and melting ice. Only two types of people deny climate change: Fools, or those with financial interests that directly conflict with common sense and self-preservation."

Reluctantly she dug out a handheld portable VHF receiver and switched it to Chanel 26 where she picked up a Canadian Coast Guard automated weather broadcast. She pressed the receiver to her ear. Matthew couldn't hear what was being said. Instead he watched her face. The news wasn't good.

"Damn," she said, looking around.

The horizon was no longer visible. Instead, in the distance the ice had become one with the sky, an obscure grey mass obliterating any discernible horizon.

"What's the scoop?" Matthew asked, also lifting his face mask. The water vapor in his breath had turned the bottom third white and frozen. He pulled it over his head and slapped it against his knee to knock the ice loose.

"We have a storm coming," she said, getting off the machine. "We're not even 100 miles out and already we're going to have to batten down."

"It's not here yet," he ventured. "Do you want to keep going?"

She shook her head. "The first rule of survival up here is to respect the weather gods. Let's get out the tent and set it up. Pretty sure we're going to be tested. Wish we were by the shore now where we could use the scrub trees as tie downs."

"Do you know where we are?"

"Yes, GPS puts us north of South Aulatsivik Island, so we've a good start at least."

They pulled out the Arctic Oven 12 tent, deployed the ground sheet, and assembled the frame and urethane-coated oxford nylon body over it. Next they brought in their fold-up cots, sleeping bags, polyethylene food bins and weapons. The tent was pitched with the opening away from the wind.

Next they drove the snowmobiles close by on two sides to form a partial, V-shaped wind break. With tent pegs hammered into the ice and snow piled on the snow flaps around the perimeter of the tent it seemed reasonably secure. For good measure, however, they used the metal rings attached to the six top corners of the tent for additional tie downs; four of them were to their snowmobiles.

By now it was snowing hard. Visibility was diminishing by the second. They checked the sled tarps were well tied down. The wind had gone from an annoying whine to a threatening shriek, sending gusts laden with snow swirling around them. Whiteout conditions.

"If you need to go, go now," Sky shouted to him, entering the tent.

"Go where?" he inquired, at a loss.

"You're original, I'll give you that," she said, almost smiling.

He got her drift, entered the tent, grabbed some toilet paper and quickly exited.

"Hold it," she yelled at him before he'd gone one foot. She ducked her head out of the tent flap and handed him a rope. "Tie it around your body or arm. You've got thirty feet."

She was right he decided as he secured the rope on his wrist. He could barely see five feet. The snow swirled around him; ice pellets stung his face. The screaming wind gamely attempted to push him over backwards as he blindly stumbled forward for 15 feet.

Matthew had heard reports of people in Labrador who froze to death mere yards from safety because they walked out of sight of their shelter and couldn't find their way back.

Sadly, one of their own company engineers had suffered such a fate on a hunting expedition. After a blizzard they found his frozen body huddled in the snow less than 200 yards from his truck.

With the light fading fast, and with much difficulty and shivering, he did his business. Then he washed his hands in the snow and returned. Once inside, he offered Sky the rope which he saw was tied to a food bin. She grabbed it and the toilet paper, and exited. She had already lit a Coleman lantern as well as one of their Coleman catalytic heaters. He removed his parka and warmed his hands over the heater. Sky ducked back in the tent, quickly closing the flap.

"Strong wind," she said, with a grimace, dropping a bucket of well-packed snow.

They used their Coleman stove to melt the snow and bring the water to a boil. Next they tore open their Expedition Foods' bags and prepared to pour their water inside up to a fill line.

"Matthew, take out the oxygen absorber sachet from your food pouch," Sky warned. She pulled a small packet out of her food bag. "See? It removes oxygen from the sealed food packets and extends the life of the contents. Keeps them fresh. But you don't want to eat it."

He smiled, shrugged and complied. He felt so hungry from all the fresh air and the physical exertion, he was sure he could eat the oxygen absorber, the food *and* the bag.

After a supper consisting of Spaghetti Bolognese, and Custard with Apple for dessert, they washed it all down with steaming mugs of instant coffee. It was dark outside so they stripped down to their insulated underwear and prepared to climb into their sleeping bags. Matthew deliberately turned his back to allow Sky to preserve her modesty. He soon learned it didn't appear to be an issue as she deliberately walked around him in her underwear and socks, bent over, and pumped up the lantern to keep it going. Despite his good manners, he found it impossible not to notice her supple figure. Even in socks she seemed to glide about the tent. She rummaged in a rucksack and came up with two black commando-style knives. She handed one to Matthew and put the other beside her cot.

"What's this for?" he asked, hefting the weight of the no-nonsense knife.

'We're in a tent with food, fuel cans, pressurized gas cylinders and lit devices," she said. "We're sleeping towards the rear of the tent away from the door. If we have a fire and can't get out the front, cut your way out the rear. If a bear visits our front door for a snack, exit via the rear. Take your sleeping bag with you if you can. Don't wait for me. I'll probably already be out."

"You think of everything, don't you?" Matthew said.

"Have to out here. If you're okay to rest now we can let the lantern go out." She climbed into her bag arranged on her cot. Then she tucked the satellite phone and a Maglite inside her bag; her Winchester lay beside her on the floor. "The heater will run all night; it can go up to14 hours on a 16-ounce propane cylinder. Keep the tent above freezing. We have ten cylinders on each sled," she explained.

Outside, the wind was accelerating in force and screaming like a coven of angry banshees. The tent flapped madly against its frame. Matthew also climbed into his bag, rolled his pants and shirt up for a pillow and settled down.

"These cots are a great idea," he said, getting comfortable.

"An insulator from the ice," she replied. "At least until we go on foot. Then we'll have to use air mattresses. Though I've never had one that lasted a complete trip without leaking."

"Know what you mean. We used them on our prospecting gigs. I think we spent more time finding the leaks and repairing them, than actually sleeping on them."

She laughed lightly, then burrowed deep in her bag and went silent. For a while they both listened to the wind moaning outside. The only other sounds was the continued slap of the nylon roof and sides against the frame and the hiss of the lantern. Slowly the light from the lantern became dimmer and dimmer. Finally, with a pop, it sputtered out. The darkness inside of the tent was now complete; he couldn't see a thing. He debated saying goodnight to Sky. If she was asleep, however, he might wake her. If he said nothing she might construe it as rudeness. She resolved the issue for him.

"Matthew?"

"Yes, Sky?"

"Goodnight."

"...uh?"

"What?"

"Can I ask one question, first?"

"You can always ask," she replied.

"Why is your grandfather giving me an expensive diamond? And why are you guiding me to where he found it?"

"That's two," she said, but he could hear the smile in her voice. "I guess I can tell you this much: he's just an intermediary."

Matthew sat halfway up in his sleeping bag, not an easy feat. "What do you mean?"

"I mean he's acting for someone else."

"Another exploration company?"

"Of a sort."

"To quote my boss: This is bizarre!"

Sky laughed, uneasily it seemed. "Bizarre? You haven't seen anything yet, my friend. Goodnight, Matthew."

~5~

A significant Arctic storm had formed off Ellesmere Island and then moved south to skirt the coast of Baffin Island and dance across Hudson Strait picking up moisture all the way. The front was continuing south and growing in scope as it followed the coast of Labrador. Meanwhile, another low pressure had formed on the North Shore of the St. Lawrence River and was moving northward like an eager suitor. It finally centered over Nain bringing snow and gale force winds. Still, it would be only a matter of hours before both storms met, merged into one and rained snow-hell down on anything in the vicinity.

In fact, the Arctic low had begun to vent its fury on Saglek Harbour and Runway 35 as the Avenger Drone appeared out of the blizzard, dove for the end of the strip, flared and touched down.

It immediately taxied towards the barely visible ramp where it would be steered into Hangar Three for protection. As it approached the huge building, two massive aluminum doors opened wide enough for its wings. It taxied inside where another two dozen UCAVs and UAVs sat in silent repose as a plethora of industrial heaters maintained an acceptable temperature.

"We've had to bring the Avenger back in, sir," Lieutenant Gary Reynolds, the RPA pilot, explained to Colonel Moorhead in the Ops Radar Center three buildings over from the hangar.

Beside him at the control console was an empty seat usually reserved for a weapons specialist who was also known as a sensor operator. There was no need for one since the Avenger flew unarmed. This way a single crew of two could cover 24 hours in two 12-hour shifts since they had been cross-trained in piloting and weapons deployment.

Reynolds' assignment was strictly an airborne Intelligence, Surveillance and Reconnaissance (ISR) mission. Here he sat at a UAV remote ground control station with his joystick, throttle and mouse in front of him. And, it was all too simply follow two lone figures on the subarctic ice as they made their journey northward.

Military fighter pilots who flew their jets in combat looked at the RPA pilots as playing video games. These games, however, often had deadly consequences. And the lives of thousands of ground forces had been saved thanks to the "eyes in the sky" that could rain down 30 mm Gatling-gun-type rounds on their enemies from above, or fire airborne missiles with devastating accuracy to take out enemy tanks or artillery.

The Colonel had arrived and hunched over Reynold's shoulder to examine his mission displays. Unfortunately they now featured nothing more than a meaningless gobo as the pilot had successfully guided his aircraft to its resting place for the night. Since there was nothing more for Reynold's camera to see, other than the inside of a hangar, he had shut it down.

"Weather is right to the deck, sir. Subjects are presently camped on the ice near Aulatsivik Island. Based on present conditions, they won't be moving anywhere tonight. And maybe not tomorrow."

Moorhead straightened up in the semi-dark room filled with multi-colored electronic readouts, red, yellow, blue and green equipment status lights, radar green screens and numerous computer displays. There were two other airmen present at another station on the far wall, but they weren't involved in UAV pilotage. They were, instead, radar controllers tracking any and all aviation in the area, their radars screens set on maximum range. They paid little attention to their CO. Instead they fixated on watching the returns on their screens. Occasionally they spoke softly into communication headsets. The first controller suddenly sat up straighter in his chair.

"Painting two high-speed targets, heading two niner zero degrees at angels six zero, 800 knots…just accelerated to 2,500 knots! What the hell are they flying? Blackbirds?"

The last sentence came out in an awed tone. They very seldom picked up targets that could accelerate to the degree he was seeing on his scope.

The Blackbird or military designation SR-71, a US spy plane, was the fastest aircraft in the world having attained an official top speed of 2193 mph with a service ceiling of 85,000 feet. Because it was based on 1950s and 1960s technology, however, it was retired in 1989 to free up money for other programs. With no viable replacement, it was reactivated in 1994.

Five years later, relying on improved satellite data for reconnaissance, the Blackbird was finally retired for good.

"Blackbirds gone bye-bye," the second controller reminded his partner, sounding somewhat bored. His own screen only had a dozen trans-oceanic, civilian aircraft showing. "Another 'weather anomaly' I guess," he ventured, winking at his friend. "Record and log it, like ordered."

"On it," the first one responded, clicking some buttons on his console and, at the same time, pulling up his log book. His radar set would automatically record the range, azimuth and speed information digitally, an exact facsimile of the radar signals available for later review.

Across the room, the Lieutenant piloting the drone twisted in his seat and exchanged glances with Colonel Moorhead before looking back at the two radar controllers.

Moorhead didn't bother to cross the room to observe their ops. The sightings were too frequent these days. Anyhow, he didn't feel like fending off questions, legitimate ones, as to what the hell they were seeing. "Heavy traffic, sir. It's been like that all night," Reynolds commented.

There was never a scramble order given for these "special" targets since, usually, they'd be gone within a minute at most. Saglek merely recorded their existence and forwarded the info to Washington.

"Not surprised," Moorhead replied.

"Radio Ops reports UHF chatter increasing in line with the visuals, sir."

"Yes. It would be interesting to know *everything* those suckers were saying," Colonel Moorhead said.

"Who, sir?" Reynolds spoke without thinking and silently cursed himself. There was no way he wanted to get in bad with the old man.

"It's all coming to a head, Lieutenant," Moorhead muttered, ignoring the man's query.

"Yes, sir," Reynolds said, again wishing he knew *what* was coming to a head. Nor would he have minded information in regards to the surprising capabilities of what he deemed to be the newest generation of foreign jets they were tracking. And, he'd also like to know how the two civilians on snowmobiles he was surveilling fit into the whole picture. He sighed. His particular job was to keep his UCAV over top of the two and covertly track their progress. It wasn't to be curious and it wasn't to ask questions.

"Orders stand, Lieutenant. Scramble the Avenger as soon as weather permits and stick with them when they start moving. I want their position relayed to me every four hours. And I want to know if they deviate more than forty degrees off their present course, unless they're following a shoreline in a bay."

"Understand, sir."

"And when they reach Saglek, I hope to God the ice is good enough for them to cross. Unfortunately, I'm guessing they'll be coming into Saglek Fiord to follow the shoreline west. And I want notification when they're five or six hours out as per the protocol posting. Understood?

"Yes, sir."

"Thank you, Lieutenant. As long as they continue north, I'm going to eventually want 24-hour surveillance on the subjects when they get near Cape Territok. Intel showed that the old man usually headed inland there, so we're assuming they'll do the same."

Old man?

"All mapped out, sir."

"Good, carry on."

Moorhead spun on his heel and exited the darkened room. He made his way down a chilly, fluorescent lit painted plywood hallway connecting two more portable units before he found The Palm Tree Club. In the hallways he took note of deficiencies in the tunnels; here and there were cracks in the plywood walls where snow had drifted in.

He could hear the tinkle of glasses, the raucous laughter of the men and women, and the music before he even entered the 30-by-30 foot room.

This would be his second time in it, his first being when it was being built and decorated.

In a direct challenge to their frozen northern location, an Airman 1st Class with an artistic flair had been let loose with gallons of paint and an array of brush sizes. As a result, the walls were covered with palm trees, grasses and tropical fauna. Two neon-outlined palm trees flanked the 25-foot, well-stocked bar, and an array of illuminated pink Flamingoes were scattered about the room. Eight bar stools along with twenty round tables with four chairs each completed the décor. Soothing Hawaiian music was pumped through four speakers set high in the corners. There were dart boards on two walls with the tropical paint job having taken more than a few hits.

The Palm Tree Club was one of two morale boosters on base. The rational had been that the men and women needed to blow off steam and if you didn't give them an outlet, they'd find one. And, that might be one the United States Air Force might not like. The second morale booster was the food in the cafeteria. The remoteness of their location and the boredom when off duty meant food became all important to the personnel on the base. So, at any time of the day or night, the cafeteria was open and staff would cook whatever the service personnel wanted, from lobsters to prime rib or filet mignon. The predictable results were offset by a small gym everyone was required to use for 30 minutes every two days – no exceptions.

Approximately two dozen airmen and airwomen were drinking and laughing in the club until the bartender saw Moorhead standing in the doorway. He immediately came to attention and called out to his clientele. Every single one leaped to his or her feet and stood at attention, some turning over chairs in the process.

"Evening ladies and gentlemen," Moorhead called out. "Just here for a drink like everyone else. As you were." It was a lie but it served his purpose.

The entire club went back to talking and drinking though at a decreased decibel level. More than a few cast surreptitious glances his way. Moorhead went up to the bar and sat on a stool. He glanced around at the assortment of base personnel.

Despite the isolation, they appeared to be relatively happy. The noise and unbridled laughter was reflected on the face of the service men and women in the bar. They worked hard at work, and then worked hard to have a good time when they weren't at work.

"Your pleasure, sir?" A young, dark-haired bartender asked. He wore a loud, Hawaiian-style shirt but Moorhead recognized him as one of the ground crew usually seen attending to their F-35's maintenance. Playing bartender was a volunteer position with regular rotation. Each and every one knew the drill. Their customers were allowed three beers, or two glasses of wine, or four ounces of hard liquor in a twenty-four hour period. There was no charge for the alcohol but each airman or airwoman had to identify themselves and sign for their drinks.

"I'll have a coke," Moorhead said.

The coke came and the colonel tossed his ID card on the bar.

"Not necessary for soda, sir," the bartender said.

Of course Moorhead knew this since he had personally set up the rules but needed to establish a little rapport with the man so he had created a small charade. He retrieved his badge from the bar.

"Thank you. Busy tonight, Airman?"

"Busy every night, sir," the bartender replied.

"Any problems at all?"

"Not sure what you mean, sir."

"I mean: Are there any air force personnel giving you a hard time as to drink limits? Or, causing any other discord? I'm not in here very often but I like to know what's happening on my base."

"Everything is A-OK, sir," the bartender asserted readily. "Any time I've been on duty the men and women have been model personnel."

"Any off-color jokes?"

The bartender stared at him in horror.

"I'm kidding, son. Don't brown your skivvies."

"The bartender let out a sigh of relief. "Sorry sir, you got me alright."

They both laughed. Moorhead stopped laughing and fixed the young man with a stare.

"But this thing I'm not kidding about, and I don't want any Bravo Sierra. Do you hear any buzz? About why we're here? Our mission? Any WAG?"

"No bull shit. And. nary a wild-ass-guess neither, sir."

"So nobody talks about it? Complete radio silence?"

He gave the man a hard look. He wanted the lowdown. His look said: Don't sugarcoat it!

The airman looked troubled for a moment but then fessed up. "I can tell you one thing that has happened, though not all that frequently, sir. Someone will ask what we're doing up here in this frozen hellhole, pardon my language."

"That's okay."

"Sure as shootin', sir, someone else will immediately tell him to clam up. Or remind him that loose lips…get sewed up tight, real quick. That generally ends the conversation."

Moorhead allowed himself a smile. "Very good. You know my

extension, Airman?"

"No sir."

It's not hard to remember, 777. If you start hearing anyone telling anyone else they know why we're here, I want you to note their name and number and give me a call. It will all be confidential and you won't be ratting out your buddies. You'll be helping us maintain the integrity and security of our mission. Understood?"

"Yes, sir."

'Thank you, John," he said to the bartender who was surprised and thrilled that the CO knew his name. He needn't have been. He'd forgotten that it was scrawled on a sign under Bartender on Duty.

~6~

The storm had continued for the better part of the second day and Matthew and Sky felt claustrophobia settling in as they waited it out in the tent. Both had been out to relieve themselves several times and it didn't seem to be getting better. Blowing snow limited visibility to a few feet. Meals helped break the monotony of waiting and Sky had listened to The Canadian Coast Guard automated weather report promised relief by the next day. Two storms had merged and now would likely move offshore to annoy or endanger shipping for a day or two.

The two of them were now preparing supper which amounted to more bags of Expedition Foods. The snow was melted, boiled, poured into the bags and sealed while they waited the required eight minutes. The process was a welcome relief from the boredom of being trapped.

Outside the wind continued to howl and scream and assault their tent.

After Sky mentioned that she'd rather be any place, even Ottawa, rather than camped here on the ice with nothing to do, Matthew thought he had an opening to find out if there was an addendum to Sky's story about her adventure in the nation's capital.

"Speaking of Ottawa," he said. "Did you ever hear from this Duane guy again?"

Sky looked up and fixed him with a level gaze which he couldn't decipher. He felt his heart speed up a bit and hoped he hadn't misjudged her mood and she'd taken offense at his follow-up. The wine had loosened her tongue a few nights ago. Now she was stone cold sober.

"After the party, you mean?" she asked.

"Yes, did he ever call to apologize or explain himself?"

"No, never heard from him again." She paused and then added: "But I did hear from Daddy."

"His father?"

"Yes. Duane knew there was no Duane Junior since he never hit a home run with me. But Daddy didn't. And Daddy didn't believe his 'oh-so-noble son' when he denied it."

"So what did he want?"

"He wanted the baby, of course. He started off by explaining how sorry he was that I had found out Duane was getting married that way. Must have been a shock, blah, blah. And he was severely chastising his son for the way he handled his personal life. He was *chastising him*, mind you. Not sure what that meant but I'm certain it didn't involve a hot poker up his ass."

"But he wanted your baby? Why?"

"Wanted to raise him as a Van Horne. He told me about all the opportunities the boy would have, the best schooling, vacations in Bermuda, a privileged life style, the works. He even hinted he would make it worth my while. After all, money can buy anything, right?"

"What did you say?"

"Remember I was pretty young by normal standards so I wanted to tell him that I sold the non-existent kid to a white slaver for a case of beer. But it had gone far enough. I confessed there was no child."

"And?"

Sky shook her head and swallowed before answering. Matthew could see that the unfairness of it all still impacted her.

"He didn't waste one more breath on me. He just hung up. I was no longer either a problem or a concern of his. The Van Horne's were safe from future infringement on their fortune or their lifestyle by an Innu bastard."

"Nice people," Matthew said.

"The very best money can buy."

They had started to eat when they heard a huge bang; a slow grinding vibration made the ice tremble under their feet.

"What the hell is that?" Matthew asked, notably alarmed.

Sky looked interested but not concerned. She didn't stop eating. "Ice heaving with the wind. Hopefully we're still part of the main ice pack."

"You mean we could be adrift?"

She reconsidered and shook her head. "Doubt it. The mainland is off to port and we have an island on our starboard side so even if we were, we won't be going far. Relax, probably just a pressure ridge forming."

"Do you want to have a look?"

"Not much use, Matthew. We can't see a thing out there. It'll have to be in the morning. According to the Coast Guard broadcast, Environment Canada is calling for this storm to clear up by tomorrow."

They finished eating supper. Then, with nothing to do, they crawled into their sleeping bags early. Matthew checked to make sure his knife was handy, and Sky moved her Winchester carbine slightly under her cot so she wouldn't step on it when she got up in the morning. If it was going to clear up, they wanted to be en route first thing. As usual the Coleman lamp continued to hiss and provide light for a time, and the heater fired away keeping the tent above freezing in a delicate balance to make it livable without melting the ice floor beneath their feet. Sky had mentioned that the ground sheet, rated at exactly -67 below, provided reasonable insulation for both purposes.

In the faint lamplight he looked over at Sky. She lay on her back watching the roof billowing up and then snapping back down on the frame with every errant gust. Shadows from the lantern played across her features. Occasionally a mixture of snow and ice rattled against the tent sides, a reminder that without their habitat and equipment, they would never survive the night. It was a sobering reality of winter in the North.

As he gazed at her, he marveled at her perfect face. She had a fashion model's jawline and her skin was as smooth as a satin sheet. Obviously the tradeoff of an arctic life without the damage of repeated summer sun tans had kept away the majority of wrinkles. She could pass for early twenties rather than early thirties, he thought. Sensing he was looking at her, she slowly turned her head and met his gaze. He felt a tingle deep in his belly and the type of nervousness he hadn't experienced since his first boyhood crush.

For a full minute they stared at each other, saying nothing. It was as if, in the seclusion and safety of the tent, they had been granted a dispensation with regard to the need for the usual social guards people put up to maintain their privacy. This magic also seemed to have granted them clemency to display their inner feelings and fears without airs, without pretensions and without reserve. Lying on their individual cots, their eyes simply explored each other with an intimacy and an openness that had not previously existed between them.

Matthew noticed that the flickering light had made her beautiful eyes grow darker with flecks of gold dancing in the irises; they were warm, enticing and almost inviting. At the same time, however, there was a hint of sadness in them. And her normal display of confidence and bravado was not there. In fact, she looked worried, even vulnerable.

To Sky, deep in Matthew's eyes, she discovered a kindred spirit, a kind person who had been deeply wounded and was desperately trying to find normalcy once again. The nature of his wounds, however, were a mystery to her. She admitted to herself that she actually liked Matthew. But, at the same time, she realized she was afraid. Afraid that she was allowing him to draw closer to her, and afraid she would again become dependent on someone else for her personal happiness. Mostly, however, she was afraid that closeness and their inevitable parting would leave her a mess, feeling foolish and disappointed. Above all, she was determined that would never happen again.

Not wanting to look away, Matthew was about to ask Sky if she was okay when she returned her gaze to the ceiling. The spell was broken, leaving him asking: What the heck just happened? Why was his heart pounding as though he'd spent an hour at the gym? *Something* had happened, his mind insisted. But what?

Not wanting to be rude he averted his gaze from her. He closed his own eyes and his thoughts drifted to Helene. They were now no longer husband and wife. It seemed that with this final step, there was zero chance of anything positive ever happening in their relationship. In a way he was angry with himself for not seeing the inevitability of their parting much earlier. After all, they'd been separated for 18 months. Indeed, he was a creature of hope, a male Pollyanna.

Helene had made it clear almost two years ago, she wanted out. They were toxic for each other, she maintained. Neither would heal after the loss of Chantal unless they moved on individually. And, more importantly, apart. He hadn't felt the same way. He wanted to be there to support and comfort her. Instead, she explained, being in the same room with him caused her pain. She wanted a clean slate. Now she had it. Deep inside herself, she must hate him, he imagined. Not that she didn't have a good reason. And, though Matthew had always been a peacemaker and fixer throughout life, he wasn't able to fix this.

"So what about you, Matthew?" Sky asked, out of the blue.

Startling as her question was, it was also a welcome intrusion interrupting his journey down a much-travelled road towards guilt and self-loathing with an ultimate destination of situational depression.

He looked over at Sky. Her face was turned towards him again and her gaze, as lovely as ever, now had a questioning look.

"About *me*?" he asked.

A blast of wind wildly slammed the urethane-coated nylon tent, simultaneously accompanied by a mournful howl that grew in intensity making him shiver.

"You're the only Matthew in this tent," she answered, with a slight smile. "I shared some of my history with you. There's not much on TV tonight and the weather won't let us step out for a draft or a movie, but we can talk."

"Sure. Why not. Me? Let's see, I started school in Montreal at St. Thomas Moore in Verdun. Later I attended McGill studying Earth Sciences, majoring in Geology."

"So we zipped over about 12 years?"

He laughed and marveled at how a few simple words from this girl made him immediately feel better. "Do you want it day-by-day?"

"Why don't you work backwards?" Sky asked. "I know nothing about you except you're getting divorced."

"Unfortunately, that's a fait accompli. I heard before we left."

"Unfortunately? So it wasn't your idea."

"No, it wasn't. But I accept it. Actually because there was little I could do about it."

"Takes two to tango," Sky said. "As I found out."

"I never asked you this before," he said suddenly, fear of the answer sitting at about 500 percent on the trepidation scale. "Are you married?"

She shook her head.

"Boyfriend?"

"No."

"You're very beautiful," Matthew said, a certain relief in his heart. "You must have had...I mean...*have* lots of contenders?"

She laughed, slightly more relaxed now. "How did this conversation become about me?"

"Oh, I just can't imagine you not being pursued –" He trailed off. "Anyhow, I attended university, travelled for a bit and returned and joined the RCAF. I trained as a transport pilot, made Captain and served in Afghanistan, I did two hitches there. After nine years of service I was honorably discharged, returned to school and got a Masters in Geology. Worked for the government till I found a home at Labrador & Ungava Diamond Explorations. And, here I am."

"Got any medals?"

"A few." As he discovered, he'd had an uncanny ability to predict and dodge ground fire, much appreciated by the air force.

"So you're a hero."

"No. At least no more than anyone else who served over there."

"Maybe I'll call you 'hero'," from now on."

He sighed: "Please don't."

"Tell me about your early life," she asked.

There was something in her tone, something in her voice that actually set the hairs on the back of his neck to attention. He wasn't sure why, but he could feel the request was laden with nuance. Her gaze, however, was blank, offering no additional info.

"Well, my father was a flying officer in the Canadian Armed Forces, Air Defence Command. Maybe that's why I joined up later in life. He was stationed at Goose Bay flying interceptors during the Cold War. Mom, Dad and I all lived on the base; I was born there."

"Really?" she said. "So you're from Labrador too?"

"Yes, though we didn't last long here after my father went missing."

"Oh," she said. "What happened?"

He sighed. Though he had only known his father as a child, he remembered the tall blond man with the huge grin who used to bounce him high in the air. Then he would let Matthew stick out his arms, and carry him around the living room playing airplane. Other memories quickly flitted through his mind including how loved and secure he felt in his father's arms. He remembered one night in particular when his father carried him to a window halfway up their stairs. There he proudly showed Matthew the shadowy 'man in the moon.'

But there was one other memory cemented forever in his psyche. It concerned another night, a much darker night when death came knocking and a light in his life went out forever. In fact, since that time, even as an adult, Matthew could never hear a lone knock on any door without feeling his heart jump.

He had just had his bath and his Mom had combed his hair and dressed him in fresh pajamas when two officers and the parish priest knocked loudly on their door in Goose Bay.

Moments later he heard his mother let out a wail of despair unlike anything he had ever heard before. For probably the first time in his young life, he felt fear. He didn't recognize the feeling but he knew he didn't like it. And, as his mother had to be helped into the living room by one of the officers and the Chaplin, he felt his heart racing and a strange trembling throughout his body.

Matthew was immediately escorted down the hall by the second officer, and carefully and gently tucked into bed. Looking down at Matthew, the man had tears in his eyes that spilled over onto his cheeks. The boy knew that for this tall, strong-looking man to be crying, and for his mother to have made such a dreadful sound, something very bad had happened.

He was right.

He never saw his father again.

"My Dad was flying a CF-101 doing a night intercept on the Labrador coast," Matthew said. "We weren't given exact details but apparently he and his navigator went down during the intercept. Air Search & Rescue was deployed immediately but a terrible storm had moved in and the search had to be suspended. When the weather cleared they tried to find his plane for a full ten days; there was no sign of it, no signals at all. They simply could not find it in the mountains. When Mom pressed for details on what happened, they said his mission was Top Secret. That was it."

"They told you nothing?"

"Nothing solid. They did bring over a medal and said he was a hero. Mom got a death benefit and a small pension. Then they kicked us off the base."

"Yes, Standard Operating Procedure, I understand," she said, distantly. "Did you know any of his friends on the base?

"I was too young but my Mom would have known quite a number. Unfortunately, she died a few years ago, strangely, on the anniversary of his death." He stopped and then continued: "It didn't seem that long after Dad crashed that we got a notification from the base that we had to move. He was presumed dead."

Sky shook her head gently, able to visualize the scene. Disbelief would be followed by confusion and finally a sense of betrayal. She decided to move away from the topic.

"Where did you meet your wife?" she asked.

"At McGill. After I left the air force and returned for my Masters. She was graduating law school the same year I matriculated. We fell in love, married and bought a condo flat in Verdun where I had lived as a boy after we left Goose Bay."

"It must have been good for a time?"

Matthew drew a deep breath giving himself time to consider if he was ready to talk about Helene or Chantal at this time. His feelings were at peak and he didn't wish to sound whiny or wimpy. He decided he'd be safe if he gave himself a moment and then kept the whole story short and sweet.

"I need some water." he said, and kicked his way out of his sleeping bag. He placed his stocking feet on the freezing floor. "You?"

"I'm okay, Matthew." Her voice was low and carefully modulated. She knew she was treading on sensitive and hurtful ground. "You help yourself."

Matthew squatted at one of the insulated food bins containing a number of bottles of water which they would dutifully replenish each day with melted snow. He felt the side of the tent slap him lightly on the butt from a wind gust.

And then, it bumped him, much more firmly.

"Jesus!" he exclaimed, stiffly holding the bottle of water and not moving from where he squatted. It happened again. Something solid bumped him through the side of the tent.

"What is it?" Sky asked, sitting up on one elbow and watching him closely.

"Something hit me in the back."

"The wind."

"Not the wind," he said, careful not to move. He felt the bump again. "Sky, there's something moving out there. Something solid."

She unzipped her bag, rolled off the cot onto her knees and brought up the carbine in one fluid motion. She stared at him hard, assessing if he was mistaken.

"There's something outside," he repeated. "No doubt."

"Get away from there, Matthew," she whispered. "Work your way over by me. Not a sound."

He did as she instructed and they both stared at the tent wall. Abruptly the material near the door moved; then something scratched at its base as though trying to dig its way inside. Sky levered a round into the firing chamber of her .30-30. She said one word: "Bear."

"You're not going to shoot it, are you?" Matthew asked quietly, though unsure of what should be done.

"There's an alternative," she whispered back. "We can let him knock the tent down, rip it apart, eat you for the main course and me for desert, or we can shoot him. Much as I hate it, I vote we shoot him."

Matthew looked around, spotted the .22 rifle propped against the tent corner and reached for it.

"That will just anger him," Sky murmured. "Adult Polar Bears can weigh anywhere from 700 to 2,200 pounds. He'll just use the .22 for a toothpick after he's dined." She stared at the flap of the tent, rifle at the ready. Nothing happened. "I can't shoot blind. And the snowmobiles are near there. Damn!"

It was quiet for another minute. They waited, barely breathing.

"Did he go away?"

"Probably not. I'm going to have to go out there."

"No," Matthew said, emphatically. "Give me the rifle." He reached for it.

"It's a *carbine* but thanks anyhow Matthew. You're a sweet man, but you'll get us both killed. I've done more hunting and shooting than you'll ever do."

Something scratched at the door of the tent again. They looked at each other. He tried to reach for the .22 anyway but Sky shook her head firmly. "I need you to open the flap. I have to see what I'm shooting. If there is nothing there, I'm going to dive through the door and out so I can get a clear shot. If I have to go through the door, I want you to head for back of the tent and get flat. I'll be as careful as I can but a live round could end up anywhere. You understand?"

"I could–!"

"Understand?" She gave him a hard look, steel in her eyes.

He nodded.

"Open it quick and pull it wide. For God's sake don't get anywhere near the opening or you could get shot."

"Okay…1…2…!"

"Open the damn thing!"

He did.

Sky threw the carbine to her shoulder, finger on the trigger, a life and death decision for the target dependent on a miniscule amount of pressure from her fingertip. As the flap opened and Matthew drew back, he saw a wall of fur.

"NO!" Sky screamed, and abruptly put up her weapon.

Atemu staggered into the tent, his eye lids almost frozen shut, his muzzle covered with ice and snow.

He stood there, unmoving, head down, trembling uncontrollably, feet braced wide apart. A gust of wind carrying more snow and ice followed him into the tent.

With much effort, Atemu weakly lifted his head and managed to get his ice-encrusted eyes open. He saw Sky, weakly wagged his tail once and collapsed.

"Atemu, Atemu…what have you done?" Sky cried, as she rapidly emptied the inner brass magazine tube of the Winchester and levered the last round out of the chamber. High powered ammo littered the floor. With the carbine rendered safe, she swept aside the rounds, propped the carbine beside the .22 and dropped to the floor beside the dog.

"Matthew, my sleeping bag, put it on the floor, open it fully," she cried, gesturing towards some open floor space.

He did as requested. She worked to peel the ice off the dog's eyes and muzzle. Then she bent down and listened to his chest. She nodded and stood up. "Help me. We're moving him over to the bag."

Awkwardly they lifted the limp dog over to the sleeping bag. He was trembling violently.

"He's shivering. That's a good sign. Turn your back."

"What?" Matthew asked.

"Turn around!"

He did so and heard a rustle of clothing behind him.

"Now, cover us!" she ordered.

He turned back to see Sky's insulated underwear lying in a heap and her slim, naked, golden body pressed up against the dog, one long limb over his belly, arms pulling him close. Trying not to stare, he grabbed the opposite side of her sleeping bag and dragged it over the two of them. Without further direction he zipped it closed. "I'll light the other heater."

"Thank you," she said, from deep in the bag. She rubbed the dog vigorously up and down under the covers. "Atemu, c'mon boy. Good dog. Crazy dog. C'mon boy."

After lighting the second heater, Matthew dragged his own sleeping bag off his cot and covered them further. Sky looked up gratefully. He moved over and sat on his cot as she continued to massage Atemu. She held the dog close, murmuring soothingly into his ear.

After a few minutes, with her still whispering to the dog and massaging him, Matthew voiced his opinion that Atemu was probably following them to retrieve the ratty ball he'd tucked in the sled. Sky just smiled up at him. "And how did he find us in this storm?" he continued.

"The nose knows," she said simply. "Guess he got away from Joe."

"But we've gone almost 100 miles you said. And, in this storm?"

"Atemu can do things other dogs can't do," she replied. "He came from the Torngat Mountains. A Canadian Ranger found him as a very young puppy running wild along the coast near Cape Territok. We have no idea what happened to his mother. But he has always been super intuitive and intelligent, and we've long suspected he is a Spirit Dog. But a *good* Spirit Dog." She continued to gently rub the dog who had now stopped trembling and seemed to be sleeping.

"What is a 'Spirit Dog'?" Matthew asked.

"It's from the Inuit and Innu culture. The name *Torngait*, from which *Torngat* has come, means Place of the Spirits. But you know that. Our belief is that there is a major spirit named *Torngarsuk* who lives in the mountains. It is believed he controls the life of the sea animals and, in the past, has taken the form of land animals such as a huge polar bear or something equally powerful to accomplish his aims.

"*Torngarsuk* was not always a good spirit, and the Inuit and sometimes the Innu wore raven claws about their necks to protect themselves from his rage. But there is also a belief that there are lessor or minor spirits inhabiting the Torngat Mountains. Some are good and some are bad. They also take the form of animals. The Ranger who found Atemu said that, though he had obviously been born in the wild, he was not afraid of humans. He almost seemed to be waiting to be found. And, even though he was a puppy, when approached, he stood his ground and allowed himself to be picked up. The Ranger took him because the mother was nowhere to be found; he was afraid the little fellow would starve to death. But he didn't need another dog so they turned him over to the RCMP in Nain. Grandfather offered a good home and gave him to me. Time and again, Atemu has shown himself to be much more aware than any normal dog. He is special. He is wise. I have never doubted that he is a Spirit Dog."

Matthew nodded. "He seems to have stopped trembling."

The dog immediately opened his eyes, raised his head, and looked at Matthew. There was a weak tail movement from under the covers. Sky felt it and laughed happily. The dog reached over, gave her face a huge lick and put his head back down on her bare arm; he sighed and closed his eyes once more. He wasn't going anywhere.

Smart dog.

"He's exhausted," Matthew said. After a moment: "Is Atemu an Innu name?

"Yes." She continued rubbing the dog all over once more.

"Does it translate to English?

"Yes, it means…dog."

"Dog? Well, obviously you worked extra hard to come up with that name," he quipped.

Sky smiled again from her sleeping bag on the floor. "It's actually from the Innu-aimun or Montagnais language. In Naskapi, it would have been *Atim*. My father was Montagnais."

"Your mother too?"

"No, actually she was Irish."

"Ah, so you're part Irish?

Sky shook her head. "No, I'm all Innu," she said decisively.

She gently disengaged herself from the dog who was now snoring softly. Unzipping the sleeping bag, she was about to roll out of its cover when she spotted Matthew's raised eyebrows. She stopped dead. He immediately reached over and returned her insulated underwear from her bunk where he had neatly folded it. He stood up and turned his back. Again he heard the rustle of clothing and when he turned back around Sky was dressed. She was standing less than a foot from him.

Her posture was perfect as usual. She stood close and her dark eyes searched his with an honesty and an intensity that was almost scary. Neither of them said a word. Matthew felt as though she was measuring or assessing him. In fact, he felt like a bug under a microscope; it was truly disconcerting. Still, his heart skipped a beat…again.

As they stared at each other, he realized with a start that he felt an overpowering attraction to her, this beautiful native girl. For a brief moment, they were leaning so close to each other he actually thought they were going to kiss. Perhaps, realizing the same thing, she stepped backwards.

"Thank you for your help, Matthew." Her tone was now formal, removed. "I don't think he would have lasted much longer."

Matthew took a deep breath. "I daresay you're right. Pretty special dog to have followed us so far and in such terrible weather. Very special."

"I'm so glad you feel that way. Really I am. So, so glad." She was smiling at him now in a peculiar way.

"Why…so…glad?" he asked, suspiciously.

"Because you and I are going to be sharing our rations with him."

~7~

The General Atomics Avenger circled over the Labrador Sea at 20,000 feet, its turbofan engine with noise reduction capabilities unable to be heard by any person below. Though it could turn on a dime, the UCAV swooped in large, lazy circles conserving fuel as it headed back towards the ice shelf extending from land.

A modern marvel for airborne surveillance, intelligence and reconnaissance, the Avenger had a service ceiling of up to 60,000 feet, and a top speed of 460 knots. It could fly for up to 20-hours without refueling. In effect, it was more than capable of tracking two snowmobiles over the ice shelf of Northern Labrador.

Right now, Lieutenant Reynolds' subjects were barely making 20 mph on the ice below. Hardly a match for his aircraft, hardly a challenge. But orders were orders.

He increased magnification on his sensor/camera and watched them on his display, two dots moving purposely northward. Though the latest high-tech scan cameras could zoom in and read a milk carton from 60,000 feet, this Avenger had arrived with older generation optics that were adequate for the job but not mind boggling. In addition, a heavy snow was falling compromising the quality of surveillance.

Abruptly he noticed something different. He switched to infra-red and raised an eyebrow. Today, he realized, he was looking at *three* heat signatures. There were three people travelling on the snowmobiles below. The third passenger was riding the lead snowmobile's sled. Where the heck did they pick up a passenger, he wondered?

He dialed Colonel Moorhead. "SITREP, sir: They've picked up a third party."

Within five minutes Moorhead was behind his chair. Sure enough, three people now.

"Can we get in any closer?" he asked.

"We have snow falling, sir," Reynolds answered. "Very thick snow and a bit of a wind. Clarity pretty much disintegrates from the moisture as we zoom in; it just gets super blurry."

"So someone rendezvoused with them last night during the storm," Moorhead said. "Sounds crazy, doesn't it? But with GPS, they could find each other even in total darkness *and* a whiteout. Which they obviously did." He watched the scene below for another minute, then thanked Reynolds and made his way to his office. He dialed nine and asked for the base operator. Connected immediately, he gave his code, verified it, and was asked what number he wanted.

"Connect me with the Royal Victoria Hospital in Montreal," he said.

Five minutes later he put down the receiver and sat back in his chair. The old fellow was still unconscious. So who rendezvoused with them? He returned to the radar/tracking room.

"They've stopped, sir," Reynolds said.

He could see the heat signature of three warm bodies separated from their equally hot snowmobiles. Two were together, obviously in discussion. The third wandered aimlessly back and forth and then picked up speed and circled the pair.

"It's a dog," Reynolds and Moorhead said, simultaneously. They looked at each other.

"Alright, who knows where Fido came from but at least we know it's not another person who might complicate things," Moorhead said, relief evident in his tone. Suddenly he was in a much better humor. "Thanks for the report. Mush on, Lieutenant."

With that he left the room and Reynolds went back to flying long, slow, boring, lazy eights over his subjects. Talk about an anti-climactic role in a top secret mission, he thought.

* * *

"We're making excellent time," Sky said, looking first at her GPS and then back down at her map. "Maybe we can make up for yesterday, get our speed up a bit." She stamped cold feet to get the blood flowing.

"I'm game," he answered.

"Just got to be careful not to get lost or we lose any time advantage we've gained. That means a whole lot more checking so we are always taking the shortest route."

The two of them stood in the gently falling snow beside her snowmobile with Atemu bounding about, happy he was now along for the ride. His playful exuberance was a full 180 degrees from the half-frozen, almost lifeless animal that stumbled into the tent the night before. Matthew shivered in the unrelenting cold.

"Didn't you say you'd been there before?" he asked.

"Yes, but the last time was years ago. There are hundreds of islands up this coast. Eventually we'd make our destination but getting lost in these islands can eat up time we don't have."

"You said seven days in and seven out. And you wanted to get there before the Winter Solstice?"

Sky watched him carefully, wondering where he was going. "That's true," she answered.

"Okay, today is the 11th. The Solstice is the 23rd this year. So we'll be more than early."

"I front-end loaded the timing," she said. "If we get there late, this won't work. If we get home late, not a problem."

They both looked over at Atemu who whined softly and wagged his tail. His nose was in the air.

"Okay," Matthew said. He shifted his attention to Atemu: "Does he smell something?"

Sky slowly shook her head, watching the dog. "No, he hears something."

Atemu continued to stare into the sky, frozen in position. His tail had stopped wagging and his ears were forward, cupped, listening intently.

"They're up there," Sky whispered, almost to herself.

"Who's up there?" Matthew asked, completely perplexed and more than a little "weirded out."

"Nobody," Sky said.

"Rin-Tin-Tin over there doesn't seem to think so."

"He probably smells a rabbit."

"You said he was listening, not smelling."

"Leave it alone, Matthew," she said, suddenly more stressed and in a darker mood. "Grandfather said they were watching him all the time. Guess he wasn't paranoid."

She swung about and stomped over to her snowmobile. "Atemu! Here!" She patted the nest she'd made for him amongst the gear on her sled.

The dog bounded over, jumped aboard, did a few quick circles and settled down on his bed between the folded tent and some tarp-covered gear. He looked directly at her and whined softly.

"I know, but we'll be okay," she said, throwing her leg over her snowmobile and starting it. She checked that the dog was secure, and made sure Matthew was ready. "Head down, Atemu."

Hearing the interaction between Sky and the dog, Matthew couldn't help thinking: Good God, she's not talking to the dog now!

Sky took off in a burst of snow that quickly created a fantail behind her, chunks ricocheting off her sled. Atemu ducked his head to avoid the worst of it. As instructed Matthew stayed forty feet behind and some feet off to the side. She was travelling at more than 50 mph now and he wondered what happened to 'slow and careful.' After a minute or two more, her sled slowed to 40 and then 30 and they eventually settled back at 25 mph.

They travelled for another four hours, at times heading west towards shore as they viewed the open sea getting closer off to their right, or circling into bays and around them. They would then continue to travel north on the shore ice parallel to the sea. The constant side trips to avoid open water were taking a substantial bite out of their 'as the crow flies' progress.

That night they made camp on the shore and used a few, very stunted and forlorn looking spruce trees, refugees from the dwindling boreal forest no doubt, as tie-offs for their tent. Matthew gathered some spruce branches and soon had a nice fire going a few feet away. They boiled snow in a pot directly over the fire and saved fuel.

For supper Atemu got his own pack of Expedition Foods. He seemed to particularly like the Beef Stroganoff with Noodles. They mixed it with boiling water into its stew-like consistency but fed Atemu off a plastic plate. They ate directly out of their Expedition bags.

Matthew motioned towards Atemu. "We eat out of bags and he gets the china."

Sky nodded, hardly paying attention.

After the dog wolfed down his ration, and he'd finished licking every last scrap off his plate, he shifted his attention to those still eating. He wagged his tail, giving them the *look*.

"No Atemu, you had enough calories for 180-pound person, so forget it," Sky said. Then, to Matthew: "Doing what we're doing out here in these temperatures we're burning up about 3,500 calories per day. But we have to balance what we need with what we have with us. So there'll be no second helpings on this trip."

They returned to the tent as the fire had sunk two feet down into the snow; little warmth radiated outward from it. Sky had largely been uncommunicative for most of the day, helping pitch the tent and moving their supplies inside while communicating via monosyllables. She was clearly worried about something. Matthew had learned by now not to question her; she'd tell him in her own good time.

Later, they lay in their sleeping bags on their cots waiting for the lamp to sputter out. Atemu formed a fur circle by her bed. So far she had still not opened up. He decided to try a short overture preceded with some humor. "This is like being married."

She bit and half turned towards him, an almost dreamy look on her face. "How so, Matthew?"

"We lie here in silence while I try to guess what the hell I did wrong."

"It's not you."

"I'm the only Matthew in this tent," he said.

The shadows from the sputtering lamp now emphasized the natural dolphin-like smile that, during most of the day, had seemed as distant as the Milky Way. Her face should never frown, he thought. In a way he wished he could ensure she never had to frown.

Don't try to get close to me. That would be a big mistake.

He tried again.

"If not me, who? Somebody pissed you off and El Canine over there still seems to be in your good graces."

She sighed. "Matthew, there are forces at work here that neither you nor I completely understand right now."

"You mean like…*supernatural?*"

Despite herself, Sky couldn't help but laugh out loud this time. It was the trepidation in his voice when he said it. She answered with a smile: "Don't worry, Matthew," she said. "No Uga-Bugga."

The relief was evident in his tone. "If you tell me what's going on, maybe I can help."

"I told you my grandfather always felt like he was being watched on his journeys northward for many, many years."

"Yes, but watched by who?"

"We don't know. Government, maybe. Other prospecting companies. Jessie Ventura."

The last name was obviously spoken in jest. Ventura was a former Navy Seal, Professional Wrestler, and Governor of Minnesota who became best known for his *Conspiracy Theory* TV show that saw Illuminati-style plotters under every rock.

"So you think the same thing? We're being followed by mining competitors?"

"By somebody."

"Somebody who wants to know where the diamond came from?"

"Perhaps. But more likely they are really interested in where we are going and why. Still grandfather worked hard never to compromise his final destination. Sometimes he had help. More often he had to use his own wits to outsmart them."

"Again, who is 'them'?"

"I'd rather not say."

"Why not?"

"Because you'd turn around and go back."

"Not true, Sky. I don't break promises. Not where the choice is mine."

She rolled on to her side in her sleeping bag and faced him full on. "I believe you, Matthew. I'll tell you when I can. Right now I'm worried I won't get you there in time?"

"Okay, my CEO has till the end of the year to prove there are diamonds up here. But if we don't make it, we don't make it. I'd like to help him but we can only do our best. Right?"

"Well, I can promise you there are diamonds at the end of this journey alright, but I don't know if it's what your boss needs. Besides, there are other considerations."

"What sort of considerations?" No doubt his patience was being tested.

She sighed. "My grandfather is paying off a major obligation."

"This is weird, Sky. There is no obligation. I don't even know him."

"The obligation isn't to you. I've said too much. Please, trust me for another week."

"I already trust you," Matthew replied. "Or, I wouldn't be out here, would I?"

He paused and tried to get a handle on why things had suddenly taken such a turn. She had said someone was watching them that afternoon. And she was looking toward the sky. Did she think there were spirits up there or something? What had he gotten himself into by agreeing to embark on this search? He sighed and finally asked her: "Look, are you okay?"

"I don't know," she answered honestly. "After today, I wonder if they trust me." Her eyes were fixed on him now, searching his, measuring him, a mixture of hope and trepidation in them. "Anyhow, please don't quit on me," she added softly. "I can't disappoint my grandfather."

"I'm not going to quit, Sky. Besides, I have far more to lose than you do."

"Maybe, maybe not," she answered. "I guess the difference is, you know what you stand to lose if we don't get there in time. And, quite frankly, I don't."

Matthew didn't comment further. Instead he closed his eyes. It wasn't long before he was visualizing a happy little girl who used to throw her arms around his neck and thought he would protect her from anything harmful in the world. Something that, ultimately, he had failed to do. If he could have one wish this evening, it would be to ask her to forgive him for failing.

~8~

Andre Jacquard wished he'd heard more from Matthew Corrigan other than a message saying they were off. Though he had Mary try to contact him on the satellite phone number he'd left, she'd been unable to get through so far. The net of it was he needed to hear immediately from Corrigan once he found the diamond site. Indicator minerals would be acceptable for now but if Matthew was able to pick up a diamond off the ground like St. Onge, and he gave Jacquard the GPS coordinates, either he or Matthew would be able to stake a claim electronically and tie up some acreage. Then he'd have investors lined up out the door. So the sooner he knew where he stood, the sooner he'd be able to sleep. Not that he didn't sleep now. A third of a bottle of his favorite whiskey generally did the trick.

Right now he need the added assurance that his man was okay. He had personally banged around Labrador in his early days as a geologist and he knew you didn't take the land for granted. It was inherently hostile, desolate and dangerous. This was mostly because of its remoteness, unpredictable weather, and ample hungry animals such as polar bear, black bears, wolves, and wolverines.

In fact, something as simple as a fall resulting in a bone break, immediately treatable in urban centers, might wait days for treatment in the hinterland of Labrador. Survivable wounds, such as a cut with an axe or knife, could turn septic or gangrenous and also kill you before you got out.

Though Corrigan had been on exploration for Labrador & Ungava Diamonds before, and had slept in his fair share of tents, this was different. This journey seemed to have no backup plan. They were attempting to remain covert and cover their tracks every way they could.

For instance, Corrigan said they wouldn't be registering any complete travel plans with the Mounties or the National Park Service. They'd be totally on their own. And since the Satellite phone obviously wasn't working now, there was no guarantee it would work in the event of an emergency.

One more variable was that Corrigan was being guided by St. Onge's granddaughter. Only God knew if she was competent enough to get Matthew back safely with the information Jacquard so desperately needed.

He sat in his office, nervously puffing on his pipe and looking at the rough gem on his desk blotter that had come back from analysis. "It came from somewhere the hell up there," he muttered to himself, trying to bolster personal confidence in the outcome.

Not that he was putting all his eggs in one basket. He had been soliciting new investors on a daily basis, giving them all the same story: It was merely a matter of time before they found diamonds in Labrador. The area had all the right geology for a major diamond find. And whoever brought in a mine would become rich beyond their wildest dreams.

In fact he had told the same story so many times, he could do it by rote now. Sometimes, just before he went to sleep at night, he found himself rehearsing the same old spiel in his mind and adding or adjusting points to make the pitch more attractive.

Initially the most promising area had been around Makkovic, Labrador, showing the largest concentration of kimberlitic pipes. He'd spent a small fortune scratching around there but the results had been disappointing. Which proved the maxim that not all pipes contain diamonds, and even fewer contain enough diamonds to make mining economically viable. So he moved his crew up to George River where the presence of tracer minerals and minor diamonds had already been proven in Ungava.

For instance, more than a decade ago, Toronto-based *Lode Diamonds* had been lucky enough to find diamonds in samples from a dyke in the Torngat Mountains east of Ungava Bay. They had acquired a 250-sq. kilometer package of land; this portion of the Torngats rested in northeastern Quebec. Their diamonds had been microdiamonds, less than half a millimeter in size in their first samplings of 200 kilograms. Those results followed the recovery of 30 diamonds, 21 of which could barely be classed as macros. They came from a grab sample gathered from kimberlite rubble at the base of two parallel dykes. But even that didn't bring success.

Now, so many years later, the only diamond mine in Ungava was the *Renard Diamond Project* in the James Bay Region of north-central Quebec. Despite initial promising results so long ago, *Lode Diamonds* still hadn't achieved the results needed to start mining.

Jacquard had hoped to open the first diamond mine in Labrador and then the first diamond mine in the Ungava Region. Neither had come to fruition yet. And, while the search might go on, and the money hemorrhaged out, the process and his window of opportunity were both finite. And now his investors had delivered a final ultimatum: no more cash until he brought home the bacon. There was one more payment due at the end of the month but that would not let them operate past the first quarter of next year.

Fortunately, what was sitting on his desk was one hell of a lot more than diamond dust. Investors would salivate once they saw its amazing size. Wherever this old man had picked it up, there had to be more. And so his company's fate now rested in the hands of St. Onge's daughter who was taking Corrigan to where he had found the diamond. Not that it was a secret; a sweep of his office confirmed three bugs present. When the security company presented them, he'd personally taken a hammer and pretended they were nails. Who planted them was still a mystery.

Tired of sitting pensively behind his desk, he had Mary find the number for the Royal Canadian Mounted Police in Nain. He had dialed it himself, 709-922-2863, and wound up with an answering machine that slowly spelled out his options in English and Innu-Aimun. He didn't leave a message. To set his mind at rest he simply wanted to ask them if they knew this Sky St. Onge, and if she was a competent guide.

Now he noticed Mary had dumped some mail on his desk including a gemologist's Diamond Grading Report for the St. Onge diamond.

He picked it up and read where it listed color, clarity, and a rough estimation that, barring surprises, it would probably cut to eight carats or more. There was a proportions drawing and a clarity characteristics drawing. Both had the word "Estimate" scrawled in pencil at the bottom. This wasn't unusual as he'd asked the evaluator to guess at what it could look like once cut, ground, polished and boiled in an acid bath. It was pretty much pie in the sky until they began cutting.

He also noted another scrawl on the form reading: "Origin –???" It was underlined twice. He dialed *Electric Blue Diamonds* and got the gemologist who had done the evaluation. He thanked him for the report.

"One thing I was curious about," Jacquard said. You wrote 'origin' and then a bunch of question marks on the report. What was that about?"

"Well sir," the man said, hesitantly. "I marked that down because the rock that half surrounds it isn't igneous rock. It isn't lava from a volcanic action.

"All right, what is it?" Jacquard asked.

"Let me explain a few things first," the evaluator said, hurriedly. "Diamonds are formed in four ways: in the mantle of the earth and carried to the surface in volcanic eruptions; in rocks that have been subducted deep into the mantle by plate tectonic processes; at impact sites where asteroids have hit the earth; and, in meteorites where they have been shocked and heated enough to create bonds between the layers."

"I'm a geologist," Jacquard finally said, impatiently.

"Okay, sorry, sir. Anyhow, the shell around your diamond is composed of a metallic and rocky material, common with what is known as a stony-iron meteorite."

"Go on," Jacquard said.

"I was curious about your specimen so I tried polishing it slightly with a diamond paste. No go. Then I tried a few other options and still got nowhere. Obviously it's harder than a normal diamond.

"Next I took it to the lab and brought in some pretty sophisticated mineralogical analyzing instruments to see how its atoms lined up. There were anomalies like I've never seen before. Still, I was able to confirm a polymorph of crystalline carbon. In effect, a diamond that is very rare in nature. But the condition of its shell, the material surrounding the gem, tells us the shell wasn't formed as a result of an asteroid or meteorite subjected to the extreme temperatures of re-entry and the pressures of impact. The shell was already formed when it arrived on earth."

"Fine with me," Jacquard said. "What's the problem?"

"No problem, sir. It's just that when you add everything up, this is obviously a diamond from a meteor. But it never impacted with the earth."

"It would have to impact the earth if it came down in a meteorite," Jacquard said.

"You would think," the gemologist said, thoughtfully. "But again, while my instruments confirmed this is a super hard diamond, the overall condition of its stony-iron shell shows no evidence of an entry into earth's atmosphere and resultant impact. It came from outer space alright, but it didn't arrive in a meteorite. It came to earth by some other means."

~9~

The sky had finally cleared and was a brilliant blue as Matthew and Sky roared across relatively flat ice at 30 mph. Ahead of him he could see Atemu was asleep in his nest deep among the equipment on Sky's sled; no tell-tale ears poked up. She had lined his bed with a woolen blanket. Sheltered from the wind, he would be enjoying the warmth of the sun on his fur. Fortunately the brilliance of the sunlight on the snow was countered by the shaded goggles they both wore. He wondered how long she planned to keep going since he really needed to stop.

Sky twisted in her seat and looked back at him and he held up his hand, palm first. She immediately throttled back. He made certain he stopped a good 15 yards behind her for safety's sake and walked forward. The dog's head popped up immediately. He uncurled himself and jumped down.

Pee break.

"Everything okay?" Sky asked, still poised on her snowmobile but, more or less, 'standing in her stirrups'."

She was a completely different person today. She must have reconciled her worries, he thought. Perhaps she'd been afraid he was going to demand to be taken back to Nain because this this was all too weird. Having reassured her he wouldn't quit may have removed one of the demons that seemed to haunt her. Whatever, she was more talkative and relaxed.

"I'm fine," Matthew answered. "Just need to take a bathroom break." He had some Kleenex tucked in his pocket.

She grinned at him. "Soon as you find one, let me know," she said.

Matthew nodded and walked off about ten yards. He looked back at her watching him. He continued on for another ten yards. Atemu was running circles around him, kicking up snow and reveling in the blue sky day. He stopped, looked back and she was still looking at him. He walked on another fifteen yards, now totally embarrassed. The ice was flat as a pancake, no place to hide. He looked back and saw she had sat down on her snowmobile seat but still seemed to be keeping an eye on him. He certainly didn't want to squat down in front of her so he walked another 300 yards. She was now almost a dot on the snow so he felt it was safe to get his business done. Atemu followed his lead.

When he returned she was watching him tramp up. "Wondered how far you were going to go," she called. "I thought I might have to give you a ride back." Though she didn't say, her reason for watching him was to keep him safe in an area where the ice wasn't necessarily secure.

He knew his face was red. "Well some of us are polite enough to turn our backs."

She smiled. "I truly wondered if you'd stop before you hit yonder mountains." She gestured towards a range of mountains at least fifty miles away.

He looked up to see a small plane, very high up, slowly flying past them heading north. As he tracked it, silver wings winking in the sunlight, he was surprised to see it make a 180 degree turn and head south again.

Still chuckling, Sky stood up, walked ten yards away, squatted, peed and was back in less than two minutes. She looked him in the eye and apologized. "Sorry, you're a nice gentleman and I won't do that again. However, sometimes we have to forego modesty up here for safety reasons where the ice isn't one hundred percent safe." She tilted her head, her eyes sparkling and gave him a nice smile. It made everything all right.

Suddenly the smile vanished from her face. She stepped back to her snowmobile, stood up on the seat, shaded her eyes and stared off into the distance behind them. Matthew turned and followed her gaze.

"What is it?" he asked.

Wordless she hopped down, dug in the sled till she found a long pair of binoculars in a rucksack and pulled them out. She removed the lens protector caps and stood back up on the snowmobile seat.

"What do you see," he asked again, as she stared through the lens.

"Somebody is following us," she said, tersely. "Look."

She handed him the binoculars and he carefully stood on her seat. He noticed they were Sunagor zoom-type, 30-to-160 X 70. With great difficulty he steadied the binoculars.

He could now make out two black dots on the ice. He adjusted the glasses and two people came into view. They wore ski goggles and were sitting on snowmobiles looking back at him. Abruptly they got off their machines and moved off looking back. For a moment he wondered if they were the two men who attacked them outside the restaurant.

He looked again. Both figures seemed to be the normal size when compared to their snowmobiles, even if though one was shorter.

Sky was digging around in another bag and pulled out a collapsible tripod. "No, there is only one way to give them the message," she said, changing her mind and burying the tripod back amongst the gear. She unclipped her sled and ordered Atemu onto the disconnected sled.

The dog sensed she was disturbed and his tail was low. Obediently he jumped up and sat down on his bed. She grabbed him on either side of his muzzle, bent down and looked into his eyes. "Atemu, stay! Stay!" He lay down.

Sky checked her .30-30 was still in its scabbard and started her machine. "Please get on, Matthew."

He did and they roared off back towards the two dots on the ice. Free of the sled they were doing at least 40 mph and it wasn't long before they arrived at the two snowmobile. One had a towing sled piled high with gear. Two parka-clad figures with telescoping hoods half closed watched them warily.

Sky stopped the machine, pulled out her Winchester, dismounted and walked towards them, Matthew trailing. Pushing back her hood, Sky called out: "Good afternoon." She rested the butt of the Winchester on her hip. "What brings you good people out here?"

A bushy-bearded face regarded them dourly from a ring of fur around his parka hood. He was about forty, thick-bodied and had a well-weathered face.

The man in the store with Bob Crummy!

"What brings us out here, is the fact it's a free country," the man said, smartly.

The second person, also sporting a similar parka and hood paused and then looked up. Bushy Beard's companion slowly turned to face them fully. Matthew watched as the hood was slowly peeled back. He saw cool green eyes, a head of blond hair partly under a wool toque, and a flawless complexion. The girl stared wistfully at him.

"Monique!" Matthew said, in shock. "What's going on?"

"Hello Matthew," Monique replied.

Sky spun towards him. "You know her?"

"Well, sort of...know her. Monique tried to hire me away from Labrador & Ungava Diamonds."

"Yes, Matthew and I are not-so-old friends," she said, perfect white teeth showing in a gleaming smile.

"Did you know they were following us?" Sky asked, angrily.

"Of course not," Matthew answered.

"This is my associate Peter Meyer and I'm Monique Boivin," Monique said, gesturing towards the bearded man. "We represent Fortune Diamonds International."

Matthew was impressed. He knew about the company. Fortune Diamonds was a major player in diamond mining. In fact, it was probably the fourth largest diamond company in the world with assets in the billions of dollars and operations in at least ten countries. But not only did Fortune conduct explorations and mine diamonds, it also did its own cutting, polishing, packaging and retailing under several dozen brand names around the world. Now Matthew and Sky faced two of its employees who were obviously bent on following them to the first diamond site in Labrador.

They stared at each other. No one shook hands. No one spoke. Finally, Matthew tried to get things moving.

"Well this is awkward," he said.

"Not to me," Sky answered softly. Then to Boivin and Meyer: "I know what you're doing so you're going to stop doing it right now. You'll get your sweet little asses on your machines and head back to wherever you came from."

"Really?" Meyer said, unbuttoning his parka and sweeping it open to expose a holstered pistol. "Or what? You're going to shoot us?"

"I won't have to," Sky said. "Because you're going back."

"Look, Little Feather, we'll go where the hell we want," Meyer said, sticking a finger over his head and wiggling it suggestively, a clear insult to Sky's heritage.

"Peter!" Monique protested.

Matthew felt anger well up in his chest and he started towards the man. He was stopped as Sky got in his way and shoved him backwards. She turned, stuck the .30-30 butt first in the snow and closed the gap between herself and Meyer. She stopped three feet in front of him.

"What did you call me?"

"Sky, I'll take care of him," Matthew said.

"Just a joke," Meyer said, grinning openly. "I apologize, okay?"

"Not okay," Sky said, staring at him. Her legs were wide apart, feet pointed straight forward, a martial arts fighting stance.

Matthew moved forward and roughly inserted himself in front of Sky, facing Meyer. She tried to go around him and he blocked her stepping left and then stepping right.

"Mr. Meyer, an apology with a grin on your face is really no apology at all," he said forcefully. "So wipe it off and apologize or I'll let her at you." He now had both hands behind his back holding onto Sky's parka for dear life as she struggled to circumvent his position. Bulky arctic clothing and semi-deep snow wasn't making it easy for either of them.

Meyer backed up two feet to get some room and said: "Me heap big afraid now!"

Mathew let go of Sky, stepped forward, placed his right leg behind Meyer's right leg, stuck his mitt in the man's face and shoved him backwards, hard. He tripped and sat down.

As Sky went for him. Matthew spun, grabbed her and the momentum took them in a wild circle with Monica screaming off to the side: "Stop it...stop it! Are you all crazy? We're business people."

Matthew was holding on to Sky who was almost purple with fury.

"Sky, he's not worth it. Stop! Get hold of yourself." Finally she quieted down, glaring at the man who had the good sense to stay sitting in the snow.

Monique was truly angry. "Peter, this is unacceptable. I'd fire you right now–!"

"I don't report to you," Meyer said from his sitting position, also angry.

He started to get up and Matthew shook his head. "You stay there bud or I'll put you down again. Only this time, I won't be so gentle! And there's no doctor out here." Even as he said it, he realized he was wrong. Beside him stood a doctor, not that she was likely to treat Meyer with anything but contempt at the moment.

"Peter, don't!" Monique cried as her companion started to get up again. "Stay where you are, dammit!"

Meyer glared at her but stayed down. "You think you could do it, Ace?" he called out to Matthew in an effort to save a little face. "You think you could take me?"

Ignoring him, Matthew said: "Better keep him in line, Monique; he'll get you in trouble."

He grabbed the carbine and Sky's arm and quickly walked her back to their snowmobile before things escalated once again. He had the feeling that if Sky hadn't allowed common sense to prevail, Meyer would not be in the greatest of shape right at the moment.

They reached the snowmobile. Matthew glanced back to see Peter Meyer still sitting in the snow.

Angrily Sky pushed the carbine in its scabbard. She got on the snowmobile and started it up. She looked over her shoulder and called: "Don't follow us. This is your last warning." She barely gave Matthew time to get aboard before twisting the throttle. They took off with a jerk.

Their journey back was conducted in silence. He held onto her since they were doing 40 mph again. A couple of times they hit small drifts and lifted completely into the air. Finally she slowed down, probably realizing she might damage something on the snowmobile.

He was guessing she was furious with him for interfering in her dispute with Meyer but he soon realized he was wrong. As they approached within sight of his snowmobile, she slowly leaned back and rested the back of her head on his shoulder. Her cheek brushed his cheek and she didn't recoil. She let her head rest there for about five seconds. They were getting close to his snowmobile now so she sat up straight and steered towards it. Farther ahead, on her sled, Atemu was sitting up straight, ears forward. He watched them closely as they stopped.

Matthew disembarked. Sky didn't look at him. She sat still, staring straight ahead.

"I'm sorry that happened, Sky. There'll always be assholes," he said, standing beside her.

"Not your fault, Matthew."

"Maybe I should have whacked him."

"We don't need an assault charge when we get back."

"Technically, I did assault him."

"Not how I saw it. You two were playing and suddenly Meyer was making snow angels."

Matthew smiled, nodded and turned. He stood on his toes and looked back. The two sleds in the distance hadn't moved. "They're still there."

"Let's hope they stay there when we start off," Sky said. "I mean, for their own sake."

* * *

Mr. Black wasn't happy. And when Mr. Black wasn't happy, no-one else in his immediate vicinity, or even within hearing distance, was happy. And, if they were happy, they usually kept it to themselves.

Black sat with a telephone receiver to his ear behind his desk in his office on Wellington Street in Verdun, a borough on the south shore of the Island of Montreal. Before him, heads hanging down, stood two sweating men garbed in suits and heavy black overcoats. Whether they were sweating because they were overdressed, or because of how their meeting was going was anyone's guess. The taller man, Agent Franklin Benjamin pulled a small piece of heavily stressed Kleenex out of his coat pocket and attempted to mop his forehead. It was like using a Wipe Knap to clean up after the *Exxon Valdez*.

"May I take off my coat, sir?" he asked.

"No," Black answered shortly. "This isn't a social call. You aren't staying."

The shorter man, Agent Levin Farnsworth, his arm in a sling, was also sweating as profusely but he just used his sleeve to try to sop up the bodily fluids leaking all over his face.

"So you are two of the CIA's finest, are you?" Black asked, still waiting on the phone.

The men looked at each other. Benjamin spoke: "Actually sir, we work for Black Ops Industrial Incorporated. We're a defense contractor supplying services to the CIA, NSA and other defense agencies."

"Great!" Black muttered, suddenly hearing a voice on the other end of the line. "Hello Alex? Stephen Black. I have two of your men here, Benjamin and Farnsworth. What the hell gives?"

Benjamin and Farnsworth exchanged worried looks as Black continued his conversation.

"Sure I asked for info on St. Onge and Corrigan. But have you read their damn report?"

He listened for a minute and sat up straight in his chair. "So they got some intel, but Jesus Christ, Alex! Did you read how they did it? They openly visited his wife for starters."

"Posing as insurance agents, sir," Farnsworth interrupted. He received a glare from Black and hastily shut his mouth.

"Then they tried to kidnap the daughter in broad daylight. They were going to use Rohynpol to extract info on where she and Corrigan were headed. We know where they're headed. We want them to go!"

"It was night, Mr. Black," Benjamin explained.

"Ask me if I give a crap," Black yelled at them.

He then slammed the phone down on his desk twice for emphasis. "You two idiots will shut up or I'll push this phone up your ass and pull it out of your mouth! Clear?"

They nodded and he went back to the phone. "They're running around a foreign country using fucking mafia tactics to get information. Is anyone in charge of them? They're off the fucking reservation conducting field ops any way it suits them. No, the end doesn't justify the means. What if these retards got pulled in by the Montreal cops? What then?! Screw up the entire operation when the fucking Canadians tell us to get out of here, and get the fuck out of Saglek!"

He listened for a minute. "Okay, that's very nice but I want these guys pulled from here. Get them back home."

Benjamin couldn't take it any longer. It didn't look like they were going to continue working in Canada anyhow. He took off his coat, turned it round, stuck his face in the lining and used it like a giant towel, desperately drying his forehead and face. Farnsworth unsuccessfully hid a smile. Black glared but was too busy listening to get involved.

"What about Jerome St. Onge? Any news on his condition?" He listened for a moment and then said: "Okay, at least we know where he is for the foreseeable future."

Black motioned for Franklin and Farnsworth to get out of his office. They departed and stood in front of his secretary's desk outside his office door. Black lowered his voice.

"Yes, I talked to Colonel Moorhead. Our analysts looked at their flights, the frequency and duration, and concluded these are not reconnaissance or retrieval flights any more. They're finishing up whatever the hell they're doing here. The code chatter also fits the scenario of a wind-up of their operation. And the cryptologist came up with some numbers they think is a date. December 23rd. So we're planning ops for that date. By then we'll know where the base is located. Obviously the girl is a surrogate for the father so we'll let them bring us to it and then move in." He listened for a moment. "Yeah, okay. And get the limo driver out of here too. Send them to Alaska for all I care until this is over. Have them chop wood or something. Good-bye Alex."

He slammed the phone down and motioned to the two men talking to his secretary. They re-entered tentatively and stood in front of the desk again.

"You two will report back to your Director of Operations. You're done here."

Farnsworth tried to mitigate the damage. "Sir, we got the intel needed –!"

Black stopped him with a wave of his hand. "Have a nice flight home, gentlemen. Or wherever the hell you wind up."

* * *

They had been travelling for two hours now on the subarctic ice shelf with hills on their left and the Labrador Sea to their right. Sometimes it loomed mere yards away and sometimes a half mile or more. They circled a few bays until Sky signaled a stop. She checked her GPS and a map she had folded in a see-through pouch secured with Velcro in the left boot well of her machine. She waved at Matthew and pointed towards a native inuksuk in the distance standing on a barren, rocky, wind-swept hill bordering the ice. The rough figure, constructed of piled stones approximated a human form with arms spread wide. Having confirmed her first landmark, she happily stuck the map and her GPS back into their waterproof sleeves.

Matthew watched her as he approached. He hoped against hope she wouldn't take out the binoculars. She did. "They're still coming. Yeah…now they stopped again."

For the last two hours they had been trailed by Boivin and Meyer at a good distance. If they turned their snowmobiles to go back towards them, their quarry immediately reversed course and sped away. Likely Monique's doing, Matthew reasoned. While she seemed intent on following them to the site where the diamond had been found, she obviously didn't want any sort of confrontation. Hence the passive-aggressive approach to following them.

It became a game of cat and mouse and Matthew could tell Sky was becoming increasingly irritated. At one point she had pulled up beside him and said: "This is costing us too much time. If they don't give up this chase, they're going to wish they had."

Now they were stopped again and Sky had her field glasses focused on them. Suddenly she stood a little straighter and muttered: "Uh oh!" Quickly she handed Matthew the binoculars."

He took them from her and focused on the snowmobiles trailing them. He zoomed in fully to get a better look. The images danced up and down; he couldn't see much.

"You need a tripod if you're using full zoom," Sky said, quickly rummaging about in her sled. Atemu jumped off as she yanked out a long canvas sack. Matthew thought it was the tripod. He was dismayed when he saw her hurriedly extract the other hunting rifle from the case. It had a formidable looking telescopic sight on it.

"What are you doing?" he asked. "We can't stop them trailing us, Sky. It's a free country, like the man said."

She ignored him, pulled out a handful of brass, high-powered cartridges, loaded the detachable box magazine, and snapped it back in the rifle with a solid click. It took her less than five seconds.

"What the hell is that?" Matthew said forcefully, though he'd have to be blind not to recognize an extremely sophisticated weapon.

"This is a .308 Ruger with a Leupold 4-12 X 50 scope. I brought it in case I had to address a problem at range." She worked the bolt action.

"Why are you loading it?" Matthew demanded.

"Why do you think?" she said simply, curling the carrying strap around her left forearm and steadying her aim using the sled as an armrest. She quickly calculated the approximate range, wind speed, and likely bullet drop based on the estimated distance to her target. Reaching up, she carefully clicked the scopes settings on top and on the side to compensate for the variables. She had to shoot fast; she prayed she would be accurate.

"What's that supposed to mean?" Matthew asked. "What the hell are you doing?"

"Quiet! Use the binoculars, Matthew," she said. "Take the zoom down. Tell me what you see. I'll have a look through my scope."

He put the binoculars back to his eyes once more and zoomed out to where he could maintain the figures of Meyer and Boivin in sight without the image bouncing too radically. "They're leaving their snowmobiles. Probably a washroom break," he said, defensively, while watching the two figures. They suddenly picked up speed, running to the right. He followed them.

He heard a tense chuckle beside him and another click of the scope. "Washroom break, indeed."

Matthew continued to watch and nearly dropped the binoculars when the .308 went off with an ear-splitting bang beside him. "What the hell–?"

"Watch, watch!" Sky commanded, using the bolt action to chamber another round.

The high-powered rifle went off with a crash a second time, the stench of cordite from the first shot already stinging his nostrils.

Matthew resumed looking just in time to see a black hole appear under the front headlight of one snowmobile, followed by a puff of yellow paint and a geyser of blue smoke erupting from its front. It must have been running. "Are you crazy, Sky?" He was furious.

"Problem solved," she said standing up, removing the box magazine from the rifle and then ejecting an empty shell from the firing chamber. She found the first one she fired and pocketed both cartridge casings.

"You shot at them, Sky. They can report this to the Mounties for God's sake."

"I told them it would be dangerous to follow us."

"You shot at them!"

"Did I?"

"You shot *at* them! For God's sake!"

"Matthew, if I had shot at them, they'd both be down now. I'm a physician. I don't take lives. I try to save them. When I can." The last sentence came out almost as a whisper. "Now, I need a moment," she said firmly. It wasn't a request.

Abruptly she walked off about ten yards, turned and faced the direction of their pursuers. She looked skyward and then bowed her head. Matthew turned and used the binoculars to see the two distant figures tentatively approaching their snowmobiles.

Sky was back.

"What were you doing?" he asked, not bothering to mask his annoyance.

"Giving thanks as I should," she replied.

"For what? Shooting a snowmobile?"

She ignored him, stored the weapon back in its case and put it on the sled. "Time to get going. We're about 50 miles south of Hebron so we'll be making camp in another hour or two. It'll be getting dark; we barely have seven hours of daylight these days so we have to make every minute count. There is no more time to chase those morons all over Labrador." She started her snowmobile and settled herself on the seat.

Matthew didn't look at her, knowing his face was red with anger. Atemu was sitting on his sled looking at the sky again, ears pricked forward. He abandoned his listening to watch him stamping away. "This is nuts," Matthew muttered. "The only place we're going is jail when they catch us."

They travelled for another half hour and Sky signaled a stop. Matthew merely sat on his snowmobile well behind her and didn't bother to approach. She stood on her seat, focused her binoculars back down the ice and then nodded her head, a satisfied smile on her face. They resumed their journey and travelled for another half hour. By now the shadows on the snow were lengthening dramatically as the sun sank lower and lower on the horizon. The temperature was again plunging, the chill settling into his bones.

Finally, Sky steered them onto an ice-covered bay. Matthew followed and was surprised to see a number of wooden buildings on the shore line ahead.

As they drew nearer, he saw most of them were in the process of gradual disintegration. However, a long, ancient-looking wooden building with a battered church steeple on top, offered relatively fresh wooden shutters covering the windows and a white-washed outer shell. Based on the obvious age of the building, the work must have been done in recent years to stabilize and preserve the structure. Two well-weathered houses and several out-buildings, all in various stages of collapse, completed the settlement.

Having travelled past the tree line, the land was pretty much barren now; not a tree in sight. He wondered where the builders had gotten their lumber.

Sky had stopped just off the ice and looked at the buildings as Matthew pulled up beside her. They sat there astride their snowmobiles like a couple of cowpokes perched on their horses surveying the herd. She said nothing. Still angry, he refused to acknowledge her.

Two can play the silent treatment game. Finally...

"This is the Hebron Moravian Mission you've likely heard about," she said, breaking her silence. "They built it back in 1831 and it was only abandoned in 1959 by order of the Canadian government. It's presently under a very slow process of restoration. Since they are only able to work here at certain times, the workers are fighting on two fronts: restoring while, at the same time, trying to prevent more damage and rot.

"The Moravians are European Protestants with a long history of missionary work who began establishing missions in Labrador in 1771. They would prefab their buildings – some believe it was done in Germany – and then ship them overseas and assemble them on various sites here. The first site was in Nain. Then they expanded up and down the coast bringing Christianity to more and more Inuit and Innu people. However, while they were adept at supposedly saving their souls, they weren't able to protect their dignity nor their freedom."

Matthew was silent, preoccupied with why she recklessly shot at

Meyer and Boivin.

"In 1880, an agent for a German zoo promised an Inuit family – Abraham Ulrikab, his wife and children and some friends – money and glory if they would come to Europe. The missionaries protested. They tried to keep them here, but to no avail. Ulrikab saw it as a way out of the inherent poverty of the area. The family was transported to Europe where they were placed in zoos and exhibited as savages before the Europeans. As the years passed, they hated what their lives had become and begged to be taken home to Labrador. Unfortunately, they were too big a draw. Then, one-by-one they got smallpox, sickened and died."

Matthew, still angry at Sky for her earlier actions, gradually felt his anger dissipating. Cautiously he sneaked a look at her. She was staring ahead, a faraway look on her face. "They were innocents, packed up like animals and put in cages for the amusement and enlightenment of the white man." She looked over at Matthew and added: "Meanwhile, the rest of the good and God-fearing English, French and other Europeans were migrating here to steal our country."

Matthew didn't comment though he was surprised it wasn't anger he heard in her voice as much as sadness. Still, he couldn't let go of what happened that afternoon. "You could have missed and killed one of those people today, Sky," he said.

"They were a good fifty yards away from the snowmobile," Sky answered. "I'm an excellent shot."

"So what will you tell the RCMP when we get back?"

"Nothing to tell."

"You could have killed them," he persisted.

"Not really."

"Goddammit Sky, you missed with one shot. *That* could have killed them."

"I didn't miss with either shot," she said simply, and twisted her throttle. Her snowmobile sprung forward.

They rode around the Mission House on the well-packed snow crust before inspecting the other houses collapsing from wind and weather. A few empty prefabs for workers stood nearby. The Mission House itself showed a definite Germanic influence in its architecture with a long, elongated steep roof punctuated by dormers and cupola. Where visible, the wood was weathered beyond what one would call barn board, cracked open in its grain and distressed by the harsh winters. The other buildings were simple squared-off structures with their own little dormers of wood that had fallen victim to the elements.

They decided against taking liberties with the site. They chose a flat spot and pitched their tent, rather than trying to jury rig shelter in the rotting buildings. Anyhow, Sky explained, the Mission had been declared a National Historic Site so they couldn't really disturb anything.

"You're telling me I can't use any of the wood from the buildings to make a fire?" Matthew asked.

"Correct," Sky replied. "The Royal Canadian Mounted Police would frown very much on that. And after they were through with all their frowning, they'd cart us off to jail."

It was dark by the time they unpacked what they needed, put up the tent and deployed their beds and other gear inside. Matthew went outside to play with the dog and found a small stick which he flung repeatedly into the darkness to give Atemu lots of exercise. It worked well till the dog returned, settled down and chewed it to bits.

"Now, what will I throw for you?" Matthew asked, in jest. "Doggie not MENSA material?"

Atemu cocked his head and looked at him for a moment, seemingly digesting the insult. Then he trotted off. He came back with a huge stick, more log-like, in his mouth and set it down in front of the tent.

Matthew took his light and followed him to where they found various sticks that were not attached to the Mission. Atemu then led him to a small pile of half-buried, chopped and weathered firewood standing off to one side of the main house. Since there were few trees for a hundred miles, the wood was obviously cut in the south somewhere, transported to the mission, and left there by workers.

Good doggie!

He carried an armful back, built a fire, stuck a large can of snow in it and watched it melt. The ratio was 10:1 so it took some time to make a bucket of water. Some would be kept for drinking and washing, and the rest was boiled to reconstitute their Expedition Food packs.

Sky had been silent throughout their pitching camp exercise and Matthew guessed he had offended her with his criticism. Still, he would not sit by and have anyone placed in danger on this trip. No diamond was worth someone else's life. Despite Sky's claim to marksmanship, it had been a long range shot; wind and drift could have resulted in a tragedy. He intended to revisit what had happened and make her promise not to do anything so foolish again.

Eventually she came out of the tent with three food pouches and a couple of granola bars. She also had some instant coffee and two tin mugs which she set beside the fire to warm. One had to be careful with metal and mouths in the North since it simply wasn't 'cool' to go around with a cup hanging from your frozen lips.

They made their food and scraped Atemu's onto his plate where he gobbled it up in short order and then, predictably, sat and stared at every mouthful they ate. His eyes shone yellow in the firelight; flames flickered and flared and they enjoyed the pungent smell of the wood smoke. The snow surrounding the fire reflected its golden glow.

Overhead, a million stars gleamed in the night sky as they ate. A full moon rising in the east completed a perfect picture of serenity.

Merely stepping a few feet away from the fire afforded them an amazing view of the heavens, one that few city people would ever be privileged to see.

They finished their supper and sipped steaming mugs of coffee staring wordlessly into the flames as they popped, hissed and crackled.

The smell of the wood smoke hung heavy in the air. Atemu had gone inside the tent and, after glancing out to make sure they were otherwise engaged, he sneaked onto Matthew's bed and curled up on his sleeping bag. Matthew slid his gaze sideways and watched him through the open flap. The Coleman lamp was firing away inside but they hadn't bothered to light any heaters since the tent flap was open.

"Walk?" Matthew asked.

Sky looked at him for a long moment as though his invitation was somehow inane. Finally she shrugged and rose. Habitually she picked up her .30-30 carbine and slung it over her shoulder. He took a Maglite.

They walked away from the mission and up a small knoll where they looked back at the tent glowing yellow from the Coleman lantern inside.

Before them was graphic evidence of the remoteness of Labrador. The whiteness of the ice-covered bay had been turned pale blue by the moonlight and stretched to the horizon in front. Behind them, in the distance, were the black, rounded shadows of old mountains.

As their vision lost the afterglow of the campfire and adjusted to the surrounding darkness, they could see surprisingly well by the stars and the moon climbing steadily overhead. Off in the distance, a wolf howled a long doleful note, soon answered by other frantic howls and barking. The air was so clean and crisp, and the silence so complete, they could hear the occasional snap of exploding sap from the wood in their fire hundreds of yards below. The grey walls of the Mission House now gleamed silver in the moonlight; the two, smaller mission houses and other outbuildings were dark lumps against the snow.

"It's beautiful," Matthew commented.

"It's Labrador," Sky answered, gazing heavenward. "I often hike up Mt. Sophie or Nain Hill at night and look at the stars and over the bay. Everything is so pure and peaceful. A perk of being close to nature."

Matthew smiled and nodded. "Look Sky, about today. Sorry I lost my temper but even you have to realize someone could have been hurt."

She sighed and shook her head. She didn't meet his gaze, instead choosing to look down at her feet. He couldn't help feeling that, somehow, she was disappointed in *him*. "Matthew, I would never hurt anyone."

"Not intentionally. I know that." He said it sincerely.

She looked up and directly into his eyes. "I saved their lives."

"By plugging their snowmobile so they'd stop following us?"

"No, that was the second shot."

She didn't say anything for another moment, content to take in the beauty of their surroundings.

Puzzled he waited for her to continue. Whereas he had been accusatory, angry and unapproachable most of the day, she had exhibited patience and calm. And that was despite the barbs he flung at her.

He couldn't help thinking Sky possessed a generosity of spirit seldom seen in his world where differences of opinion habitually exploded too quickly into incidents best forgotten. Her challenge to Meyer today had to be an aberration. The man had revealed an uncanny and irritating ability to find and push people's buttons. He had done so by insulting Sky's heritage.

She looked up, met his look and gently asked: "Matthew, tell me what you saw through the binoculars?"

"I saw them both running away from their snowmobiles."

"Looking for a washroom, right?" She said, with a slight smile. "That's what I thought."

"As I said, I hit what I was aiming at both times, as I usually do."

"You didn't shoot both machines, did you?"

"No. Remember when I told you that anyone heading into a National Park, like Torngat, isn't permitted to carry a weapon, unless they are Innu or Inuit?"

"Yes."

"So they were unarmed, except for Meyer and his tiny, toy pistol."

"You're losing me," Matthew said.

"I fired at two targets. The first was what they were running away *from*. A very angry and aggressive polar bear who was about to make dinner out of them. Meyer's pistol would have been useless against that bear. That's why they were running. The second shot...." She smiled: "That was the bonus round if I hit the first target."

"You shot a polar bear and *then* their snowmobile? A polar bear?"

"Yes. But I left them one machine so they could retreat home. As I said, I usually try to help people, not hurt them."

Matthew stared at her suddenly realizing he'd been completely wrong. He began to feel more than a little remorse over his earlier condemnation.

"You really didn't see the polar bear to the left of their machines?" she inquired. "He was coming across the sea ice and really, as you would say, 'hauling ass' to get to his dinner."

"A white bear against white snow? No, I watched Meyer and Monique running to the right."

"Well, Nanuq was about 100 yards to the left of their machines when I saw him. And 10 yards from them when I fired. And he gave of his spirit willingly or I never would have made the shot."

"You hit *two* targets dead on!" Matthew said. "Seems he didn't have a chance."

"Oh no, you're wrong, Matthew. You see, when the Innu and the Inuit kill game, we do not see it as a conquest over our prey. Animals have great spiritual power and it is only if they are willing to die that we are able to kill them. That is why I gave thanks to Nanuq's spirit. I know, I'm a scientist-based doctor and shouldn't believe Innu lore, but the old ways die hard. In fact the longer I am home up here, the more real they are to me once again." She trailed off. "

Matthew nodded slowly. "I'm sorry Sky. Why didn't you tell me you were saving them from that bear?"

She shrugged. "You weren't in any mood to listen. And grandfather says that those who won't listen, seldom wish to learn. They are slaves to their personal beliefs and agendas." She gave him a gentle smile. "Head back to camp?"

Matthew realized that he had received a very mild rebuke, as rebukes go, and he felt lousy about how he had treated her all day. He should have known better.

Sky looked at him, head cocked to the side. She motioned down the hill again. It seemed that as far as she was concerned, the matter was closed and forgotten already.

"I'll join you in a minute," he said.

As she started down the slope, Matthew took a final look around. The snow-covered and icy sea shore glittering in the moonlight, bordered by the low hills behind him, all under a deep, navy night sky peppered with stars was the perfect picture of a winter wilderness. Throw in the yellow tent below, a glowing refuge beside the orange campfire and the scene was eerily dreamlike.

He watched Sky making her way quickly and expertly down the snow-covered slope and realized that his respect for her was growing exponentially. In fact, he admitted to himself, he was more than a little in in awe of her quiet strength and reserve.

All things considered, she was one truly remarkable young women.

For a moment he allowed himself to imagine the barriers she would have had to overcome in her life: to have the courage to let go of her northern home and enter the modern world; to win acceptance to medical school; to study, graduate and intern; and, then to go on to become a surgeon. Yet, remove her from her hospital surroundings and drop her in one of the most inhospitable regions in the world, and she still thrived. She not only survived, but she took care of people around her.

Even people she didn't particularly like.

Inwardly he chuckled: not everyone skilled in the precise use of a surgeon's blade could also fire a .308 at range and squarely hit a well-camouflaged, rapidly-moving target. And yet, her sense of self did not demand she mount a defense against his accusations until he insisted on clarification. Only then did she open up. Knowing she had done the right thing was enough for this young lady.

And, tonight, two people were still alive…because of Sky St. Onge.

PART THREE

Shadows on the Snow

Thoughts are the shadows of our feelings – always
Darker, emptier and simpler…
Friedrich Nietzsche

~1~

"Trouble in paradise, sir," Lieutenant Reynolds said to Colonel Moorhead standing over him and staring at his video displays. The screens showed the Avenger was still flying lazy circles over Sky and Matthew's position at the Moravian Mission. Since it was dark, the infrared sensor showed several heat signatures: a tent, two people moving around it, and a dying fire. Ten yards away the dog was motionless, probably attending to his toiletries prior to turning in.

"There was an altercation today between our subjects and two people following them with one being knocked down," Reynolds continued. "Later the trailing snowmobiles continued following our subjects. But every time our subjects turned around and chased them, they retreated. Cat and mouse."

"Yes, I got your earlier message," Moorhead replied. "We're checking on the pursuers. Eventually they headed back?"

"On only one snowmobile, sir. The other was obviously disabled. I'm pretty sure one of our subjects shot it, along with the bear I mentioned. From more than 1,000 yards I'd say. Hell of a shot."

"Obviously they didn't want them tailing them."

"Yes sir," Reynolds said. "But not enough to leave them as dinner for Yogi."

"Yogi?" Moorhead asked.

"Uh...Yogi Bear, sir? Hanna-Barbera? Pic-in-ic basket?"

Moorhead simply stared at him.

"Never mind, sir." Reynolds eased his yoke on the control console to the left and turned the Avenger once more. "They took out a polar bear charging towards their pursuers."

"So it all worked out," Moorhead said. "What time do they usually leave in the morning?"

"Just before first light, around 0900 hours, sir. Imagine they'll leave the same time. Now they're stationary, I'm about to bring my aircraft back for refueling. And I plan to deploy again bright and early at dawn. Though I don't know how bright it will be. When they start to move, I'll be right there to watch them"

"Very well. I estimate they'll enter Saglek Bay around 15:00

tomorrow so I've ordered a moratorium on all flights at noon," Moorhead said. "Everyone stays indoors, quiet and out of sight. I want them to bypass us, follow the ice across the bay and continue their journey. They've had some delays so hopefully they'll be more interested in making tracks than visiting a deserted military base."

"Do we know where they're headed, sir?" Reynolds asked.

"Up to Cape Territok and then inland from there. That's all we know so far."

Lieutenant Reynolds was beginning to believe that he was building a good rapport with the Colonel and he was itching to know exactly how this scenario all fit together. Military exercises in the subarctic were one thing but closely following two civilians on snowmobiles didn't exactly jive with testing drones under Arctic conditions.

"Sir, if I may, why are we following these two?"

"Need to know, Lieutenant. Need to know."

"Sorry sir."

"You're bringing her in now?"

"Roger, departing Hebron Mission, all systems green."

"Very well. Keep me informed of anything new or odd that happens." He strode to the door and then said: "Carry on, Boo-Boo."

Moorhead exited the Radar Ops Center as Reynolds grinned. Boo-Boo? The old guy did have a sense of humor, after all. He swung the drone west and took one last look at the campsite. The tent and the remains of the fire were the only heat sources outside. Everyone below appeared to have settled down for a long winter's nap.

He turned the Avenger and headed north through the dark towards Saglek. As soon as the aircraft was 10 miles north of the campsite, he began a rapid letdown decreasing altitude from 10,000 feet in prep for landing. His display finally showed the glow of the lights of the base miles ahead. He cross checked their local weather with Goose Bay's ATIS on 128.1 MHz. ATIS continuously broadcast non-control, aeronautical info. This included active runways in Goose, not of much use to him. The weather stats, however, including temperature, humidity, wind direction and strength were all valuable. It was the closest automated weather system they had.

Now he turned the drone towards the sea. He would fly past Saglek, loop over Big Island and then put it to his left with Shuldham Island and

Handy Island to his right. Then he'd do a long, slow turn onto final approach over the bay to land on Runway 17.

Sometimes, he mused, it was easier at night with the runway lights on max and the wind having settled for the evening. During the day, in fog or drizzle with hilly terrain all around the airport and a 1,000-foot ridge to the southeast of the strip, it could be more than nerve racking. Nobody wanted to be responsible for crashing a $14 million drone whether they were in it or not.

"C'mon baby," he said to himself as he looped out and then turned 180 degrees towards Big Island. Ahead, well over the island and across the bay, he could make out two tiny parallel strips of lights. "Honey, I'm home," he said, aloud. "Let's just–" Abruptly Lieutenant Reynolds paused and then exclaimed out loud: "Jesus Christ!" He tipped his craft and turned his surveillance sensor fully to starboard.

Behind him a radar controller echoed his surprise. "Lieutenant, we're painting a target off your starboard wing, less than a quarter mile. Just popped up. Making 280 knots," the operator called out.

"I see him," Reynolds said tensely, gazing at the navigation lights of an aircraft on his right side; for all extents and purposes it was pacing him. "Any idea what it is?"

"No sir," the controller said. He spoke into his head mic and then: "Duty Officer notified," he announced.

The second radar controller was on the phone. Moorhead appeared in two minutes flat. He bent over the lieutenant's shoulder watching Reynold's approach to Saglek Harbour. He hadn't let on he'd seen anything, his sensor split between watching the unknown on his right and keeping the runway in sight. He dropped lower.

"Where'd he come from?" Moorhead asked.

"I never spotted him till I turned onto final, north of Big Island," Reynolds responded. "Brazen as hell, full navigation lights on. Pretty sure it's an Ivan, sir. "

"Just popped up off the coast," the radar controller confirmed behind them. "Could have been hiding behind Big Island."

"But full navigation lights?" Moorhead said. "Did you check with NORAD? Do we have anything up?"

"Nothing except Lieutenant Reynolds," the radar controller said. "Goose is shut down for the night. Like the lieutenant says, probably a

Ruskie."

"So it's definitely an aircraft, right? An Aircraft?"

"Yes sir," the controller replied, looking strangely at the Colonel. *What the hell else would it be?*

"Any others?" Moorhead asked, inwardly cursing his slip.

"Not unless their bellies are wet, sir," the controller responded. In other words none unless they were too low for the radar to catch them, flying almost at sea level. An oft used trick to avoid radar, with any sort of range, was to use the nap of the earth for cover staying on the deck until they were ready to make their presence known. This had often been done by former USSR aircraft approaching Labrador during the Cold War. They would then rapidly gain altitude so they would "pop up" on radar. The sole purpose was to judge interceptor response time for fighters out of Goose Bay, Labrador, or Bagotville, Quebec.

"Very well," Moorhead said.

The Colonel now stood over the radar controllers and watched the two targets side-by-side. Reynolds maintained his final approach.

"Orders, sir…?" he called out.

"Bring her in, Lieutenant. Okay, let's not make them think we're asleep. Any radio response?"

"We broadcast on multiple frequencies; no response from bogie, sir. Duty Officer issued scramble order," the radar controller confirmed. This meant two F-35 Lightning pilots were already running down a hall from their quarters. Ground Crew would be opening hangar doors and pulling away chocks from the wheels of the interceptors. It would be the radar controller's job to vector their fighters to the target.

"Make sure they know we have an Avenger inbound on 17."

"Yes sir!" the radar controller said. "Target has turned, heading now zero six five degrees…zero seven five degrees… tracking back towards Big Island. Now climbing and heading north of Big Island."

The phone on a desk behind Reynolds rang. Moorhead picked it up.

"Colonel Moorhead," he said. "Yes. I'm heading for the tower now."

* * *

With the Avenger down and clear of the active runway, Captain

Ladd Heldenbrand and his wingman lifted off from runway 35, the airport landing lights and blue-lit taxiway dropping beneath them as they climbed into the night sky. He pulled his F-35 in a steep vertical climb to 3,000 feet, leveled out and turned onto a heading of zero nine zero degrees.

"Saglek Control, Foxtrot Echo zero one, requests vector to target, over," Heldenbrand radioed.

"Foxtrot Echo zero one, Saglek Control, target vector zero three seven degrees at angels one five," the controller replied. "Distance 90 nautical miles, speed 400 knots, over."

"Roger, Saglek Control, steering zero three seven degrees and going to afterburner. Climbing angels one five," Heldenbrand confirmed, as he pulled the nose up and maintained a comfortable five-thousand-feet-per-minute climb ratio.

Beside his aircraft, his wingman, also in an F-35, matched him in motion and speed.

"Foxtrot Echo zero two, estimate intercept five minutes, over," Heldenbrand told his wingman.

"Roger, Foxtrot Echo zero one. Let's get 'em," the second pilot answered as the two jets screamed over Saglek Bay in hot pursuit of their target.

Far below the full moon cut a silver swath across open water. It was obvious the intruder had no intention of making it easy for Heldenbrand or his wingman as they soon found out. Because they did not have the bogie on their own radar sets, they were relying on Saglek to vector them to the target.

"Foxtrot Echo zero one, Saglek Control. Assume new heading zero four seven, angels unknown, target descended rapidly behind Big Island. NORAD confirms intrusion, over."

It was obvious the target had decided to play some games rather than simply accept the intercept as was usually done.

"Roger, Foxtrot Echo zero one and two on new heading zero four seven, over."

Once an "unknown" penetrates the contiguous zone of the North American Air Defense Identification Zone (ADIZ) without identifying itself or broadcasting a transponder signal, it was assumed to be hostile until proven otherwise.

Heldenbrand knew that while neither the US nor Canada claimed sovereignty over this North American "transition zone," (which circumscribes the coast of North American) they closely monitored it and requested information from all targets entering the zone. In a post 9/11 world, when there is no response from any aircraft or ship, an intercept was ordered.

There was, however, an exception to this rule now in place for Saglek Base. No scramble orders were issued for what were termed "weather anomalies" around and north of Saglek. These anomalies appeared as solid targets, generally off the Torngat Mountain section of Labrador. They exceeded known flight parameters, conducted instant, physically impossible 90-degree turns, and disappeared as quickly as they appeared. The radar controllers seriously doubted that solid targets, though only appearing briefly, had anything to do with weather. But they had been ordered to keep radio silence regarding these phenomena. And, to keep their mouths shut.

And so they did.

On the other hand, this intruder tonight seemed to be displaying a "flesh and blood" signature, and so they were happy to be dealing with it as a true unknown. Know thy enemy was once again a solid dictum.

"Foxtrot Echo zero one, Saglek Control, bogie reappeared east of Big Island. For intercept, vector one, one five degrees. Target is on the deck, speed 510 knots, over."

Heldenbrand confirmed reception. He and his wingman were well north of Big Island now. The bogie had cunningly dropped out of sight, then flown south around Big Island as the interceptors flew north. He was now cruising full out, probably at 300 feet or less heading into international waters. More and more it looked like a Russian training flight. NORAD generally allowed these flights to do their job but still dispatched an "escort" for them.

Heldenbrand and his wingman pulled a 180 degree turn and powered back around Big Island boosting their airspeed as they dropped like stones from 15,000 feet.

Within five minutes, the F-35s had caught up to their target and closed carefully. Once the 'unknown' realized the jig was up, it climbed to six thousand feet and throttled back to 400 knots. Approaching "in trail" again, they could see a huge red star on the aircraft tail immediately identifying it as Russian.

Heldenbrand and his wingman pulled level with the Russian aircraft identifying it as a TU-95SM, built in the late 1980s and 90s. Heldenbrand flashed his landing lights to ensure the pilot of the Russian bomber saw him and his wingman in the night sky. The bomber also flashed its landing lights as return acknowledgement. The cockpit lights in the bomber came on and, using a WAC chart to exaggerate his hand movement and be seen, the co-pilot waved. The heavy bomber cruised on, its four sets of contra-rotating props winking in the light of the moon. Neither side wanted an accident that could trigger an international incident.

"Saglek Control, Foxtrot Echo zero one, we have a Tupolev Bear bomber in sight, over.

"Foxtrot Echo zero one, Saglek Control, confirm one TU-95 intercepted."

"Saglek Control, affirmative. Still in Canadian airspace, over?"

"Foxtrot Echo zero one, estimating one minute to international airspace, over."

"Saglek Control, orders, sir?"

"Escort them out, Captain, and return to base."

"Roger," Heldenbrand said, carefully watching the huge bomber beside him.

While still in the zone, the bomber would soon be hitting the 12 nautical mile limit that defined Canadian airspace and water. While Canada, at this point, had the right to demand that the bomber fly to the nearest Canadian airport and land because it had violated Canadian airspace, not a word was said. They wanted him out of there.

Back at Saglek, watching a radar scope, Colonel Moorhead saw the Russian make international waters, their interceptors turn back towards base and all become right with the world. He returned to his darkened office, dialed 9 for an operator and gave his code and a second verification code. A satellite line out soon responded with a far-off ringing sound.

He slumped into his chair, not bothering to turn on the office lights.

"Black," a gruff, somewhat sleepy voice answered on the other end.

Colonel Moorhead, sir," the Colonel replied. "Had an incident tonight, Bear Bomber penetrated ADIZ and made it within 10 miles of base before we picked him up."

"Meet and greet?"

"Yes, two F-35s sent him on his way."

There was a pause at the other end of the line and finally Black said: "Evasive action?"

"Yes, but in hindsight, it seemed more of an afterthought. He came out of nowhere with navigation lights on, flew beside our Avenger drone for a few minutes, made sure he was seen, and then peeled off. When we scrambled our fighters he retreated behind Big Island, dropped under the radar and flew south as our boys flew north looking for him. They barely caught up one minute from international waters."

"So he wanted to be seen."

"Apparently," Moorhead answered.

"Well their satellites know all about our physical activities, so it wasn't a reconnaissance mission," Black said, slowly.

"No sir."

"So it was a message."

"Telling us they know?"

"Well, telling us they know something is up, at least. They must be seeing…weather anomalies…as well."

"And our stockpiling of assets."

"So they've put it all together and concluded we're going to move on something."

"Yes sir," Moorhead said. "But they can't."

"Not without starting WWIII," Black agreed.

Moorhead could hear movement at the other end of the telephone and Black becoming more awake all the time. The phone was put down for a second and immediately picked up.

There was some fumbling, a curse and an annoyed female voice at the other end. Was Black married? He hadn't given it much thought before but it seemed he was. Or had a lady friend.

"Colonel, I am going to put this before our committee tomorrow and move to get the State Department to lodge an official protest with the Russian Ambassadors. We'll have it done in Ottawa and Washington, and tell them in no uncertain terms that if they stray into Canadian airspace again, without notifying us, we can't be responsible for what happens. We'll use the pretext of 9/11, an anticipated potential terrorist plot, and itchy trigger fingers on the part of our boys. We'll request they restrict all training fights near Labrador for a few weeks as a generous gesture of cooperation and good will. Only until we get things under control, of course."

"Roger, sir," Moorhead.

"And Colonel, what the hell kind of operation are you running up there if they can get within 20 miles of your base? And where the hell was NORAD? Out shopping?"

The Colonel knew excuses were useless. Terrain, nap of the earth, stealth, poor radar technology, weather anomalies, God's will, or bubonic plague, nothing would satisfy his master. What Black really wanted to know was: What actions would Moorhead take to ensure it never happened again? "I am going to put an AWACS up 24/7 until this is over, sir."

That would mean they would have airborne radar on station, off the coast, 24-hours-a-day, landing only after being replaced by a second radar plane.

"See that you do."

There was a click on the other end and Moorhead slowly put his phone back on its cradle. "I should have taken that job as an aluminum siding salesman," he said, to no-one in particular. "Commissions, car allowance, benefits…and no fucking government spooks giving me orders."

~2~

Sky and Matthew broke camp under a brilliant blue sky. For some reason they had slept so soundly they only awoke when the sun actually started to slightly heat the tent. The Mission House shone grey and white in the sun a few dozen yards away. Tiny wisps of snow curled off the tops of the hard-packed, white snow dunes with the ever-present wind continuing to make its presence felt.

There was little doubt it was much warmer since three-foot icicles hanging from the roof of the Mission House were dripping in the sun. Both Sky and Matthew arose and worked without benefit of parkas. Their thick, wool ski sweaters provided enough warmth on an unseasonably warm day.

Quickly collapsing the cots, they rolled their sleeping bags, folded the tent and moved the food bins onto the sleds.

Atemu bounded around burning off steam knowing he'd be confined to the sled for the day's journey. They had deliberately not packed the Coleman stove so they could heat snow into boiling water and mix it into Expedition Foods' packets of scrambled eggs, potatoes and mixed peppers. The dog finished his breakfast in one minute flat; Matthew cleaned his empty plate in the snow and then poured the remainder of the boiled water over it.

Sky had pulled out their satellite phone and tried to contact the Royal Victoria Hospital to check on her grandfather. Nothing happened. She took off the back, checked the battery and then reassembled it and tried again. "It's not working," she said. She substituted a spare battery. It lit up but she couldn't dial out. Finally she turned it off and put it back in its leather carrying case under her parka. "We'll see if we can fix it tonight."

She urged him to finish packing as quickly as possible. They were getting a late start. She wiped her forehead, looked at a pocket temperature gauge and said: "No wonder, it's a balmy -5 degrees."

"Where are the darned beach towels?" Matthew demanded, pretending to rummage about as he packed one heater on each sleigh, one sleeping bag and one cot.

"Strange we didn't wake before this," Sky said. "But I remember sort of being in a quasi-sleep, and hearing whistling sounds in the sky, even a couple of booms, one after the other."

"So did I," Matthew replied. "There's still NATO tactical flight training out of Goose Bay. They were probably doing night exercises."

"I know. We've been protesting their low level flights for years. They disrupt the annual caribou migration. More than a decade ago they tried to increase the training flights from 8,000 to 40,000 a year. And then the government tried for a NATO contract that would have meant 100,000 flights a year. These flights scare game and make them unpredictable so my people couldn't hunt successfully."

"I thought they adjusted the flight levels out of Goose."

"They did after our hunters started shooting at them."

"That wasn't a good thing, Sky."

"Maybe not, but suddenly the government mysteriously started to listen to our band chiefs and elders. For the first time. Coincidence, eh?"

She looked around and then out at the bay. "This thaw isn't necessarily a good thing for us. The ice is tenuous at best so we'll have to be extra careful."

They were soon packed up and on their way. After three hours of uninterrupted travel, the temperature growing colder by the hour, they could make out a weather front growing out of the horizon. It was an ugly, nasty, grey and black color. Sky stopped her snowmobile and Matthew hung back as usual. He pulled up his goggles onto the front of his helmet and squinted at the brightness as she spoke to him on his helmet radio.

"That's another storm coming from the northeast," she said, gesturing towards the clouds.

"Will we keep going?"

"Yes, at least to our fuel cache up ahead. We'll refuel and try to get halfway around Saglek Fiord today. Everything will depend on the condition of the ice. Saglek is on the south end of the Torngat Mountains. Once we're north of Big Island, we'll be entering the boundaries of the park."

Matthew paused for a moment and pulled off his helmet. He was sure he could hear the whine of an aircraft and he looked up. Sure enough, a small plane, likely a Beaver or Cessna, was slipping through some clouds overhead. It was at about five thousand feet he guessed. Probably a mail plane, he thought. Obviously Sky couldn't hear it with her helmet on, so he decided to ignore it. No use stressing her over nothing.

"We seem to be making good time," he radioed back, after pulling his helmet back on.

"This is the easy part," she replied. "Once we leave the snowmobiles, we pull toboggans with our gear. After that, we use snowshoes and knapsacks. Also some climbing involved."

"Climbing?"

"Don't worry, it's not technical rock climbing; we'll be using the pitons and ropes more as safety measures."

"Good."

"But there is one spot where we'll be climbing more than 3,000 feet straight up...."

"Don't be cruel," he tried singing over the radio.

She actually laughed for a change. "Don't quit your day job," she advised re his singing.

Their journey had forged well ahead and being able to talk about entering the park seemed to make Sky happy. Also, she admitted she was very much relieved that their "trail buddies" had abandoned the chase. While Matthew had so many questions for Sky regarding *who* did she think was watching them, *who* used to give her grandfather help, and *why* he would make trips up here anyhow, he held them in abeyance. She seemed a little less stressed, so why get her upset again?

Ahead, she waved her hand and off they went. They were still making only 15 mph at best. Soon the sky greyed up, the sun vanished and the clouds thickened. A stronger wind was also beginning to whip up snow in front of them. Matthew saw Atemu had his head down, probably with his nose in the wool of his blanket. It was getting colder by the minute. Sky only paused once very briefly to hop back and cover the dog's head so he was well protected. Though, being a Husky he could sleep in a snow bank, their speed resulted in a wind velocity that penetrated his natural insulation and cooled him at a prodigious rate.

They travelled for another hour with the temperature plummeting and the snow getting thicker by the minute. Sky was stopping to check her GPS more frequently. The helmet earphones crackled: "Matthew, listen up please. This is getting unsafe. I'm going to take us into shore. We must be right on the entrance to Saglek Fiord. I glimpsed open water about a mile ahead just before the wind increased. These gusts are affecting the ice where we're sitting. I felt it heaving a moment ago.

"When we reach the fiord, it should be frozen farther in. So we'll circle inland till we hit solid ice and then we'll cross. I hope we'll be able to cross somewhere between Jens Haven Island and Rose Island. Then we'll follow the north shore east and finally head north deeper into the park."

"Roger," he answered, but she had already started to move. He wiped snow off his compass on the snowmobile. This would take them on a heading of 270 degrees meaning due west magnetic. He pulled his goggles over his eyes, wiped a layer of snow off them and started to follow her. The visibility declined even further.

Suddenly Sky stopped again. The wind gusts died for a moment and far ahead he could make out a section of black water. But it wasn't north, where she had seen it before. They had already turned towards shore according to his compass. That put the water west of them, right across their intended path to land.

A huge gust of wind sent snow swirling about and he lost sight of her completely. Behind him he heard an explosive crack that made him physically jump. He looked back. Through the heavy snow he saw the ice was buckling, breaking apart and then falling into a newly created channel of black water. It was widening rapidly, barely a hundred feet behind him. With the intense wind, it widened further as he watched. Spray now whipped off the tops of newly formed white caps in the ever widening channel. More ice seemed to rise up and crack off the edges, then settle back down leaving more open water. The wind strength intensified.

"Sky," he radioed. "Open water south of us." He could just make her out ahead.

"North and west too," she radioed back. "Not what I would have ordered, Matthew."

The wind picked up even more. The snow swirled and he lost sight of her for a moment. They were now experiencing whiteout conditions. To move anywhere without being able to see would be suicide. For sure there was no escape to the east as there was nothing there but the Labrador Sea. More and more it looked like they might be trapped on an ice flow. Their only chance lay to the north. There might still be a section connecting them to the mainland.

Matthew jumped from his snowmobile, pulled off his helmet and trotted through the storm up to Sky. "Think we're adrift, captain?" he yelled. He tried to keep it light and sound like their predicament was still manageable. Cleaning snow off her goggles, her look told him he was wrong; there were dire consequences in the offing.

"This is really dangerous, Matthew," she shouted back. "The wind and snow are getting worse. And we need to find if we're still connected to land. If so, we have to get off the ice, pronto. But, right now, this storm is making it deadly to move."

"What do we do?" he asked, no longer feeling quite so cavalier about their situation.

Sky removed her helmet, placed it on the sled, and pulled up her hood. She yelled over the shriek of the freezing wind: "We wait and pray this dies down so we see where we're going."

"Think there's still a connection to shore? North of us?"

"Might be," she called back.

"But we have to stay put?" He cradled his helmet under his arm and yanked up his own hood. The wind was increasing in strength, screaming its fury and virtually blinding them.

"Right," she yelled. "We can't see at all so we'll wait for a break in the storm and then carefully explore up ahead. Bring your snowmobile up near me. We don't want to suddenly find ourselves on separate ice flows."

As he turned to fetch his own snowmobile, Matthew stumbled; he was sure the ice had moved under his feet. He flinched as more explosive cracks sounded around him. The ice under his feet vibrated as it broke apart and collided again somewhere off in the veil of white. He heard a foreign sound and looked at Sky, not moving.

Though the wind was roaring full force, they both began to hear the new sound, a loud whistle piercing the moans and howls of the storm.

At first Matthew thought it was the wind increasing again but Atemu was sitting up and staring at the sky overhead. The snow above them began to rotate in circular gusts. In fact, snow and ice seemed to be bouncing upward from the ground, scattering outward and leaving a circle of bare ice. The intensity from above was blowing everything flat, including the dog's ears. Atemu cowered in the sled. It grew louder, a high-pitched whine, almost a devilish scream. For a second Matthew thought *helicopter*, but then he knew the sound of a helicopter; this wasn't it.

Is this what she's talking about?

"What in the hell is up there?" Matthew yelled, looking skyward. A blast of warmer air hit his face and he was forced to close his eyes for a moment. All around, it was getting darker. He could feel, rather than see, a gigantic indistinguishable presence descending towards them.

Sky grabbed his arm and for the first time since they'd met, he saw fear on her face. Abruptly she dropped his arm and dove for her .30-30 in the scabbard. She plucked it out and rolled over the seat of her snowmobile coming to rest on her back in the snow with the rifle pointed upwards. He saw her levering a shell into the firing chamber. Whatever was over them had to be huge to be making this sound; a crippling shot could bring it down on both of them.

"NO!" he yelled, dropping his helmet and rushing around the machine towards her. He dived on top of Sky knocking the rifle aside as it discharged.

"Stop Matthew, let go!" she screamed, trying to dislodge him. "They're here...they're not supposed to be here!"

Matthew stayed on top of her pinning the rifle between them. As they struggled, he twisted around and saw a dark triangular shadow come partially into view overhead. Just as quickly it vanished from sight in the blowing snow.

What in the hell?

"Please Matthew, let me up...let me up!" Sky screamed.

He realized she was past being reasoned with; she was terrified.

"Sky, we're okay...we're okay!" he yelled back as she fought gamely against his weight, her beautiful eyes wide, her lips open. He could feel her whole body trembling through multiple layers of clothing as they struggled.

She looked desperately at him, finally realizing she was helpless. Tears of frustration and fear spilled onto her cheeks. He had never, in all his life, seen such horror on another person's face.

He didn't know what to do to calm her down but he desperately wanted to comfort her, to subdue this apparent dread and to make everything better for her. She was in full panic mode still trying to twist beneath him, to crawl away.

Then, without any clearly planned course of action, both logic and rational thought seemed to flee with the wind. There was nothing to lose now. He gave in to a natural impulse that was something totally out of character for him.

The whistle had grown into a deafening shriek; wind and snow beat down on his back, and all visibility was lost in a virtual vortex of white.

He looked at Sky underneath him and leaned down and kissed her. He kissed her softly and then kissed her with more urgency. She resisted at first. Then he felt her relax and she was kissing him back just as hard. The noise stopped for him, the wind died to nothing and every sense was tuned to the warm softness of her mouth.

Peace…

Silence…

Calm….

And then, as though sharing a mutual cue, they broke apart, gasping for air.

The screaming shriek was back, the wind was buffeting them and snow and ice pellets were being driven downward and ricocheting off their bodies. He rolled off her taking the rifle with him and squinted upward at what was casting a giant shadow on the snow. The mass darkened their world, bringing a sense of impending doom.

Slowly, a strange, other-worldly shadow came into view. It was black as the night and looked like someone had imposed a triangular shape over the outline of a manta ray with two angled shapes towards the back and a sharp nose. The craft had ceased descending and hovered menacingly over them; its details were obscured mostly by blowing snow with an array of lights barely confirming its shape. The adrenaline from the past few seconds was fleeing from their muscles now and neither Sky nor Matthew could move. They lay on their backs staring upward at the massive object. But, for Matthew, his air force training imposed on him the reality of what they were actually seeing.

"F…"Mathew gasped. "F….F–"

"Go ahead, say it!" Sky said, resisting her instinct to finish the expletive for him, her attention fully centered on the huge shape less than fifty feet above them.

"N-no…no…F…F-35 Lightning," he finally choked out.

Squinting through the maelstrom at the VTOL stealth jet, they could make out the helmet and visor of the pilot looking at them as he tilted his aircraft nose down. He wasn't going to do a vertical landing after all. His gloved hand came up, made a circular motion and then pointed behind him. The plane slowly pivoted towards where he had pointed a moment before. It vanished in the blowing snow again and then reappeared. Slowly it began to move away.

Atemu jumped from his perch and raced up to them. He licked Sky's face, turned, licked Matthew's face and then went back to her. He then dashed away directly under where the aircraft was moving. He ran back again, his tail wagging so hard it made a circle. He barked frantically.

"We have to follow him," Sky shouted at the same time Matthew also realized what they had to do. The aircraft was getting harder to see in the wall of snow as it moved away. He leaped up, pulled Sky to her feet and shoved the carbine at her. "Let's go!"

He ran back towards his snowmobile, barely hearing hers start over the whistle of the aircraft. She was beginning to move but looked back through the blizzard to make sure he was coming. He started his machine, twisted the throttle and raced towards her. Seeing him coming, she darted ahead. As he approached where she'd been, he spotted something silver in the snow. It was his helmet. He didn't slow at all. Racing by the helmet, he bent down and scooped it up like a rodeo rider. He tucked it forward of his lap as he steered.

Mindful of Sky's advice, he didn't get too close to her as they rode. Though they couldn't see the aircraft anymore, the whistle of its engines was still all around them. Thankfully Atemu could sense which way it was moving. Sky and Matthew followed him as he ran ahead.

With an icy wind cutting into his face, he wished he had his helmet on but there was no time for that. Then he realized he didn't need the severe visual restrictions it placed on the wearer. If anything, he needed to use every one of his senses just to stay alive. And, sight was a primary one.

There were now chilling expanses of black water on both sides of them as they roared along on an ice-path barely 15-feet-wide. Every moment or two, on one side or the other, the wind gusts would force ice flows to collide and rear up while geysers of water exploded into the air with massive booms sounding like whales exhaling. The water geysers soon lost their upward momentum and Matthew was hit by the slap of spray raining down on his back and covering him in a watery deluge. Fortunately, before it soaked into his parka, it froze. The wind continued to whip the ocean water into a frenzy, and pieces of ice were breaking off on both sides of them. The width of their escape route was quickly being reduced. He prayed it wouldn't end with black waves ahead waiting to suck them down to an airless grave. Still, they had little choice. They had to trust the pilot.

Matthew glanced at his compass. Their heading was dead on 355 degrees; they were heading north towards the open water Sky had seen earlier. More ice buckled on his right, sank under the black water and then reared back up. Geysers sprayed into the air with hisses…

…On his left.

…And, yet again on his right.

Explosions came from near and far. The gusts sent massive ocean waves under the ice to lift it, fracture it and drop it hard with the ebb; the buildup of pressure and release brought cracks, rifts and havoc everywhere.

Abruptly Atemu stumbled, then scrambled to his feet, and altered his course 90 degrees to the left. Sky and Matthew followed him, steering towards 270 degrees as they continued racing forward. He could barely make out her red taillight through the snow, and only occasionally glimpsed her looking back to make sure he was still with her. A hundred yards ahead, the aircraft turned a full 360 degrees to check their progress and then moved resolutely forward, disappearing into the blizzard again. Without Atemu, they would have been travelling blind.

Matthew heard a crack loud enough to sound over the roar of his own snowmobile engine and the whistle of the aircraft. He glanced behind in time to see another channel of black water open up. Any attempt to retreat was gone. They'd bet their lives on the mystery aircraft.

So it was full steam ahead.

Or drown.

By now Matthew had lost sight of Sky and Atemu so he concentrated on keeping his snowmobile in the middle of the ice path and away from the water on either side.

His heart pounded as he bent low, squinting through the driving snow. A three-foot expanse of black water suddenly opened up ahead of him. There was no choice; he gunned it and breathed a sigh of relief as his snowmobile hit the water and its momentum allowed him to water-ski safely over the break.

Suddenly, over the wind and the jet's engines, he heard a shrill scream. Had Sky and Atemu gone into the water? Her snowmobile would go down like a rock. His heartbeat accelerated with fear. "Jesus, stay afloat…stay afloat!" he screamed aloud, in desperation.

The realization that he might have lost her was unbearable and he felt the same type of fear he had experienced so long ago as a boy when two RCAF officers pounded on their door to tell his mother that his father had crashed.

With growing dread, Matthew twisted his throttle to full speed; he had to reach them before they went completely under. His machine roared ahead. Seconds later it was only his quick reflexes that saved him from a head-on collision with a snow-covered boulder. He managed to swerve to the right just in time. Then his snowmobile's nose pointed skyward and he found himself climbing a small hill. He powered through a frozen bush, its branches snatching the ice off his parka.

Land…land…land! Dear, sweet, precious, wonderful land!

They made it.

He backed the throttle off to zero speed. His machine came to an abrupt halt throwing him painfully against the steering bars. Further up the rise, he saw Sky and Atemu. She was off her machine and had her arms in the air waving at the jet pilot. The downdraft from the VTOL aircraft was still creating an intense snow storm around her but she seemed not to notice. He could hear her yelling: "Thank you…oh…thank you!"

The F-35 Lightning, nose tipped down, with the USAF emblems on the underside of its wings, did a full celebratory rotation. He could make out the pilot giving them a thumbs up, white teeth showing below his green helmet visor as he grinned. Then the tenor of his engine increased to a deafening scream and his aircraft ascended straight up into the storm. In a second he was out of sight like a mystical guardian angel; mission accomplished. A moment later, far overhead, the whine turned to a thunderous roar. Though they couldn't see it, he knew the aircraft was streaking away. Within ten seconds, there was no sound except the continued howling of the wind.

Matthew gave the throttle a little gas and coasted up beside Sky and Atemu. The dog ran up to him and he grabbed his fur and pulled him close. He gave him a big kiss on the muzzle, and received a lick in return.

Who cares about doggie germs!

"Good dog," Matthew said. "Good boy! You may not have saved Timmy from the well but you saved us from a worse fate. You knew what to do before we did."

"He's smooching everybody today, isn't he, Atemu?" It was Sky approaching from ahead of him. "Maybe we'll call him *Smoocher* from now on," she added.

Matthew looked at her, his face going red. For a moment he wanted to apologize, to mention she had kissed him back. Instead he decided to leave it alone. The storm was calming down and they stared at each other, neither saying a word. He became aware his heart was running amok again; he was experiencing feelings he hadn't felt in years. Finally, though a smile played briefly at the corner of her lips, her words were like a dash of cold water full in the face. "Remember what I said, Matthew. Getting close to me would be a big mistake." She turned away and began arranging Atemu's travelling bed on her sled.

Anxious to change the subject, Matthew gave Atemu a final hug and stood up. "That was a close one."

"Where did he come from?" she asked, continuing to work on the sled contents since they appeared to have shifted.

"I don't know but he saved our lives."

More suspiciously she said: "And, how did he know where we were in this storm?"

"As a former air force guy I keep up with military aircraft and their capabilities," Matthew replied. "The F-35 has an Electro-Optical Targeting System. Its sensor has forward-looking infrared, and an infrared search and track functionality. We would have shown up as two…actually three…heat signatures on the ice. Three heat signatures in a lot of trouble."

"American."

"Yeah. Had to be out of Goose Bay. Sometimes low-level flight training isn't all bad, is it?" He raised his eyebrows.

She turned and gave him a look. "No," she agreed reluctantly. "Sometimes it isn't."

* * *

"Saglek Control, Foxtrot Echo zero one, they're safe, sir," Captain Heldenbrand radioed as he pulled his F-35 into a right turn and headed out over Big Island. A few moments later, he turned onto his base leg in preparation for landing at Saglek. With the blowing snow he still couldn't see much, so it was strictly IFR all the way, and an instrument landing to look forward to as well. Again he thanked the air force gods for coughing up the dough to install an Instrument Landing System (ILS) in Saglek.

"Foxtrot Echo zero one, Saglek Control, thank you, Captain. We have you on approach. Other traffic also in-bound, in trail, over," the controller radioed. He was letting the pilot know the drone tracking Sky and Matthew was coming in to land behind him so he should clear the runway A-SAP.

Heldenbrand turned onto his final approach and began his descent. The aircraft bucked and slewed sideways but he managed the rudder pedals and quickly brought it back into alignment for an almost perfect approach. He placed the aircraft in a 20-degree crab to counter a heavy crosswind as the flashing ILS guided him down, a life-saving beacon in the snowstorm. At the last moment, with the array in sight taking him to the end of the runway, he straightened the aircraft and with one wing slightly down to address the cross-wind, the F-35 touched down. Behind him he knew the drone was also lining up. It had helped guide him to where he could pick up the figures on the ice on his own sensor.

As he turned onto the taxiway he knew exactly when the Avenger touched down because the array and runway lights were immediately switched off as per a previous notification. Soon the base would be locked down and they'd all be hiding in their holes like rats. Weird assignment or what?

Within a few minutes Heldenbrand was taxing into the hangar where his plane would be sequestered. He marveled at the dozens of drones crowded inside, nose-to-nose and tail-to-tail. They would also remain behind locked doors; not a single aircraft nor any other vehicle would be visible on the base.

The orders were clear. Not one door would be unlocked, not a single electric light bulb would be on, and all generators would be turned off. In anticipation, thermostats had been turned up to 95 degrees to build up heat in the domiciles and hangars; no-one seemed to have any idea of how long the lock-down would last. If Command knew, they weren't saying. During this time, not a single soul was allowed to be within sight of a window and a minimum amount of movement was stipulated. If anyone positively had to use the can, they walked quietly to it in their socks. And no flushing, yellow or brown.

In fact, Heldenbrand knew at this moment most base personnel were already in their bunks. Ground crew were hurrying towards him in the hangar as he removed his helmet and prepared to disembark from his jet.

In his office, Colonel Moorhead was very happy. Despite almost dooming their two subjects, the storm couldn't have come at a better time. Snow was covering all tire tracks on the runway as well as footprints or any other sign of habitation. To anyone approaching from outside, this would be a ghost base, reactivated at some time obviously, but now deserted.

Moorhead watched his battery-driven clock on his office wall. Major Stone sat in front of his desk watching him watch the clock. Not a word was exchanged. The time hit 1200 hours and all the white noise delivered by heat ventilators, fluorescent lights, computers and printers and shredders ceased. No buzz, no hum, no idling of any type of electronics permeated the air. Total silence and darkness for one second. At that point, a pre-selected series of battery-driven emergency lights clicked on, one in Moorhead's office since it did not feature an outside window.

"Let there be light," Stone said, dryly.

"It's just till they pass," Moorhead assured him. "St. Onge isn't a stupid woman. There's every chance she might figure out why we're up here."

"Smarter than me, obviously," Stone shot back. Then added: "Sir."

"Major...Paul, I've been involved in the genesis of this operation. First on the periphery and in later years, almost full time. You were brought into this mission because you have expert organizational skills from early in your career. You always found a way to get things done, to source equipment, get crews to do overtime to meet schedules, and ingenious ways to skirt approvals if necessary. If you were asked to set up and equip an outpost in Siberia, everyone knew you'd find a way. And you did a great job spearheading the revival of this base."

"I didn't do it alone, Bob."

"Of course not. But like always, you got it done. Now we are going to access skills from your latter years. In fact, once my work is almost done here, yours will be just beginning."

"How so?" Stone asked, hoping this time to get a full answer.

Moorhead sighed, a sure sign he wasn't about to reveal all. "Look, your current specialty is foreign technology, correct?"

"That's right."

"And, you've talked to your predecessors in the job."

Stone nodded.

"What about old guys? Guys from the 50s or 60s and beyond?"

"Sure I've talked to some of them, the ones still alive," Stone admitted. "Mostly when I'd be handed something I didn't recognize, I'd consult with them. If it was straightforward stuff like who could make the best use of a piece of a crashed Chinese jet or the parts of a fire control system from a MIG 29, I could handle that. But they always seemed to know who would benefit most from these strange pieces of gear I used to get. They'd advise me on who could look outside the box and leverage new applications from what I received; who should get A or B piece...or both pieces; who was the best company to back-engineer the strangest looking circuit board I'd ever seen? Stuff like that."

Moorhead nodded. "Did they talk about the products they handed industry in years gone by? Stuff that kept us just that much more ahead of our enemies?"

"No. Just *how* they did it."

"Right. Well, like you, those old guys were sworn to secrecy and they took that stuff seriously. They were handing our military contractors remnants recovered from crashes: pieces of burnt plastic that weren't plastic; strange glass wires; mangled wafers that contained so many circuits that even a scanning, tunneling microscope couldn't count them; cracked and broken pieces of optics; and, other stuff that looked, most often, like it had been pulverized by a wrecking ball. And then there were the organic pieces nobody has figured out yet."

"I know. Lots of rumors but nobody would pinpoint where this stuff came from," Stone said. "I heard it originated with the Nazis, Atlantis, Stonehenge, the Egyptian Pyramids, Area 51, the Bermuda Triangle, and crashed spaceships...pretty much the whole spectrum of nonsense."

"So they never really revealed the source?" Moorhead said.

"Nope. Said they didn't know. But I knew they were lying. They said they passed stuff on to Raytheon, General Dynamics, McDonnel Douglas, Northrop Grumman and United Technologies to name a few. The idea then – like now – was to salt the military industrial complex with what looked like evidence of new technologies so they could exploit, improve, or innovate from them. Eventually they'd hand the

Pentagon something they could use. And this technology often gave our military a definable lead in product weaponization.

"Eventually these technologies were declassified, and found their way into the private sector generating new commercial products including fiber optics, micro-circuitry, nanotechnology, night vision and more. The leap forward in the 60s, 70s, 80s and 90s was tremendous."

"Right," Moorhead said. "Cut to today. You know we aren't discovering or recovering new technologies at the pace we did in the past. And now, more than ever, we need to develop the next generation of weaponry. Consider this: the Middle East is still a tinder box, even after 3,000 years of murdering each other; Ukraine is in civil war over rejoining Russia; anarchy, as usual, rules Africa; and, Iran is still trying to go nuclear despite our latest agreement. And let's not even talk about the Red Chinese. We don't know what those mothers are doing except holding too much of our debt, accepting all our jobs, and creating the largest military force in the world. Hell, soon we'll all be eating egg rolls every day and worshiping Confucius."

Stone chuckled. "I think Confucius was a philosopher, not a deity. So what's next? Are we up here merely to follow the St. Onge girl and see if she disappears like her grandfather?"

"You're smarter than that, Paul," Moorhead answered. "But this stuff is above Top Secret." He paused: "Not time to open up yet. However, let me tell you what I can."

"Do tell," Stone answered.

"Okay. As you know, the importance we attach to the Air Defense Identifications Zone has waxed and waned according to the political state of the world. Since 9/11 we've been looking at it more closely. And this new attention highlighted how many intrusions we've actually been experiencing off Labrador, though it's mostly wilderness. I mean NORAD saw them, you understand. But they were there and gone before we could blink. And we couldn't afford to scramble interceptors for every transgression. We knew by the time we got there, all we'd find would be a memory."

"Understood," Stone said. "The Russians have been getting more aggressive in their demands for sovereignty in parts of the Arctic we always assumed belonged to North America. They've been flying in and out and pushing their seeming dominance."

"Yes...them too," Moorhead said, enigmatically.

Just as Stone was about to comment further, a light on the colonel's phone lit up. He picked it up and listened for a moment. "Damn," he said. "I was hoping they'd by-pass us but they're headed right for the base."

~3~

Major General Sergei Topkolov looked around the oak conference table at the six other representatives of the *General Staff of the Armed Forces of the Russian Federation*. All held a general's rank of varying levels. As head of the task force charged with *Operation Phoenix*, the study of the reactivation of the Saglek Harbour base, General Topkolov had selected reps from the: Main Operational Directorate; Main Intelligence Directorate; Main Command – Ground Troops; Main Command – Air Forces; Airborne Troops Command; and, Main Organizational Mobilization Directorate. Coupled with his six choices were numerous Military of Defence staff overseers in the form of Advisors to the Defence Ministry. While their contributions were few, they would record and report everything that happened in their meetings directly to the Minister.

For the past week, the *Phoenix* task force had sat in the General Staff's main conference room on Znamenka Street in the Arbat Military District of Moscow. They actually worked together to explore reams of intelligence data secured by: satellite, ground based operations, radar transcripts, telecommunications intercepts, US Defence computer system intrusion, stealth overflights, and, other surveillance methods seldom openly discussed. For this operation they had even activated a sleeper agent who flew up to Nain, Labrador, and nosed around to glean what he could.

Topkolov was actually amazed at the cooperation that had taken place between the General Staff and the Russian Ministry of Defence whose bureaucratic battles were legendary since the breakup of the Soviet Union. Many times, over the two weeks, he had wondered if someone had slipped Prozac into the water jugs to effect such a spirit of openness, cooperation, and harmony.

Now, near the end of their session, he had finally come to the conclusion they were all in good humor because they were preparing an operation they understood, one against their old adversary: the United States of America.

The Chechen, Georgian and Ukraine operations – where Russia should have been welcomed rather than scorned and hated – hadn't made sense to any Russian, let alone a military high command used to kicking butt and sending people away trembling from a single hard look.

This adversary, however, they knew. This adversary they trusted. At least, they trusted it to operate in a traditional and defined fashion. It had never changed its spots. It continued to present an imperialistic-based foreign policy while preaching choice, freedom and democracy in a schizophrenic schism that brought great comfort to the Russian High Command. This was an enemy who wasn't even embarrassed about invading such featherweights as: Panama, Grenada or Haiti. The more unofficial invasions (backed by the US government) such as Cuba and a cornucopia of South American regimes, might not be outright invasions, but they certainly involved financing and arming so-called "civilian" freedom fighters or clandestinely toppling heads of state.

In fact, officially the US had invaded or bombed 22 countries in the last 20 years, and yet went ape-shit when Russia rightfully tried to reclaim Ukraine as part of its Federation. And as for the Crimea, the majority of its citizens were Russian anyhow and wanted to rejoin their mother country.

That must be it, Topkolov surmised. They're slapping each other's backs like old comrades, and passing sandwiches back and forth because they are finally allowed to mix it up with their old, familiar and very predictable enemy.

Who said: "War is hell?"

The ultimate findings of the task force wasn't what he had expected. In fact, the scenario they put together had many possibilities. Still, once they added up all the data, the events, the actions and the current operations in progress, the most likely conclusion was the US military was preparing to attack someone. And, that someone resided on Canadian soil.

As outrageous as it sounded, the idea of *who* they intended to attack on Canadian soil was even more outrageous. So the task force needed two things: confirmation that what might appear to be nonsensical was, indeed, sensible and accurate. And two, a way to stop the American mission. If they were right, a successful outcome for the Americans could once again tip the balance of power in favor of the West.

The decision of the *Operation Phoenix* task force was unanimous: irrefutable proof could only come from close-up, clandestine surveillance, which, in turn, translated into boots on the ground in Labrador. It would be a high-risk mission at best. And if these boots confirmed their findings, outrageous though they be, then they had no choice other than to prevent the US from successfully completing its mission.

At all costs.

* * *

The *Phoenix Team* of three Spetsnaz, Special Forces paratroopers, rose as one from their seats in the lurching IL-76 transport aircraft and shuffled towards the open ramp where a black, wintry sky awaited them.

Once the twin doors had been opened, the temperature inside the aircraft had immediately plummeted into sub-zero figures. The thunder of the four turbofan engines filled the cabin. Almost in competition, the wind moaned like a tortured fiend waiting somewhere below in the chasm of the Canadian night.

The jumpmaster, who stood beside the open ramp longer than anyone else, was clothed in a full-body, insulated suit, hood and full plastic facemask to prevent frostbite. He kept his gloved hand up, while staring intently at the red, amber and green signal light on the aircraft wall. Only the red light glowed at this point.

The men had to jump at a precise time, and land on a precise patch of shore ice selected from satellite photos taken that day. They could only hope that what had been photographed was still in position. Once their chutes opened, they would each drop a five-second flare to aid in their landing.

If they missed the patch of ice they were aiming for, they could well wind up dropping into the water and freezing to death in the Labrador Sea.

Being a low altitude jump, each man's static-line was clipped to a metal wire. Once they stepped into space, their chutes would deploy immediately and the latest Arbalet-2 Special Parachute System would guide their drop from a mere 700 feet altitude. Their three Canadian-sourced snowmobiles and supplies would then plunge after them. The second everything had been dumped out the door, the aircraft would then drop back down to 100 feet and employ its sophisticated autopilot to run for international waters while hugging the surface terrain. In this case it would be the ocean.

Dimitri Onegin, 29, was the first paratrooper in line. He was a blond, blue-eyed, baby-faced, cold-blooded killer who had long been diagnosed as a sociopath. His Canadian name was now *Wolfgang Schaeffer* for all intents and purposes; he would not answer to any other name while in character. He spoke flawless English with a northern Canadian inflection. His ID identified him as a second generation German-Canadian born in Sudbury, Ontario. Despite his social character flaws, he was also a qualified physicist. Indeed, if anyone could blow up the world and feel guiltless, it would be Wolfgang. His other strengths included a fierce dedication to duty and a mission focus that had always bordered on the obsessive. He didn't fear death because his ego simple could not conceptualize his own demise.

He was followed by Pietro Perezhogin, 23. His Canadian name was *Allan Hoover* and he'd supposedly been born in Calgary, Alberta. His English contained a distinct twang and cowboy idioms that most Canadians would associate with the western province.

His specialty was Advanced Chemistry and he knew exactly what made the *99-Rasplavleniye* tick and how fast it would kill them all. However, he was nothing, if not a loyal Russian. Orphaned at an early age he'd been raised by his grandparents. And after listening all his life to their tales of the murder, rape and torture committed by Axis troops invading Stalingrad during WW II, he was willing to make the ultimate sacrifice. Never again would a foreign power gain the upper hand and send troops onto Russian soil. His grandparents were gone now and he told the psychologist examining him that he had no living relatives and no wife or girlfriend. He was an ideal candidate. And, if this mission was so important the Federation was willing to lose three soldiers to complete it, then he would be proud to be one of them.

The oldest member of their troop, Ivan Medvedkov, 38, was motivated by his personal demons that had included alcoholism, drug use and a latent homosexuality. More than once he had been put on notice by the military. He was saved again and again because of his formidable martial arts abilities and his amazing shooting skills. They had wanted to send him to a special sniper unit, however, he threatened to leave the forces if they did so. It would have driven him crazy to remain motionless for hours in the confines of a "Ghillie" suit, awaiting a target.

His Canadian name was *Yves Legrand* and he now spoke English with a French accent. He could also speak French with all the Quebec inflexions and slang handed down from the early Habitant settlers. His cover was as a Montagnais guide from Labrador West taking two environmental tourists into Torngat National Park. His Slavic features were perfect for the job. His specialty was computer science and they hoped to be able to electronically eavesdrop on the American base. Of the three men, he was the one who almost didn't make the team.

The psychologist who interviewed him wanted to know why he was willing to die for Mother Russia. He had simply told her it was his sworn duty to do so. Soldiers did it all the time on the battlefield. Why the big fuss? She had probed and prodded him until she was blue in the face but couldn't find evidence of a death wish or any other form of psychosis or neurosis that might compromise the mission. He stressed his love of country and that he was a loyal Communist Party member. Period. When he tired of her game, he had turned the tables and asked how a psychiatrist could argue with his motivations, unless she was ideologically compromised herself?

He was quickly given a pass.

Formerly of the 76th Guards Air Assault division, the three men had all known each other for more than three years in the service. No blue berets tonight, however. Each one was clothed in a Sun Ice, North Face or Sears Logan Hill Parka. Even their undergarments were Canadian: Stanfield's unshrinkable underwear, complete with "drop seat." Hard to get more Canadian than that.

"Prigptov'sya!" the jumpmaster yelled at the three men.

"Speak fucking English to me," Wolfgang Schaeffer screamed.

"Da," the jumpmaster answered. "Get ready, Comrades!"

"Jesus Christ," Wolfgang answered. "Comrades!? What a tool."

His companion jumpers grinned at him and readied themselves. The before-jump drill had been explained to them, so they bent their knees slightly, steeled themselves and waited.

Within a few seconds the huge aircraft suddenly clawed its way upward to 700 feet putting enormous pressure on everyone standing. Once they hit their altitude, the red light went directly to green.

"Go, go, go!" the jumpmaster shouted, chopping his hand downward as the three men trotted forward awkwardly, packsacks swinging loosely between their knees.

Without hesitation they jumped into the black void and were gone.

Two cargo wranglers immediately pushed three wooden crates on rollers out the back door. Static lines attached to the crate chutes would deploy the large parachutes as soon as the crates were clear of the aircraft. Unfortunately neither the crew, nor the jumpers, would be able to see if the chutes had all opened.

The hydraulics on the back doors whined. Even as the doors closed, the jumpmaster and cargo crew felt their stomachs lurch again as the aircraft plunged back down to 100 feet; the engines then opened up on full throttle.

They had probably been at 700 feet for less than 45 seconds. If all had gone as planned, NORAD radar had not picked them up. Or simply slotted them as one of the frequent and strange "unidentified" blips they were used to seeing. After all, in the past these radar blips had become almost commonplace, both in North America, and rest of the world. The Americans had seen them, the Russians had seen them, and surely even the Chinese had seen them. Not to mention the Belgians, English, Germans, Swiss, Iranians, Saudis, Africans and Australians.

These radar returns were unpredictable and unidentifiable and, so far, the Russian military had been unable to intercept them. And, surely, that went for the rest of their world neighbors as well.

Hopefully a 45-second radar blip would seem minor compared to the usual strangeness of the Torngat Mountains.

* * *

After raiding one of the St. Onge fuel caches, filling up and then replacing empties with full 10-gallon jerry cans on the sleds, Sky and Matthew were proceeding single-file through blowing snow. The storm had calmed only slightly and they stayed as close to the shoreline as possible to avoid the sharp slope of the mountains now rising beside them. Both were shivering, despite their insulated clothing.

While the ice on the bay extended out quite far, their height on the land delivered the advantage of being able to see the center portion of Saglek Bay; it was open water so far. The season was still early so they had to proceed west and further up the bay, prior to being able to cross. Once on the north shore of the bay, they'd head east, and then north up the Labrador coast.

Drawing close to where Sky knew the old Saglek military radar base had existed, she wondered what shape it would be in now. The last time she had been here was more than a decade ago.

As a defunct base, she was also aware that the only time the airstrip was now used was in summer to bring in eco-tourists with a desire to hike and fish in the Great White North. Though there were still some older buildings, most of the radar equipment, and anything else of value, had likely been removed.

Indeed, the last time the area had seen any form of occupancy was in the 1990s. That was when the joint Canadian-US base had undergone a thorough cleanup of PCBs which had seeped from transformers and other equipment into the ground during the base's 20-year life.

It was only after significant levels of PCBs had been found in groundwater, as well as in local birds and fish living around old arctic military bases, that alarms had gone off.

Government clean-up crews then flew up to Saglek where they worked until they reduced PCB readings from 1,120 parts per billion (PPB) to less than 77 PPB, a level considered relatively safe in the civilized world.

Other, similar defunct bases in the subarctic and the Arctic were also mandated to be cleaned up. The contamination hadn't been deliberate; it was simply a matter of the occupiers of the base, and those who worked in many other pristine environments, having no idea of the extent of the damage their chemicals could do to a land they thought was inexhaustible.

As a teen-ager, Sky remembered a summer ride up the coastline on their old 32-foot Boston Whaler all the way to Saglek Harbour with her grandfather. They went ashore and watched the crews excavating more than 20,000 cubic meters of PCB laden soil around the upper and lower base for chemical and incendiary destruction. Some of it would be destroyed there while other waste would be shipped out to safe disposal sites in the south. Her grandfather wanted to impress on her the sacredness of their land and how it was finite.

He had looked at her and said: "Princess, where the white man goes, he often harms the earth. He considers it, the air and the oceans and lakes inexhaustible, and so he throws his waste into them. Then he is surprised to find the waste makes the land, the water, animals and the fish and the fowl sick.

"We, the Innu and Inuit, have a sacred trust to respect the land and the wildlife on which we depend for our sustenance. We never take more game than we can eat. We never cut more wood than we need for shelter or fire. We never exploit and damage the earth where we live. We look for balance and harmony to please the Creator. In turn, the Creator keeps us safe and our cooking pots full."

And Sky had innocently asked: "Do the white man not want balance and harmony too, Grandfather? Do they not want to please the Creator?"

"Their god is a strange god," her grandfather had said. "They seem to do everything to please their god. In fact, this god trumps all, and they do unspeakable things to each other and to the land in the name of it. Their bases leave poison. Their mining rips up the ground. And our Innu brothers in the west tell of logging practices stripping mountaintops bare so the wind blows the topsoil away and nothing ever grows again. They murder the land and then sometimes try to fix what they have destroyed."

"Why, Grandfather, why?" She asked, the distress so obvious on her young face.

"For Profit, little one. For the one god the white man worships above all else: one they call Profit."

Three months later, from when the cleanup began, the base was declared safe; silence and the purity of the North was returned to Saglek Harbour.

Matthew's earphones in his helmet crackled. Sky was about to transmit to him.

"There it is," she radioed from ahead, standing up on the running boards of her machine.

They had come round a bend and travelled up a small hill where she stopped and stared through binoculars towards the old military base. It was situated on a bluff overlooking the entrance to Saglek Harbour. The most dominant feature usually was the ball-like radar dome. She could barely make it out through the blowing snow.

Matthew caught up to her and stopped his snowmobile parallel to hers. She handed him the binoculars and he pulled up his goggles and adjusted the focus. From the angle they were at, he could make out the peaks of roofs and the dome.

"We'll head over there and then use their trails to go down to the lower base," she said.

"Lower base?" he asked.

"The base is split into two sections. Up there where the radar unit was positioned for best coverage, and down below where it was viable enough – meaning flat – to build an airstrip. Come on."

She popped the binoculars into their case and off they went. They were travelling cross-country now making for the old base. They soon bypassed it, a group of dilapidated buildings and started down a hill towards where the airstrip should be. Of course there were no longer any roads visible with the snow so deep, but the trail Sky chose was relatively smooth. No rocks stuck through the windswept snow on the slope.

As they travelled down she seemed to be standing higher and higher on her machine, peering ahead as though puzzled. Finally she stopped. Once again he pulled up beside her.

"What's the matter?" he shouted.

She yanked off her helmet and gave him a look.

"Sorry" he said, realizing he had shouted in her ear via the radio.

"What's going on down there?" she asked, perplexed. She pointed down the hill into the small valley. Then, unwinding the carrying strip from the binoculars, she took a good look and shook her head in wonder. He could just make out multiple buildings. She handed him the binoculars. He changed the focus again and inspected the area.

First he saw a long, flat uninterrupted surface with snowbanks. It was obviously a runway. At its end was a gleaming aluminum antenna array. Also, midway off the strip was a two-storey building with a third storey raised center portion that had to be the base control tower. But there were many other buildings as well. And, contrary to what he expected, none of the buildings looked old and faded. Rather than being warped by time and exposure, with peeling and chipped paint like the "upper base," the wood and aluminum buildings seemed pristine and freshly painted. He scanned further.

There were also *two* gleaming white geodesic radomes on formidable and very high pedestals overlooking the bay area. Obviously they must house radar antennas. And, in various locations near the apron of the runway, four substantive, white aluminum hangars were parked; they looked brand new.

On the other side of the main building there were five, long prefab structures that could only be military personnel barracks. He knew this from having flown into, or having lived on Canadian military bases across Canada. These buildings were lined up parallel to the runway but slightly behind the main building.

A series of other outbuildings and eight large, round, silver fuel tanks completed the picture. The barracks, three hangars and the main buildings, topped by what was obviously an Air Traffic Control Tower, were all connected by a series of battleship-grey painted, box-like wooden tunnels

"All this wasn't here when I visited years ago," Sky said. "They were cleaning up spilled base chemicals long after closing it. They must have opened it again."

"Looks new," Matthew agreed. "But it also looks deserted. Where are the aircraft? Where are the people? Even in this weather there should be some activity."

"Let's take a quick look," Sky said.

They gunned their machines and in ten minutes were pulling up in front of the three-story Air Traffic Control Tower building.

Off to one side, a lanyard rhythmically clanged in the wind against the side of a bare flag pole, its chimes the only sound in the morning air.

Sky checked what appeared to be a main entrance to the building but it was locked. They checked the hangars, also locked. The outbuildings and barracks, silent and locked. Even the refueling nozzles on the fuel storage tanks were locked down with shiny, new padlocks. Not a soul appeared to occupy what was obviously a brand new base.

They looked at the roofs but not one metal chimney or any of the other multiple exhaust pipes gave forth any hint of smoke or steam. There was not a single light on outside the buildings, and no generators hummed inside. Sky and Matthew looked at one another. They said nothing though both felt something was wrong with the whole scenario.

They travelled further onto the airstrip and Sky looked up and down and then ran her snowmobile, open throttle, to the south west end. She came back in a few minutes, Atemu riding high on the sled, his tongue hanging out. "This runway is definitely longer," she said. "And I dug up some snow down there. They widened it. And here they added a long taxiway. But, why?"

"Right and it's been plowed recently," Matthew said, observing the snow banks bordering the strip. Everything was now covered with an unblemished coating of newly fallen snow. No tire tracks nor any other sign of life.

Sky dismounted and dropped to her knees. Gently she blew aside the cover of newly fallen snow until she reached the well-packed base. She then widened her dig and exposed multiple tire tracks wedged in the snow. She ran her fingers along the ridges. "These are fairly fresh," she said. "Hours old, I'd say."

They rode their machines further around the base, and down a road to a burned out garbage dump, also cold and pristine with newly fallen snow covering it. Underneath were fresh ashes.

They returned to the main building. More and more it was beginning to feel eerie, if not downright post-apocalyptic.

"Now why would they set up a base, construct brand new buildings and install new radar equipment if they aren't going to man it full time?" Sky asked, completely puzzled.

"Many of the Pinetree Line radar sites in the 60s and 70s were automated," he said. "The only personnel going there were Marconi technicians for maintenance."

"Did they have barracks built beside them?" Sky asked. She knew a barracks when she saw one. "Maybe there's still some Northern Warning Radar here....but all this?" She swept her hand around.

"Good point," Matthew said, nodding.

He knew many of the old sites were essentially a radar tower with a hut containing bunks and a small kitchen. The Canadian Marconi technician, along with a cook, would arrive by RCAF helicopter to the remote station, perform the required maintenance and be retrieved within a few days. Most sites were eventually automated and then some closed as satellite capabilities made them obsolete. Still, the DEW line, the Mid-Canada line and the Pinetree line had been critical during the Cold War.

Sky and Matthew were now parked on the ramp in front of the control tower looking around at the deserted post.

"Is this where the F-35 came from?" Sky wondered aloud.

"I don't know," Matthew replied. "But you don't launch an aircraft like that from a closed base. He must have originated from Goose."

"This whole place feels strange," she said, motioning Atemu off the sled. "I can feel a 'presence' here and yet it's all locked up."

Atemu raced for the door of the tower building and began sniffing and scratching at its base. With no results he finally wandered off down the building to a corner where a connecting tunnel made an alcove. He raised his leg.

"I think Atemu is expressing an esteemed opinion," Matthew said.

"Then we'll act on it," Sky declared, smiling.

The dog rejoined them and they headed west along the shore, hoping to soon encounter solid bay ice farther up the fiord.

~4~

That evening they chose to stay on the south side of the West Arm of Saglek Bay. The fiord featured huge mountains, formidable, ice-encrusted rocky giants devoid of vegetation or other signs of life; they swept down out of low clouds to frame the bay in an icy embrace that likely wouldn't let up until early June of the next year. Much to Sky's relief, they had finally found a solid ice bridge extending across the bay.

They began unloading their supplies for the night. The sun had already sunk behind the mountains as they unpacked. The wind had decreased slightly but remained just strong enough to complicate pitching their tent.

After setting up camp, Sky declared they would cross the ice early the next morning to the north side of the fiord; they'd be in the park in hours. "When we hit Cape Territok, we'll head inland until we reach a certain rock fall. Then we'll leave our snowmobiles and cart our supplies into the mountains," she said. "We'll use the fiberglass toboggans first. When the terrain becomes a little…steeper, we'll switch to knapsacks."

She smiled to herself.

"How long before we reach the site where your grandfather found the diamond?" Matthew asked.

"I'm hoping three days."

They fixed supper and ate it in silence, each lost in their own thoughts. Sky tried the satellite phone again but with no result. Though the batteries indicated an almost full charge, and the phone lit up, there was no connection. The night before Matthew had also taken it apart to see if he could find a loose wire or cracked resistor, or some other damage to the microelectronics. Admittedly he was far from a technical wizard; he didn't notice anything obvious. Atemu had finished his supper by now and was inside the tent, likely on Matthew's cot. They began the clean-up ritual, flattening their empty meal pouches, packing them in their plastic storage bag and washing their cups and utensils in the snow and remaining hot water.

What you bring in, you carry out.

The silence was starting to become uncomfortable and Matthew was sure the spontaneous kiss under the jet was the reason for the awkwardness between them. For idle chatter and to keep the lines of communication open, he decided to find out what Sky meant when she screamed out a warning during their recent crisis. "Sky, mind if I ask you something?"

"Go ahead," she said.

He could already feel her defenses going up. Still he pressed on: "When that F-35 was coming down on us, you said something curious." He didn't elaborate on the fact she'd pretty much been in an uncharacteristic meltdown.

"I did?" she answered, not looking at him.

"Yes, you said: 'They're here…. they're not supposed to be here.' What did you mean? *Who* wasn't supposed to be here?"

He noted she stiffened slightly but quickly covered it up by continuing her clean-up. She was packing up the utensils, cups and Atemu's plastic plate, seeming to make herself busier than she needed to be.

"Did I say that?" she finally asked, feigning innocence.

"Yep."

"I suppose I meant…the United States Air Force. This is our

country, after all."

"But we didn't even know what was coming down on us that time. It was just a giant black shadow on the snow."

"I saw it," she said.

"I don't see how," he responded.

"Simple, I was looking up. You, on the other hand, were on top of me and had other things on your mind."

Zing! Bam! One for the Gipper. Now what?

"I'm sorry," he said, lamely.

"That's okay." She said it kindly. "I admit, I lost it. And the kiss did calm me down." She turned away.

"Me too," he said, trying to make light of the whole thing."

After a moment she added: "Despite the circumstances, it was a nice kiss."

For some stupid, adolescent-like reason, Matthew felt a surge of joy at the remark. Then he waited in trepidation for the inevitable and dreaded reminder not to get close to her. It never came. He felt great relief at this and covered by also making himself busy.

He went over to the snowmobiles. They always parked them along the two walls facing the prevailing wind, giving themselves additional insulation. He adjusted the small tarps over each and made sure the bungee cords holding them to the frames were secure. Then he fiddled some more until she moved away. Coming round to the front of the tent again, he found she was already inside. Through the nylon he heard her admonishing the dog about something.

"No Atemu…bad dog! Get out of there. Lie down."

He entered the tent in time for Sky to whirl with a guilty look. Atemu lay in the corner, a picture of innocence with a "who me?" expression on his face.

"What's up?"

"Oh, nothing," Sky replied, quickly.

"Was he into the food?"

"Our spirit dog was into something, that's for sure."

The heater was already lit and they soon crawled into their sleeping bags on the cots. Atemu had curled up on a blanket in the corner. As usual, they didn't pump additional air pressure into the Coleman lantern and so it soon sputtered out. Only the gas heater continued providing a welcome, though modest amount of heat. Matthew had begun leaving his shirt off when he slept, and he started scratching almost immediately. It was as though someone had poured itching powder into his sleeping bag. He tossed. He turned. Still, despite his machinations, the itch remained; it was on his back, on his side, on his legs. He groaned and scratched.

"What's the matter?" Sky asked, out of the darkness.

"I-I don't know. I'm itchy as hell!"

She made a strange muffled sound.

"What?" he asked.

The muffled sound came again.

And then she laughed outright. He couldn't help feeling annoyed since she seemed to be finding immense merriment in his discomfort. More sounds from her bag. It was obvious she was trying to suppress her mirth but not having much luck.

"Again, I ask: What!?" he groused.

After a minute she managed to control herself. "You-you know how Atemu has been sneaking onto your bed before we come inside?"

"Yes."

"I found him *inside* your sleeping bag when I came in a few minutes ago. And, as you can see, he's one hairy mother." She started to giggle and then it erupted fully into peals of laughter.

Dog hair and lots of it.

"Damn," he said, grumpily. He jumped out of the bag and unzipped it in the freezing cold. She got up, still laughing. He soon found himself joining her.

He relit the lantern and together they brushed out his sleeping bag as much as possible. Knowing a superfluous brushing wouldn't do the trick, Sky got a blanket and lined the bag, bade him lie down, folded the blanket over him and zipped it up. Atemu watched innocently from the corner.

"Who the hell would think he'd shed in this weather?" Matthew grumbled.

"He loses hair 24-7 no matter what time of the year it is," she answered. "We'll clean the bag better in the morning and put a bin on it from now on once we set up at night. I can't say 'bad dog' to him; at this point; he'd have no idea what he did wrong."

Unable to fall asleep right away, Matthew heard Sky turn over several times. Knowing she was awake he decided to try some conversation.

"Are you practicing medicine in Nain, Sky?" he asked, hesitantly.

"No," she replied. "But I'm going to have to make some decisions after we get back."

"When did you leave the Royal Vic in Montreal?"

"Last year."

"Why?"

"It's a long story. With an unhappy ending."

"We have lots of time."

She sighed and he could hear her stirring in her bag, deciding. Finally....

"I studied to become a general surgeon and had finished my internship, residency and fellowship," she said. "I was assisting with a routine tonsillectomy on an eight-year-old girl. During the surgery she started to hemorrhage. Everything went very bad, very quickly. The bleeding was acute. This was no easy fix and we called a code. We tried to cauterize it, without success. We couldn't pump blood in her fast enough. She was bleeding out in front of us when she went into cardiac arrest. We couldn't get her back."

"I'm sorry," he said quietly. "Why did she start bleeding?"

"It's called a spontaneous tonsillar hemorrhage. It's rare but it happens. An undetected weakness in a vascular wall."

"So what happened after that?"

"There was a hospital board of inquiry and the surgical team was cleared. All the protocols were followed. They concluded that once it started, there was virtually no way to save the child in the time we had before she crashed."

"So why did you leave?"

"The patient was an Innu girl from Rigolet and her parents were very happy to know that I, also Innu, would be assisting in the surgery. I guess I felt I had let them down. This was a sweet, little eight-year old who wanted nothing more than to go home to play with her dolls. We should have been able to send her home, not to the damn morgue!" The frustration and anger was such that Matthew wished he hadn't started the conversation. He tried to fix things.

"Sky, I'm assuming the board of inquiry was composed of very learned doctors and medical specialists," Matthew said, evenly. "And they agreed everything was done that could have been done."

"Look, I'm not naïve," she replied. "Every surgeon has to learn to live with the fact they will lose some people. That's life and I'm a big girl. But I think of her every day. *Every* day. Her death was the straw, I suppose. I left right after the inquiry. But...!" She hesitated for a moment. "...there were other factors."

"Such as?"

"I'm Innu, Matthew. I have been educated as native since I was a girl. I've been taught our language and history, and the ways of our people by my grandfather and our native teachers. But I have also been educated in the white man's world. Often I feel I have one foot in my world and one foot in your world. But I belong to neither fully. I felt it was time for a revaluation of my life."

"You have wonderful skills you can use to help your people in the North."

"I suppose that's why I'm back up here now. Trying to decide if I should remain in the North or return to a southern hospital. It's not an easy choice. What I'd be treating up here would be anti-climactic to what I'd be doing in the south. Here it would be endless days of upset stomachs, cuts, bruises, alcohol-related battery, or the occasional hunting accident. Anything serious would likely be medivaced to Montreal."

"A conundrum...."

"Anyhow, I decided to leave The Royal Vic. Call it a rest, call it a sabbatical, or whatever you want. I'm out. At least for now." She sighed. "Anyhow, enough about me. What about you? Have you wrapped your head around your divorce being final?"

Matthew thought for a moment and then said slowly: "No choice, really."

"Were you married long?"

"Nine years."

"Are you still in love with her?"

"No. For the past 18 months it was more like I was in love with how our marriage used to be. Near the end, I have to admit it was a rather anemic rendition of what had once been a beautiful relationship."

"What went wrong? Or do you know?"

"Oh, I know alright. Anger, guilt, and regret slowly poisoned our marriage. Finally it killed it off completely."

"Regret? Guilt? Over what?" Sky was paying closer attention now.

"An accident," he said, slowly. "You see, I also lost a little girl."

* * *

They rose the next morning and packed as quickly as possible. Before long they were on the ice and crossing the fiord. It was still dark.

The temperature had plunged once more and it was now hitting -25 degrees. Despite the parkas, balaclavas and mitts, it wasn't long before the cold began to penetrate their layers of clothing and seep into their bones. The combination of a constant wind from their movement, and the fact they were static on the snowmobiles and not using muscles to generate additional body heat, was a double whammy. They stopped once to dig out and don extra wool sweaters.

The sky was cloudy and the ever-present wind began stirring up loose snow augmenting the snow discharge spewing from Sky's snowmobile. It was becoming increasingly difficult to see and Matthew finally gave up trying to anticipate the terrain ahead. In this crossing, it had been decided Matthew would follow Sky, who would already have blazed a safe trail. He dropped back to improve visibility.

Now he carefully watched her machine turn, pitch and yaw, so that he could prepare for a similar ride a few seconds later. Occasionally he would look ahead at her snowmobile, violently pitching about on the ice, the formidable shadows of the mountains in front and behind them, and wonder what vagaries of fate had brought them to this moment. He also became aware of how truly alone they were. In this wilderness, there was no backup. They couldn't even call for help.

Because it was so early in the season, the ice had buckled in many spots in the fiord. The freezing and melting process, compounded by the water movement underneath, cracked the ice first, and then forced it against itself to form formidable, volcano-shaped pressure ridges. In other cases, the ice merely separated leaving water holes filled with grey, half-frozen slush effectively hiding their potential for disaster. This was early in the winter season. Nature seemed to be daring them to try to cross what Matthew described as 'a semi-frozen minefield of death.'

They travelled cautiously, giving their full attention to the path ahead. If they were farther north they might be travelling on multi-year ice that remained frozen from year-to-year. On Saglek Bay, however, they were now travelling on new ice that hadn't yet frozen to its maximum depth. Certainly it was in the process of thickening for the season, but not quite there yet.

Both breathed a sigh of relief when they reached the north shore of the bay. They now travelled east to hit the coast. The land wasn't even and Atemu was finding his ride rougher than normal. He sat up in his nest and tried to anticipate which way the sled would tilt so he could throw his weight in the opposite direction to counter it.

The wind had strengthened even more. Ahead, Matthew could barely see the red glow of Sky's taillight bobbing erratically in the drifting snow. His chin felt frozen; he pushed it deep in his collar for warmth.

Finally they turned due north and were on what seemed to be fairly firm shore ice. Occasionally the wind would pause and he'd see a formidable, sheer, and very black rocky wall off to his left as he rode.

After a couple of hours, the wall of the rock cliff ended abruptly and he glimpsed what seemed like the beginning of a valley. It vanished from sight whenever the wind increased in strength.

Sky shifted their route 45 degrees left and the terrain became much less rugged. It was a relief not to be battling with the steering bars of the snowmobile. After hours of struggle, his back, neck and arms ached. Not to mention his butt after banging over treacherous ice for hours.

If he had one wish, he thought, it would be for the wind to take a break and lay low. He also wouldn't mind a drink. Even beside the sea, the air was dry and his lips were chapped.

Finally the wind lost some of its force and visibility improved. Matthew saw that they were descending a steep slope onto what was obviously a deeply carved, U-shaped glacial valley offering a relatively flat, snow-covered plain. They were heading towards two sets of older, rounded mountainous growths that reared out of the plain in semi-circles facing each other. One might call the opening a canyon, but it would only be in the broadest sense of the word. The plain was so wide, the mountains on either side of it seemed like afterthoughts. The curious semi-circles of hills facing each other in the center were certainly no more than two or three hundred feet high, looking more like giant anthills.

They circled the first hill which took about two minutes. As they approached the second one, Sky aimed her snowmobile directly at it and climbed the incline. It took about five minutes to reach the rounded top where a fifteen by ten-foot hunk of shale formed a nipple of sorts. She pulled up beside it, paused and waited for him to join her.

Matthew stopped and pulled off his goggles, helmet and balaclava; he welcomed the light but cold breeze that now cooled his face and scalp.

Atemu jumped from Sky's sled and peed on one of the front skis.

"Nice manners, Atemu," Matthew commented. "Now I need a car wash." The dog simply looked at him and wagged his tail.

"I call these the *Plains of Pharsalus*," Sky said. She removed her helmet and shook her head. Her flattened "hat hair" took on more life, surrounding her face with soft curls and waves.

"Pharsalus? Interesting name. Is it Greek?"

"Yes. In 48 BC, during Julius Caesar's Civil War, he and Gnaeus Pompeius Magnus faced each other at Pharsalus in central Greece. Caesar had 22,000 legionnaires and Magnus had almost 50,000 including cavalry. After several months of dares and threats, pressure from senators who had escaped from Rome with Magnus, forced him to reluctantly engage in battle with Caesar. Magnus was defeated. These hills we see here, resemble the position of the armies facing each other. Both were hoping to starve each other out rather than fight. So, fanciful girl that I am, I call here the *Plains of Pharsalus*."

"More like the plains of a frozen moon," Matthew said. He looked down at the lowland and over at the other hills. Everything was encased in ice and snow. Indeed, the scene looked like some white, sci-fi scene painted for the cover of an *Other Worlds* magazine.

Sky stared back down the hill, her gaze carefully following their trail. With the wind finally calm, their vantage point allowed them to see their twin snowmobile tracks snaking back towards the mountainous cliff framing the southern side of the plain.

"Should we grab some food?" Matthew asked, not sure what they were doing on top of the rise. They seemed to have strayed from their route, and while the perspective was interesting, he didn't believe they were up there for the view.

Sky didn't reply, continuing to stare. Her mood had definitely taken a downturn. Finally she pulled out her binoculars and aimed them down their trail to where they had come around the mountain wall on the coast. Though visibility was better, the crest of the mountains was still hidden in some low lying mist or cloud. He wondered how far up the cliff went.

"Damn!" she exclaimed. "I knew it!"

"What?" Matthew asked.

"Two snowmobiles stopped down there near the rock wall. See them? Two dots."

She passed the binoculars to Matthew and stood, hands on her hips, a stance he'd seen before that showed her displeasure.

After adjusting them slightly, the two black dots jumped into focus. The snowmobiles were stopped within a few feet of the corner of the rock, their riders remaining immobile. Though he couldn't make out details, he sensed they were looking right back at him through binoculars.

Suddenly they turned their machines and silently melted back around the corner of the rock wall, out of sight.

~5~

After landing in the snow without injury the previous night, Wolfgang Schaeffer, Allan Hoover and Yves Legrand had set up camp in pup tents and waited till the morning to find their three supply modules.

They uncrated their snowmobiles, buried the wood from the crates in the snow and ensured everything worked. They were now aboard their Bombardier machines, one hooked to a sled loaded with a four-man tent, communications gear, sleeping bags, gas, food and other supplies. It also contained one other piece of equipment critical to the overall success of their mission.

Pausing on the ice, they compared their map to the GPS unit.

"So we have to head south to Saglek," Schaeffer concluded.

"And carefully. We don't know where their security perimeter starts or ends," Legrand cautioned. "We just observe and report."

The plan meant every 12 hours they would send an encrypted message with a report on their status via a microburst transmission to one of three Russian Molniya communications satellites following a high elliptical orbital path over the northern hemisphere. Their first deadline was in four hours; they were anxious to have something concrete to say.

Hoover listened to his companions with half an ear. It was only their second stop of the morning and it allowed him to check out his Remington 783 .30-06 caliber rifle. It was a beauty he thought, with its black composite stock and 22-inch barrel. At seven pounds it was a nice weight. Mounted on it was a Simmons 3-9 x 40 mm scope, perfect for shorter range problems. Hoover qualified as Marksman on the range but had never fired an American Remington. He was eager for the chance but Schaeffer had forbidden him from taking a few practice shots. Though Hoover tried to convince Schaeffer that he needed to "sight it in," their de facto leader had simply reached over and put his finger in the barrel and said: "No."

"Hey, Hoover, stop fooling around with the rifle," Legrand called over. "Put it away. I'm the only one supposed to be armed, anyhow." Slung over Legrand's shoulder was a WW II vintage, sporterized Lee Enfield .303. As their "Innu guide" he was legally qualified to carry a weapon within the park boundaries. What observers could not see was that each man carried a Smith & Wesson .38 revolver in a belt holster easily accessible through Velcro-sealed slits in their parkas.

Hoover joined the other two. "We're an eco-tourist party, like any other, so we don't have to hide," he reminded them. "Even if we run into soldiers, the National Parks of Canada computer system will show we filed a travel document with it two weeks ago."

Indeed, if anyone did attempt to verify their story, the Russian Federation's *Directorate X: Science and Technical Intelligence* had easily hacked into Parks Canada's system, registered them and issued the proper permits for their three-week journey. All fees had been "paid" and i's dotted and t's crossed. It was amazing what a few keystrokes from several thousands of miles away could accomplish. Their paper documentation, given them before they left, also matched their virtual declarations in the system.

Schaeffer closed the map and nodded to his companions. "Then let's move, eh?"

The three climbed back on their snowmobiles and proceeded south. They followed the shelf ice, butted against mountains and hills. So much of the park shoreline was simply mountainous cliffs with five or six hundred yards of ice extending outward.

It wasn't long before they found relief from the ever-present cliffs on their right side as they passed a plain of sorts extending deep into the interior. In the distance they could see snow-covered hills but failed to spot two people atop one near a rocky outcropping. Focused on the trail ahead, they kept riding. It wasn't long before Hoover stopped his snowmobile and pointed. In the snow, about 100 yards ahead, were two fresh snowmobile tracks heading off to their right onto the plain.

"They coming or going?" Legrand asked.

"And who the hell are they?" Schaeffer added. "Eco-tourists? I thought this place was virtually deserted in winter."

"Maybe Innu hunters," Hoover offered.

Schaefer got off his snowmobile and examined the tracks. The rear discharge of sprayed snow made it easy to tell the direction. "They headed northwest and we're heading south. Doubtful we'll meet them."

He looked towards the hills on the plain, scanning it trice. Through the binoculars he checked one or two suspicious bumps. Nothing. The three continued south.

Everything was working out well.

* * *

"I don't believe this," Sky said out loud. From atop the hill she was looking directly east towards the coast to where three snowmobiles were charging southward, fantails of snow behind each." It's like Times Square down there."

"Hunters?" Matthew asked.

"There's no hunting allowed in Torngat National Park except for Innu and Inuit," she replied. "As for eco-tourists, they're few and far between up here in the winter. Most people come in the summer months when the weather warms."

"So who are they?" Matthew asked, absentmindedly. "Could they be soldiers from the base?"

"There was nobody there," Sky said. After a brief pause: "Or was there?"

"Maybe they're guards. After all, they couldn't leave all the new buildings, hangars and fuel tanks unguarded, could they? And maybe they happened to be away when we stopped."

"Maybe," she replied. "Something fishy is going on. I don't know what, but I feel like we're part of some game. Only we don't know the goal of the game or the rules. Look, first we get in trouble on the ice and a military plane miraculously appears in a major snowstorm and leads us to safety. Next we encounter what looks like a brand new military base, but nobody is home? Now we're seeing soldiers, or somebody, racing around down there like it's a major highway."

"There's only five people," Matthew corrected.

"Matthew, encountering five people on a trail up here in winter is like accidently running into a group of 5,000 people on a side street in Montreal. Doesn't happen. Especially in winter."

Matthew shrugged. "Okay, it's simply a military patrol. Those two snowmobiles we saw near the cliff down there were waiting for the rest of the patrol that went north for a bit. Now the five of them will meet, go back to the base and resume their guard duties."

Sky sighed. "You may be right. But when grandfather went on his trips up here, he always said he felt he was being watched. And it wasn't by the others."

Matthew looked at her strangely. "What *others*?"

There she had done it again. Opened her mouth before engaging her brain. Now she'd have to lie. Now she'd be the one ducking and weaving. Her mind raced and she picked the lesser of the two evils.

"The spirits," she said, innocently. "Torngat means *Place of the Spirits*. Grandfather is a shaman, in case you didn't know."

He gave her an intense look. She wanted to look away, to let her gaze slide to the side so he wouldn't see the lie in her eyes. But she knew that if she did so, he wouldn't buy it. And he'd keep pestering her until she made another slip. So she looked straight back at him and tried to bluff. They looked at each other for a full minute until he broke eye contact. He looked away, sighed, looked back at her again. Then he shook his head. It was plain he didn't believe her. Quickly she decided to use one of his own ploys against him: comic relief.

"White man realize he be with crazy Indian lady and make heap big, steaming pile in the snow," she blurted out. Matthew couldn't help himself; he started laughing. And then, so did Sky. The tenseness of a moment broke in a welcome ebb, and they laughed until their sides hurt.

Finally, struggling to catch his breath, Matthew gulped out: "You got that right!" This sent them back into more peals of laughter.

Atemu regarded them happily and wagged his tail; he didn't know what brought about this new feeling of positive energy, but he liked it nonetheless.

"Let's get some lunch," Sky said, ruffling up Atemu's fur. "That sound good, boy?"

They had begun to pull out the Sterno, pots and meal packs when the faint sound of three quick, sharp crack echoed to them on the wind. Sky stopped and looked over. "Did you hear that?"

"What?" Matthew asked, struggling to light a can of Sterno in the breeze. They needed to melt a pot of snow to reconstitute their meals.

"Sounded almost like...shots," Sky said, a perplexed look on her face.

"Just ice cracking," Matthew ventured.

Sky looked troubled but then conceded: "Yes, you're probably right."

They settled down to eat their lunch.

* * *

Colonel Moorhead stared at Lieutenant Reynold's screen as the Avenger looped over Schooner Cove and headed out over the Labrador Sea. It didn't travel far before it made a 180-degree turn and headed back inland. Falling snow continued to inhibit its sensor's effectiveness.

"Orbit over the trio, Lieutenant," Moorhead said. "I want to know who the hell we have out there."

"They just *appeared*, sir," Reynolds said. "Yesterday they were nowhere in sight and this morning they were camped near Iron Strand. They just popped up."

"And the other two are the Fortune Diamonds people? I thought they'd give up long before this."

"Afraid not," Reynolds said. "Report said their company bought a new snowmobile in Nain, ferried it up aboard a Snowcat BR400 with an aluminum haul deck and met them on the ice. We saw them meet. Had them up and running and back on the trail within 24 hours. I've been watching them run like hell to catch up to our subjects. I think they caught up around Deacon Head. The Fortune Diamonds' people watched our subjects through binoculars and after they reached the plain, they stopped and retreated back around the cliff out of sight. Right over there." He pointed at the screen.

"Took cover because they probably didn't want another snowmobile shot out from under them," Moorhead mused.

"Yes, sir," Reynolds said, turning the Avenger once more. An inshore wind was stirring up the sea less than a half mile away. The pilot watched the temperature climb slightly and thicker snowflakes appear. With more snow, visibility deteriorated further.

"Tell me about the three men again."

"I think they're men, sir, but not certain, Reynolds said. "They came roaring southward out of nowhere. They're about to rendezvous with the Fortune Diamond people."

"I have Major Stone checking up on them with Parks Canada," Moorhead replied. "They have to have permits to travel up here, so they had to register their trip. We'll know who they are soon enough."

"But how did they get up there without us seeing them, sir?"

"They may have been up here for a while, Lieutenant.

"Sir, I've often flown north more than a few times after standing down," Reynolds confessed. "Just to practice some low level flying, keep my hand in."

"You mean to relieve the boredom of lazy eights," Moorhead answered, understanding perfectly how tedious the job could be when in surveillance mode.

"That too, sir. I think I would have seen them if they were up there. At least picked up some sign of them. I found polar bears, foxes, a few Muskoxen, lots of caribou and several wolf packs. But never any people."

"Well they didn't appear out of thin air, Lieutenant, so they were up there somewhere."

"If you say so, sir."

"And that's our subjects down there." Moorhead, pointed to the right of the screen.

"Yes, sir" Reynolds confirmed. "They have a small heat signature between them, probably a cooking stove fueled by propane or Sterno. Looks like they're having lunch up there on a small hill."

"How soon before those other three rendezvous with the Fortunate Diamond people?"

"I'd say about 15 minutes, sir. Maybe twenty."

The phone rang beside one of the Radar Ops behind them and he answered it. He immediately called out: "Colonel, sir? Major Stone asking if you could drop in and see him A-SAP?"

"Roger, Sergeant, tell him I'll be there pronto."

Moorhead turned on his heel and left the room, calling back. "Let me know if anything changes, Lieutenant."

* * *

Peter Meyer and Monique Boivin sat astride their snowmobiles and looked at each other.

"I don't think they saw us," Meyer said, though he wasn't sure at all. "But if so, I don't want fucking Little Feather shooting at me again."

"Stop it, Peter," Monique said, angrily. "They saved our lives."

"And took out my snowmobile."

"It might have been a wild shot, you don't know."

"Really?" Meyer spat. "She hit that bear below the right ear and shut him down like he never existed. She knew perfectly well what she was shooting at when she put the next one in my machine's engine."

"Which proves my point. She wasn't shooting at us."

Meyer disembarked from his snowmobile and trudged through the snow over to the edge of the rocky cliff. The corner of the cliff was almost an abrogation of nature. It was so well defined and sharp, it might have been constructed by a carpenter except it was obsidian-type black stone with an 80 degree vertical rather than 90.

He peered around the edge, looking out onto the plain. It was deserted except for the two sets of snowmobile tracks.

"If those are anthills," he said, looking at the 300-foot high hills, "I sure don't want to be around when the ants come out in spring."

"What are you saying?" Monique called to him.

"Talking to myself. Is that okay?"

Meyer came back to the snowmobiles and took a backpack out of the single sled they were towing. "Hungry?" he asked.

Monique nodded. He pulled out two military MREs and placed

them on the side of the sled. They had made extra coffee that morning and filled a large aluminum thermos bottle. He took this out also, along with two cups. Next he took another large insulated pouch out of their sled.

He opened their MRE boxes, added some bottled water from the insulated pouch, and activated the chemical-based, flameless ration heaters. Monique watched him closely. He was an odd bird and she was beginning to think he might have more than a few mental issues. She wasn't sure if she was comfortable with him preparing her food.

Meyer then wrapped the "heaters" around the pouches containing their chicken and dumpling main course, and waited the required ten minutes for them to heat.

"I'm starving," Meyer said.

"We'll have to hold back for a while when they get started again," Monique said. "We just follow their tracks, so no need to be that close."

"We can do that until we see Corrigan taking samples," Meyer agreed. "I wonder if they've tried to use their satellite phone yet. They must know it's not working."

The night before Sky and Corrigan left, Meyer had taken a walk by her grandfather's house and seen the two packed sleds outside. Since the lights were off in the house, he had taken his flashlight, and explored the sleds. He'd come across the satellite phone in a knapsack and couldn't believe his good luck. He opened it, peering at the innards with his flashlight. No battery, but that was okay. He'd taken his pocket knife and carefully scraped some printed circuits at the corners in three spots; enough to break the connection but devilishly hard to find.

Then he packed everything back the way he found it and continued his late night walk. Sometimes fortune smiled on the brave, he mused. But then he quickly put that thought aside. It didn't fit in with his personal philosophy; you make your own luck.

He caught Monique staring at him. "What? What's wrong now?"

"How do you know their satellite phone isn't working," she asked, puzzled.

"Oh, let's say I got 'lucky' when I was out for a walk the night before we left."

"You went into their house?" she asked, disbelief in her tone.

"No, they left their packed sleds outside the night before. You know how trusting people in the North tend to be? Or should I say, imprudent?"

"What did you do?"

"What do you think I did?"

"Don't fool with me!"

"Alright, alright. Jesus! I found the phone on the sled and my pocketknife may have accidentally damaged a connection or two on its circuit board."

"You sabotaged their emergency phone?"

"Hey! It isn't only for emergencies. You know once they get where they're going, they'll power up a laptop, patch through to the net using their Sat phone, and access Land & Forests' On-Line Mineral Claims Staking System. Then they'll nail down the lease."

"Which is exactly what Fortune wants us to do once we locate the site," Monique replied.

"Except now they won't be able to do that. And we will."

Monique sighed: "I never should have accepted this assignment. I should have resigned."

"Oh, don't tell me you're having an attack of conscience," Meyer laughed.

"They saved our lives."

"And we…that means you and I…still plan to do them dirty. So don't play the saint. At least not with me."

"I'm far from a saint," Monique snapped. "This is business. This is the prospecting business. And we can still win. As long as Beauregard Diamonds or one of the others up here doesn't beat us to it."

"Did you hear anything further on them?"

"Only what Gordon said before we left: Beauregard will likely make a concentrated effort to watch Corrigan and the St. Onge woman. And then attempt to beat them staking a claim."

"It's a bloody race, is what it is."

"With very high stakes."

"All's fair in love and war…and business," Meyer chuckled. "Though there's not much traffic up here. I mean, if the Beauregard people were around, you'd think we'd notice them." Indeed, within minutes his words seemed to turn prophetic.

Monique didn't answer. She appeared to be listening. Sure enough,

Meyer heard it too. A far-off, mix-master sound thinned by the atmosphere. It certainly wasn't a buzz saw since there were no trees for hundreds of miles.

"Those are snowmobiles," Monique said. She put down her MRE ration, stood up and looked northward.

"Son of a bitch," Meyer said, also rising from his seat on his snowmobile. He ran to the cliff and peered around the corner. Then he returned, snatched his binoculars from their case and looked out on the plain, but further north towards the coast.

"Are they coming back?" Monique asked, a hint of worry in her voice.

"No. They're still there. I can see them by the outcrop on top of the second hill." He swung the binoculars to his right and swept the ice shelf closer to the sea. "Jesus! Beauregard Diamonds. Must be. Those bastards."

"Are you sure?"

"Who else? Three of them. Heading right for us."

"Why are they heading south?"

"Maybe because they're missing the Lone Ranger and Tonto? Obviously they haven't seen them on yonder hill," Meyer said.

"Or, they've already found the diamond site," Monique ventured, not looking forward to more unpleasantness.

"Leave it to me, okay? Don't say a word. Maybe, if they found the place, we can cut a deal at least. I'll pretend to know more than I do. And tell them I'm going to report them as claim jumpers since we tried to file first. Nobody likes it when the waters get muddied up and there's doubt about a claim. Half a loaf is better than a lawsuit dragging on for years and years with no production taking place."

Monique felt dismay and a little confused. The only reason for Beauregard to be up here would be looking for the diamond site. And the only reason for them to be heading south would be if they'd found it.

The three snowmobiles arrived with a flurry of snow and noise as they ground to a halt about twenty-five feet away. Three men stared at Meyer and Monique, the leader sporting a big wolfish grin.

"Howdy partner," Wolfgang said, jovially. "Didn't know there was anyone else up here in this godforsaken land." He grinned at them again.

Beside him, Hoover and Legrand merely nodded by way of

greeting.

Meyer stood up from his snowmobile, his jacket fully open exposing his pistol. He glared at the three. "Don't fucking 'howdy' me, partner. We know exactly who you are and what you're doing up here." He held up his phone. "And we're about to report you."

The trio exchanged glances with each other. Then they rose from their snowmobiles, all the while smiling and rolling their shoulder as though unwinding from a long ride. The leader who'd spoken looked at the others. They advanced a few feet and suddenly moved as one.

The sound of three Velcro-sealed pockets being ripped open simultaneously seemed particularly loud to Monique. As she saw what was coming out of their pockets she opened her mouth to scream a warning.

She was too late.

~6~

"The Parks Canada guy is totally 'gob-smacked'," Stone said. "I think that means 'surprised' in Canadian."

"Over what?" Moorhead asked.

Stone pushed some sheets of paper across the desk with three names highlighted in yellow and a *Parks Canada* logo on top. "This. It's a copy I printed of a permit for two eco-tourists and an Innu guide to enter Torngat National Park, dated from last week. The problem is, so few permits are issued at this time of the year, the clerk swears he would remember it. And he has no idea where it came from. Nor does his department. It just appeared in their computer system. Complete with travel plans, and fees paid up.

"And it doesn't stop there. These guys are supposed to have left from Nain to head north. But we've got a guy there, Bob Crummy, who keeps us in touch with what's going on in Nain. For a fee. And he doesn't remember them. In fact, he swears they were never there."

"Well, surely he can't know everybody," Moorhead insisted.

"Sir, this fellow trades in information. He's the Gladys Kravitz of Nain, the busybody neighbor who knows everything about everyone. He collects and sells info to prospecting companies, provides consulting services to hunters or other travelers, keeps tabs on who is going where and sells it. If these three had been there, he'd know it. In fact, he's the guy who told us about Meyer and Boivin trailing Corrigan and St. Onge."

"So who are these other three?" Moorhead was getting impatient with Stone.

"I can't tell you that, Colonel," Stone said. "But I can tell you who they are not."

Moorhead didn't say a single word. Instead he merely stared at him. He wasn't in the mood for guessing games.

Stone pointed at the copy of the permit. "They're not Allan Hoover of Calgary, Alberta, Wolfgang Schaeffer of Sudbury, Ontario, or Yves Legrand of Schefferville, Quebec."

"Are you certain?" Moorhead asked, alarm bells starting to go off.

"Yes, unless they rose from the grave."

"They're all dead?"

"As doornails," Stone said, nodding.

"Stolen identities..."

"...because dead men don't complain," Stone finished

Moorhead weighed the possibilities. Could they be rendezvousing with the Fortune Diamonds' people because they had some deal going on? But why the fake identities? And now Lieutenant Reynold's query took on new importance: *Where did they come from?*

The Colonel thanked Stone and retired to his office. He didn't like a bunch of poseurs running around a mere day or so from his base. Whatever business espionage was taking place, it was going to have to take a back seat to his mission. He'd have an Away Team scoop them up pronto.

What he wanted, indeed, what he needed, was for St. Onge to lead Corrigan to the old man's diamond site. Not for the diamonds, but for what else was there on the periphery. The evidence that had been collected on St. Onge over so many decades pointed to one thing. He had been regularly meeting with someone or *something* in the Torngat Mountains for decades.

Further, when it was added to the UHF chatter they had been able to decipher, and the change in the pattern of abnormal vehicular air traffic around the Torngat Mountains, it sure looked like his there were preparations taking place for a Winter Solstice departure.

Therefore, the timing of everything was becoming more and more relevant as the Winter Solstice approached. And it was critical that Moorhead's military operation wasn't compromised by anyone.

He picked up his phone to dial Black and then thought better of it. He'd solve the problem first and then report to his Lord and Master. Right now, his first priority would be to send out a fast patrol and haul everybody in for questioning. Without spooking Corrigan and the girl, of course.

Even if they were simple poachers, they had to be removed. And the trio could scream all they wanted. Once they knew Moorhead was aware they were using fake IDs, he was pretty sure they'd quiet down.

The telephone on his desk rang. It was Reynolds. He wanted Moorhead back to the radar ops room A-SAP.

* * *

Sky and Matthew cleaned their utensils and packed away their empty meal pouches. Atemu trotted over and obediently jumped aboard Sky's sled where his bed lay. He watched them kick snow off their snowmobile skis, buckle up their helmets, and do a quick radio check. Next they opened and tied down their solar panels on Matthew's sled to trickle charge the exchange batteries for their helmet radios.

The clouds had started to drift off, compliments of a fairly strong wind; a blue sky was also rapidly forming overhead. The sun peaked out from behind the remaining few clouds and the ice crystals in the snow sparkled like millions of diamonds. Both Sky and Matthew pulled on their dark goggles to again stave off snow blindness. Without dark goggles, within an hour or two, they'd be unable to keep their eyes open.

"Before goggles or sun glasses, my people carved pieces of caribou antlers to fit our faces and then cut a thin strip in the bone to let in only a small amount of light," Sky said. "Used a strip of caribou hide to tie them on. Worked fine until you stepped in a hole you couldn't see."

Matthew laughed. Then he stopped abruptly. He was sure he'd heard a sharp crack in the distance.

"What?" Sky asked.

"Ice breaking up some more," he said, and threw his leg over his snowmobile.

They were soon powering down the hill and heading across the plain towards the shore ice. It was only this ice that allowed them to travel along a relatively flat coastal route without having to cross hilly terrain, or climb mountains. Matthew noticed they were proceeding directly east rather than swinging northeast.

"Sky, why are we not swinging more north?" Matthew radioed.

There was no answer but they had checked out their communication gear so he was pretty sure she could hear him. He tried again: "Sky?"

"I'm thinking," she said, in a no-nonsense tone.

"Well, after you're done, let Atemu and me know what's going on," he radioed back. "He's getting worried." No laugh. No comment. No acknowledgement.

They continued east until they'd reached the shore ice. She stopped and sat astride her snowmobile. She looked north and south and then south again. He pulled up behind her.

"You worried about those guards or whoever they were?" he shouted.

"Something doesn't add up," she yelled back over the snowmobiles' engine noises.

"Well if they're following us, we'll soon know it, I think. It looks pretty flat and straight along the shore."

"The three snowmobiles we saw heading south weren't following us. If we hadn't detoured we would have met up with them," she declared.

"Doesn't it make sense they came from the base? Other than Saglek, the nearest settlement is Nain isn't it? A week's travel?" Matthew asked.

"I think you're right after all. The base looked too 'occupied' to be empty."

"So there you have it," Matthew said, somewhat pleased with himself.

She nodded and turned north. Matthew began following her. They hadn't gone five miles before Sky stopped, her hands on her steering bar.

Matthew's radio crackled. "We have to go back," Sky said.

"Why?" Matthew asked.

"I want to see where the five of them met up; that they really were a single party of guards from Saglek."

"Roger," Matthew said, sighing. He turned his snowmobile. "Shouldn't take too long."

Sky roared up beside him as he rode. She then pulled in front as they headed south again. In fact it took them 25 minutes to arrive at the corner of the cliff where the snowmobiles had obviously met up. Sky and Matthew got off and explored the scene. Atemu rose to disembark also but Sky stopped him.

"No, stay there boy. Stay! You peed an hour ago and there's no need for you to be messing around here." The dog whined at her but she stuck to her guns, twice telling him to *sit!*

A melee of boot and snowmobile prints covered the snow. The site was mostly trampled flat with a formidable pile of snow at the base of the cliff as though someone tried to clear a campsite. Three granola bar wrappers rested on the snow pile.

"No concerns about littering," Sky said. "Okay let's follow them south for a few miles to make sure they're heading back. That way we don't have to keep turning around to see if someone is on our tail."

They jumped back on their snowmobiles and followed the tracks southward.

Sky could see multiple tracks in front of them as they rode. Some looped in and out, crossing over one another or riding in tracks of tracks. At one point, where the ice widened and the snow was well packed down, the tracks no longer converged. That was likely where they had the opportunity to pick up speed and separated to avoid the fantail of snow from the other drivers. Sky held up her hand and stopped.

"What's wrong?" Matthew radioed to her.

"This is odd," she replied. "Come over here."

He ran his machine up beside hers but she was already getting off. She knelt down exploring the snow for a dozen feet away in either direction. She was counting.

"What did you find," he asked, walking up to where she knelt in the snow.

"Nine sets of tracks."

"Okay, that's about right, isn't it?"

"Two of them are made by foxes."

He looked at her trying to understand her point. "So, you have seven sets of tracks."

"Look Matthew, how many sets of snowmobile tracks should be here?"

"Counting us and the other two snowmobiles coming north…four…and five of them going south. That means we should have nine sets, not counting ours that we're making now."

"How many snowmobile tracks do you see in front of us?"

He counted. "Seven."

She crawled around until she'd examined all snowmobile tracks and then stood up. "Based on the patterns, the way the snow was discharged from each snowmobile thread, we have four coming north – us and two others – and just three going south."

"There should be five going south," he said. "Five guards, right?"

"Exactly." Sky looked around, worriedly. She explored the ridges and cliffs bordering the ice where they stood. Her instinct demanded she be on full alert. "I hate being here in the open."

"What's going on?" Matthew didn't like this one bit.

"That's what I'd like to know." She edged back to her snowmobile and loosened the .30-30 in its scabbard and took it out, still looking at the high ground to their right.

"Jesus, Sky!" Matthew exclaimed, now spooked himself.

"Okay, let's assume the trio we saw met the other two sleds hiding around the edge of the rock face."

"Okay."

"And those two didn't come south. Just the trio did."

"Okay."

And we know the two didn't come north because we were there, watching. And we went north and there were only three sets of tracks in front of us, the trio coming south. And they continued south, after meeting up with the others at the wall."

"Right."

"So where are the other two people?" Sky asked, her gaze still scanning, her right hand ready to lever a round into the chamber of her weapon.

Matthew was at a loss for words. He looked at her but she never took her eyes off the ridges and cliffs.

"Again, where are they, Matthew? Think about it."

"They're still there," he said softly, his heart sinking.

"That's right. Now I want you to get the .308 with the scope out of my sled. You know where it's stored. Be casual. There are two loaded ammo clips with it in a side pocket of the rifle case. Take them out of the side pocket and hand them to me with the rifle. You take my carbine here and put it in the scabbard on my snowmobiles and tighten the straps. Got that so far?"

"What are we doing?"

"We're getting the hell away from here."

"What are you looking for up there?" He motioned towards the hills and cliff nearby.

"A flash, a reflection off something. Now listen. After you hand me the rifle, you are going to get on *my* snowmobile and get yourself and Atemu out of here. At a fast pace. In other words, you are going to go like the devil was after you. Got it?"

"I am not leaving you here alone, Sky."

"Before we set out on this trek you promised to do *what* I said, *when* I said it. Remember? That was the deal."

"Yeah, well I meant I'd get water, cook your food or carry your bags."

"There's probably nobody up there and I'll be right behind you. Please, get out of here now!"

"Can't do it. I've already lost someone I –." He stopped abruptly.

She stared at him for a moment and then went back to scanning. "What did you say?"

"I said I can't...no...I *won't* leave you here. But I'll get the rifle."

He was back in less than a minute and exchanged the .308 for the .30-30. She immediately slapped one of the two clips in it, worked the bolt action and threw it to her shoulder. Using the scope she conducted a hurried inspection of the ridge nearby.

"I'm not leaving, Sky."

She sighed. "Alright, start both machines, get on your snowmobile and let's backtrack. I'll be right behind you."

"*Right* behind me," he insisted.

He started both machines and Sky walked backwards, weapon ready, until she reached her machine. She spun around: "Go, go," she said to him, jumping aboard her snowmobile.

They roared off along the ice at top speed. After a minute, when they rounded a turn and she figured they were no longer exposed, Sky radioed him to slow down. Then she gradually reduced her speed to 30 mph and then dropped it to 25 mph which was comfortable for towing.

In 20 more minutes they reached the cliff face where the wide plain began. They could see the three granola wrappers as they pulled up. For a moment they sat looking at the scene. It was pretty much chewed up by all the snowmobiles that had been there. They both found themselves staring at the ten-foot high mound of snow heaped against the black cliff base.

Thick, fluffy flakes had begun falling again. Within a minute the ever-present wind reappeared.

"Atemu, go boy," she whispered softly.

The dog exploded off the sled in a giant leap and immediately raced to the left side of the pile of snow, sniffed it and then ignored it in favor of the right side. He began to dig. Snow flew from between his hind legs as he worked frantically. Sky and Matthew rummaged around in their sleds and quickly found their small aluminum snow shovels. They went to work on the left side of the pile. Their faces were grim.

The more Sky shoveled, the more certain she became this was dug-up snow, flung there to bury something. It was light and loosely packed, and it wasn't long before she heard a clunk sound as Matthew's shovel hit something; it had to be metal. He and Sky exchanged glances.

"Oh damn it all," she said, in dismay. They soon uncovered a blue and white Polaris snowmobile with rider. Lying back on the seat was Peter Meyer, his eyes wide open, pupils fully dilated and already cloudy from potassium in the blood cells breaking down. His parka sported a small red stain on the front. Matthew could see two holes almost dead center; he'd been shot. They tried to sit him up and saw a massive red stain on the back of his parka.

"Meyer," Matthew said, shortly.

"He's dead," Sky said, examining his eyes. Still, she pulled off her mitt, and checked his carotid for a pulse anyhow.

Nothing.

They turned to Atemu who had uncovered the front skis of a yellow snowmobile at his spot. He stopped digging, climbed up the side of the pile and began renewed digging near where a driver would sit. Matthew steeled himself for what he knew they were about to find.

"Atemu, here!" Sky said firmly, but the dog ignored her. He kept digging frantically, whining as he did.

"Here boy, I'll do it." Matthew got his shovel and gently scraped away the snow where the seat would be. Atemu forced his way in between him and the snowmobile. He continued digging until he was scraping snow off a blue nylon parka. Matthew reached down behind the parka and carefully lifted Monique Boivin out of the shallow, snowy grave and set her down on the ground. Her eyes were closed, her skin pale, head lolling to the side like a ragdoll. There was a single hole right over her heart where the bullet had entered.

Atemu jumped from the half uncovered snowmobile and began licking her face.

"It's no use, boy," Matthew said, feeling himself starting to shake and hoping he wasn't going to be sick. Sky came round and knelt beside him. Gently she placed a hand on his shoulder and eased him back so she had room. He sat numbly in the snow.

She pulled Monique's hood down and inserted her fingers under her collar. She found the girl's ear and dropped her fingers until she found the carotid artery. She looked at Matthew and shook her head. Atemu whined and pawed at Monique's face.

What was the matter with that dog?

As she was about to withdraw her hand…

…Sky felt a flutter.

Impossible, she told herself. Still she pressed down more firmly and felt a pulse. It was weak and thready, but it was definitely there.

"My God, she's still alive," Sky said, tearing off her other mitt and reaching both hands down to cup Monique's face and neck, searching for both carotids. "She's breathing!"

Matthew was looking at her in disbelief. "Are you sure?" he asked, jumping to his feet.

Sky checked one eye pupil, tore open Monique's parka and saw her yellow ski sweater was soaked with blood. She pulled up the sweater and yanked a sodden wool shirt out of her pants.

"Hold this clothing up," she said to Matthew. He grabbed the bunch of clothing and held onto it. Sky reached into her pocket and opened a clasp knife which she used to cut off Monique's bra.

The bullet had not gone into her heart but rather into the upper left quadrant of her chest above the nipple of her left breast. Her chest was a mass of blood and her breathing was shallow and intermittent.

"She must have been turning when they fired at her," Sky muttered. "Looking at her parka, it looked like they hit her dead center. But they didn't."

"She's alive! I can't believe it," Matthew said, still in shock. "Should I check Meyer again?" He waited for Sky to give him the go ahead but soon realized by her behavior that it wouldn't be forthcoming.

"No, Matthew," she said. "He's definitely gone. She's lost a lot of blood and she's in shock. Get my medical kit off my sled…never mind…here press this mitt against her wound and hold it as tightly as possible." She dashed off and returned a moment later lugging a 10-gallon red gas container. She propped Monique's legs in an elevated position. "Make sure they stay elevated," she said, and dashed away again.

Back within moments she dropped a backpack with a red cross on it in the snow beside Monique. Pulling it open she extracted multiple gauze and bandage packages. Again she checked her patient; Monique was still breathing.

Next she took out a bottle of saline solution, a tin of surgical tape and unrolled a cloth Medic Emergency Roll pouch containing shining forceps, scalpels, retractors and other surgical instruments. "We have to get the left arm out of her parka and sweater," she said, donning a pair of blue nitrile surgeon's gloves and liberally splashing the front of the wound with the saline. "She'll need surgery but if we can stabilize her now, we might keep her alive long enough to get it."

Together they worked to remove her bloody garments, Matthew pulling and Sky cutting with her scissors. She examined Monique's front and back. A slightly larger, ugly exit wound in her back was steadily oozing blood. She checked her pulse and breathing again. "Through and through," she said, tearing open gauze pads with her teeth. "No bullet to worry about." Using her forceps she picked pieces of fabric out of the wound while Matthew opened more bandages.

"Have to pack the wounds front and back and stop the bleeding. Then we'll warm her. I need to get fluids in her somehow."

After irrigating the wounds and cleaning them with saline-drenched sponges, Sky used her forceps to pack both wounds with ribbon gauze. Next she covered both wounds with pressure dressings which she taped in place with white surgical tape. Matthew helped her wrap the wounds tightly with Elastoplast bandage looping it around her shoulder and across her chest. She secured the end with two metal clips and gently lay her back on her parka.

"Bastards buried her alive," Matthew said, bitterly.

"That's likely what kept her living," Sky replied. "It was a light covering of fluffy snow so she could still breathe. And the cold slowed her heart rate and her metabolism so it thickened her blood and it flowed more slowly. The cold also caused her body to send blood from her extremities to where it was needed most, the brain and vital organs. It did her more good than harm. Now, get some blankets and some of our hand and foot warmers!"

Matthew carefully packed Monique in blankets supplemented by several activated chemical hand and foot warmers, and then re-elevated her legs. Sky checked her pulse and breathing, and nodded at Matthew encouragingly.

"I think it's a little stronger," she said, noting the day was already losing its light. "But she's not out of the woods by a long shot. She needs fluid." She looked around again. "It's too late to travel today. It would be virtual suicide to blunder around on this ice in the dark. So we have to get our tent pitched, stat, and get her warmed up."

"Will she survive a trip back to Nain?"

"Doubt it," Sky said, bluntly. "That's why we're not going to Nain. First thing tomorrow we're going back to Saglek. The base may be closed down but it's relatively modern and probably has a comprehensive medical facility on site to treat emergencies."

"But if there's no one there and she needs surgery…?"

"That's where I come in," Sky said simply. "I'll have to do what I can."

Matthew looked at her again in wonder. Events made him forget she was actually a surgeon as well. His respect for Sky grew even more. Throughout this trip and its hardships she had never lost her direction or her drive. She never lost her poise, courage, or confidence.

Except maybe…once…

"…*They're here…they're not supposed to be here!*"

He pushed the memory out of his mind. There were bigger problems at hand. "Suppose those were military guards and they shot her –?" He left the sentence unfinished.

"Think about it later," Sky said. "Right now, to have even a small chance of saving Monique, she has to be warmed."

They set the tent up and got the two catalytic heaters and the Coleman lantern going in record time. Matthew set up the cots. They gently carried Monique into the tent on one of the toboggans they had for carrying supplies on the second leg of their trip. She groaned. Her eyes fluttered open for a moment but then she closed them again. Her breathing was more noticeable now.

"On the cot," Sky said.

They put her down and she moaned again in pain.

"I'm going to save the pain meds until she's fully conscious," Sky said. "She'll need them more at that point. Matthew, do you know your blood type?"

He thought for a moment and then replied: "Type O…"

"Damn…"

"…Negative."

"O Negative? The spirits are smiling on this girl, Matthew," Sky said, a look of incredulity on her face.

"How so?" Matthew asked.

"Because O Negative people are the only ones who can give blood to everyone. And you, my friend, are about to become a donor."

Within 15 minutes Matthew was lying on the cot in the tent with Monique lying on a folded tarp on the floor beside and below him. He had a needle – taped for stability – inserted in his arm with a plastic tube leading directly to a similar needle inserted in Monique's bared arm below. He was rhythmically squeezing Atemu's ratty, chewed-up, rubber ball to help pump his blood down the tube into Monique's vein. Gravity was also helping.

"It's not the best but at least we're getting some blood into her," Sky said, checking to ensure neither needle had pulled out. She had a blood pressure cuff around Monique's upper arm and pumped it up and then watched it deflate. "100 over 60. Better than I could have ever hoped for. It was in her boots when we started." She didn't bother to unwrap the cuff from the arm.

"My hand is starting to cramp up," Matthew said.

"Stop whining, hero" Sky replied, and for the first time in hours, smiled.

Matthew looked at her and smiled himself. "Sorry."

"That's enough anyhow, Matthew. We've taken about a unit. If we take any more I'll have two patients on my hands." She disconnected them both and placed cotton wool and band aids on their arms. She then pulled a container of orange juice from their insulated bag, jammed a straw into it and handed it to Matthew. "Stay where you are and drink," she ordered.

He took a sip and then a second sip and looked at her in surprise. "This isn't orange juice, this is a Screwdriver. And a pretty potent one," he said in surprise.

"Vodka prevents the orange juice from freezing," she replied.

"Yeah, well based on the percentage of alcohol in here, I don't think I'll be stiffening up any too soon."

It was only when he saw an involuntary grin cross her face that he realized the double entendre he'd put out there, Despite the cold, he could feel his own face reddening again. It wasn't that he was a prude. He just couldn't help feeling embarrassed over blatant sexual innuendos.

Sky pulled out a vial of a broad-spectrum, powdered antibiotic and reconstituted it. She shook the vial to help it mix, let it settle down, inserted a hypodermic needle into it and drew the liquid into the needle. Then she pulled down the blankets and inserted the needle into the deltoid muscle of Monique's left arm. As she withdrew it, Monique groaned again. Her green eyes opened.

She stared about in confusion and suddenly began to thrash, and sat up. The pain of her wound hit her and she cried out and started to collapse. Sky caught her and carefully eased her back.

"Monique, you must stay still," Sky said, adjusting a pillow fashioned from a rolled up blanket under her head. "I'm a doctor and you've been shot. Do you understand?"

After a moment, Monique nodded her head. "W-water?"

"Yes, we'll give you some water. If you are able, I also want you to swallow two pills. Can you do that?"

She nodded again and said one word: "Why?"

Sky and Matthew exchanged glances. They didn't bother asking her to be more specific. They knew what she meant. Sky sat her up partway and gave her several sips of water which she sucked down. It was followed by two capsules and more water.

"That's enough for now," Sky said. "Monique, were they military people? The ones who shot you?"

She closed her eyes and didn't say anything for a moment. Finally: "They…were just…people. We thought they were Beauregard Diamonds' people." Suddenly she opened her eyes again. "Peter? Where is Peter? They shot him too."

Sky shook her head. "I'm sorry, Monique; he didn't make it."

Monique turned her head to the side and tears leaked out from under her lids. After a moment, Sky reached down and sat her partway up once more. She gave her more water.

"We don't know who they are or why they did this," she said to Monique. "Right now, however, our priority is to get you to a hospital. Tomorrow we'll head for the Saglek Air Base and see if we can find a radio or a satellite phone that works."

"We-we have a Sat phone," Monique said, her eyes still closed. "Peter had it in his hand when they shot him."

Matthew grabbed his Maglite from his pack and was out the tent flap in less than five seconds. He shone the light around the camp site, taking in their snowmobiles, Monique's sled, the glowing tent and finally the body of Peter Meyer lying half covered with snow on his snowmobile. He approached the body and, using one of the shovels stuck in the snow, uncovered him further. He checked the snow around the snowmobile but found nothing. Finally, reluctantly, he checked Meyer's pockets trying to avoid the clouded stare of the dead man.

Still nothing. Monique said he had it in his hand when he was shot. Could the killers have overlooked it? He began examining the snow around the campsite. As luck would have it, he felt himself step on something solid. It was the Satellite Phone. He picked it up, sighed and re-entered the tent, quickly closing the flap.

Sky didn't give him a chance to say anything. "Matthew, you know those three cracks I heard that we thought were ice breaking?

"Yes."

"Those were shots!"

"Yes," Matthew replied, "And I heard a fourth one. The one that did this."

He held up a piece of mangled plastic, once a satellite phone. It had a bullet hole drilled directly through its center.

* * *

Colonel Moorhead and Major Stone hovered over Lieutenant Reynold's shoulder in the Radar Ops unit. They watched the two screens relaying what the Avenger drone was picking up as it circled high over the single tent on the ground. It was dark and they were looking at an infrared rendition of everything occurring thousands of feet below at Sky's campsite.

"Where are the other three men?" Moorhead asked, as he yawned and stretched. He and Stone had spent the last five hours visiting and revisiting the unit, trying to make sense of the story occurring on the ice.

"Right now they're camped out on the opposite side of Saglek Bay to us, sir," Reynolds answered. "They're down for the night, but they'll probably be able to see all our landings and take-offs."

"Okay. Let me do a reprise of what happened here today," Moorhead said. "Corrigan and St. Onge were heading north followed by two reps from Fortune Diamonds, Boivin and Meyer, right? These are the ones following them since the outset, trying to beat them to a claim."

"Correct, sir," Reynolds said.

"Corrigan and St. Onge went off, seemingly on a side trip for a time, and had lunch on one of those hills on the plain."

"Yes, sir."

"Three men – at least we assume they are men – appeared out of the north heading south and encountered Boivin and Meyers. Without any provocation we could make out, the three men shot them and buried them in the snow."

"Correct," Reynolds said, looking baffled. "Why? We have no idea, Colonel."

"Corrigan and St. Onge then head north again, decide to turn around and retrace their path southward where they by-pass the shooting scene. They almost catch up to the three men but, at the last moment, they stop. For some reason they turn around. They return to the scene of the shooting, discover the bodies and find one person alive. Do you know which one?"

"No sir," Reynolds answered. "Snow too thick for a good image."

"They appear to have treated the survivor and now have him or her in the tent down there."

"Yes, sir. We have seven individual heat signatures in the tent. Probably a lantern, couple of heaters, the dog and three adults."

Stone watched the Colonel and posed the question he knew Moorhead was considering: "So what do they do now? After all, we're assuming the trio thought both were dead so the victim must be seriously wounded."

"You know what they're going to do," Moorhead responded.

"Yes, Colonel, they are going to head right back here because they'll figure there has to be a medical facility on this base, deserted or not. And St. Onge, being a surgeon, will hope to find an operating theatre here. Except this time, if we don't answer the doorbell, she'll blow the lock off and kick her way in."

"And we'll have a lot more than egg on our faces," Moorhead added. "Those three assholes that did the shooting may have screwed up our entire mission. I want an Away Team out at first light to take them into custody. Their adventures in the North are over!"

"I'll get right on it, sir."

"Once the mission is complete, we'll turn them over to the Canadian Mounties."

"There will be questions asked," Stone cautioned. "Questions we may not want to answer. And if we tell the Canadians exactly what happened, they'll want proof of those murders, proof like those scenes from our Avenger."

"You're right, Paul. We'll decide what to do with the three men after the mission. The Labrador Sea is a mighty big body of water."

"One other thing, Colonel. There's something that might convince Corrigan and St. Onge to continue on their journey."

"You mean if they could find help for the gunshot victim?"

"Yes. We could render assistance," Stone said.

Moorhead shook his head. "We can't do so overtly or they'll know we're watching them. They could assume the F-35 was a stroke of luck, but another intercession? They'd know they're under a microscope. We have to wait for them to come to us."

"What happens at that point?" Stone asked.

"I have an idea," Moorhead replied. "I need you to find me a camera, sound system and an electrician. Oh, yes…and break out two hazmat suits and a biohazard flag. This base is now doing chemical warfare experiments. Prepare for some live theatre that will explain all the cloak & dagger to our friends."

* * *

Major Paul Stone stood in the conference room and used his laser pointer to pinpoint the exact position of the trio of hunters on the map displayed on the 55-inch digital monitor. Ten fit looking men in battle fatigues sat around the 15-foot, oval spruce-top table and watched him.

"The 'enemy' for want of a better word, is camped here, probably planning on crossing Saglek Bay…right up here if they want to continue their journey south," Stone said. He moved the pointer to approximately where Corrigan and St. Onge had crossed Saglek Bay.

"You said they're civilians, sir?" Sergeant Ed Tucker said, lightly tapping his pen on a pad in front of him. Tucker was no more than 25-years-old, and sported a 1950s brush cut. With his blond hair and fair complexion he could have doubled for 50s movie star Tab Hunter.

"That's right, Sergeant," Stone replied. "But we also have to remember they attempted to kill two people yesterday and succeeded with one. We know they're using fake identities and have reason to believe they may have hacked into the Parks Canada system and created bogus permits and registration for travelling in the Torngat Mountains. We have no idea who they are or what they are up to. Nor do we know where they came from."

"So they should be treated as hostile, sir?" Tucker asked.

"Definitely, Sergeant," Stone replied. "You are not to let your guard down for a moment. We want you to disarm them, secure and blindfold them, and then transport them back to base. They are to be treated as extremely dangerous."

"No problem, sir. I think the ten of us can take on a few civilians." He looked around at his men. They laughed.

Stone surveyed them and thought: the folly of youth. Confidence, perceived invincibility and the strength of numbers was already making them complacent.

"Sergeant, your attitude gives me great pause as to whether you are up to this job. I have told you…in fact…I've told you *all* how dangerous these three are, and yet you seem to regard this assignment as something more suited to boy scouts? Is that pretty much it, Sergeant?"

Tucker turned red and sat up straight, as did his men around the table.

Stone continued: "These three are dangerous people who have already killed and you are not to let your guard down for a moment. Do not engage them in conversation. Do not approach their tent. Do not expose yourself or your men. Surround them, order them out of their tent, and take them prisoner. Have I made myself clear?"

"Yes, sir," Tucker replied. "Sorry, sir. Permission to speak, sir?"

"Go ahead," Stone said.

"Begging your pardon, sir, but we meant no disrespect. We intend to take all measures to ensure a safe and successful mission."

Stone nodded, keeping eye contact with Tucker. "One other thing, Sergeant, there will be a Predator on station tomorrow morning with two Hellfires aboard. Just in case. However, we'd prefer to question them rather than toast them. Try to make that happen, won't you?"

~7~

"I think we're screwed now," Hoover said to Schaeffer and Legrand. "I think we are Gulag screwed." He was chewing on a granola bar from an MRE box and sitting cross-legged on his sleeping bag on the floor of their snow-white, camouflage tent.

They had pitched it close to a dark rocky outcrop with the hope that if anyone saw it, they would focus on the black rock and slide right over the white tent with the snow heaped halfway up its sides.

Outside, all three snowmobiles and their sled were also lined up outside the tent flap covered with snow-white nylon tarps so they also resembled nothing more than big, snow-covered boulders.

At the allotted time, they had pulled out their small transmitter and uploaded their status report to the satellite where it would be routed to the *Operation Phoenix* Command Centre. They would not be able to receive a reply to their report for another eight hours. It would arrive at the same time they sent in their second report. The fact they had already been compromised seemed almost impossible. And yet two dead civilians lay in snowy graves

The men had a single propane heater and three candles lit, and it was freezing in the tent. None had bothered to take off their parka.

"How the hell did the little prick know who we are and what our mission is about?" Legrand asked, staring at a candle flame. "How could that be?"

Schaeffer had been giving the matter much thought since the afternoon and he was beginning to believe they might have jumped to a wrong conclusion. The fellow hadn't revealed any extraordinary knowledge of their mission. He merely insinuated he had it.

"Maybe he was talking about something else," Schaeffer ventured. "Maybe he thought we were poaching. Maybe he thought we were fucking polar bears. Maybe he thought we were little green men from outer space."

"He had a pistol," Hoover reminded them.

"Not in hand," Schaeffer replied. "He didn't even reach for it. Would you do that if you thought you were facing down three Russian agents who'd kill to keep their mission secret? In a spot where you couldn't exactly call..." he hesitated and then added, "...9-1-1?"

"Doesn't make any sense," Legrand agreed.

"No it doesn't. That's why I think we overreacted," Schaeffer said. "Like amateurs."

"The problem is we aren't spies," Hoover interrupted. "We're soldiers. We weren't supposed to meet anyone. We're supposed to dig in, and observe and report."

"Whatever," Schaeffer said. "If they talked to the base and mentioned three guys out here, we might have had a visit from a military patrol, sooner rather than later. They had to be terminated."

"We have impeccable credentials," Hoover protested.

"It's not about identity," Schaeffer argued. "Even if they bought our story, hook, line and...?"

"...sinker," Hoover offered.

"Okay, sinker. Even if they bought it, they could still tell us to get the hell away from their base and make sure we travelled far enough to be useless as ground watch."

"True," Legrand said.

"So we eliminated a potential problem."

The others agreed. After a moment Legrand said: "Too bad about the girl. Very pretty."

"And we have very pretty girls at home too," Hoover asserted. "My baba told me that during the Battle of Leningrad, we had more than a million casualties. In one, single week, Axis bombs killed 40 thousand civilians alone. During the battle, tens of thousands of our young girls and women were taken from their homes and raped before being murdered."

Silence descended on the tent, each man lost in his own thoughts.

"That's why I'm here," Hoover continued. "We must never again weaken, never allow foreign troops to invade our country to rape, pillage and kill our people. Never!"

"Okay, settle down, Attila boy," Schaeffer said, "And by the way, it's your grandmother, not your baba, Hoover. We're in fucking North America. Remember?"

* * *

Sky and Matthew took turns sitting up with Monique all night. She slipped slip in and out of consciousness; they closely monitored her temperature, checked on her breathing and Sky took her blood pressure frequently. Though, initially it had been way down, she had responded nicely to the transfusion and liquids they fed her; Sky made sure she took water every half hour. Her body had a lot of blood volume to replace.

They had moved Monique onto a cot after the transfusion, and Atemu slept beside her, obviously sensing her distress and providing support the only way he could – through companionship.

Sky had pulled out a plastic washing pan and slipped this under Monique to allow her to relieve herself. She carefully checked the contents. Monique needed to excrete 30 ccs an hour to avoid kidney shutdown. She wasn't there yet, so when Matthew took his turn, Sky urged him to press her to drink more. She told him to wake her if there were any toiletries involved.

Sky knew that if the wound was infected, her patient would start to spike a temperature by the morning. In fact, that was the likely scenario. The bullet would have carried bacteria, some gunpowder residue and material from her garments deep into her shoulder. She needed to get Monique into an OR, thoroughly clean out and debride the wound, and repair what damage she could. Then fill her with IV antibiotics. Saglek Harbour was their best bet.

By morning, Monique was awake and Sky was keeping pain meds in her keeping her marginally comfortable. She was able to talk and anxious to know why her attackers had killed her partner and very nearly killed her?

"Did you recognize them?" Matthew asked. "Have you ever seen them before? Anywhere?"

"No, we never saw them before. Peter thought they must be from Beauregard Diamonds," Monique said, avoiding their eyes and, obviously, embarrassed at her own role in the event. "Beauregard is also trying hard to find out where your grandfather found the diamond."

"Is that who they were?" Matthew pressed.

"I don't know but I've never heard of anyone in our business shooting someone over information. Even if it is worth a fortune." She began to cough and the pain it inflicted was evident. After a moment she settled back, taking a deep breath.

"They came from the north," Sky said.

"That surprised us too," Monique whispered. "We thought maybe they found the diamond site already. Peter tried to bluff them with some ludicrous charade about reporting them as claim jumpers or something. He thought maybe they would offer Fortune Diamonds a partnership for our silence."

"We're going to have to pack up and get going," Sky interrupted.

"You're sure they weren't military police or soldiers?" Matthew pressed.

"They weren't wearing uniforms. Peter held up his Sat phone and said he knew exactly who they were and what they were doing up here. Then he said he was going to report them. They looked at each other, pulled guns from under their jackets and started shooting. That's all I remember."

"Okay, try to rest," Matthew said.

He and Sky packed all their gear. They left the tent and Monique's cot for last. Sky had displaced Atemu from her sled, and piled more gear on Matthew's. She rigged a bed of sorts for Monique cushioned with blankets and sleeping bags and ultimately the tent.

Monique was propped on Matthew's snowmobile and watched carefully as they finished packing. They both supported her walk to the bed on Sky's sled, helped her lie down, and covered her with blankets. They knew she was hurting. Still, she kept her silence and merely gritted her teeth with every movement. By the time she was settled, her face was soaked with sweat.

Sky took out an old fashioned thermometer she kept in her shirt pocket against her body to keep it warm. She checked Monique's temperature again.

"Damn," she mumbled.

"How high is it?" Monique asked, fear in her voice.

"It's okay, nothing I didn't expect," she said, evenly.

She joined Matthew at his snowmobile and dropped her voice. "It's 39 C so she definitely has an infection going on. I'll have to get out my kit again, give her another antibiotic shot and an anti-inflammatory. I can hold it off for a bit, but the wound is likely beginning to fester. Eventually she'll go into septic shock and I have a limited spectrum of antibiotics. I think we can do this trip in one day?"

"Okay," he said. "But at the speed we'll be going, it'll be dark when we cross the bay. And we have to remember, we're heading the same way those killers went."

"Since *they* weren't wearing uniforms I think we can rule out base security. So they might by-pass the base and continue south. Who they are and why they tried to murder two people is a question still to be answered."

Matthew looked at her. "I think you were right when you said we're part of some larger game being played, and we don't know where we fit in."

"I agree. And, just in case, I stuck the .30-30 in your gear there and I'll have the .308 in my scabbard," she said. She shook her head in frustration. "Should have had a back-up phone."

"You checked it before you took out the batteries for charging."

"Yes but I should have checked it again before we hit Unity Bay. When we could still turn around and borrow another phone."

She accessed her medical pack and then crossed to Monique who lay asleep. She gently woke her, pulled down the blanket, and gave her the injection. Then she helped her swallow two 500 mg. of A.C. & C. with codeine.

"We're going to take it easy," Sky explained to Monique, "but there will be discomfort for you on our journey. We're hoping somebody will be at the Saglek base which appears to have been refurbished. If not, we'll break in and hope there are medical facilities there. Or, at least communications gear so we can summon an air ambulance and get you to a proper hospital. If that doesn't work out and I have the equipment I need, I'll have to go in and repair your wound as best I can."

Monique looked at her with evident trepidation. Sky smiled in her best bedside manner: "Don't worry, we'll take good care of you."

As they prepared to depart, Sky radioed Matthew. "I'm glad I front-end loaded our trip, Matthew. But to get you back to the Torngats in time, we need someone to be at that base. If there's nobody there, or we can't contact somebody, I've no idea what we'll do."

* * *

By nine o'clock the next morning, dawn was beginning to break as Hoover awoke. He looked over at Legrand and Schaeffer; both had their eyes open, not moving a muscle.

"What?" he whispered.

Schaeffer slowly lifted a finger to his lips, not moving any other part of his body. He motioned toward the door and all four walls of the tent and then made a circular motion with his finger and pointed towards his ear.

Hoover began to breathe quickly, on the verge of panic. Legrand reached over and rapped him with a knuckle on the side of his head.

Schaeffer was telling them all that he had heard noises on many sides and there was a good chance they were surrounded. Not one of them moved.

All three lay there listening to the wind moaning outside for five minutes. The tent flapped intermittently, the only sound any of them heard. And yet, *something* had awakened them. There was a muted glow from outside the tent so they knew the first streaks of dawn were appearing. Since he was on an active mission, Schaeffer's "soldier" instinct was now on full alert. With sleep deprivation common on assignments, even weary soldiers would still awaken on full alert when a sense of danger prodded them. It could come from a footstep, a cracking branch, a sudden silence, or simply from a warning generated deep in their primal nerve center.

Something isn't right.

Five minutes passed and still not a sound. Legrand began to think their warning systems had gone awry, generated a false alarm. That's when they all heard it.

Faint though it was, no soldier could mistake the rack of an automatic weapon being cocked somewhere close by.

"Fuck," Schaeffer whispered, still not moving.

They waited for another minute but didn't hear a second sound. Hoover was hoping against hope they'd been mistaken. That they'd heard a piece of rock falling, or an errant icicle shattering. Still deep in his heart he knew it wasn't so. Those had been metal-on-metal clicks.

Could there be a hunter outside? One who was taking precautions with obvious strangers in a strange land? If so, he wondered how many legitimate hunters used automatic weapons in the Canadian North. That had definitely been the rack of an automatic weapon. The answer to how many hunters used automatic weapons was probably nil. So, if it wasn't a hunter/poacher with a huge personal quota, it had to be someone in the military. He picked "military" as his new word of the day.

Then Schaeffer finally said the words both Legrand and Hoover hoped they wouldn't hear for many days. Indeed, somewhere in the deeper recesses of their minds, it would have been impossible not to have a faint hope they'd get out of this alive. Through some miracle they wouldn't have to self-destruct. The eternal hope for a last-minute reprieve. Schaeffer spoke. "We can't be captured," he whispered. "We all know that, right?"

Hoovers eyes were as big as saucers as the thought of his own demise hit home, hard and bitter. It was too soon. They hadn't even begun their mission. They had contributed exactly zero to command headquarters. So they were going to die for naught. It wasn't fair.

His thoughts shifted to the *99-Rasplavleniye* built into the bottom of their sled. He knew it was a derivative of concentrated white phosphorous carefully insulated in a container of carbon disulphide to ensure it didn't oxidize prematurely, but spiked with some nasty unnamed accelerator and enhancer that turned it into one of the most lethal destructors of their time.

He'd been told that once the process of detonation began, there was no stopping it. Although, he admitted to himself, detonation wasn't exactly the right word; it was more like a furious, exponential burn that grew hotter and faster with every passing second. He had seen graphic demonstrations of this new weapon; it wasn't pretty.

But it was effective.

Their instructions had been for the three of them to gather tightly around the sled, lean over and press their heads as low as possible down towards the center of the sled before activating the bomb. That way, as it incandesced in the first few seconds, their brains would begin melting, beginning with the frontal lobe that monitored intelligence, reasoning and movement. They wouldn't be able to recoil, understand the significance of the pain or even scream. By the third second, the simultaneous destruction of temporal and the parietal lobes would kill any sensations whatsoever. Within another second, it would hit the brain stem taking out any reflexive attempts to breathe, even if there were muscles left to do so. By the sixth second their heads and upper body would be liquefied and the burn would begin its insane acceleration in earnest to the point where subsequent destruction would be catastrophic.

The burn would expand outward to incinerate everything within a 50 to 75-foot radius. It would continue to grow in intensity for another 20 seconds or so, enough time to ensure the total obliteration of them, their snowmobiles and their gear, not to mention any immediate ice, earth, and rocks beneath them. Only ash would be left.

Hoover remembered how proud the weapons specialist, who explained it to them, had been. Of course, the specialist wasn't the one whose ass was going to be turned into a Roman candle.

While post chemical analysis would be able to determine the makeup of some of the materials incinerated, there was no way anything could be identified as to its origin.

"Okay," Schaeffer said, interrupting Hoover's thoughts. "Whoever is out there is going to expect us to exit and take a few moments to orient ourselves. So we have some leeway. The worst scenario is if we tried to shoot our way out and were wounded and taken prisoner with no chance to destroy everything. So that's not an option.

"If there are soldiers out there, they will undoubtedly assume we are civilian hunters; ones who are surprised and confused over any orders they give us. They will be hesitant to shoot Canadians on their own soil. I'm betting as long as we're not seen as an immediate threat, they'll delay long enough for us to surround our sled and complete our assignment."

"But we haven't completed our assignment," Hoover protested.

"If there are soldiers out there, we have," Schaeffer said, in no uncertain terms. "It's all over. We're going home. On angel's wings."

"Oh, man!" Legrand said, his tone hopeless.

"For any of us to be captured would be the greatest act of disloyalty, the greatest betrayal we could do to Mother Russia. Right up there with Igor Gouzenko," Schaeffer growled.

Gouzenko was a cipher clerk from the Soviet Embassy that, in 1945, alerted the Western world to the espionage activities of the USSR in North America. Later he was recognized as one of the most influential instigators of the Cold War. To Russian, and rightly so, he was a devious traitor.

"Do you think we could talk our way out of this?" Hoover asked.

"Maybe," Schaeffer answered. "But what if we can't? I am sure they are as proficient at making people talk as our dear, departed KGB used to be. There's only one way out of this and it's to show Mother Motherland how much we love her."

"Right on!" Legrand whispered, fiercely.

"Okay," Hoover agreed, reluctantly.

Quietly they climbed out of their sleeping bags and stood up. Schaeffer looked at three MRE boxes longingly. "Wouldn't mind breakfast," he said.

Legrand unzipped the tent flap a few inches and peeked out on a blue sky day. He could see a portion of the partially frozen Saglek Bay with a long snowy slope leading to it but little that was suspicious. The three snowmobiles and sled were a mere five feet away. He squinted at a mound in the snow about 200 feet away. Was that a lump of snow or the white hood of some cammo gear? He watched it for a minute but nothing moved.

"Let's eat," Schaeffer said. "Hell, we're entitled to a last breakfast, eh? Whether or not there's anyone out there."

"They broke out the MREs and used the chemical packs to heat pouches containing sausage patties, hash browns with bacon and eggs. They also ate wheat bread and jelly. Unfortunately, they had no water bottles to thaw for their cocoa beverage; they were on the sled.

"Coffee would go good, right now," Legrand said.

Schaeffer agreed. Hoover was silent. He wasn't eating.

"Hey Allan, eat up. I don't think you're going to get another chance," Schaeffer laughed. "If we have visitors, I'd like to wait until they get close enough before setting this little sucker off. Take a few of them with us." He grinned.

Legrand grinned back.

Hoover was silent.

"Okay, boys, time to get this show on the road," Schaeffer said, standing up. "We'll do the dishes later." He dropped the meal pack where he stood.

Above them on a snowy ridge, Sergeant Tucker put down his field glasses and moved the parabolic microphone ever so slightly to the right. It only seemed to operate intermittently but he had picked up the words *KGB* and *Mother Russia*. That seemed to seal the deal. Commies for sure. He took off the mic's earphones and held up three fingers high above his head and motioned towards the tent confirming for his men that there were three inside it.

He turned the mic a few degrees to the left and then back to the right, trying to fine tune it to hear further sounds from the tent.

Everything was silent for a minute and then he heard whispering again. He pushed the earphones tight against his head, straining to make out the words. At least, whoever they were, they were speaking English.

He picked up the words: *...setting this little sucker off!* Were they taking about an explosive device? He gave his men a second signal, the signal to pull back. They were supposed to do so in 50-foot increments. They were positioned to fire on the tent using the classic L ambush position so none were in the direct line of fire of anyone else. Obediently his men squirmed back another 50 feet in the snow. They had forsaken radios since sound carried so devilishly well in the freezing air. Sergeant Tucker checked the megaphone he was about to use. Hopefully it worked better than the parabolic mic.

Down below, a man stepped out of the tent, yawned, stretched and then sauntered over to their sled. He was wearing a sidearm on his belt but no other weapons were in evidence. He pulled a white tarp back and uncovered a sled attached to a snowmobile. Leaning down over the sled, he moved some gear. Then he straightened, turned and leisurely scanned the area. Suddenly, in something akin to whistling at night in a graveyard, he began to sing a sea shanty – Blow the Man Down. He kept it up repeating the only verse he knew, over and over.

Meanwhile, he scanned the four points of the compass; what he saw he didn't like. He stood there and gradually let his singing die a natural death. His eyes were narrowed against the sun now breaking over the sea to the east and casting long shadows on the snow. He was pretty sure he wouldn't be seeing the sun set that evening.

"Bastards," Schaefer said as he turned back to the sled, moved some gear aside and pulled the two-foot trigger-wire handle up on its hinge until it was within easy grasp. He looked back up at the ridge and caught a movement. A man was watching him through binoculars. He didn't show any reaction and looked about as though enjoying the morning. It wasn't difficult to make out at least seven other men in attack positions. Some were near rock outcroppings, others hunkered down in their snowy foxholes, and one used the lay of the land and his white cammo suit to conceal himself. Numerous black rifle muzzles were pointed at him.

Somebody at home had obviously fucked up big time on this mission. Their first day resulted in running into two civilians who threatened to report them; and, on their second, they had a military welcome party and they didn't appear to have brought a cake, balloons, or a brass band.

"See anything?" Legrand called from inside the tent.

"Oh yes," Schaeffer drawled, nonchalantly. He stretched his arms high over his head again, pretending to stretch. "Everything's set if you and Allan want to get yourselves out here. And bring the transmitter. Let's make sure it disappears first-hand with us."

On the ridge, Sergeant Tucker put down his glasses. Enough of this. He'd prefer to see them all out of the tent. That way he'd know what they were doing. But, as the Rolling Stones sang: *You can't always get what you want.*

"Attention hunters in the tent," his megaphone barked. "This is the United States Air Force requesting you come out with your hands in the air. You are completely surrounded. Do not...I repeat...do not pick up any weapons. You, sir, standing near the sled, raise your hands immediately!"

Nothing happened.

Schaeffer simply grinned up at the ridge and leaned back, half sitting on the sled, his arms folded.

Tucker repeated the warning.

Still no reaction.

Tucker debated the wisdom of firing a burst over the man's head.

The man below finally yelled up at him: "We are Canadians. Who the hell are you?"

Legrand and Hoover slowly came out of the tent, their hands in the air.

"Put your fucking hands down," Schaeffer said, to the two men joining him. Facing the ridge and still smiling, he unfolded his arms and nonchalantly reached back towards the detonation handle now sticking up almost to the top of the sled's side. All he had to do was give it a good yank and the world would disappear for the three of them.

The megaphone spoke again. "We are the United States Air Force. Please listen closely. Stay away from any weapons, put your hands in the air, and turn around. Begin to walk backwards towards me with your hands up until I say to stop. Do you understand?"

"We are Canadian citizens, sir, and you are on Canadian soil," Schaeffer yelled back. "We do not have to obey you in any capacity. You say that you are American soldiers? Then you are transgressors in a sovereign country. What do you want?"

"Sir, this will end badly if you do not listen and obey. We know you are not Canadian citizens, your identifications are fake, you attempted to kill two people yesterday and you are in this park illegally. You are under arrest. All three of you, put up your hands and turn around. If you do what you are told, I promise you, you will not be harmed."

"You guys ready?" Schaeffer asked, a big grin still on his face.

"Looks like the jig is up," Legrand said.

"Wait, let me talk to them," Hoover said. Suddenly he whirled and strode towards the ridge.

"What the fuck!?" Schaeffer said, taking his hand off the trigger. "Pietro, get back here!"

Pietro Perezhogin, alias Allan Hoover, suddenly began to run. His boots sunk into the snow dramatically slowing his progress. Still, he ran like death was chasing him, gasping for oxygen, spittle flying out his mouth and eyes wide in terror as he imagined a bullet tearing into his back. Desperately he yanked his boots out of the snow, throwing himself forward.

"That son-of-a-bitch isn't going to talk, he's surrendering," Schaeffer shouted, as Hoover's hands shot into the air and he ran faster.

The Americans were screaming: "*Freeze! Freeze!*" To Schaeffer it was a ludicrous and comically unnecessary command since it was easily -20 below and everything was freezing. He dragged out his revolver and fired towards his fleeing partner but Hoover kept on trucking. He was easily 100 feet away. Schaeffer was about to fire again when the M16A2 5.56 NATO-chambered round hit him in the chest blowing a saucer-sized hunk of flesh out of his back and sending him reeling backward to land in the sled.

Ivan Medvedkov, alias Yves Legrand, meanwhile had drawn his own sidearm and was taking careful aim at Hoover who was running for his life. Hoover's hands were in the air and one boot was now off. "Fucking coward," Legrand screamed. He snapped off the shot. Almost simultaneously a round hit him somewhere in the gut and doubled him over. He felt his bowels give way at the same time the pain hit.

On the sled, Dimitri Onegin, alias Wolfgang Schaeffer, was gurgling noisily as he tried to breathe with a punctured lung. He labored to sit up and reach the trigger-wire handle for the bomb but blood was pumping out of his chest and down his arm like a river. His bloodied hand kept slipping off the handle each time he grasped it. He felt so weak, so tired.

There were more screams of *Halt* and *Freeze* and *Surrender* shouted at them as Legrand staggered over and collapsed face-down on the sled. He looked up at Schaeffer beside him and gasped: "Man, we're the Volga without a paddle."

"Fucking Pietro and all his outrage over Stalingrad," Schaeffer said, and coughed out a bubble of bloodied phlegm. Then he threw up a geyser of blood, mucus and MRE bits that ran down onto his sweater. "Ivan, please! You have to do it…I can't move," he gasped.

Legrand heaved himself over till he had a firm grasp on the handle. Around them, soldiers in white cammo suits were standing up, their weapons all pointed at Legrand and Schaeffer. Seemingly far off voices continued to frantically scream hysterical instructions at them.

"Shall I wait till they get closer?" Legrand whispered, nodded towards the soldiers who looked ready to advance.

"No time," Schaeffer gasped. "Hurry! Do it!"

Numbness was beginning to creep over his body and Legrand looked over at Schaeffer sitting awkwardly half in the sled, his legs and arms dangling uselessly now. "Dimitri, we're-we're…supposed to…press our heads down here," he gasped through the all-encompassing pain.

"Sorry Ivan, afraid m-my ass is going to…have…to do," Schaeffer murmured.

Legrand nodded and allowed himself to imagine hearing the strains of Russia's new national anthem: *Patriotocheskaya Pesnya.* Using every ounce of his remaining strength he managed to raise his arm and hand into the air, the middle finger extended in an international salute.

Then, humming to himself, he leaned down and yanked the detonator handle on the phosphorous bomb.

~8~

It was close to noon under a grey, cold sky when Sky gunned her snowmobile to make it up a small rise and then, remembering Monique lying in the sled, immediately slowed. Though she occasionally caught cries of pain from behind when they hit a frozen ice ridge, or eased over a particularly rough stretch, her patient never openly complained nor begged her to go slower. But the fact Sky heard her over the snowmobile's engine meant it must have been particularly painful. She tried to pick the smoothest route but sometimes there was simply no smooth route over the ice. She shivered and wished for a hot coffee.

Matthew was riding behind keeping an eye on Monique and glancing worriedly back at Atemu perched precariously on his overloaded sled. Since they had displaced a sizeable amount of gear on

Sky's sled to make room for their patient, it had all wound up on his own. There was barely a light depression left for Atemu.

Ahead, Sky constantly scanned their trail and the hills beside them to see if any of the three snowmobiles they were following appeared. The real problem was that the killers could have travelled straight ahead for a half mile, and then doubled back off the ice and hidden in the hills beside them to set up an ambush. She was on high alert for anything that wasn't white or grey. Their main advantage was that the trio probably didn't know they were being followed.

Eventually she held up her hand and her snowmobile ground to a halt. Quickly and unobtrusively she checked the surrounding terrain once more, her hands never far from her carbine. The frigid wind continued to blow and clouds scuttled across the sky. There wasn't that hushed sound that she had come to associate with danger.

Matthew also stopped and waited for a sign from her to approach. He soon realized she was checking Monique. Holding a water bottle Sky helped her sit up, and eat two more tablets. Monique nodded her thanks and sank back on her makeshift bed. Sky quickly inserted a thermometer in her mouth, checked the results and gave Matthew a look.

She left Monique and approached him as he got off his sled. "Temp is still 39 C degrees," she said, quietly, "so it's up there. If she isn't treated soon, the infection will worsen and her temperature will rocket up dramatically. We have to be close to the fiord crossing now, so we're not stopping until we reach the base."

"We'll cross the bay in the dark?" Matthew asked, remembering her reluctance to do so before.

"We don't have any choice Matthew. We'll look for our old tracks, try to retrace them. As I said before she could go septic on us. Time is our enemy. The wound needs to be cleaned and we want to load her up with a ton of IV antibiotics, A-SAP."

"Okay," Matthew replied, remembering the many ice sinkholes they had barely avoided on their first crossing in broad daylight. "I'll take point when we reach there."

Sky thought about it for a moment and saw the wisdom. "Okay, but go slow. And I want a tether around you."

"Sky, thank you but you know it won't work. I'll be running over it with my sled, or worse, you'll run over it, I'll accelerate and yank myself right out of my seat. Then Atemu will be driving. And I hear he has a heavy foot."

She smiled at him, loving the way he often defused tension with gentle humor. "Okay, you're right. But when we reach the bay, Matthew, no taking chances."

For some reason her concern made him feel good. But then he realized it was likely situational concern rather than anything personal.

A half hour later, they unhooked their sleds, left Atemu with Monique and made a five minute run up a hill to check the route ahead. Gazing south, they were shocked to see a brilliant yellow fire cluster explode in the hills ahead. It lit up the dark bluish clouds and then quickly faded with a distant rumble. A pillar of smoke slowly dispersed.

"What the hell is that?" Matthew radioed.

"Dynamite?" Sky ventured. "I don't like this. At all. We have to be extra careful, Matthew." They returned to their sleds, hooked them up and pressed on wondering what they'd encounter further up the trail.

Soon after they ran into a rancid odor in the air. The intensity of it brought them to a halt. Matthew pulled up beside Sky. Monique was sleeping on the sled, only her nose visible amongst the blankets.

"What's that smell?" he asked, his nostrils testing the air again.

A heavy and putrid stench resembling burnt garlic was coming steadily at them via a strong, southern headwind.

"I've never smelled anything like this up here before," she answered. Then, a moment later her olfactory memory kicked in, and it hit her: Chemistry lab. "Phosphorous! When we burned phosphorous under the chemistry lab hoods, I'd get a whiff. It smelled like this."

"Phosphorous?" Matthew said. "Has to be from that explosion we saw. What the hell are those three guys up to? Other than killing people."

With no ready answers they resumed their journey. Sky was still in the lead so far. The grey clouds were beginning to dissipate as they travelled farther south. As more blue sky appeared, the sun broke through the clouds. Because they were travelling fairly slowly, it warmed their faces. An hour later, at a stop, they both heard the far-off clatter of a helicopter. *Something* was going on.

For them the stench hadn't waned, In fact, it was building. Sky was pretty certain they were going to reach the source very soon.

By mid-afternoon they had the bay in sight. The sun was already sinking much too swiftly towards the tops of the mountains in the west. Around them shadows lengthened. Once it went behind the nearby peaks, darkness wouldn't be far behind. Sky checked her watch. By the time they reached the path across the ice, it would be certainly dark.

They finally reached a gentle snow slope leading all the way down to the bay. They could still see the three sets of fresh snowmobile tracks, the ones they had been following all day. The tracks led half-way down the slope towards a melee of other tracks, both man and machine. All the human tracks, however, appeared to stay away from a 70-foot diameter hole in the snow. Surrounding the hole were a series of aluminum poles with yellow tape attached, the type used by police to mark crime scenes. From the midst of the hole, smoke sifted up into the deep blue sky. A blackened, burned rock stood to the side. It was plain where the smell of burned phosphorous was coming from.

Sky and Matthew rode their vehicles down to the edge of the "crime scene" tape and both disembarked. Matthew ordered Atemu to "stay" in no uncertain terms. He watched them from the sled, ears cocked on alert.

The hole was about eight feet deep with the bottom stacked with grey ashes, to what depth they had no idea. Wordless they watched the yellow and green smoke seep up from various spots in the ashes only to disappear and then reappear in new spots a few seconds later.

"Late season Bar-B-Q?" Matthew asked.

"I'd hate to be the guest of honor," Sky answered. "Any ideas?"

"Not one. But look at the ridge over there. Several sets of tracks up and down. And over there and there."

They checked on Monique who was still sound asleep, then trudged up towards the ridge. Off to one side, a lone set of tracks led upward. As they traced them backwards, they could see they came from the vicinity of the hole. They crossed the snow towards the trail.

"I don't want to waste time for Monique's sake but we better understand what happened here and what we could be facing," Sky said. "Look at this."

She reached down and pulled a single boot out of the snow and examined it. A Sorel Tofino man's right boot with laces not done up. "That's strange. If you lose a boot in winter in Labrador, you retrieve it; it's never up for debate."

Matthew looked at the trail plainly leading up the small ridge.

"Look at the width of his strides. He was running from something."

They followed the tracks upward and then found a spot where the man had obviously rolled in the snow to put out a fire. All around the roll marks were burned pieces of wool stuffing, melted bits of nylon and oodles of black soot.

"So he was on fire when he was running, at least for these last few steps," Matthew mused. "That would be a very good reason for a lack of concern over the current status of his footwear."

Sky gave him a look. She then examined the two sets of tracks that descended from the ridge and met up with the man on fire at the spot where he rolled. Three sets of tracks then led upward, one obviously minus a boot. There was splashes of crimson mixed in with the snow near the boot. It had to be blood.

They looked down the slope at Atemu who had jumped off the sled and moved over to sit beside Monique. "He's smelled the blood," she said. "Now he's on guard for her."

"As long as he doesn't go near that pit," Matthew cautioned.

On top of the ridge they could see the imprints where three men had lain down with a good view of the hole. Matthew caught a glint of brass and found an empty casing from a 5.56 mm slug. "This is a NATO round," he told Sky. "Someone was shooting at something or someone from here on the ridge. Obviously Mr. One Boot was not being shot at or he wouldn't have been running towards the shooter. He was trying to get away from someone below. Maybe received covering fire from up here."

Sky looked at Matthew. "You sound so authoritative."

"We all went through basic training, even pilots," he responded.

Sky closely examined snowshoe tracks as well and pointed at a particularly good one. "These aren't Innu-made snowshoes," she said. "See the roundness of the outer structure? These have an aluminum or metal frame of some sort."

Matthew could also see seven other positions down below where snow had been disturbed with tracks leading from them. They were set in the classic military ambush "L" position so no man was shooting towards his or her comrades. But who, exactly, was being ambushed? Where had that hole come from? Who was ambushing who?

After considering all the information for a few minutes, Matthew advanced his theory of what happened: "We've been cautiously following the three sets of snowmobile tracks belonging to the killers all day," he said. "And you can see they lead to the 'hole.' But no snowmobile tracks come out of the hole. Just a single set of man tracks running towards the ridge."

"Okay," Sky said.

"At some point, an ambush was set up around the hole since all the positions have imprints of men facing it. Also, the high position fired one shot, at least, based on the cartridge we found. There could be more lost in the snow."

"So you think the hole was the campsite of the three men who shot Meyer and Monique?"

"Probably," he said, shrugging.

"What did they do? Nuke it?"

"It almost seems like that," he said. "From what I can see, before the shooting started, one of them – Shoeless Joe – decided to save his tail and ran for enemy lines to surrender, losing footwear in his haste. Probably that didn't set well with his compadres. Based on the length of his strides, I'd say he feared his partners. They may have been trying to take him out. Hence the blood in the snow." He pointed down at the stains that had pretty much turned pink by this time.

Sky nodded. She felt Matthew's assessment made more sense than anything she could come up with.

"When the explosion came, he wasn't quite out of range and got singed. But it seems like he made it; he rolled to put out the fire. And two sets of footprints came down to help him."

"So you think the hole was where the people who shot Monique were camped?"

"I do," Matthew replied.

"Which brings us back to: What the hell did that?" She pointed at the hole.

"Something very bad. Remember, since time began we have always been finding bigger, better and more expedient ways to kill each other. Our shoeless wonder may have been running since he knew something was about to explode."

"Okay, so *who* did all this?"

Matthew looked far across Saglek Bay and gave it some thought before he answered. "You remember when you said that the odds of running into five people out here in the dead of winter were astronomical?

"Yes."

"How about running into another ten?"

"Impossible, unless there was some sort of military—!" She stopped dead. "Saglek Harbour Base!"

"I'd say this clinches it. Definitely not as deserted as we originally thought," he said.

* * *

In the dark, Matthew's snowmobile headlamp gyrated wildly from highlighting the snow on the trail crossing the bay, to losing itself in the night sky overhead. He was driving over drifts as high as his shoulder. The trick was to mount the drifts forcefully and slow immediately just over the top as the weight of the sled he was towing bore down trying to force his vehicle to speed up. Looking back he could still see Atemu's furry silhouette perched on his sled compliments of Sky's headlamp following about 15 yards behind. Nightfall had offered them colder temperatures for a decrease in wind. Not a bad trade but still he shivered.

They had been progressing steadily across the western arm of Saglek Bay. They didn't have to search for their previous trail since it looked like an armada of snowmobiles had followed their original route both coming and going. If he found himself heading for virgin snow, he knew immediately he was going off trail and corrected his heading.

Reaching a relatively smooth spot he steered with one hand while looking at the glowing hands of his watch. It was 4 A.M., and he figured they'd be across in another hour. That meant they could make it to the base by first light. It was taking much longer this trip since they were trying to minimize Monique's discomfort. Thankfully she slept most of the time despite the rough trail. Of course, this was aided by Sky administering the codeine-based tablets.

At that moment, Sky's voice crackled through his headset: "Matthew, I think it's time for a rest; give our arms and shoulders a little time out."

"Good idea," he radioed back, and cut his engine when he reached a flat spot.

She stopped well behind him and pulled off her helmet and balaclava. Despite the warmth they provided in the sub-zero weather, it felt good to escape the claustrophobic confines of the helmet and feel cool air flow over her scalp.

Matthew followed suit, disembarked and went back to Atemu. Though he had made him a better bed lined with a wool blanket (which Matthew had drawn over him when they started) it hadn't been long before he was sitting up, a second pair of eyes for driving. Fortunately he was a wise, and therefore silent, back-seat driver.

Though their progress was slow, the crossing wasn't as bad nor as dangerous as they had assumed it would be. A couple of times they saw where the many snowmobiles had veered from their original tracks on the way over and branched farther up the bay. They chose to follow them rather than stick to their original trail. Obviously, the riders had been suspicious of the trail and it was better to be safe than sorry. Their path soon turned back towards the opposite shore.

When they finally reached land, Sky signaled for a halt and took Monique's temperature. She was awake and cooperative but obviously in more pain. Sky read the thermometer and walked a good dozen yards away from the snowmobiles. Matthew followed. Atemu watched them from the sled.

"Her temperature is up," she said, wiping the thermometer, and storing it in an inner pocket of her parka. She put her mitts back on and stared at the sky.

The stars were no longer in sight and the unremitting cold was taking its toll on them both. The only welcome concession was the continued lack of wind.

Sky called Atemu to join them. Then they did a brusque walk around the vehicles for five minutes, made sure Monique was comfortable, and resumed their nighttime journey. They elected to leave their helmets off and blink their running lights if they needed to stop.

Reaching land, they coped with a new challenge. Most of the trail was on a 20-degree slope leading to the mountainous terrain on their right side, so they were constantly fighting to keep the sleds from skidding to the left behind them. They proceeded slowly but this still resulted in the occasional bounce as the sled slewed sideways and hit an outcropping. More than once Matthew heard a sharp cry of pain and then

Sky calling out an apology to Monique.

Finally, with the sun on the horizon and morning light flooding the frozen white countryside, they glimpsed the lower base of Saglek Harbour. They travelled until they hit the end of the runway, a relatively flat surface and therefore an easier ride for Monique.

Sky pulled up beside Matthew and they stared at the base before them. It was well lit with lamps around the grounds; yellow light spilled from multiple windows onto the snow.

"Not as deserted as we thought," Matthew mused, confirming the obvious.

"Not this time," Sky agreed. She pointed down at the runway surface where they sat. The tire marks from multiple takeoffs and landings of aircraft could be plainly seen, as well as piles of freshly plowed snow to the sides and at their end of the strip.

They slowly motored towards what they considered the main building sitting under the Control Tower of the base. As they neared the front door, Matthew pointed towards what had previously been a naked flagpole. Now it was adorned with a flag snapping in the breeze. But it was not a Canadian flag. Rather, the yellow flag plainly displayed three partially completed circles superimposed over a fourth circle. It was the international symbol for biohazard activity, or the presence of biological materials carrying a significant health risk.

What the hell was going on?

He exchanged looks with Sky who rode beside him now. As they approached closer, he stared up at the Control Tower; it looked deserted. She stopped about 100 feet from the front door. He did the same.

Nothing stirred, nothing moved.

"Biohazard symbol," Matthew commented.

Sky nodded and then called out loudly: "Hello?"

Silence except for a groan from Monique on Sky's sled.

Sky had the .308 out of its scabbard and had worked the bolt placing a round into the chamber before Matthew saw what she was doing. She pointed the rifle away from the building and towards the hills and fired a shot. The crash echoed off the buildings and the round wound up somewhere in the remoteness of the countryside.

"Aren't we supposed to fire in the air?" Matthew asked, nervous about discharging a weapon on a military base. By rights, MPs should have been swarming over them by now.

"You do and the gases and sound disappears into the air with a pop and nobody hears it, she said. "Fire horizontally and the sound bounces off everything around you."

She was right; his ears were still ringing.

Still no reaction from inside.

They both disembarked, cautioning Atemu to stay put. Sky and Matthew approached the front door with her high-powered rifle in hand.

Nothing stirred.

They looked at the doorway which featured a five-by-five foot snow roof over top of it. The door itself was made of solid-looking heavy wood. As before, it featured a formidable, commercial grade security lock sporting an aluminum-buttoned, key-touch pad. It had been built extra wide with no window. Sky glanced up to her right at the top corner of the porch where a speaker was positioned. Beside it a small lenses was mounted. It was pointed directly at them.

"Was that thing there before?" she asked, motioning towards the speaker/camera combo.

"I'd think we would have noticed," he replied.

She pounded on the door with the butt of her weapon.

No answer.

Sky looked about; there continued to be an absence of life signs. The sun was rising higher in the sky now, heralding a sunny day. She moved backwards from the door, her left hand moving Matthew back with her. "If they want to be assholes, let them be assholes," she said.

Judging they were back far enough to avoid splinters, Sky pulled another round into firing chamber and aimed deliberately at the door lock six feet away.

"Stop!" a deep voice ordered from the speaker.

Sky lowered her weapon and they walked forward and looked up at the camera.

"Attention," came the voice again. "This is a Canadian-sanctioned, secure and sealed United States Air Force military site and you are trespassing. You cannot be here and if you persist, you will be arrested and prosecuted to the full extent of the law."

"Is there any other extent?" Sky asked, dryly. She looked at the camera and her tone clearly conveyed she was at the end of her patience.

"Listen whoever you are–!"

"Leave your patient!" the voice interrupted.

"What?" Sky asked, in surprise.

"Leave your patient."

"I have a female gunshot victim here with a major wound in the upper left quadrant of her chest. Infection has set in and she needs immediate medical attention."

"Leave....her!" the voice commanded. "She will receive all required treatment from our medical staff and be medivaced to an appropriate medical facility before the day is out."

"I'm not about to leave her out here in the snow," Sky said, angrily. "What the hell is the matter with you people? Show yourself."

"This is a *sealed* installation! There are biohazards involved. Leave your patient and move to the opposite side of the runway. She will be retrieved. But do it *now!*"

"We'd better do as he says," Matthew advised. "They don't sound like they're in a mood to bargain."

Sky looked at him. "Who the hell do these people think they are?" Her eyes were hard. Not a happy camper.

"Doesn't matter," he replied. "If they don't come out and get her, we'll come back over here. Then you can shoot your way in like Wild Bill Hickok. Deal?"

"Alright. But only in the interests of Monique."

They carefully lifted her, swaddled in blankets and gently deposited her a dozen feet from the doorway. Sky looked down at her. She could read the brightness of fever in her eyes. "Monique, we have brought you to an American facility at Saglek Harbour. You must have passed it in the last few days on your journey. They have promised to have you taken to a hospital today. Due to some stupid rules, we have to leave you here but we'll only be a hundred yards away. If they don't take you inside immediately, we'll be right back. And *I'll* bring you inside! Do you understand?"

Monique nodded weakly, a film of perspiration on her upper lip, the blond hair protruding from under her hood still soaked with sweat. She raised a hand and beckoned them both into her field of view. "B-both of you...thank you so much. For saving my life. For getting me here. For not pressing on to look for your diamond field when you had every right to do so. Instead, you helped me."

"Thank Sky," Matthew insisted. "She's the one who resuscitated you, treated you and kept you alive, Monique. I'm pretty much a pack mule."

Monique smiled through her pain: "A very nice pack mule. I want to say I'm sorry to you both. I wish I had let my personal ethics rather than my business ambition guide my actions. You two are very special people. I-I wish Peter had seen that. Thank you." Exhausted by the simple effort of talking, she closed her eyes and drifted off to sleep.

Matthew and Sky jumped on their snowmobiles, pulled them and the sleds in tight 180-degree turns, and roared off across the airport runway where they stopped on the other side and faced the building once more. They kept a careful eye on the small, lone figure of Monique lying wrapped in blankets in the snow in front.

They didn't have long to wait. Two people in silver, aluminized hazmat suits complete with oversized helmets and faceplates emerged through the front door pulling a stainless steel gurney covered with white sheets. They gently lifted Monique onto the gurney, strapped her in and vanished back through the front door which snapped shut the second they were through.

Sky and Matthew looked at each other in amazement and shook their heads.

"What in the hell are they doing in there?" Sky asked.

"I don't know," Matthew replied, "but those are definitely air force hazmat suits; I know them from emergency response drills."

"So who is being protected? The men inside? And from what? Us? Monique? The air out here? What's going on in there?"

"Maybe all those things," he ventured. "My worry is: Did we expose her to something more dangerous than her wound?"

"Well we're not leaving her till we're sure she's safe." She gunned her snowmobile.

Matthew watched her for a moment feeling a strange welling up of emotion. Again the thought: This girl is probably the most impressive person I have ever met in my life.

He followed her and they arrived at the front door again. Sky knocked while they stared up at the camera.

"This is a Canadian-sanctioned, sealed and secure United States Air

Force military base. You are trespassing and cannot remain here. Please do yourselves a service and leave immediately." It was the same voice, the same monotone.

"Based on what we observed, two people in biohazard suits, we are concerned we may have exposed our patient to something far more serious than her wound," Sky said loudly. "And this way of communicating is ridiculous. Who am I speaking to, anyhow?"

"Your patient is in good hands, and is already receiving treatment by our flight surgeon," replied the voice. "You must leave this area now or you will be detained. Our next response will be an armed response placing you under arrest and quarantine. Do you understand?"

"Less and less," Sky said. She turned to Matthew. "What do you think?"

"We came here with the intention of demanding treatment for Monique. I'd say we've achieved our goal. This is a US Air Force installation. They'll do their best for her."

Sky looked back up at the camera. "Thank you." She said it simply, turned and walked back to her snowmobile.

Sky motioned Atemu off the sled. He quickly relieved himself on a snowbank and leaped back aboard. They pulled their sleds away from the base and backtracked up the Western Arm of Saglek Harbour as, once again, they continued on their original journey.

* * *

"I'm sorry, sir," Airman First Class Smyth said after Colonel Moorhead gave him permission to speak. "Captain Stoiber asked me to tell you the patient died five minutes ago."

"Damn," Moorhead lamented, turning towards Major Stone. "Can't seem to catch a break."

They were sitting in Moorhead's office. The airman remained at attention.

"I'd say the patient shares your view, sir," Stone commented.

Moorhead gave him a look that plainly said: Don't be so damn smart. He looked back at the airman. "Tell the doc to prepare the body for shipment to Washington on the incoming medivac flight. That's all."

"Yes, sir," the airman said, saluted, spun on his heel and left.

"Dropping Miss Boivin off on the way as well?" Stone inquired.

"Yes. I spoke to Goose Bay. Apparently the catchment area for up here is Montreal. Doc said she's stable enough to travel to that Royal hospital."

"Royal Victoria Hospital, Colonel."

Moorhead nodded. "So, no answers from Allan Hoover who really wasn't Allan Hoover."

"According to Sergeant Tucker, he almost made it to their line but one of the other two combatants snapped a second shot off before they detonated the charge. Caught Hoover in the back, right through his lung. Major damage. He was drowning in his own blood by the time they got here. Amazed he lasted as long as he did."

"Any news re photos or prints? Be nice to know exactly who we're dealing with up here."

"No sir. OSI says no match for Hoover whatsoever from IAFIS, and the info has been run against all their databanks: fingerprints, electronic image storage, criminal histories, and physical characteristics such as scars, tattoos, and even aliases. They will check his DNA against the national DNA databank when they receive the body," Stone finished.

"All right," Moorhead said. "That was a military grade phosphorous bomb of some kind to literally vaporize them and all their gear. Never heard of anything like it before. Not a hint of a clue left. The sergeant said they mentioned Russia in their tent so it had to be a Russian reconnaissance team of some sort."

"I agree, but for them to risk such a bold move, they obviously know the stakes are pretty high here; we really have their attention."

Moorhead picked up a stainless steel letter opener and absentmindedly began to drum it on the desk. "There have been official protests lodged with the Russian Embassy over the flight incursion the other night but so far Black says they're playing dumb. They claim they're looking into it and say if one of their bombers inadvertently strayed into Canada airspace, to please accept their apologies."

"Our interceptors are on Quick Reaction Alert," Stone answered, "and the AWAC is up as you ordered. If they return we'll be ready for them."

Moorhead rose and paced in his office. "Major, I want perimeter guards doubled and two 24-hour Away Teams with night optics patrolling the base perimeters a few miles out as well. If Ivan dropped a recon team here God knows what else those crazy bastards might do. And one armed UCAV on station at all times looking for strange heat signatures anywhere near our base. If they find one and it's an unknown, I want to be notified immediately. Then we'll decide if we smoke 'em."

"Roger," Stone said.

"They'd better stay the hell away from *our* country or we're gonna send 'em to that big vodka factory in the sky."

Stone was bemused and showed it. "Canada, sir. No offense but we're guests here ourselves."

Moorhead nodded. "Of course. You know, one of their prime ministers, Pierre Trudeau I think, once said that being neighbors with the United States was like sleeping beside an elephant. No matter how friendly or even-tempered is the beast, one is affected by every twitch and grunt."

"Your point?"

"If the Ruskies start screwing around here, this elephant is going to do more than twitch and grunt."

~9~

"They missed their fourth transmission window," Major Oleg Serdyukov said to his grim looking guest. "We must assume they were discovered and self-destructed."

"Can we be sure they used the *99-Rasplavleniye*, Comrade?" General Sergei Topkolov asked in a too-smooth, oily tone devoid of any accusation or blame but nevertheless sounding threatening.

"There are no guarantees, sir, but they are…*were* some of our best men." Serdyukov looked nervously around his oak-paneled GRU office. How much longer would he reside here? Would his next posting be smack in the middle of Siberia? Someone was going to pay for this failure. He'd tried to cover his ass through notes and memos to bring everyone in the canoe. How successful he'd been was yet to be determined. Even though the GO or NO-GO decision had been made way above his pay grade, the generals and bureaucrats were very adept at shifting the blame for any malfunction down to the lowest acceptable level. In other words, his men had fucked up and so, in the end, he would be held accountable. His only hope was Topkolov.

"Yes, we can hope, can't we?" Topkolov was saying. "However, I have come from a briefing at the Central Intelligence Service where I was told our satellites show the Americans have doubled their foot patrols, put up a 24/7 AWACs aircraft and have two F-35s on a scramble alert. We see hangar doors partly open. Their actions must be motivated by something unique that has happened. Wouldn't you say so?"

"Yes," Serdyukov replied, nervously. "No sign of our men, of course?"

"None, Comrade. Unfortunately we can't risk any more inadvertent fly-overs. We have to rely on satellite imagery. Not always the best with that schizoid Labrador weather. And no current intelligence."

Serdyukov nodded, desperately wondering the best way to play his hand. Should he offer hope their team's communications gear had failed? That would probably give him a reprieve of a day or two at best. Or, should he own up and place the blame at the feet of fate? After all, he had assembled the best team he could. Surely the high command wouldn't blame him for what happened on the ground a half-world away?

Yes! Of course the Kremlin would see reason. And, maybe there was a Saint Nicholas and an Easter Bunny and a Grinch who did steal Christmas from the children of Hooterville.

He sighed at his own naivety. One thing, he knew for certain. Missions didn't fail without someone paying the price. It was *so* now. It had always been *so*. And it would be *so* in the future. And, since General Topkolov had cut him out of the loop by attending the Central Intelligence Service briefing without him, it looked like he was being lined up as the sacrificial lamb.

Not that he believed he'd be lined up against a stone wall. He was pretty sure that the new Mother Russia had dispensed with the muss and fuss of having to carry out the bullet-ridden bodies of those who displeased her so the Black Marias could cart them off for a private forest burial. At least, he hoped so.

He tried a delaying tactic. "Are there any thoughts of a second mission?" he asked.

"Surely you jest, Oleg? If the mission was successfully terminated, and they have no proof that we placed soldiers on the ground, then we dodged a bullet. How big a bullet we'll never know. Nevertheless they know something was attempted even if they have no tangible proof. To try the same thing again would be tantamount to spitting in their eye. This time they would undoubtedly take the matter to the UN Security Council and once again we would be on the defensive. Surely they would not sit still and do nothing. There would be reprisals."

"The imperialistic Americans aren't exactly saints," Serdyukov protested. "They have been peeking over our borders with their U-2 flights and their SR-71s for decades. How dare they take the high road!?"

His indignation was genuine but he knew the general would pick up on the fact he was trying to find a way to deflect or mitigate responsibility by playing the outraged Party member. He felt his face flush and felt ashamed of his machinations towards self-preservation. Did he not receive the *Order of Lenin* for past successes? Was he not a good Party member and a dedicated soldier? Did he not read fucking, useless *Pravda* every day and regurgitate party philosophy like a trained seal?

General Topkolov grinned at him and stood up. "Something to drink, Oleg?"

"Of course, General," Serdyukov said, quickly. "I can have some tea brought in momentarily."

"I said a *drink*, Oleg, not pussy juice!"

Serdyukov hesitated but only for a fraction of a second. He dug into a lower desk drawer and quickly dragged out a bottle of Stolichnaya Gold Vodka and two water glasses.

He filled them both half full and handed one to the general. They clinked glasses and both downed at least three ounces of the liquor in a single gulp. Serdyukov felt the fire in his belly and his limbs beginning to relax. There was a lot to be said for a quick anesthetic when your privates were about to be roasted like Saint Nicolas' chestnuts.

Topkolov looked at him and shook his head. "Oleg, I will try to protect you as best I can. We had a unanimous vote on proceeding. The mission was well planned. And, as you say, the men were our best. Anyone would agree we had little control over what happened once they were deployed. It truly is not your fault. Nor mine."

"Thank you, Comrade," Serdyukov said, relief flooding through him as quickly as the warm numbness from the 100-proof premium vodka he'd downed a minute before.

"Of course, if the Americans come calling again demanding blood, we may all have a problem."

"Deny, deny, deny," Serdyukov hastened to recommend. "There is not one shred of anything they carried that was not either manufactured in Canada or by another company that exports to Canada or the United States. And the '99' would ensure nothing survived anyhow."

"Unless it wasn't exploded."

"They'd still have nothing."

"Live prisoners they could interrogate."

Serdyukov felt a chill run through him. That would definitely not be a good thing for any of them.

Truth be known, Serdyukov was worried. Even though these were Russia's hardened, superbly trained GRU Spetsnaz soldiers, every human had his or her breaking point. If they were captured, would they stand up to American interrogation techniques? After all, these techniques were becoming highly sophisticated and refined. This wasn't the era of Russia's notorious Lubyanka Prison where prisoners went in and either talked quickly or came out in small, digestible pieces. Now they used psychological torture, deception and incentives.

In his heart Serdyukov knew that if they had been taken alive, they would eventually break. Every human would. It was a question of time.

This would be followed by a show trial and the United States would express its indignation and moral outrage like a violated virgin. It would scream and exploit the high ground even though their CIA black projects regularly violated the sovereignty and the privacy of its closest friends and allies. He sighed again.

His telephone rang and he looked over at Topkolov who nodded. Both prayed it wasn't from a superior officer now sitting in his Kremlin office.

Serdyukov picked it up, identified himself and listened to one of the sweetest messages he'd ever heard. He smiled, thanked the caller and hung up. He spun to his computer, signed in with his password, read for a moment and then turned back to the general.

"Sir, two days ago, at 0918 hours, our glorious Persona-3 satellite system reported a very bright flash via Kosmos-2506. It has a 1300 kilometer image swath and so happened to pick up the flash and residual burn, as well as log it. It was only discovered this morning. But from initial reports, it occurred on the north side of Saglek Harbour in Labrador, approximately 50 kilometers, as the crow flies, from the American base. This would approximate the location of the *Operation Phoenix* team. I think our boys did their duty."

Topkolov nodded and smiled. "Let us hope so, Oleg, for all our sakes." He reached for the vodka bottle.

* * *

Sky and Matthew had crossed the bay and were headed east towards the sea to pick up the shore ice for their journey north. Though it was now December 17th, she was pressing them forward at an unprecedented speed. Storms and being Good Samaritans was eating up their travel time. They couldn't afford any more delays.

Having repacked their snowmobile sleds, Atemu now rode with his mistress again. But, periodically he still raised his head and kept a wary eye on Matthew following diligently behind.

Matthew lifted an arm and waved at Atemu. He was surprised to see the dog actually wag his tail, as though in acknowledgement.

As evening approached, they reached the vertical cliff edge bordering what Sky named the *Plains of Pharsalus.* Meyer's body rested where they left it, now covered with a thin coating of snow. Sky pulled out her GPS and made sure the coordinates were entered so that they could tell the RCMP exactly where the body could be found when they returned to Nain. They both recognized that, crazy or not, this was an official crime scene so they decided not to move him. Instead, they buried the body under a few more feet of snow in the hopes it would discourage any wolves or polar bears from chowing down.

"We'll have to camp here again," Sky said, looking around. "Starting to get dark. Should have left the tent up."

They again pitched the tent in the same spot, ate supper inside and then exited to wash their utensils with the remains of the water they boiled.

The frozen landscape was cast in pale blue moonlight. Though it was only a half-moon, without air pollutants, it was exceptionally bright so they could easily see the blackness of the cliff looming beside them on their left; on their right was the shore ice with the ominous black swells of the Labrador Sea less than 500 yards beyond. As Matthew looked away from the moon, the brilliance of millions of stars carpeting the sky almost made him dizzy. Their tent glowed yellow from the lamp inside as they stood in front of it and took in the beauty of the subarctic night. He watched Sky go off by herself to check the tarps on their sleds and snowmobiles. Again he felt a great warmth for this beautiful and lonely looking girl. He fought the feeling; she had assured him there was no future for them many times.

To the side, Atemu sat in the snow and watched them. Matthew ruffled his head and joined Sky. They walked over and peered around the wall of the cliff onto the plain, also lit with the moonlight. Indeed, it still resembled a gleaming, icy alien terrain. They paused for another moment, enjoying the magic of the dreamlike panorama, and then heard the far-off howls of two wolf packs competing for air time. The sounds lent an additional, albeit eerie, dimension to the scene.

Finally, spent and weary from their journey, Sky and Matthew slowly walked back to their tent, called Atemu inside and zipped the opening closed.

Sky completed her nightly ritual of handing him a Commando knife in case he had to cut his way out of the tent, and placing her loaded carbine on the floor beside her cot.

She then stripped to her long underwear, bent over and turned off one of the two heaters. The Coleman lamp would expire when it ran out of pressure.

Once again he couldn't help looking at her tall, gamine figure with the slight swell of her hips and breasts augmented by her proud carriage. When she moved in her stocking feet, her lithe form had the grace of a sleek, feline predator.

This time, however, she looked over and caught him watching her.

He immediately blushed and mumbled an apology. "Sorry…I-I…just wondered if you'd like an extra…blanket," he stammered. He felt for all the world like a letch, despite his singular thought being one of admiration.

Rather than giving him a look of resentment, she smiled briefly and shook her head.

They turned in and lay on their cots looking at the tent roof which, for once, wasn't flapping madly against its frame like a demented bat. The evening was relatively calm; the subarctic coastal winds were taking a breather for a change.

One could only wonder what else it had in store for them, Matthew thought. Every day brought a new challenge, generally more bizarre than the previous day.

Sky lay there lamenting the fact she hadn't thought to ask the "voice" at the base if they could find out her grandfather's condition. Though she wasn't vocal about it, he was constantly in her thoughts. The only consolation was that she was doing exactly what he had asked of her in the hospital. A further question that nagged at her was: What would she do with Atemu when they reached the mountain? Was she prepared to sacrifice her best friend? The answer to that was an emphatic No. Would he be safe if she left him behind, on the ground? Not really.

From outside, the howl of a single wolf sounded intermittently, a wilderness song repeated nightly in Labrador. It was definitely closer. Lying in a corner on his blanket, Atemu growled softly but didn't lift his head.

"Think that wolf might try to go after the food we left on the sleds," he asked.

"Don't worry," she replied. "If he comes anywhere near camp, Atemu will wake us up."

Sky then turned on her side away from him. He was disappointed she didn't want to talk. His heart was telling him he liked her more than a little. In fact, the pheromones seemed to be working overtime lately. On his part, anyhow. Ridiculous when he put everything into perspective. But still true.

No longer in any doubt that his admiration for her was morphing into more serious feelings, he knew he had to face certain realities. Juxtaposed against his growing fondness was the knowledge she had been terribly hurt by a callous and opportunistic rich boy. Worse, however, this baggage seemed to have stayed with her for far too many years. Surely such an accomplished and attractive girl had many suitors over such a long time. And, obviously, none had worked out.

Not a good sign.

But he had another concern when acknowledging his feelings. Sky's intuitiveness was obviously on high alert; she had warned him more than once that getting close to her would be akin to looking for trouble. But still, the idea that their adventure would inevitably end, and they would part company was almost unthinkable to him.

If he ever hoped to get to know her better, or entertain the notion of a possible relationship, he knew he could not be too overt in making his feelings known. Instinct assured him any telegraphed notion of romance would drive her away in short order. So he became more and more self-conscious when they were in close quarters.

Matthew decided he had to clamp down on his feelings until their assignment was complete. Then, if he dared, he could risk telling her how he felt, or say good-bye forever. He looked over at Sky's back for indications she was awake. A sigh, a cough, anything.

He heard nothing.

She must be dead tired from an exhausting day on their increasingly bizarre odyssey. A secretive military base, biohazards, murder, mysterious explosions, ambushes, and Sky's feelings they were being watched were all combining to make this prospecting trip more like a Spielberg adventure movie. He hoped most of the strangeness was now behind them and they could get on to their final destination. If that was even possible.

Matthew tried to rein in his thoughts and relax. Both would need their strength the next day, he told himself. With a little luck there wouldn't be any more surprises.

He tossed and turned for some minutes before drifting off to sleep.

On the cot next to him, sleep wasn't coming easy for Sky neither as she estimated the number of days to the Winter Solstice versus the distance they had yet to cover. Timing had become a real concern and she was glad she had made allowances for storms and the like.

In addition, she worried constantly about her Grandfather's condition. Had he come out of his coma? Was he getting well? Was he, in fact, dead and she didn't even know it. The latter scenario filled her with dread. She tried to find solace in the fact that if something terrible had happened, she was sure her instincts would tell her.

Still, her grandfather had stressed they must reach their destination by the Solstice deadline since the other people had to leave by that time. God forbid they choose an early departure, she thought. Idly she wondered where they were going, or why they were leaving at this time.

In fact, it was a mystery she never expected to understand. She only knew that they had been here for many decades and that their work was winding up.

What had begun so long ago was now culminating in a moral-based decision by the other people to partially right a wrong. And because of her grandfather's illness she was right in the middle of it; this despite the fact that returning to the site was one of the few things in life that frightened her.

Though these people had never done anything overt or pernicious to warrant or cause her fear, she simply could not be near them without feeling an abject terror. And, after her first visitation with them, the feelings of fear that she experienced, shadowed her for months afterwards. Of course, to their credit, once they realized the reality of her feelings during that first visit, they had pretty much stayed out of sight during her second visit. And being sympathetic to her feelings, her grandfather made sure he only met with them in private.

But there was also another concern keeping her awake. More than a few times she had experienced the notion that something was up with Matthew. When they were around each other he seemed nervous and even uncomfortable. In fact, he appeared to be making a deliberate attempt not to sit too close, or even touch her. If he inadvertently did brush against her, he apologized. Prior to a few days ago, they seemed like buddies who had taken each other's measure and found a comfortable working relationship. Now he treated her like a china doll.

Not that he didn't continue to display an immense respect toward her. However, she did notice the occasional lingering glance or a quick avoidance of eye contact as though he was afraid she would read something in his glance. Now she wondered if this avoidance was because he was finding it harder to hide his inner feelings. After all, she had warned him more than once that she was best kept at a distance.

If he was just horny it would be one thing, she thought, amused. But she sensed this wasn't the case. Putting her ego aside, she was reasonably sure that there were major feelings starting to percolate. And, while she might be able to turn him off with a few sharp words, they wouldn't address how she was beginning to feel about him.

Indeed, while she had avoided close relationships with men for years, she was confused when it came to Matthew Corrigan. He was somehow different. Maybe it was nothing more than they were both free of relationships, forced together by circumstances. Or a kinship felt because they both suffered personal losses in their lives. Or, maybe it was simply that she liked his spirit, his sense of humor, and his sensitivity and kindness.

When they first met, she had seen how easy it was to hurt the man as she unfairly took out her anger over her grandfather's illness on him. In turn she felt regret at her behavior as she discovered he was a decent fellow caught up in a situation not of his own making. After all, she had no right to assume his motivations were anything other than honorable. What would he think when he found out *where* she was leading him? That was another matter altogether. She prayed that all would go smoothly and he would understand why she had to do what she did.

She really couldn't stomach the idea he might wind up hating her for involving him in something so strange it might affect him for the rest of his life.

The thing was, in truth, she had no choice in the matter.

PART FOUR

Canyon of the Winds

"If an elderly but distinguished scientist says that
Something is possible, he is almost certainly right, but if he says
that it is impossible, he is very probably wrong."
Arthur C. Clark 1969

~1~

The proverbial beans had finally been spilled.

After holding the final 411 Mission Briefing for all planning and operations personnel at Saglek, as well as RPA Pilots, Sensor Operators and Mission Commanders stationed in far-off places such as California, Colorado and other states, Colonel Robert Moorhead had finalized the mission orders.

Though there had been extensive prep work performed by Mr. Black and his largely unknown "contingent," Moorhead still fielded dozens of questions on strategy, tactics, exposures and withdrawal. Of course, this wasn't a surprise; this was pretty much SOP for any operation of this size.

The subarctic War Game simulation, code named *Operation Flashbang,* was a GO. Of course, there was still a hold on the actual launch date but everyone involved knew that it was coming very soon.

War Games generally featured two components: *Field Exercises* and *Command Post Exercises.*

Field Exercises involved the moving of men and equipment to strategic positions to carry out attack scenarios on defined objectives such as airfields, communication centers and other worthy military targets. Live ammunition was "verboten." Electronic sensors mounted on people, vehicles and buildings tallied the damage done.

Command Post Exercises, however, often operated virtually using computer simulations, either scripted or unscripted, to elicit and test command decision making.

With the briefing over and heading back to his office for a meeting with Major Stone, Moorhead asked himself: So when is a War Game not a War Game? Though the question was rhetorical, his answer was definitive: It's not a damn War Game when the Field Exercises are conducted using bullets, missiles and bombs and other unnamed but live ammo against a designated target. Even if it was a stone wall.

Which would be the case during *Operation Flashbang*.

Stored UCAVs at Saglek were being serviced, tested, and fueled, and would be fully armed once the mission was imminent.

Primary Satellite Link Communication suites, and Ground Control

Stations in Saglek and four states had undergone rigorous testing so remote control piloting and payload delivery for the Saglek UCAVs, would operate flawlessly. The command structure was in place; nothing further was needed other than a countdown. Targets had been assigned to cause maximum noise, and limited destruction in the hope of instilling panic and confusion. The objective was to cause a speedy evacuation of a base by their quarry. When a base was evacuated in panic mode, often things were left behind. And the USA was anxious to consume any leavings. To the participants, it was theatre. To the top ranks, the exercise was deadly serious.

In case the UCAVs were rendered ineffective through jamming or other defence initiatives, a Strike Squadron of 12 Fighting Falcon F-16s and five F-35s from Saglek, armed with missiles and laser-guided bombs, would be their backup. But they would be used only as a last resort since nobody wanted to explain lives lost.

The GO or NO-GO directive on a secondary strike would only come from Mr. Black, and off-site advisers who, he had once coyly hinted, included some members of the Joint Chiefs of Staff. And now Mr. Black was obviously in consultation with his so called shadow government. On the surface *Operation Flashbang* might be classed as a subarctic war game but, as Moorhead knew, their true agenda had little to do with testing preparedness. This was a live operation.

Indeed, when it came right down to it, this operation might be the biggest blunder in the annals of history. Or one of the United States military's biggest triumphs. If they were successful and reaped the rewards they hoped for, it would assure them of a giant leap forward in their technology. The only flaw in the strategy was that because a force appeared to be benign, it didn't mean it would remain benign if cornered.

To try to mitigate retaliation, the strike force was tasked with attacking the mountain where they expected the facility to reside; they were, however, forbidden from attacking any craft or "personnel" encountered. With luck, their quarry would simply flee. If not, and their quarry took exception to the eviction, *Operation Flashbang's* epitaph might read: *Here lies the death of US Imperialism; slain by underestimating the innocent of the universe.*

Meanwhile, without all the drama currently taking place in more than a dozen military installations farther south and west of Labrador, high above the ice-bound coast of the Labrador Sea, Lieutenant Reynolds kept his Avenger on station. The routine seldom varied: Fly a lazy-eight pattern and watch two civilians and their mutt move northward.

In his office in Saglek Harbour, Colonel Moorhead had already switched gears. He was pleased with how smoothly everything had gone in dealing with St. Onge and Corrigan. "Excellent charade, Paul," he said to Major Stone sitting across his desk in his single office chair. "No doubt they think we're engaged in some sort of chemical warfare testing."

"What if we lose them?" Stone asked. "You say you've lost Jerome St. Onge in the past. He vanished from his tent for days and you only rediscovered him after he returned."

"True, but this time we have a slight advantage. The girl takes her .30-30 with her everywhere and when they went to the Northern Store in Nain, our operative, was very busy. He entered her house, drilled the stock out under the butt plate and left a micro GPS transmitter inside. Once they're near their destination, we'll remotely turn it on and track her anywhere she goes for up to two weeks."

"Why the cost of a drone following them if they can be tracked via GPS," Stone inquired.

"Because a GPS unit only tells us where they are," Moorhead explained, patiently. "Drones tells us where they are, what they're up to, who they meet, and what transpires. In fact, they wouldn't even be alive if we hadn't rescued them on the ice."

"Works for me," Stone replied. "By the way, I met with the rest of the Mission Recovery Team when they arrived this morning. Actually I worked with several of the scientists over the years at Wright Patterson. Didn't realize how we are all 'getting on' till I saw all the grey hair."

"Thought you'd be pleased," Moorhead said. "Mr. Black said you'd feel right at home with these fellows. We've done everything possible to make the recovery operation run as smooth as silk. Your team is the last wave. Once you land, get in there as quickly as possible. We never can tell if there'll be a delayed reaction and some payback coming our way. So you and the Mission Recovery Team will use the mountain as shelter."

"Roger." Stone opened a red binder on his knee, turned to an overview page and began to read. "It says we are to use extreme caution since we don't know what we'll be facing once we enter. That's got to be an understatement." He read some more. "The hazards or lack thereof are unknown. Full hazmat suits with individual air supplies are an option but team members will use their own judgement."

"We hope you don't need them," Moorhead replied, "but we can't be too careful. Tomorrow your team will get a look at some of the equipment you'll use: AIRSENSE Analytics for gases, Geiger Counters, the latest Fiber Optic Biohazard Detectors, Infrared Sensors, Motion Sensors, transceivers and recording equipment. You should be well aware of what's ahead of you as you engage.

"By the time you arrive, we'll have knowledge of a possible entry point. We're expecting our subjects to lead us to some sort of main entrance."

"Will we go in the same day?" Stone said.

"Yes," Moorhead answered. "We've asked our pilots to avoid targeting the entry point once we've identified it. And the Bell UH-1 Yankee will set you down as close to there as possible." Moorhead stopped for a moment and looked at the major. "Once you're in, done your initial assessment, and grabbed anything you can, we have a crew of other scientists who will come in over the next few months and go over the place inch-by-inch."

Stone raised his eyebrows: "How do you know there is a base?"

"Because they don't return there year-after-year without some sort of fixed base in operation. We think it's been their home for as long as we've been tracking them."

"Why haven't you faced them down? They are on NORAD's radar, right? This is Canadian territory, right?"

"Let's just say they're *special*. Look Paul, so far we're not asking you to climb mountains or do anything fancy but you know we can't predict the site conditions once we move. That's why four of your team are not recovery specialists, but Mission Specialists trained as Advanced Military Mountaineers, purposed with helping you gain entry. One Mountaineer for each of you. They'll fly in via a Cessna and land not far from you."

"Well, I'm sure they'll earn their money hauling our asses around," Stone said, wondering if he wasn't too old for this sort of game. "You know the average age of our team members, Bob, so I am assuming we'll be also be issued walkers."

Moorhead laughed in spite of himself. "You'll do fine, Paul."

Stone knew his own expertise on foreign technology was needed to quickly evaluate captured technology, and that knowledge only came with years of experience. He and his team had, at least, brought that much to the table. Curiously, they still hadn't been told if they were going after a Chinese, Russian or what kind of base. Deliberately so, it seemed.

Moorhead was standing up, a sign of dismissal. Stone also rose, tucking his binder under his arm.

"I would estimate we have about four or five days to get you ready," Moorhead said. "Your equipment will be available in Hangar One at 0800 hours tomorrow where you'll be able to try it on, test it, and familiarize yourself with the controls and readings. Specialists will be there to answer all questions."

"Right, sir. As you know, I've evaluated foreign technology but I've never actually been on a recovery mission going in after it," Stone said.

"Well, we're hoping this will be the icing on the cake for your career, Paul. With some luck, we'll clean up."

* * *

Sky slowed her snowmobile and angled it inshore. With the change in direction, Atemu immediately sat up on the sled.

He'd kept low since she had been pushing them up to 35 mph around the bays and even taken them overland where the terrain permitted.

Matthew knew her self-imposed deadline of reaching their destination before the Winter Solstice didn't have the padding it once did. Several storms and the journey back to save Monique had consumed days of their timeline.

Soon, Sky had said, they would leave their snowmobiles and proceed on foot. It really wasn't something Matthew was looking forward to, but she had carefully explained to him that there was little choice.

As they motored towards the shore, Sky pointed towards the top of a nearby hill. Matthew saw again a stone Inuksuk on the rise, a large flat rock forming the arms of a figurine composed of piled stones.

After viewing the first one, Sky had told him the message inherent in an Inuksuk was often simple: Sometimes to simply tell other travelers that someone had been there. Or, it was used as a navigation marker, as a marker for fishing or hunting camps, to mark a place of veneration, or simple to mark a food or fuel cache. The native people did not attempt to hide their caches any more than they would lock up their log cabin, often containing ammunition, food or firewood. With the remoteness and scarcity of help in the North, Canada's Native peoples were always willing to share; someone's life might depend on gaining access to their stores or their shelter. It would be against their way of life to deny them. In turn, visitors tried to leave behind anything they did not need. Hence, what one traveler used, another might replenish.

Far below the Inuksuk, Matthew saw a rough lean-to of stripped spruce logs covered with a yellow tarp barely visible under a snow drift up ahead. A ten-foot whip antenna sporting a yellow flag bent in the chronic wind. He now recognized a St. Onge fuel cache when he saw one. Sky had explained that her cousin had hauled the logs up from further south, built the lean-to, and made several trips per year, via boat or snowmobile, with refilled fuel containers. This enabled her grandfather to visit the area whenever he liked.

He pulled up beside Sky as she took off her helmet and called over to him: "We'll fill up and only take one more container each. That should enable us to get where we're going and return here in a few days." She was all business again.

Her hair was tousled and sticking up wildly, her nose was red from the wind and there may have been a few more crow's feet at the corners of her eyes where she'd been squinting against the glare of the snow. Still, she looked beautiful to Matthew. There was no longer any doubt in his mind how he felt about her. He looked away, disembarked from his vehicle and began dragging gas containers out of the deep snow. One went on each sled and two more were sufficient to refill each of their snowmobiles.

Sky dug around in her sled and came up with a box of ER granola-type survival bars. She passed him two, gave herself two, and peeled the wrapper off a fifth for Atemu. He sniffed it, appeared disappointed and looked off at the horizon. "Atemu, this is it, boy," Sky warned. "No time for a gourmet meal. Eat!"

Her tone brooked no nonsense and the dog turned back. He gingerly took the ER bar from her hand. His demeanor spoke volumes: He would eat it but he refused to enjoy it.

Hippie food.

"God, what am I going to do with him?" she said, aloud.

"He's eating," Matthew assured her.

"No, I mean when we have to…go where we have to go. He can't come. I'll have to leave him behind in the tent and come back for him."

"Why can't we take him with us?" Matthew asked.

"He could complicate things and we have no time for that," Sky insisted. "You'll understand later." Without another word she spun about, motioned Atemu back onto the sled, donned her gear and started her snowmobile. "Okay, time to move out." The stress was back in her voice.

They travelled for another four hours with the sky becoming more and more overcast immersing them in a world of grey. Matthew tried to ask Sky how she was doing but either her headset was turned off, or she didn't feel like answering. All he got was dead air. He tried again with the same result. And again. Was she ignoring him? Was this her way of saying she knew how he felt about her and she was having none of it?

With so many hours travel behind them, his arms ached from steering around ice patches and snow mounds, and wrestling his machine over hill and dale. They had gradually entered a mountainous region that offered black cliffs shooting straight up from the shore ice for what looked like a thousand feet before fading into the grey gloom overhead. He wondered how far up the cliff went and then remembered Sky mentioning that some of them shot up over 2,000 feet straight out of the sea.

The good news was the surface was smooth, more resembling a skating rink butted up against a granite wall rather than a torn-up battlefield of ice. Traction and steering, however, weren't the best and Sky slowed them to 20 mph for that section.

Finally they emerged from the cliffs and travelled along beside a range of small hills that slowly gave way to flatter terrain sloping down to the ice. Sky pointed her snowmobile inland and they came off the ice and over a rise to see a huge expanse of snow extending towards a formidable mountain range in the distance. Two of the mountain peaks stood out above the others even if they were a good fifty miles away. Both were noteworthy because they appeared almost round and sported relatively flat tops. Even from this distance he knew they had to be many thousands of feet high.

Sky stopped her snowmobile and hauled off her helmet. Matthew pulled up beside her and did the same.

"I tried calling you on your headset," he said, letting his annoyance show. "Are we not talking or something?"

Sky gave him a funny look and then examined her helmet. "Sorry, it's turned off," she said, and then added: "What's the matter?"

Realizing how petulant he sounded, he immediately felt foolish. After all, it was a trivial matter. He tried to gracefully extricate himself. "I thought we were keeping them on for safety reasons. That's all." Unfortunately, he realized, he still sounded pissed off. Not what he wanted.

"I'm sorry, Matthew, I must have turned it off when we refueled. I wasn't ignoring you," she said sincerely. She continued staring at him, trying to understand where he was coming from.

If anything, Matthew was also confused at his own sensitivity. Why was he turning something minor into something major? Was it because his feelings for Sky had him overreacting to a perceived slight? One that she assured him wasn't even real? He turned away towards Atemu who was also staring at him as though he had two heads. Great, he thought. Even the dog thinks I'm off my meds.

"Sorry," he mumbled, shaking his head. "Just worried." He walked a few feet away and stared off at the distant mountains. Sky joined him but didn't say a word. "Is that where we're going?" He motioned towards the peaks.

For a moment she didn't answer. Finally she nodded, and said: "Yes, but we'll camp here for tonight and leave at first light. By tomorrow evening we'll be in the foothills in front of the mountains and have to leave the snowmobiles behind. We'll pack our gear on the small toboggans and head into the mountains."

They did the usual drill of unloading their gear and pitching their tent. By the time they finished, the light had vanished and the stars were becoming visible. There was no moon but they could still see pretty well.

After eating, they sat outside on their polyethylene food bins and took in a spectacular display of the Aurora Borealis sweeping across the night sky in waves of blues and greens and yellows and reds. The Northern Lights snapped and crackled as their eerie glow danced and rippled, collided and broke apart. While watching their personal light show, Sky worked with a punch, leather straps and lacing. She was fashioning a harness and sling for Atemu.

When they had gone outside, Atemu had immediately entered the tent. He looked out the flap to see Matthew watching him closely so he carefully lay down on the groundsheet beside the cots, a picture of innocence. Matthew returned to watching nature's impressive show.

"Scientist say it's unlikely that the Northern Lights make any sounds," Sky said, gazing upward. "But, my people have heard them for centuries."

Matthew nodded: "A well-known science writer, Arthur C. Clarke, once said that if a scientist tells you something is *possible*, he is probably right. If a scientist tells you something is *impossible*, he is probably wrong."

Sky laughed softly. "Isn't that the truth? White people believe reincarnation is impossible but the Innu and Inuit believe in animism. When someone dies we believe they come back as an animal. The totem for my family is the wolf."

"So you'll come back as a wolf," Matthew asked.

"I will only know when it happens," she said, quietly. "Though I think once around has been enough for me."

"Why are you so hard on yourself, Sky?" he asked. "All this: Don't get close to me…danger, danger Will Robinson…stay away? You're a very accomplished person. You're a doctor for God's sake. You're self-reliant, capable, smart and resourceful."

She shook her head. "But in the personal department I'm a mess, Matthew. I've had one steady boyfriend in my life, and a hundred first dates and very few seconds. I don't do well in relationships. I just wind up hurting people or hurting myself."

"Why?" he asked.

"Trust issues, I suppose. Don't know where they came from," she said, her tone dripping irony.

"Maybe you haven't met the right person," he replied, trying to be objective.

"I'm okay on my own," she said and then added in a whispered. "At least…I used to be."

He stared at her, the ones and zeros in his mind clicking madly, trying to decipher what he'd just heard. She just sighed and looked away.

Both continued to sit on their food bins with their parka hoods down, balaclavas rolled into toques so they could appreciate the full scope of the aerial display as it rolled across the heavens in colorful breakers. Neither said anything further. Suddenly Sky rose and Matthew felt disappointment that she was heading into the tent already. Instead, she came and stood over him. To his surprise, she sank to her haunches, took off her mitts, pulled off his, and then took his hands in hers.

He noticed Atemu had exited the tent and was sitting down watching them.

"Are we okay, Matthew?" she asked, looking closely at him. "You've been very patient, very courageous and very understanding, all qualities I love about you."

He didn't move, didn't blink, and was almost afraid to breathe in case the moment evaporated. His mind raced. He tried to decide what to do or say. Her touch had his heart pounding. The warmth of her fingers had his hands trembling. His mouth had gone dry. He prayed she wouldn't feel the tremor through his fingers. The fearless military pilot, the daredevil who dodged missiles and other ground fire in Afghanistan, was frozen by her touch.

They continued staring into each other's eyes.

"Are you afraid?" she asked, quietly.

He swallowed and slowly nodded. Finally, he managed to speak. "Yes," he said, gently.

"There are dangers ahead," she admitted.

"That's not what I fear, Sky," he whispered, conscious they were still holding hands.

She tilted her head sideways, her brows knitting. "No?"

Without breaking eye contact, he shook his head; he didn't trust himself to speak again.

"Can I do anything to make this easier for you," she asked, still holding his gaze, the pressure from her fingers on his hands, even and warm.

"I really don't know," he whispered, and cleared his throat. "I no longer know what is possible and what is impossible...with you."

She nodded. "You know," she said. "Someone told me that a wise man said that if you think something is *impossible*, you're probably wrong. So maybe you shouldn't worry so much."

Matthew swallowed desperately. He had to keep his emotions in check even though what he was feeling at the moment seemed more intense than anything he'd felt in years. At the very least, he was totally enamored with Sky. But in all probability, he was hopelessly in love with her. Then he noticed that as she gazed at him, her eyes were misting over. There was a tremor in her breathing.

"I'm going to do something," he said quietly, "and I hope you don't take this the wrong way."

With that he leaned forward, hesitated for a moment, and then placed his mouth over her lips and kissed her softly.

She opened her lips and kissed him back. It was a gentle kiss, lacking in urgency but full of sincerity, promise and sweetness. Gently she disengaged and pulled back.

For a moment, Matthew felt his heart sink. Then she reached forward and resumed their kiss. The warm wetness of their mouths mingled as they moved their lips gently against each other and then slowly and tenderly explored each other's mouths.

After a good minute, she pulled away, smiling softly. Maybe even a little sadly.

For Matthew, however, he didn't remember ever feeling such joy.

"Matthew," she said. "Right now we have no idea what the future will bring, so we have to put any thought of plans on hold. I think I know what you're feeling. And I know what I'm feeling. But with what lies ahead, the last thing we need are distractions. No matter how pleasant they may be. Please don't be angry, but I am really going to need your trust, cooperation and focus in the next few days. In fact, more than at any time during this trip. Do you understand?"

He nodded because that's what you do when someone asks you a question, even if you aren't listening. Sometimes even when you *are* listening. Whatever she was saying, he would swear that the entire color spectrum of the Northern Lights was reflecting in her eyes. What else could make them shimmer so? How else could they be so bottomless and so full of promise? In addition, her lips were beckoning to him again and he wanted nothing more than to caress them with his own.

Her hands still held his. Hands that could fire a high-powered weapon with amazing accuracy. Hands that could heal and bring joy and relief to many. And, hands that could make his heart sing and his whole body tremble with their touch.

"Earth to Matthew?" Sky said, still holding his hands.

"Oh," he said, shaking himself out of his reverie. "I-I'm sorry, Sky. Was that okay?"

"Yes, Matthew," she said. "But now we have to concentrate on business. Can you 'roger-wilco' that, Captain?"

"Got it," he answered, barely preventing a goofy smile from spreading across his face. For a moment he wanted desperately to confess how he felt about her. On consideration, however, everything she was saying told him it was best kept for another time. He contented himself with analyzing what she'd said about possibilities.

Sky let go his fingers and handed him his mitts. "Put these on. Nobody likes cold hands." She rose, picked up her food bin and moved it inside the tent.

He watched her duck inside.

Wait a minute! Nobody likes cold hands?

"We need to get some sleep," she called from the tent. "Long day tomorrow."

Okay, scrub that pipe dream, Sherlock.

Still, Matthew couldn't have been happier. It was only in a very tiny corner of his mind that a small voice asked how he could go from love for Helene to falling head-over-heels for Sky. The answer came back instantly. There was no longer anything between Matthew and Helene. She had ended it long ago. Anything that existed for the past two years resided solely in his imagination. Now, it seemed he'd finally found the strength to grow up and accept that the past was long gone. And, to be willing to move on. Amen!

"We're on our way," he called back, as he picked up his own food bin and motioned for Atemu to enter. The dog trotted into the tent and he followed.

Sky was already in her sleeping bag gazing lazily at him as he entered. Briefly he couldn't help wondering if there was invitation in her gaze. She followed his movements as he put down the bin carefully avoiding the heater and Coleman lantern, zippered the tent flap closed and shrugged out of his parka and outer clothes. For some reason he felt embarrassed, and avoided looking at her. He made himself as busy as possible, climbing into his sleeping bag, rolling up his pants and shirt for a pillow. He even threw in a fake yawn.

Finally he dared to look over.

She was on her back now gazing at the roof of the tent lying limply against the aluminum struts. There was barely any wind, so all was quiet. Too quiet. Finally, he allowed himself to give in to his feelings; he had to know if there was more to all this than a kiss.

"Sky?"

"Yes, Matthew?"

"I'm trying not to push you. Mostly because I'm afraid of the outcome, I suppose. But I just want to say, I never expected to feel what I'm feeling for you. Not in a million years."

"Gee, thanks," she said, dryly.

They both broke out laughing. Humor again, the great slayer of tension.

Her gaze swung to him. "Maybe we each deserve a second chance, Matthew. And if we can get through the next few days, I'd like to explore that possibility." The dolphin grin appeared. "Am I being too sappy for you?"

"You're a regular romantic alright," he said, also smiling. "I'll have my people contact your people and perhaps we can take a meeting or do a lunch to discuss merger possibilities? That work for you, Doc?"

"Sounds like a plan," she said. "Goodnight, Mr. Corrigan."

Goodnight, Doctor St. Onge," he replied.

They both retreated into their own thoughts and within minutes had succumbed to their dreams.

~2~

The morning came earlier than usual since Sky was determined to get moving before the sun came up. After heating and eating their packaged breakfasts, which Atemu enjoyed much more than an ER bar, they rolled up the empty pouches and stored them away in their refuse bag.

There wasn't much conversation between Sky and Matthew. They moved their gear out of the tent, took it down and packed the sleds while making sure there was a nest for Atemu. They did, however, exchange the occasional smile. Once, she deliberately bumped him with her hip and then apologized profusely though they both knew it was a flirtatious move on her part. He grinned, knowing that he probably looked like a lovesick teenager, but not caring.

With everything loaded, they topped up their gas tanks and then roared away across a very welcome, flat snow surface. It was still pitch dark and so Sky used her compass to navigate. Matthew simply followed her red tail light blurred by a fantail of snow. Even though they weren't on ice any more, it had been decided he would still follow her in case there was a rock or some other obstacle in their path. Not riding parallel provided some insurance against damaging both snowmobiles simultaneously.

Today, the headsets were on: "Sky, did you say we'd make those mountains today?" he asked.

"Yes, Matthew. Sometime this afternoon. I wanted an early start so we can get to the base ASAP."

"What base?" he asked.

"The base of the mountain peak we're going to climb," she said.

Static crackled through their radios and for a moment Matthew thought they were going to quit working. He wondered where the interference was coming from; they were in the middle of nowhere. Could it be the electric display of Northern Lights from the night before? He'd never heard of residual interference, but then, why would he? He decided he'd pull out the helmet linings and check their transmitters for a possible short when they stopped.

"Which peak?" he pressed.

"The big one," she replied, in a matter-of-fact tone.

"Naturally," he answered, nervously. It was strange but he could fly an aircraft at 35,000 feet, stretch his tether to the limit while checking on a parachute drop from a Hercules open ramp, or even step into space and parachute without a problem. But if he leaned over the edge of a building roof, he could feel some invisible force trying to drag him over the side. In other words, he didn't like heights that were static. He *really* didn't like them.

"Don't worry," she radioed. "It's a strenuous climb but most of it is up a well-hidden chimney and there are preset pitons smacked in all the way up. The bad news is that it's more than 3,000 feet high. It'll take today and part of tomorrow to scale it. Especially with Atemu."

"We're taking Atemu up the mountain?" Matthew asked in surprise.

"Now you know why I was so upset when he joined us," Sky responded. "We can't leave him at the bottom. We can't abandon him."

"No, no, of course not." Matthew was thinking hard: Heck, the way up couldn't be that steep if they were bringing the dog. So, in a way, this latest info provided some relief. He didn't know how wrong he was.

The sun finally rose revealing a beautiful blue sky day as they travelled. With the sea well behind them, the air had warmed up to about -15 degrees. The wind was also absent for which they were both grateful. Travelling with sun glasses on was mandatory, however, to counter the blinding whiteness of the countryside. In the distance, he saw a vast herd of animals slowly making its way southeast. Sky radioed one word: "Caribou." By the time they reached them, the herd would have passed; she stopped her snowmobile anyhow.

He joined her and noticed a group of smaller animals patiently trailing the caribou, about a mile behind. Sky didn't have to tell him what they were: a wolf pack, obviously with caribou listed as their evening's main course. They were waiting for a calf or older animal to either stop for a rest, or separate from the herd for some reason.

Then things would happen rather quickly, he knew. He'd seen enough Animal Planet episodes to know that a wolf pack wouldn't be inclined to show mercy. Survival of the swiftest and the fittest.

"Wolves are perfect snow hunters," Sky said watching the pack. "Their front feet are larger than their back so they can really shovel through the snow. They can trot at eight-to-10 mph all day long but when they go after their prey, they can easily crank that up to 40 mph. If their quarry is any distance from the collective protection of the herd, it's game over."

"We saw a few in Ungava," Matthew said. "Never really bothered us."

"Don't be fooled Matthew. Your wolves obviously weren't starving. Wolves can smell you from almost two miles away, and can hear you for about six miles in the forest and ten miles on open ground. Their bite comes in at around 1,500 pounds per square inch, twice that of a German shepherd so they can fracture the biggest bone in your body, your femur, with a single snap. They can also hear your heart beating from up to ten yards away. When their prey's heart beat is racing so fast the animal is virtually petrified and paralyzed, they go in for the kill."

"You said your family's totem is the wolf," Matthew remarked, eyebrows raised.

"Yes," she said, and then smiled. "So be a good fellow and try not to piss me off."

He gave her a brief salute by way of acquiescence. No way did he ever want to be on her bad side.

As their two machines churned through the snow, the mountain range grew closer and bigger every minute. Jagged triangular peaks loomed over them, severed by deep valleys or connected by craggy ridges or rocky saddles. They were mostly bare rock except where punctuated by sweeping layers of snow or frozen moss; they looked sharp, unfriendly and unforgiving.

Two of the closer mountain peaks, however, stood out above the others, mainly because of their height and odd shape. More than anything, Matthew thought they resembled the famed Devils Tower in Wyoming. With one notable exception; they were was easily three times its height. And God appeared to have double-downed on the formation since one peak stood behind the other.

He looked at them again. They stood cold and silent, twin rock sentinels of the Torngat Mountains.

Sky radioed him with information about what he was seeing and where they were going. Pointing ahead at the two massive hunks of cylindrical granite brazenly thrusting their way into the sky, she said: "Even though there are two summits, it's called *Castle Peak* because they resemble two castle turrets joined by a saddle. You can just see the second summit behind the first. Further, behind that is what we call the *Canyon of the Winds*. Many Inuit, and also my people, have reported seeing strange lights coming from there and hearing terrible noises in the night. It keeps natives and even game from wandering too close. A wise move, I'm sure."

Before he could ask why, she altered course to the left taking them on a more direct route towards the cylinders.

As they got closer, Matthew began to feel smaller and smaller. It always amazed him how the grandeur of young mountains made him feel so insignificant.

Of course 'young' was a relative term up here since the rock of the Torngats and the tectonic plate shifts that formed the mountains, dated back billions of years, the result of five major events. As a professional geologist, he knew that only two places in the world featured rocks older than the Torngat Mountains: Canada's Northwest Territories and Australia. Right now, he was certainly looking at episodic proof of the modern earth's violent birthing and settling process.

And, thanks to his associated studies, despite the mountain's forbidding climate and harsh landscape, he knew there were cultural archeological sites dating back more than 7,000 years in Torngat National Park. Maritime Archaic Innu, Pre-Dorset and Dorset Paleo-Inuit, and the Thule culture had merged over thousands of years to form the modern day Inuit. Indeed, as a visitor to the area, he was definitely a Johnny-come-lately.

From what Matthew could see, Castle Peak continued to appear to be almost cylindrically shaped though Sky had explained earlier it appeared so simply because of the angle from which they were viewing it; she assured him, that once on top, its oblong shape would become more visible. And directly behind it, mostly out of sight, the second peak resided, slightly lower and out of sight at their present angle of approach.

Gazing up through the frigid air, he thought: Sky must be kidding about scaling that beast. And trying it with Atemu in tow would be impossible; he wasn't exactly a Chihuahua. Looking again at the sheerness of the sides of the mountain, he was sure the only way to the top involved a helicopter and some passengers with a death wish.

Sky stopped her snowmobile and he joined her. They both removed their helmets and balaclavas, their hair sticking up in all directions. Sky looked at him and smiled.

"Do I look like you do?" she asked, pointing to his hair.

"Of course not," he lied. "You look like you just stepped out of a Hollywood salon."

She gave him a doubtful look.

"Okay, maybe one that had just been hit by a tornado."

She smiled and then became serious. ""Matthew, we're going to head to an area north of Castle Peak where we'll leave our snowmobiles. There's a rock fall up ahead that we can't get through with our machines. We'll repack some supplies onto our two toboggans and trek to the base of the mountain. When we get there, we'll transfer our gear into two backpacks. I have pretty much worked out a harness for Atemu but it's going to be very difficult to get him to the top."

"Why do we have to go up there?"

"Because it's required," she said, simply. "I'm not being rude, it's just that up there we're exposed and we can be inspected."

"Inspected? By who?"

"The other people."

"Who are 'the other people'?" he asked, by now sure she was talking about some ancient Inuit tribe that kept their diamond mine a closely guarded secret. "The diamond your grandfather left for me? It came from them?"

"Absolutely," Sky said, carefully. At least that wasn't a lie. "But there is a protocol for contact. And we have to follow it. I asked you to trust me. Do you?"

"Of course, Sky," he said. "I'd trust you with my life. I *am* trusting you with my life!"

"Good," she said. "Let's go."

They travelled on through the snow until they reached some low foothills fronting Castle Peak. Rather than a smooth field that gradually sloped up to the base many miles away, they found themselves facing a windswept and barren area composed of a light dusting of snow mixed with gravel and punctuated by hundreds of medicine ball-sized, sharp black rocks. They were scattered haphazardly on the plain, making it impassable for their snowmobiles.

As Sky directed, they pulled out the two toboggans from their sleds and loaded them with food, cooking pots, and their second, smaller Coleman Hooligan 3-person tent…

"In the smaller tent I'll need your body heat and you'll need mine…"

…an assortment of ropes, pitons, a hammer, locking D-shaped

carabiners, climbing helmets, the Coleman lantern, one heater, two knapsacks, a groundsheet, air mattresses and sleeping bags. Last but not least, the .30-30 Winchester was strapped to Sky's toboggan.

She then pulled out two sets of Ojibwa caribou hide snowshoes and handed one to Matthew. "For after we pass the rock fall," she said.

"Are these people dangerous?" Matthew was tempted to press for more information but feared it would be interpreted as a lack of trust.

"They could be if they wanted to be," Sky answered, rather perfunctorily.

He tried one more question: "Are they indigenous to this region?"

"That's a big negative, good buddy," she answered, mimicking a southern trucker, a tight smile briefly touching her lips. She quickly moved off to store their snowmobile helmets in the tow sleds.

Matthew did as instructed and covered both their snowmobiles and sleds with tarps, and secured them with multiple bungee cords. Finally, Sky extracted a telescoping plastic rod from a corner of her sled. She pulled it up as one would extend a collapsible fishing rod and attached it firmly to the sled's side. At the end of it, a plastic yellow flag unfurled in the wind. This would make it much easier to find their snowmobiles and gear in the snow when they returned. For insurance, Sky also recorded the coordinates in the GPS she'd removed from her snowmobile.

A light wind began heralding something stronger in the offing. They both buckled on their snowshoes, raised their hoods and peeled back the wire snorkel brims for better vision. Atemu waited patiently.

Matthew made sure both of their toboggan loads were well tied down. He grabbed the tumpline for his toboggan and looped it over his shoulders and behind his neck. Sky picked up hers as Atemu pranced eagerly in the snow.

"Let's get moving..." she said, and pointed towards the mountains.

They set out on what Matthew thought would be a half-hour tramp to the base. When, after the half-hour, they seemed no closer, he realized how huge Castle Peak truly was.

"My God," he called out, breathing hard. "It looks like we haven't moved an inch."

Sky removed the tumpline from across her forehead and nodded. "Deceptive, isn't it," she said. "Remember, they're both more than 3,000 feet high."

Atemu sat in the snow, his tongue out as he panted. The debris field of rocks was now behind them. The snow had gotten considerably deeper and the slope leading to the base had steepened. The sky was grey with no cloud definition.

Sky dug in her pocket and handed Matthew an ER bar and ate one herself. Atemu wandered over and accepted one with all the enthusiasm of a condemned criminal taking a last meal.

"Sky, no offense, but I can't see how we're going to climb that monster," he said motioning toward the massive butte.

"Very slowly, Matthew. That's why I want to get started today. At about a thousand feet there's a ledge where we'll spend the night. Hoisting Atemu up will be the real challenge."

"Well, just to alert you, I'm not good with heights."

"You're a pilot."

"Different type of height."

"Don't worry. Where we're going, you won't be aware of the height."

"Fabulous."

"Unless you look down," she said.

"You know, you've got a perverted sense of humor," he replied. "Definitely warped."

"But you love me anyway," she quipped, and then froze, realizing what she'd said.

For a moment he felt himself getting very serious. Then, to give her a break, he laughed and said nonchalantly: "Doesn't everybody?"

The look of relief on her face was almost comical. But then she reconsidered, sidled over and gently put her arms around his waist and looked up into his face. "You're a pretty special guy, you know that?"

He dropped his mitt, lifted her chin with his fingers and gave her a simple kiss on her forehead. "You're also a very special girl, Sky. I really want to know you better, but at a pace that's comfortable for you."

"Thank you," she said simply, gave him a squeeze and went back to her toboggan.

They continued walking for the next two hours; the weather grew worse. The wind picked up, whirling loose snow around them. Its whistle grew in intensity, rapidly building to the 'Labrador shriek' with which he had become so familiar. They both deployed their snorkel hoods and half closed them. Soon they were leaning forward into the wind just to stay on their feet. Their sole purpose centered on putting one foot in front of the other to gain ground, not an easy feat on snowshoes. They trudged on, heads down so the wind didn't snatch their breath away.

Suddenly a huge gust of wind hit them.

Caught off guard, Sky was whirled 180 degrees and dumped on her face, feet tangled in her snowshoes. Matthew shrugged out of his tumpline, and ran awkwardly through the snow to help her. It was a struggle to stay on his own feet. One sideways step with the snowshoes and he'd also be down. He held out a hand and helped her up.

"Ghost Winds," she yelled to him over the howling, and pointed towards the vague outlines of the mountain range. "They're gusts caused by sudden wind shifts that scream down from the mountain peaks at high velocity. And they can come from any direction, even ignoring the direction of the prevailing wind. They'll probably get stronger as we get closer."

"That looked strong enough," he shouted back.

She nodded, now checking her GPS and leaning close: "These blasts originate in the *Canyon of the Winds* on the other side of Castle Peak. I've experienced them before."

Retrieving a coil of rope from her toboggan, she paid out twenty feet, tied one end to her own arm and one end to Matthew's arm. Large snowflakes had joined the snow being picked up from the ground; the whole mess was being driven horizontal by the wind. They reached into their hoods and pulled their balaclavas down as the gusts drove ice crystals into their faces at high velocity.

Atemu kept shaking himself to dislodge the snow sticking to his fur. He stayed close to them, also head down and leaning into the wind. Occasionally he stopped and pawed at his muzzle, clearing his vision. Sky kept a wary eye on him.

Roped together, they slogged on, fighting their way through the squall, the Ghost Winds intensifying. Atemu staggered behind using them as a shield. Finally, the weather began to calm down as they approached the base of the mountain. The closer they got to the relative shelter of the base, the more the wind weakened. Sky pointed to a spot in the perpendicular grey cliff and headed for it. Much to his amazement, Matthew realized she was making for a well-camouflaged cleft of rock with a piece bent back on itself to effectively hide the entrance to an opening.

Atemu raced ahead but then stopped dead at the entrance. The hackles went up on his neck. He stared at the dark mouth of a cave and growled.

Sky breezed by him and pulled her toboggan inside, beckoning Matthew to join her. "Now we ditch the toboggans and repack our gear into our knapsacks," she said, her voice echoing hollowly in the cave. She began stuffing her knapsack without pausing to examine their surroundings. "No time to waste."

They were in a cave about 20 feet wide and ten feet high. The depth wasn't easily determined as the back wall disappeared into the dark. Atemu sat just outside.

With their knapsacks full, they secured their sleeping bags on top of their loads. Matthew had the tent tightly rolled up and clipped to the underside of his knapsack. Each had 180 feet of Maxim Glider 9.9 mm dry rope slung crosswise over their shoulders and a climbing helmet on their head. There wasn't quite enough room for two wool blankets she'd brought so they left them on the toboggans inside the cave.

Sky picked up her .30-30 and placed it in a crevice of the cave, almost a natural gun stand. She frowned, picked it up again and put it to her shoulder.

"What's up?" Matthew asked.

She shook her head, started to put the carbine down again and didn't. Instead she put out her hand and rested the weapon on her extended forefinger to test for balance. It immediately fell, barrel heavy.

"What's going on?" she asked, catching the carbine.

"What's the matter?" Matthew asked.

"I've had this carbine since I was 13-years old," she said. "I could always balance it perfectly, resting in on my finger at this point. Now it won't balance. Barrel heavy."

She began examining the weapon carefully, finally arriving at the butt plate. She rose, took it into the light at the mouth of the cave and examined it. There were faint, but unmistakably fresh scratches on the screws. She returned, sat on a rock and used a pocketknife to unscrew the butt plate; she sat back in surprise.

Slowly, from an obviously drilled out opening, Sky withdrew a black, plastic box with a small antenna and passed it to Matthew. "Son of a bitch!" she said angrily, her face flushing.

Matthew read the label: *Sat-Gear GPS Tracker*. An artist's rendering of an insignia featuring a globe was stamped in gold on it. "Who did this?" he demanded, holding up the tracker.

She ignored his question. "Look what they did to my carbine." She showed him the hollowed out pocket in the stock. Reaching inside, she pulled out a canvas bag. "Lead shot to provide a counter balance. Still suspect I'm a little paranoid? And don't bother asking me 'who did it' again. You probably wouldn't belief the answer, anyhow."

She grabbed the GPs tracker back from Matthew and used her boot heel to crush it. "If I find the guy who did this to my carbine, I'm going to send his ass to the Happy Hunting Grounds, one piece at a time!" She reinserted the shot bag, refastened the plate and stood the carbine in the corner. Finally, she calmed down, the redness leaving her face.

Sky held up the harness she created for Atemu but then had to force him to enter the cave before buckling him into it. Looking around for a moment, the dog fixated on the darkness at the back and emitted a low rumble of a growl. Sky took the last items off her toboggan, two sturdy-looking body harnesses featuring stainless steel loops from which hung a selection of carabiners and pitons and a small hammer on each. She helped Matthew into one harness, explaining its features and then buckled the second around herself.

"Now to find the elevator," she said, her focus back on their task.

She shouldered her pack, pulled out a flashlight from her pocket and led them deeper into the cave.

Matthew noticed she was leading Atemu on a leash attached to his harness. When he tried to pause, she gave a small jerk. Tail down, he fell back into step, but not without another ill-tempered growl.

Proceeding along a rocky corridor, shadows jumped at them from both sides as her light played against the walls. Finally coming to a halt, she pulled out two LED headlamps with headgear from another pocket and handed one to Matthew. "Buckle this on your helmet," she said.

"So how do we climb from in here?" Matthew asked. He was slightly bent over since the ceiling of the corridor had become shorter and shorter as they progressed.

"Look up," she said and flashed her light vertical. "It's called a chimney."

Overhead a black hole yawned, proceeding up as far as the light could reach. It was roughly about five feet in diameter and he could see what appeared to be stone outcroppings every few feet. That gave them almost four feet of uninterrupted clearance.

"A natural stairway," she said.

"Maybe for Rambo," he replied, cautiously.

"Falter not, hero, you're in the big leagues now."

"Stop calling me that. How far up does that thing go," he asked.

"All the way."

"All the way to the top?"

"More than 3,000 feet." She uncoiled her rope. "My grandfather climbs it and he's 75."

He looked at it doubtfully and then opined: "Piece of cake, do it with one arm tied behind my back, maybe go up backwards."

"Oh, I get it," she said, with a knowing smile. "GI Joe bravado, spit in the face of danger, laugh at death, moon the devil and his disciples."

"Would you rather I do what I'd really like to do and collapse into a quivering mass of Jell-O?" he asked. "Cause I can do that. Right now."

"No, I prefer Matthew the Hero." She quickly knotted the rope into a ring on the top of Atemu's jacket-sling and uncoiled about 50 feet of it. "Make a step for me, would you?"

Matthew linked his hands and braced them on a bent knee. Sky stepped on them and quickly pulled herself into the shaft, complete with knapsack. She vanished in the chimney, the rope uncoiling as she climbed.

He stood under the hole and lit up the interior with his headlamp. She was moving upward extraordinarily fast, jumping from one outcropping to another as she climbed. Small pebbles and loose dirt occasionally rained down. Matthew sheltered his eyes with a hand. "Bloody hell, she moves like a gazelle," he grumbled to himself, more than a little concerned over his own impending ascent.

Atemu looked up into the hole and whined softly.

Sky went up about 40 feet and then inserted the end of the rope tied to Atemu's harness through an existing piton hammered into a crack in the rock wall. Next she looped the free end around her forearm several times. Holding tight to the rope with both hands, she made ready to kick off. "Okay, Atemu, here I come," she called out, her voice echoing from the hole. Suddenly Atemu rose into the air and vanished into the mouth of the chimney.

Matthew heard the words: "Good boy" echo from the hole as Sky squeezed passed the dog on her way down. A few seconds later she landed in front of him, knapsack and all.

"Grab the rope," she said. "Hold tight."

He did, feeling Atemu's weight trying to yank it out of his hands.

"I'll climb up, secure him there and then you can come up."

Understanding the concept, Matthew asked: "Are we going to 'leapfrog' him up 3,000 feet?"

"That's the plan."

He nodded and sighed.

"Alrighty then! You good?" Rather than exhibiting hesitancy, Sky seemed energized.

"Guess so," he said, still doubtful.

She bent down. "First I'll attach Atemu's rope to your harness with a 'figure-eight, follow-through' knot." She worked her magic with the rope. "After I tie him off up there, you come up. Do just as I did. As you climb, I'll be shortening your safety line so you can't fall."

A frantic bark echoed out of the hole. Plainly, the current resident of the chimney was asking if they'd forgotten something. Perhaps the *dog*?

"Good boy!" Sky yelled upward.

She reached above her head, was able to grab two outcroppings and, without help, hoisted herself effortlessly back into the hole in the cave roof. Holding Atemu's rope tightly, Matthew's headlamp revealed Sky again bouncing from outcropping to outcropping. She appeared to be climbing little more than a rough staircase.

The rope loosened as Atemu was secured to a piton. He sighed and made ready to follow Sky's lead. But would he be able to hoist himself high enough in the chimney? Using every bit of his strength, he pulled himself upward like he was doing a chin up.

The first time, his knapsack hit the side of the hole and he dropped back down. He tightened the straps so it hugged his body. In the second attempt he made an allowance for his load and pulled himself inside. Reaching the halfway point, as his wrists passed his waist, he found he was now pushing down to keep himself from falling. He swung a leg up and slammed his boot against one side of the chimney while jamming his back against the other side. He was wedged tight. But he couldn't move. He felt paralyzed.

"Your safety line is tied off, Matthew," Sky hollered down. "Trust it and let go. Then get one foot on a step. Once you get started, it's easy."

"Sure, sure," he muttered, unconvinced

Taking a deep breath, he let go and felt the harness digging into his flanks as he dangled freely in the air. Swinging one boot onto the first "step" he used it to lever himself vertical. Then he found a second step, steadying himself with his hands. He was taken aback by how even and well-spaced were the outcroppings. Carefully he climbed, step-by-step, to where Sky was perched, tied off by a rope attached to two pitons.

Atemu looked positively pitiful dangling in his harness. He stared at Matthew with soulful eyes.

Get me out of here and I'll give you my Kibbles for a year!

Balancing on two steps, Matthew couldn't help feeling sorry for the dog and rubbed his ears playfully.

Sky smiled at him. "You did well for a pilot afraid of heights."

He smiled back, catching his breath. "I've never even heard of a chimney that goes up 3,000 feet. Must have been formed by a volcanic eruption of some sort. But it almost looks like it was designed. Even the steps seem more formed than natural. They're so smooth they look like they were melted. And so evenly spaced–!" He stopped, realizing Sky was refusing to look at him.

"We'd better get going," she said, abruptly. "It's going to take us many hours to get to the ledge where we can camp. And, pulling doggie up means we're gonna sleep well tonight."

True to her word, this was one of the most exhausting efforts Matthew had ever undertaken. Hoist the dog, tie the dog off, climb back up further than the dog, hoist him up again using your weight in a free fall drop. And on and on. Working together they soon found shortcuts without compromising safety as they indeed leapfrogged up the chimney.

The *bad news* was they were working in the dark with only their headlamps for illumination. The *good news* was they were working in the dark with only their headlamps for illumination. That meant Matthew couldn't see the sure-death drop below. Instead he was fully focused on the task at hand, tying and untying ropes, and taking turns with Sky kicking off into the air to allow his or her weight to pull the dog up.

He soon found the trick was to look down using his headlamp to illuminate and select two steps, nine or ten feet down. Then, using Atemu's weight and natural friction to slow his descent, he'd land on his targeted steps hoisting the dog up with his weight. Three or four jumps used up the free rope and Atemu was then tied off, having ascended 30 or 40 feet. Both he and Sky had a safety rope attached to their harnesses.

It would have been hard enough unencumbered, but each also wore a knapsack with a good 20 pounds in it. Sky's pocket thermometer showed the chimney was a balmy -5 degrees. And they had no wind. It felt almost tropical after the endless freezing nights they'd endured. Both removed their leather mitts and opened their parkas as they climbed.

Four hours later, they reached a rock shelf that was about twelve feet long and ten feet wide, large enough for the three of them to lie down. Sky called a halt to their climb and they gratefully shrugged out of their harnesses and knapsacks.

Matthew noted that there were numerous metal pitons already hammered into cracks in the rock wall giving them more than adequate tie offs. "Your grandfather certainly believed in safety," he commented. "Did he discover this chimney?"

"He was told about it," she replied.

For the first time they were able to stand without leaning into a wall or grabbing a handhold. It was also the first time Atemu's four feet rested on a floor in as many hours; his first order of business was to wander over to a far corner and anoint it. Sky then tied him to one of the pitons letting him wander a few feet but keeping him away from the edge of their vertical tunnel.

They sat on the stone floor, switched off their LED lights and ate survival bars. Sky and Matthew also drank "orange juice with a kick." Atemu got two cups of water; they would melt snow on top and give him more the next day. Cradled by hundreds of millions of tons of solid rock, the darkness was complete.

With lights back on they blew up their air mattresses, unrolled their sleeping bags and settled down with Atemu curled up in a corner on their unrolled tent. Both took off their parkas, and inner clothes, and slept in their insulated underwear. No longer generating heat by exerting themselves, the cold soon began to penetrate.

Sky was lying with her back to Matthew and moved closer spooning with him for warmth. As she squirmed to get comfortable, she wound up pressing her rear into his stomach. He sneaked an arm out of his bag and put it over her shoulder. She didn't protest. Tired as he was he felt himself reacting and tried to pull away. He knew she felt his hardness through the bag. He swore he heard a soft giggle.

"Sorry, Sky," he said. "This is embarrassing."

"No, Matthew," she answered. "It'd be more embarrassing if you *didn't* react."

They both laughed openly.

"Unfortunately, I think we both smell like a couple of overripe skunks. When we get to where we're going, we'll take a bath."

He chuckled. "You toy with me."

She rolled over his way and he felt her lips close over his. He kissed her back. They broke apart gasping. He tightened his grip around her but she resisted. "I want to as well, Matthew, but I'd like to be clean."

"You're right," he said, backing away slightly.

"Don't see this as rejection," she said. "Consider it anticipation."

"I do," he said. "I'm all anticipated as hell. It's the animal in me."

At the word 'animal,' they heard a whimper from the corner.

"He thinks we're talking about him," Sky laughed, and then called out. "Good dog! Go to sleep."

Atemu gave a short bark, then exhaled noisily and Sky knew he was putting his head down on his tent mattress. She waited a minute.

"He'll be out in about another minute," she whispered to Matthew.

No response.

"I'm sure it's as stressful for him as it is for us."

No response.

"Matthew?"

Only a soft snore answered her.

"I've reconsidered your offer big boy…take me. Take me now!"

Another snore.

"Huh!" she said, thoughtfully. "Maybe I'm not quite as hot as I think I am."

* * *

General Sergei Topkolov knocked on Major Oleg Serdyukov's door wondering where Oleg's secretary was this time. He regarded the vacant desk, papers scattered about, an empty coffee cup and a ringing multi-line phone. One of the lights across the base of the phone illuminated cutting off the annoying buzz. He figured Oleg had answered it himself from his office. The light went off almost as quickly as it had come on. He was about to knock when a pale-looking girl appeared and quickly sat at her desk.

"Comrade General, I am so sorry. I was in the little girl's room."

"No problem, doushenka," Topkolov said, magnanimously.

"I shall announce you, sir?" she asked, almost afraid to look at him.

"No need. Why worry the Major?" he asked, with a smile.

The girl looked at him in fear, sensing this was bad news for the major.

"No, no, everything is fine," he hasten to assure her. He smiled to back up his words. "I shall surprise my good friend." With that he pushed through the door, closing it behind him.

Major Serdyukov looked up, and then quickly gained his feet and saluted. "Comrade General," he said, a litany of questions and concerns loud and clear in his voice.

"Relax Oleg, Nobody is going to the wall," he said, with a chuckle.

"You have news?"

The general sat down and dropped his hat on the major's desk. "Yes. Our *Operation Phoenix* team indeed used the bomb and obliterated every trace of two of them. A third, we don't know which one, was captured but was apparently shot during the capture. He died. Our informants say that he was too far gone to reveal anything. The Americans are going wild trying to find his fingerprints, a photo, or his DNA in their databases. That's going to take a while."

"Like…forever, Comrade," the major said.

The general started to laugh and Serdyukov joined in. After a moment, he reached in his desk without being asked to do so, and out came the premier vodka and two glasses. He poured two generous shots as his superior talked.

"We positioned it with the politburo as the Americans are chasing their imagination up in Labrador and we are sure they will find nothing."

"And they accepted this without reservation?"

"What choice do they have?" the general asked. "And, even if the Americans do find something, I'm sure they aren't going to report it to Moscow."

"Well, St. Matrona has spared us," Oleg said.

"There is one thing, however, Oleg," Topkolov said, then downed the vodka in one continuous swallow.

"Uh oh!" the major said. "You said nobody was going to the wall."

"No, no," the general said. "But you know someone always has to pay."

"Da."

"How do you feel about retiring, full pension and benefits? Big send-off. Glorious servant of the Russian Federation?"

"That would work for me," the major said, quickly.

"Probably no second *Order of Lenin*," the general said.

"Ask me if I give a shit," the major responded. He poured more vodka into the two water glasses, this time filling them almost to the brim.

"Whoa Oleg!" the general said, with a laugh, his mood already altered by the first drink.

The major raised his glass and the general joined him. They clinked their glasses hard.

"You're lucky, you'll be out of it, Oleg," the general said, seriously, a half smile on his lips.

"Surely you're near retirement age, Sergei?"

"I put my fucking papers in this morning," the general suddenly yelled, roaring with laughter, stamping his feet and pounding on the desk at the same time. He began coughing and gasping but finally regained control. He grinned insanely at Serdyukov and shook his head as he pondered his future.

They both drank some more and slapped their glasses down on the desk. Oleg took out two Cuban cigars from a drawer. He handed one to his friend who had protected him all the way. They both lit up.

"So, what will you do, Oleg? Any plans at all? An extended fishing trip? An ocean cruise? A vacation in Cuba?"

"Actually I'm going to do something I've wanted to do all my life, Comrade General. All my life."

"What's that?" General Topkolov asked, truly curious.

The major looked off into the distance, a smile on his lips. "I'm applying for an American visa. And then, my friend, I'm going to Disney World."

~3~

Sky woke first but didn't move. Her eyes were open but she couldn't see a thing. She shivered in the damp coolness. Somewhere in the blackness there was the hollow sound of water dripping. Remembering where they were, she reached over and switched on the Maglite and looked at her watch. It was 6:30 AM; time to move.

Instead she lay there thinking of the man snoring softly beside her. There was little doubt she truly felt something for him that she hadn't felt for anyone in a long time. Part of his attraction was undoubtedly his gentleness and his humor. Also his moral compass and basic honesty. She could feel that he sincerely respected her and her Innu beliefs; unlike so many others, he was not a judgmental person urging her to get with the 21st Century and forget her traditions.

But there was something else. She felt he made *her* a better person. First, his sense of humor was catching. Second, even when she felt angry or upset, his calm gaze and a few words seemed to have an uncanny ability to dissipate her anger and make her see reason. In fact, she had come to admire this degree of calmness. When he did take charge, such as stopping her from firing at the American jet, or preventing her from decking Meyer, he didn't hesitate. And yet, he didn't try to take away her power. He was smart enough to realize he was in her element in Labrador; he allowed her to do her job without his male ego demanding he take the lead. Except when he thought she had shot at someone, of course. He'd refused to let that go until she revealed she'd shot a polar bear to save lives.

But Matthew also had a tenderness about him that had seized her heart like no other had ever been able to do. This both frightened and attracted her. And despite her admonishments not to get close to her, secretly, she wasn't all that displeased with his attention.

And he had demonstrated a few times he wasn't a bad kisser. She shivered at her memory of the night before and how close she had been to saying "yes" and be damned with the bath. The reality of their travels was they were probably equally smelly.

Quietly she crawled out of her sleeping bag. She took a plastic bottle out of her knapsack, went over to a corner and carefully peed in it. She closed the lid securely and placed it in the back corner of the ledge. As she shone the light around, it revealed about ten other similar bottles, some full, some empty. Atemu was up and straining at his leash.

Rousing Matthew, they both dressed silently, packed up their gear and then all three ate an ER bar.

"Are you okay for the bathroom?" she asked him.

"Gonna have to do number one," he said.

She chuckled at his reluctance to use the word 'pee' in front of her and pointed the Maglite at corner. "There's an empty container over there. Use it and leave it. Next trip they will all be removed."

"Next trip?" he said, shocked. "Oh, you mean when your grandfather comes again."

"Or me. Many have been carried out over the years," she said. "Remember, we are in the place of the spirits. We don't soil a holy place."

The next seven hours were as hard as any Matthew had ever experienced. His arms ached, his legs ached and his back ached. If he hurt that bad, he wondered what this dog-hoisting extravaganza was doing to Sky. He groaned more and more often, but she was stoically silent. Finally, he stopped feeling sorry for himself – poor baby – and kept his moans silent.

At one point they reached another small ledge. Swinging his headlamp around, Matthew discovered a seven-foot, almost perfectly round hole in the side of the shaft. It seemed to be a tunnel leading somewhere. He called to her and pointed to it excitedly.

Sky, standing on a single step above, vehemently shook her head and pointed upward.

"Do you know where it goes?" he called.

Sky nodded, but again pointed upward. Obviously no time for sightseeing.

They continued their arduous, perpendicular journey.

Matthew could scarcely believe it when he looked up and saw a faint light overhead. He glanced over at Sky and she smiled at him in the glow from above. He realized her headlamp was off.

That was all incentive they needed to redouble their efforts. Within twenty minutes they pulled themselves and Atemu up over the lip of the shaft, and rolled from under a rock overhang covering the opening. They shook off their harnesses and knapsacks and dropped prone, exhausted and relieved. Nor were they the only ones. Atemu stood looking around realizing that the nightmare was finally over. Surely he was free?

The sky was blue, the sun dazzling and blinding. Exhausted they lay on patches of snow, breathing in the mountain air so pure, it made them light-headed.

Squinting, Matthew looked back at the entrance and realized the overhang would make the shaft invisible from above. In fact, it was much like the entrance to the mountain far below, almost impossible to find unless you knew exactly where to look. He thought: If I didn't know better, I'd think this was all engineered. Now lying in the bright sunlight they were both forced to keep their eyes closed.

"Sure know how a mole feels," Matthew said, enjoying the crispness of the air and the warmth of the sun on his face. Though the wind soon found where they lay, after the claustrophobic environment in which they had operated for the past two days, it actually felt good. At least until their noses began to freeze. Of the same mind, Sky and Matthew retrieved their balaclavas from their pockets and pulled them on.

Beside them, Atemu tried to rid himself of his harness. Sky put on her sunglasses, unbuckled him, and let him race around like the proverbial mad dog, barking and peeing on everything he could find. Finally he raced over to the edge of the flat mountaintop and looked fearlessly over at a vertical drop of almost two thirds of a mile.

"Atemu!" Sky screamed, somehow finding the strength to stagger to her feet. Matthew also dragged himself up, squinting and grumbling as they headed over to where the dog looked at them curiously, his tongue out and panting like a derby winner.

"Here, boy!" Matthew called.

"You fall off this mountain after us dragging your tail up here and you'll never see another doggy treat, I promise you!" Sky shouted at him.

Sensing someone was not happy he trotted over to them, tongue out. Nothing was going to spoil his good mood over being released from the infernal sling.

But rather than delivering a scolding for something a dog would naturally do, Sky bent down and hugged him tight. After a few seconds of mothering, Atemu began to squirm and she let him go.

Matthew approached the edge of the cliff and tried to look over the side. He saw dark grey rock and a vertical drop; it went straight down. The familiar strains of vertigo tried to nibble at his balance and he quickly pulled back from the edge, breaking the spell. "Me and Jimmy Steward," he mused, turning to rejoin Sky.

"Real food tonight, Atemu," she called out, a happy grin on her face.

"You really love that puppy, eh?" Matthew said. "To do what you did for him."

"What *we* did, Matthew," Sky said. "Going down should be a little easier, I think."

He nodded, looked at his watch and noted that it was 3:10 PM. The sun was rapidly sinking in the sky. It would be dark in another hour at most. And not a time to wander around a hunk of rock where one misstep could turn you into a Torngat Mountain statistic.

Sky was right; the top of Castle Peak was oblong shaped, about 300 feet wide and about 1,500 feet long. It featured a coating of snow and ice interspersed with reams of mostly flat, windswept rock interrupted only by small crevices and depressions. There wasn't a boulder or a knob higher than a few inches, other than the tunnel entrance over to the side.

He took some minutes and wandered to the end of the oblong-shape to see another flat summit about 100 feet below and about 500 feet away. It was slightly smaller and rounder with a rough diameter of maybe 1,000 feet at the top. It was much, much larger at the base, he noted. When he gingerly looked down, Matthew saw a rocky saddle connecting the two peaks far below. These were dramatic and unusual summits side-by-side. But the smaller summit, opposite where he stood, was different; it featured an almost round patch of gleaming ice covering most its top, a convex shape bulging towards the heavens like an artificial skylight. Idly he wondered what had caused such an unusual shape.

Unfortunately, both peaks were deserted; there was no secret society of Innu or Inuit elders living on top. Or anyone else for that matter. So where were these "other people?" Why were they up there in the first place? Rather than put Sky on the spot, however, he approached her and simply asked: "Now what?"

She looked at him and then over to where their fully laden knapsacks rested. "Now we make camp." She waited for a well-deserved show of impatience or protest; it failed to materialize.

"Roger," he said and tramped back towards their gear. The wind had started to build again. And the unrelenting cold increased.

She really did like this man!

They camped at the southern end of the rock surface hoping for a modicum of shelter from an adjacent mountain peak. Pitching the tent in a strong northwest wind proved to be a major challenge as it flapped and billowed and tried desperately to escape. Sky sat on part of it as Matthew managed to secure a "corner" with a piton he hammered into a crevice in the rock. After that it went much easier. Though it jumped, swayed, inflated and deflated with the gusts, nothing short of a catastrophic tear would free it. They hammered in multiple pitons to further secure it. Neither wanted their tent to be picked up by an errant gust in the middle of the night and to find themselves rolling over the edge.

Next they gathered snow and heated it over cans of Sterno, adding more snow as it melted. Finally they were rewarded with a half pot of boiling water. Recognizing the drill, Atemu sat beside them and stared; he was destined to get a hot meal at last.

After eating, they blew up their mattresses, unrolled their sleeping bags and lit their single heater for the small tent. The wind continued to howl. It wasn't long before they lit the lantern to see. Sky dragged out the satellite phone hoping their altitude would facilitate a connection. She desperately wanted to check on her grandfather's status.

"I don't understand it," she said, getting no sound whatsoever.

"Maybe it got slammed when we hit a bump," Matthew said.

"Maybe. Now I'm kicking myself for not having Saglek call the Royal Vic for me."

"We had other things on our mind. Not to be insensitive, but without the Sat phone I won't be able to access the online claim database, neither," Matthew replied.

Sky looked at him for a moment, understood his concern, and realized it wasn't really a concern. Of course, he didn't know there was no diamond claim to stake.

Exhausted as they were, they went outside and sat together on a piece of polyethylene. It kept their bums from direct contact with the freezing rock as the last sliver of gold faded from the horizon and the stars became visible over the dark silhouettes of the surrounding jagged peaks. Without any ambient light pollution, and sitting at an altitude of more than 3,000 feet, they were treated to a spectacular star show of winter circumpolar constellations. They picked out the Big Dipper and Cassiopeia. Between them was Polaris – the North Star – gleaming brightly overhead.

"The North Star has always been special for me," Sky said. "Grandfather used to say that if you kept your eye on the North Star, you would never lose your direction in life."

She moved closer to Matthew and he put his arms around her. She nestled her head against his chest and he heard her sigh with what he took to be contentment. His own heart was beating slightly faster now. Finally she tilted her head back and he reached down and they kissed. The kiss was long, slow and honey sweet. He had never thought of a kiss being two people making love with their mouths, until now.

"Oh, Matthew," she murmured, nestling closer.

"Sky, when this is over, will you…will you…?" Not having thought his request through, he was at a loss for words.

"Wear your sorority pin?" she asked, mischievously. "Walk the dog? Wash the dishes? Sing you a lullaby? Have your baby?" She began to chuckle.

"Hey," he protested. "I'm out of practice."

"Well, when this is over, I hope you still feel the way you do now."

"Oh, I will…I will," he replied. "We have so much to talk about. Anyhow, why would anything change?" He was sure she stiffened, just a shade.

"You're going to find out some things that are going to change your perspective on…" she hesitated, "…everything. I hope you can deal with it. And forgive me if you can't."

He didn't say anything. Finally, a trifle uneasy, he said: "Forgive you for what?"

"For not being totally candid. For serving someone else's priorities."

"There are no diamonds?"

"Oh, there are diamonds alright," Sky said. "But not in the

traditional sense."

"Sky, I don't think of myself as an uninformed person," he said. "And, I respect your beliefs and your ways. But I have to say, right now, I'm confused as hell."

"Telling you why you're here is still premature and could even be damaging. Could you trust me for another day or two?" Her tone was pleading. "For the first time in years, I think I've found someone I want to be with and I don't want to lose you."

"You won't lose me, Sky. But to be frank, I'm feeling a little nervous."

"Nothing will hurt you, I promise."

"How about you? Could anything hurt you?"

"No, they are not interested in me."

"Who are 'they'?" he asked. He looked around. "Where are 'they'? Are we meeting 'them' up here? And if so, why? If not, why not?"

"They are people who simply want to right a wrong," she said.

"What wrong? I've never met them. And that chimney we came up? It wasn't volcanic activity that formed it. Not with those steps."

"Please, Matthew? Soon I'll be able to tell you everything. Okay?"

He nodded and tightened his grip around her.

"Thank you," she said, giving his arm a squeeze. She looked up at him with a gaze that melted his heart. But then she slowly disentangled herself from his arms, gave him another squeeze and said: "Now to bed, hero. Morning will come earlier than usual for us."

* * *

Getting to sleep wasn't a problem. Staying that way, however, was difficult. And more than a touch unsettling.

Matthew seldom dreamed. Or, at least, remembered his dreams. This night, however, perched high on a peak in the Torngat Mountains, he felt like a sacrificial offering to the Gods of the North as he drifted to sleep with the wind moaning and the tent flapping against its frame. He dreamt that something was forcing him to approach the edge of the summit. Though he fought the force valiantly, he found himself looking over the edge...and suddenly he was falling, falling...!

He woke up!

Mired in a foggy quasi-sleep, he experienced a phenomena called the *Hag* by those of a superstitious bent, and *Sleep Paralysis* by the scientific community. No matter its label, it soon became a terrifying experience for him.

Half-awake and half-asleep, he found he was frozen, unable to move. He felt an urge to sit up, and leap off his air mattress and run. He wanted desperately to escape down the shaft that had brought him to this strangeness. What he'd be running from, or for that matter, why he was running, wasn't exactly clear. But somehow he felt he needed to flee.

Still, what about Sky? His mind screamed at him: You can't abandon Sky!

When the thought of her entered his mind, he was relieved to see her sleeping safe and sound beside him. But then he realized he hadn't turned his head. Because he couldn't. And yet he could see her, see both sides of the tent, and the door and the back of the tent, all at once.

How the hell can I see her? How the hell can I see everywhere!?

His heart began to pound, and he began to sweat, even in the sub-zero temperature. Strange noises were emanating from the exterior of the tent. He could hear electronic humming sounds that waxed and waned with the sudden coming and going of exterior lights. The lights were so bright, they were making the nylon sides of the tent translucent.

Indeed, directly outside the tent he could plainly see eye-ball searing flashes of colors: vermillion and cobalt blue, yellow and thulian pink, tangerine, and emerald green. They were so dazzling they illuminated everything in a fusion of colors growing and fading, blending and merging, shifting and separating. Other, pure white lights darted in and out of his sight, seeming to pass over their tent, dip below the rock tower and then shoot back up. But then one came closer, much closer.

A fiery red light, like a huge, round spinning sawmill blade cut a swath through the tent. Slowly, methodically, it moved up his and Sky's bodies from their feet towards their heads. Still frozen, he had the feeling it was scanning, searching for something. Finally, it paused at Matthew's chest. A thinner, brighter crimson laser-like beam sliced down through the wider blade of light and pierced his chest. He could feel it slowly enter his body, a cold probing rod that slipped through his skin, pierced his pectoral muscles and penetrated bone and tissue. Though he could feel it moving about in his chest, its coldness seemed to numb and negate the pain he should be feeling from such an intrusion.

Suddenly, in his mind, he heard a calm, gentle voice telling him to take a deep breath and hold it. Without a second thought, he obeyed and felt three small burning sensations in his lungs and instinctively coughed and exhaled. He mentally apologizing for doing so. The voice informed him that it was all right; it was over.

What was over?

Abruptly the laser beam withdrew so quickly he thought it had been snapped off. The wider, spinning blade of red light continued slowly up their bodies, past their heads and finally disappeared through the tent wall.

Everything went silent.

The lights outside appeared less frequently and then, finally, vanished altogether.

Silence....

He was again looking at nothing but darkness. And, he could move again. He sat up.

He looked down at Sky beside him. She was fast asleep, her breathing rhythmic and natural. Had she seen the lights? Had she heard the sounds? Was he going mad? Was it some sort of magical ideation? A ubiquitous hallucination brought on by a bad ER bar? An aurora borealis phenomena? Or something else?

He'd heard friends talk about the effects of magic mushrooms and other hallucinatory drugs, and he imagined he was experiencing similar effects. It certainly couldn't be any weirder. He took a deep breath and slowly lay back down in his sleeping bag. He looked protectively at Sky again.

But Sky kept her breathing even. She didn't move. She didn't look up. Then the message that she had asked for, that she hoped for, and that she had prayed for, came to her. Indeed, one she thought was her due.

Sleep, your grandfather has been made well.

Then a second message informed her that her companion had also been helped. The voice explained further.

Sleepily Sky reached across for Matthew and embraced him.

For a moment he felt her trembling and decided it was a natural physical reaction brought on by the cold. He held her gently pressing her cheek against his chest, and allowed his lips to brush her forehead...

...so he didn't see her smiling through grateful tears.

* * *

Colonel Moorhead stared at Lieutenant Reynold's display. The Avenger circled at 15,000 feet over Castle Peak. The two Radar Ops glanced back across the room to where the Colonel stood over the Avenger pilot. They turned back to their sets.

"As you know, they went into an opening at the base of the mountain yesterday, sir, and came out of somewhere on top late this afternoon," Reynolds said, carefully working his joystick to keep the drone on station as ordered. He was flying a wide orbit with his sensor targeting the heat signature of a tent far below on the flat rock of the summit. He pointed to a second red splotch signifying a slightly warmer spot, several dozen feet from the tent. "It seems likely that's the opening of a shaft, sir," he said. "While we didn't catch them until after they were on top, they had to have come up the inside; there was no other way they could reach the top."

"I was here after they emerged on the summit, Lieutenant?" Moorhead reminded him. "Why did you call me now?"

"I'm speaking for all of us in here, sir, but something came in from the north and lit everything so bright our sensors were useless; couldn't see anything with IR for a few minutes." There was a chorus of murmurs of assent from the radar operators behind them.

"So you switched from active infrared illumination to regular optics and what did you get?"

That's just it, sir, we could still see very little other than an array of colored lights bouncing off the peaks and whipping down into the valley, over the twin peaks and sometimes right through the rock. They were flat balls of light speeding north and south, and east and west. They climbed, dove and generally acted in a haphazard and random fashion. Despite this they appeared to be under control. But their brightness prevented our Avenger from seeing details."

"Something was carrying those lights, Lieutenant. Could you make out *any* solid craft?"

Reynolds shook his head. "No planes or helicopters, sir."

"Anything else?" Moorhead persisted.

Like what?

"No sir...nothing solid. They seemed to be lights, mostly."

"Why do you say *mostly*, Lieutenant?"

"Well, a couple of times our Radar Ops painted a solid target for a few seconds but then it morphed into nothing. It lost its form, consistency and from what we observed, turned back into a flat ball of light."

"Go on."

"Then a huge, bright red, round, flat light...like a dinner plate...it looked some sort of laser, or ionized, or 'living' energy, sir...hovered over the tent and a spinning red ray seemed to scan the tent up and down. During this scan, or whatever it was, another thinner and brighter red beam appeared and slid down through the wide beam and disappeared in the tent. Then it switched off...or at least it disappeared. The red ball took off like a bat out of hell and all the other lights followed.

"What was their heading when they left, Lieutenant?"

"That's what's totally weird, sir. They only shot off about a hundred yards and then all the colors merged into a bluish ball."

"Which direction, Lieutenant," Moorhead asked, impatiently.

"No direction, sir...they didn't go anywhere. The blue ball shot straight down into the center of the rock of the north peak."

"Jesus!" Moorhead exclaimed. "Into solid rock?"

"Yes, sir, I called you immediately on seeing the lights arrive, sir."

"That's okay Lieutenant. You caught me in a shower so it took some minutes."

Moorhead looked at his watch and squinted at the date indicator. He realized it was December 21st.

"Maybe Santa was making an early run, sir," Reynolds said, hoping he wasn't stepping over the line.

"Let's hope so, Lieutenant," Moorhead answered, without a smile. "The United States of America would like a nice Christmas present about now."

* * *

The next morning wasn't morning. Except by the strictest definition. When Sky shook him awake, he checked his watch. It was exactly 5:00 AM. He could barely see her dressed in a stiff, full head-to-toe dark suit that bent and crinkled as she moved. She was wearing her helmet and headlamp under a hood drawn tight. Over everything, she wore her climbing harness.

"What's going on?" he asked, looking around, and then at his watch.

"Time to go, Matthew," she said.

"What are you wearing, Sky?" Just as quickly he realized it was one of the two suits that had hung on her bedroom wall.

"It's an anti-nightvision camouflage suit made by a German company," she said. "It has a thermal IR coating that eliminates heat signatures."

"That's interesting," he muttered, vaguely. "Always nice to be in fashion."

"Yours is over here," she said, picking up a second one from the tent floor.

Atemu looked at it curiously. Matthew noticed he had a long rope tied to a leather collar. Though the dog sat inside, the rope was obviously tethered outside.

"We have to leave," she continued. "And we don't want to be seen."

"Seen by who?"

"Whoever has been watching us? As I said before, Grandfather knew he was being watched. He read about infrared technology that could track a person in the dark, and also about available countermeasures. He ordered two suits and used them here. Fortunately he had one on when they appeared one night."

"Who appeared?" Matthew asked.

"Soldiers."

"Soldiers?" Matthew said, incredulously. "What the heck did soldiers want with your grandfather? And how did soldiers get up here?"

"They arrived in a stealth helicopter, likely from Goose Bay. Very quiet, very efficient."

"Did your grandfather confront them?"

"No, but he knew they were coming. He was warned by the other people. He exited the tent and hung over the edge of the cliff on a rope, sheltered by a crevice."

"What did they do? These 'soldiers'?"

"They checked his tent and then left."

The tiniest of doubts began to pick at the edges of Matthew's mind. Was the grandfather a little off? Paranoid? Delusional? Neurotic? Even psychotic? Had he taken Sky in with his tales of soldiers in the night tracking him for some nefarious purpose? The fact the old man found a diamond didn't in any way support his contention he was being followed everywhere. Nor did it repudiate the possibility that Matthew – as Jacquard had insinuated – was dealing with a family of Looney Tunes. But then, who put a GPS locator unit in her carbine?

Never having talked to Jerome St. Onge, Matthew had no personal basis on which to judge the old man. But he'd come this far with Sky and, indeed, strange happenings were afoot. So, he crawled out of his sleeping bag and began to dress. "Why would soldiers follow your grandfather? Think about it, Sky. There's really no reason on earth."

"Actually, Matthew, there is every reason for them to be interested in him." Sky said, sensing his doubts coming to the fore again. Despite everything that had happened during their trip, despite his assurances to the contrary, she could feel his confidence in her slipping.

On his side, Matthew now realized all he had to go on was Sky's perspective and judgement. She was watching him. He stopped dressing. She was obviously worried; she knew he was doubting her.

"Sky, I'm a pretty tolerant guy, but this is getting nuttier by the minute," he said.

She nodded her understanding.

"It's becoming more and more bizarre," he reiterated.

She swallowed and nodded again. He sighed and looked at her, then at Atemu. And then back to her.

"But that's good enough for me," he said finally, realizing his judgement was copiously clouded by how he felt about her.

Sky threw her arms around him and held on tight. Atemu moved in and tried to insert himself between them.

Matthew laughed out loud: "Either he's jealous or he wants in on this group hug." He, grabbed the dog and was smothered in slippery kisses for his trouble. "So what'll we call this? Love-In at 3,000 feet?"

Sky stopped him from donning his parka before putting on the IR suit and harness. She explained he wouldn't need heavy clothes where they were going. They settled on a light insulated jacket and sweater under his suit.

"Is this some long lost tribe we're meeting?" he queried, adjusting his helmet under the IR hood. "If so, they have some damn strange rituals. We could have booked a conference room in Montreal and settled it all there, you know."

"Never happen," she answered, grateful to see him smiling. "Atemu will stay here until we get back. He's tied to a piton outside but we'll leave the tent door partially open so he can squirm in and out when he wants shelter."

In a corner of the tent, Matthew spotted three ER Survival Bars broken into thirds and placed near where Atemu slept. Sky reached over and gave the dog another hug: "You eat snow if you're thirsty. But not the yellow kind. Now be a good boy. We'll be back for you, I promise."

With their IR suits on, they moved to the shaft, rolled under the overhang and switched on their headlamps. The light bounced off the black rock all around them. They sat hunched over the abyss, their feet dangling freely in the chimney. Sky would lead.

"Don't worry, we're only going down about 800 feet," she said, attaching a doubled safety line to a piton, and beginning the descent.

"Great," he said, somewhat relieved. He also attached his safety line.

"Be careful," she called up.

"Okay. By the way, I had the oddest dream last night," he said, carefully placing his feet on the steps as he spotted them with his headlamp. His voice reverberated hollowly.

Though they moved purposely, they did so with caution. The protocol was to descend 40 or 50 feet, untie the double safety line from their harness and pull one end through the anchored pitons above. Then they would thread it through a new piton sunk in the shaft wall. Once tied firmly to their harness, they again moved down, protected by their double lines. They kept repeating the process, making good time. Matthew thought the absence of a 60-pound canine was no small matter.

"What sort of dream?" Sky finally called upward to him.

"I woke up and thought I was seeing dozens of weird, colored lights buzzing us outside. Then one sent some sort of wide scanning beam into the tent accompanied by a thinner laser beam that hit me in the chest. You're going to think I'm crazy, but a voice in my mind told me to take a deep breath, which I did. Felt some pressure and then the lights vanished."

"That *is* weird, Matthew," Sky replied from below, breathing hard from the exertion. "By the way, did you ever smoke?"

"Smoke? That's a funny question, isn't it? What does smoking have to do with anything?"

"Did you?"

"A pipe, for about ten years. And, may I say, I looked very intellectual and sophisticated. Why?"

"Lung cancer," she said.

"I don't have lung cancer," he declared, slightly put off.

"No you don't," she said, lightly.

They climbed down steadily, barely talking now.

Sky was about 30 feet below him when he saw her suddenly swing sideways and disappear; he was sure she had entered the round mouth of the tunnel he'd seen on the way up.

He continued to make his way down, cautioning himself not to hurry lest he become careless and make a fatal error that, in posterity, would be recognized as his *last* mistake. A moment later he joined her.

Helping each other, they stripped off their IR suits and helmets, and left them, as well as the ropes, by the mouth of the tunnel. Matthew shivered despite wearing a heavy wool sweater and jacket; he wondered if it had been wise to leave their parkas on the summit.

"Matthew, might as well save your headlamp," Sky said, leading him into the opening. Her own light danced on the walls as she moved. He turned his off and followed.

They walked swiftly through the rock tunnel and again Matthew was amazed that the walls were relatively smooth. It was almost as though something had melted the rock. And, while lava from a volcanic action might spew upward, forming a chimney, it didn't often spew sideways to create passageways for wayward travelers.

In fact, the texture reminded him of the so-called "steps" in the chimney. And those were not mere oddities of nature neither; they were designed and planned. How they were formed, or by who, was the big mystery. He hoped there would be answers at the end of their journey.

After they'd been walking for about twenty-five minutes, Matthew began to feel warmer.

"Sky," he called ahead, "Where are we going?"

"To the meeting," she answered.

"So I take it we're about to negotiate mineral rights or some sort of partnership with these people?" he asked, all business.

She didn't respond but pointed forward instead. In the distance he could make out light. They must be exiting the tunnel, he thought, and wondered why he didn't feel cold air. He became aware of the sound of rushing water. A minute later he stood in stunned silence beside Sky.

The tunnel opened into an enormous rock grotto. It was lit from above by morning's first light streaming through what seemed to be a concave sheet of ice serving as a roof. In places, shadows hovered where snow covered the "roof." The air was hot and humid thanks to what looked like a 200-foot-wide waterfall on the opposite side of the gigantic cave; various sized ponds radiated steam upwards. Several tinkling streams also made their way through a wide variety of tropical looking fauna. These included many different ferns, flowers, and other exotic-looking plants. Small palm trees and Yucca plants dotted the landscape. Birds chirped from somewhere and he spotted a bee pollenating yellow flowers nearby. Heady overtones of sweetness resembling honeysuckle, magnolia, tuberose and wisteria, offered a potpourri of smells.

In effect, they had come upon a complete biosphere with a very effective ecosystem hard at work in the Torngat Mountains. Things were no longer merely bizarre, he thought. They were now off the scale.

Matthew couldn't even guess the dimensions of the cave, much less its height. He was sure, however, that one or more football fields would fit comfortably inside it. "What in the name of God is this?" he asked, too astonished to process everything he was seeing.

"Hot springs and a natural ice roof," she replied. "The moisture from the steam rises, hits the opening up there and, over time, has frozen solid. Grandfather says that for a month or so in the summer season, it is very thin, or it partially melts leaving a small hole in the middle. It freezes over again in the fall. He says this cavern is probably millions of years old."

"You've been here before?" he asked.

"Sure," she said, the nonchalance in her tone a bit forced.

"But aren't those tropical plants?" he protested, pointing.

"Most are native to North America," she replied. "But a few are certainly tropical and probably resulted from seeds frozen here for millions of years. When the right combination of forces came together and formed this…" she pointed around, "…then they sprouted."

Matthew knew there was ample evidence that less temperate and even subarctic zones had once been tropical, of course. He also knew that deep down in the earth, scientists had discovered fossilized tropical plants and trees, and even sea shells, all where no jungles or oceans existed today. He stared at his surroundings as he unconsciously removed and carried his jacket and wool sweater. "It's like a Shangri-La," he said.

"As far as I know, only Grandfather and I and the other people know about it. And now you, of course."

"This is crazy!" he said. "Obviously it's been here for centuries or, more likely, thousands of years. So you'd think it would have been discovered. Particularly with the dramatic improvements in optics and spectral analysis that we've seen."

He looked up in awe.

"My God, look at that!" he continued. "Heat must be escaping from somewhere and infrared satellite photos would have revealed an unknown heat source in Northern Labrador. That would have piqued the curiosity of scientists and eventually there would have been a scientific expedition up here to find out where it was originating. Middle Earth conspirators should have been going nuts. In fact, by now, there should be tour companies selling tickets to visit the subarctic 'Jungle in a Cave'."

"Right, well we may have had a little help with preventing that," Sky said.

"What kind of help?"

She smiled. "From the other people. Grandfather says they adjust the satellite data before they allow it to be transmitted back to earth."

"They? Who exactly adjusts it?" he asked. "And how?"

"Matthew, I have something I need to show you," she said, ignoring his question. "But first we need to test our destiny with each other."

Without waiting for a comment or more questions, Sky moved off at a rapid pace; she jumped from rock to rock, and onto clear areas of grass and sedge.

Matthew remained rooted to where he stood for a moment and

simply watched her. Again it was impossible to ignore the grace with which she moved.

As she worked her way across the grotto, and grew smaller, in the process, he was able to compare her figure to the overall size of the cavern. Indeed, it was bigger than he first realized. We must be in the second peak, he thought. Looking upward again, he realized he was looking at a virtual glass ceiling, but one made of ice. It had to be the ice he'd seen from the southern tower.

When he saw Sky reach and stop at a large flat rock bordering a fair-sized pond about 300 feet across, he began to make his way over to her.

She stood on the rock beside the pond and took off her mitts and her rolled-up balaclava. Then her jacket, sweater and shirt. Her back was to him as she faced the water and removed her bra while kicking off her boots. Next came her socks. Lastly she slipped off her trousers and insulated underwear and a tiny pair of pale blue panties in a single motion. She dropped everything and stood there, naked. He gaped as he looked at the graceful curve of her spine, her trim buttocks and beautiful long, gently tapered legs. She half turned and looked at him over her shoulder. Though her eyes were serious for a moment, gradually the dolphin-like smile emerged like the sun rising on a perfect day.

Then, without further ado, she crouched and leaped upward to peel off in a perfect, half-moon dive, her slim body slicing into the water with hardly a splash. A moment later she surfaced, her hair wet and even darker, perfectly complementing her eyes. Effortlessly treading water, she swept her hair back and called to him. "Bath time, Matthew!"

"Works for me," he called back, wishing he had some genius-sounding retort. Desperately he looked around for a place to change; a rock, tree, anything would do.

"What are you looking for?" she called out, continuing to tread water and smiling broadly. The mist rose around her; she looked like a mischievous water nymph hailing from a Captain Nemo story.

He looked at her grin and saw that she damn well knew what he was looking for.

"The change room is right there," she called, pointing to the spot on the rock she had occupied moments before. Her clothing rested in a heap beside him. She watched him turning red with embarrassment.

"I'm not as gorgeous as you," he called back.

"Says who?" She turned and swam towards the opposite side of the pond, cutting him some slack.

As she did, he literally threw off his boots and clothing, and leaped into the water with all the grace and dexterity of a hippo. Sky turned at the gigantic splash and deliberately and swiftly swam straight back, her gaze fixed on him as a predator eyes its next meal. He found he was shaking like a leaf as she approached and it wasn't because the water was cold; it was as tepid as a warm bath.

Sky swam right into his arms and wrapped her legs around his waist. Her hands cradled his face as she kissed him. They both went over backwards still locked in the kiss. They sank underwater. Amidst bubbles they surfaced, still in each other's arms and laughing with the abandon of teenagers. They dove, swam, chased each other and spent several minutes rinsing their bodies. The clear water tasted fresh and clean rather than giving off the sulfurous odor often accompanying hot springs.

Finally, out of breath, they paused with Sky again wrapping her long legs around his body in a scissor hold. He could feel her heat on his stomach and he felt himself growing hard.

"Okay, Mr. Corrigan," she grinned, catching her breath. "You wanted to talk...talk!"

He looked at her without a trace of a smile: "I think I'm in love with you, Sky."

"Love? That's a pretty big word –?"

He cut her off. "I'm serious. And this isn't some crush brought on by our working together in an unreal environment."

She also stopped smiling and they gazed at each other. "How do you know this is love, Matthew?" she pressed. "Could it simply be infatuation? After all, I'm the only girl in the neighborhood." She squirmed closer.

"Oh God," he moaned, "Don't do that."

She smiled, using her arms to stroke the water, her legs still pinioning his body.

"Hell, you're going to give me a heart attack if you keep this up."

He looked at her perfect breasts rising above the water, the dark nipples standing out like twin sentinels. He pulled her close. Her breasts flattened against his chest and he saw her gaze wavering and her eyes half-closing; she continued the pressure against his belly.

Finally, he asked the question that would make or break the deal: "Sky, I fell in love with you the moment I saw you; but I have to know where you're coming from."

"Well, let's see, Matthew," she said. "I've got my arms around your neck and I'm rubbing my naked body against you. Any clues there?"

"But I don't know if this is a one-act play or what," he replied. "I need to know there's more."

"How much more do you want?" Though Sky was questioning him, her motivation wasn't to make him question his own feelings, but more to reassure her.

"I want everything, Sky," he said. "Did *you* feel anything for me when we met?"

"At first, not really," she said, honestly. "But over the last weeks, I've gotten to know you. I've gotten to know your kindness. I've gotten to know how sensitive you are. I've gotten to see how you treat people, animals and even potential enemies like Meyer. And, I saw your courage when you defended me in Montreal, as well as readily abandoning the diamond hunt to help save Monique. Finally, I've seen how you treat me personally with caring, compassion, loyalty and…even more.

"So no, I'm not just horny. Well I am, but it's backed up with some powerful feelings for you, Mr. Corrigan. To answer your question: Yes, I am in love with you. A whole lot. And I hope you won't end up hurting me."

"Never!"

"Promise?

"On my life," he said.

"Then, answer one more question," she said.

"Anything."

"Do you want me?" she asked, not in a teasing way but almost in desperation. "Do you?"

"God, yes, I want you more than anything in the world."

But she wasn't about to let the mental nor the physical foreplay end. She continued to rub against his chest and belly. "Well that goes two ways," she said, looking him right in the eye. "So, what's your next move?"

"I want to make love to you," he gasped.

"How?" she demanded hungrily, her jaw set and her eyes flashing.

He knew what she wanted and he tossed away any inhibitions. "I want to kiss you all over, every inch of your beautiful body and make you crazy with desire."

"Oh God, yes!" she gasped, pressing hard against him.

"Sky, have mercy…!"

"Do you really love me, Matthew?"

"Love you? I adore you," he gasped. He moved, trying to enter her but she would have none of it.

"Not yet," she said. "First I want you to make me feel every fiber of my being."

"Sky, I'll do anything you want," he moaned in sweet agony. "Anything…but let me do it *now*!"

"Work for it, hero." She pulled away from him. In a few strong strokes she reached the side of the pond and scampered up on the flat rock. Before he could reach her, she scooped up both sets of clothing and ran towards the near side of the grotto. He followed her and they entered a small cave-like room. By the far wall was a thick bed of dead grasses. Someone had slept here before. Who had done so, at the moment, certainly wasn't of concern.

Quickly he took their clothes, spread them on top of the grasses and sat down. Despite her prior boldness, she moved to him slowly, even hesitantly. He noted her long athletic legs, her slim waist and her deep belly button above a soft cluster of down. She approached and looked down at his nakedness. She stood there just long enough for Matthew to fear that she was reconsidering. Then she moved forward eagerly; he enfolded her in his arms.

"Oh, Matthew," she said. "You know I want this as much as you do."

"I sincerely doubt that," he whispered, with a smile.

They kissed softly and then more urgently, tongues probing, exploring each other's mouths. He turned her over until he was on top and then kissed her body all the way down until he reached the juncture of her thighs.

"Oh…sweet Lord," she gasped.

He kissed each inner thigh and moved higher, pausing only briefly when he reached her center. He felt such a deep love for Sky, he wanted nothing more than to please her completely. He continued his explorations with them lying side-by-side.

Sky gasped and laid her head on his shoulder. He kissed her forehead tenderly. God, how he loved this woman. How he cherished this woman. And, in his heart, he knew he could never let her go.

He slipped down and tenderly mouthed her nipples. Her gaze was now unfocused and unseeing. She had surrendered to the feelings coursing through her body.

For Sky nothing existed other than a heaviness creeping into every limb, and a delicious ache in her loins. She yearned for satiation.

Mathew went from one breast to the other, kissing them, worshipping them. She threw her head back exposing her throat and he kissed the hollow there as he lifted her breasts and tenderly squeezed them repeatedly. She sighed and moaned softly. He kneaded them, his thumbs rubbing the nipples lightly, slowly, feeling them harden even more.

The experience was all too delicious, and despite the increasing urgency she felt for penetration, she didn't want it to be over until he had maximized her pleasure. In this she would be needful. In this she would demand all. In this she would have absolute togetherness.

Indeed, she knew the physical could not be happening with such completeness and such intensity except for the fact she was deeply in love with Matthew Corrigan.

Sky pushed him away and sank down. As a physician she knew the most sensitive points of his body and capitalized on this knowledge.

"No…" he said, desperately pulling her up. "I won't be able to stop it."

In turn, he started to move down once more but she shook her head and instead took his hand in hers and guided it up to her mouth. Slowly she licked his palm. Seizing his fingers she brought them up to her mouth and licked each appendage, nibbling on the ends. As several fingers were drawn deeply into her mouth and lavishly devoured, Mathew emitted a low, hoarse groan.

Meanwhile he held her tightly against him and continued his ministrations with his other hand. Her breathing quickened and her stomach muscles expanded and contracted ever more quickly. They continued kissing, barely able to get enough of each other and he stroked her until she was digging her fingers into his neck, holding him close. He kissed her again and again.

"Oh my God, Matthew!" she exclaimed, as he rose.

She was now scratching his back, leaving gouges both red and angry. But he didn't care. There was pleasure in feeling the pain, pleasure in knowing he was making her happy and pleasure in the anticipation of joining with her.

"Matthew…please…now!" she finally gasped.

He was ecstatic and eager to oblige. Poised above her, ready to make their union complete, he saw her looking up at him with those beautiful eyes, her full lips and mouth open with desire. He couldn't help himself; he couldn't wait any longer.

Together they luxuriated in their feelings as they joined as one. Both were almost frozen with the intensity as they moved against each other. He kissed her hard forcing his tongue against her tongue until they were intertwined and caressing one another's mouths.

What he couldn't believe was the heat and softness surrounding him, and the feelings of love and of being wanted again. Augmenting this, having obviously not engaged in love making for some time, her own desire heightened his pleasure a thousand fold.

For her, the foreignness of his entry caused her to want more, to want to keep him within her. She pushed her pelvis forward, feeling him fill her entirely.

Gone for both of them was the shyness and the discipline of the past weeks. Gone was the doubt, hurt and uncertainty.

The sound of their lovemaking was both sensual and motivational as they tried to enhance each other's pleasure.

It wasn't long before they both abandoned any semblance of maintaining control. He groaned in delight. "Oh, Sky," he breathed. He was rapidly heading towards the point of no return with this amazing woman.

"Now, my love, now!" she whimpered, as a particularly powerful wave of pleasure started small, grew rapidly and then urgently exploded through her lower body. The feelings flooded up to her breasts, enveloped her whole being and refused to stop. Above her, he also moaned in ecstasy as he entered that brief and elusive realm of feeling that could never be achieved or duplicated in any other way.

"I love you, I love you, Sky…" he whispered.

Spasms wracked both their bodies.

Below him, despite his own feelings of pleasure, he marveled at a transformation that magically took place in his beautiful partner.

At the apogee, Sky's eyes went from their bottomless darkness to a silver, glistening sheen; in fact, they glowed with a life that was almost alien in its intensity.

Finally, they collapsed into each other's arms, gasping desperately for air, not saying anything, simply welcoming the relief and happiness of release.

After a moment, Matthew gently rolled off Sky onto his back. He was breathing like a marathoner and his body felt as though his bones had dissolved. He didn't have the strength to even sit up, let alone stand. One thing he knew for certain: loving Sky was everything he could hope for in the world. He thought that if he died at that very moment, it had been enough. He'd certainly leave the world a winner.

Sky couldn't ever remember losing control the way she had for the last ten, 20, or was it 1,000 minutes? Random questions floated lazily through her mind. What had happened? Where had all these feelings come from? Physiologically she understood them, of course. But personally she was sure she had never experienced such all-encompassing bliss.

And, as her cognitive abilities returned, she realized she knew full well why it had been so pleasurable. She was finally with the right person. After all, the greatest sex organ was the brain; couple the physical with love, respect and admiration, and you obviously had a sure-fire recipe for success. She almost laughed aloud, giddy in her happiness. After all, where did she find the person she had wanted and needed all her life? Deep inside a prehistoric cave in a frozen wilderness that French explorer Jacque Cartier had called: *The Land God Gave to Cain*. Who could have imagined this, she mused.

Luxuriating in the afterglow of their lovemaking, she allowed her mind to drift to their initial meeting and how her opinion of him had changed radically as she got to know him better.

At first Matthew had come to her disguised as just another opportunist or 'man with a mission.' And, even after her grandfather had told her who he *really* was, she had only softened slightly. But during intimate and unguarded moments alone in their tent, he had slowly revealed himself to her as a sensitive and loving individual brutalized by a tragedy, and yet one who refused to give up on a doomed relationship until the decision was torn from his hands.

When she looked deep, she realized that everything she had learned during their weeks together showed he personified courage, fortitude, charity, fairness and strength. Not in a loud or brash way, but in a quiet and tolerant fashion. He was the sort who would dash into a killing fire, save someone and leave the scene, never looking for acknowledgement nor reward. Finally, she knew she had found someone she could truly respect and love.

Beside her, Matthew was seeing a virtual vision of loveliness, a girl-woman whose lithe body now showed her neck, arms and upper chest flushed red from their love-making. Her flat belly slowly moved up and down, her arms were relaxed at her sides, and her head was lying limply to the side, a stunning artist's model in repose. She didn't move. Her eyes were hooded, half-open, but likely not seeing much.

His admiration for her had grown quickly during their journey as they were repeatedly tested by danger, hardship and moral choices. He'd constantly been surprised at her resolve and her dedication to their task. And through adversity, she had maintained her honesty, courage and generosity even to the point where she had twice opted to save their competitors' lives without a thought to exploiting a potential advantage.

There was no sound in the cave other than their mutual breathing and the growing roar of cascading water which inserted itself back into their world. She moved her hands over her belly for a moment as though lamenting the loss of him. She half rolled over and clutched him tightly about the waist. With this act, she was his and she prayed that he meant what he said; he was hers.

Matthew gradually became aware of the distant thunder of the waterfall outside. He realized that if anyone had asked him about it two minutes before, his response would have been: What waterfall? He smiled at the thought.

Sky was moving beside him and he suddenly realized she was crying. Alarmed, he raised himself on his elbow and his mood went from joy to fear. What had he done?

"It's okay," she gulped, seeing his concern and patting his hand.

"That was beautiful."

He took her in his arms and held here for a long time. Finally she took several deep breaths. The tears had ceased. He looked down at her: "I love you."

"And I love you, Matthew" she said.

"Then why are you crying?"

"Didn't you know? Girls cry when they're happy. I may seem like a hard-ass but I have my moments."

"I could never figure that out," he said. "Girls cry when they're happy. They cry when they're sad. They cry when they're touched by something. They cry when they're angry."

"It's true," she said, with a smile, pretending to toss it off. "But it's also been a very long time. Since I was so *happy*, I mean" she emphasized, the hint of a mischievous smile on her face.

"Me too," he replied. "So, it was okay?"

"Men really are inherently insecure aren't they," she laughed.

"I haven't done it in a while."

"It was wonderful, Matthew," she reassured him.

"Course it took the right man," he joked, regaining his composure, feeling his oats.

Yes, hero, go outside, climb up on that big rock and beat your chest!

But she merely laughed, happy for him that he was feeling good.

"So how come…?" He left the obvious dangling.

"Oh there were a thousand opportunities, Matthew," she said. "Especially with the med students during university, or the docs at the hospital. But it never seemed the right time or the right person. Or it was the right time but the wrong person, or the wrong person at the right time. Or, maybe, as one disgruntled fellow said when I wouldn't play ball: I'm just a cock-tease refugee from a funny farm. I actually thought about becoming a nun at one point." She laughed at herself.

He looked down at her face. Tenderly he kissed her cheeks and forehead and eyes. "I love you so much, Sky." After a moment he continued: "Do you realize, it's the 22nd today? Christmas is just around the corner and I've just received the best Christmas present any mortal could wish to receive."

"Well Merry Christmas, my love," she said, reaching over and kissing him. "I know I got the best Christmas present I could ever hope for also. And I didn't have to wait until the 25th to open it. That was a bonus."

"Are you happy?" he asked tentatively.

"Yes, Matthew, I'm happy."

He burrowed his nose into her neck. She laughed, reached for him and hugged him.

"But, you know something," she continued, voice breaking again. "Idealistic and 50s as it sounds, I'm glad I was very selective, Matthew. It makes it more special. And I really have fallen for you! Head, heels, the whole enchilada!"

"And, I'm crazy over you, Sky," he answered, feeling a lump in his own throat. I think, that all things considered, we're both pretty lucky."

She looked up, inspecting his face closely. Then she stroked it with her hand, shaking her head slowly from side to side at the wonder of it all.

In turn, he felt his heart pretty much leap for joy at the love he saw within her.

But then she gave him a gentle smile that turned into the wider dolphin-like grin, and in turn, morphed into something that could best be described as crafty. When she spoke, her voice was low and husky: "Can you make me *happy* again, sailor?"

~4~

It was the day before the big day and Stone and his team had been fully briefed. Now he understood the necessity for the secrecy, and the critical nature of their mission. What happened in the next two days could, literally, change the future entirely, depending on what they recovered.

Activity at the Saglek Harbour base had gone from almost nothing to looking like a busy modern airport. Hangar doors slid open and closed regularly, ground support personnel scurried from building to building, some with heavy toolkits in hand, and a Caterpillar D-8 bulldozer moved tons of snow to accommodate aircraft emerging from hangars. Fuel was being pumped, systems checked and rechecked, and thumbs-up being given.

On the runway, a Komatsu Motor Grader rolled up and down removing snow almost to the tarmac and grading it to the side. Lights were on over the hangars and other buildings, the Biohazard flag had been replaced by the Canadian Maple Leaf flag and the Stars & Stripes directly below it. Two-man snowmobiles patrolled the perimeter of the base with heavily armed and vigilant guards riding them.

The hangers had been pretty much emptied now resulting in lineups of cammo-painted Predators, Avengers, Reapers, Global Hawks and other unmanned aerial combat vehicles waiting in orderly rows on newly plowed areas beside the airstrip. The six brand-new, heavily classified Super Eagle Drones carrying the devastating 30,000 pound Bunker Buster bombs were still in their hanger to avoid being photographed by spy satellites. They would emerge right before take-off.

Five of only 115 F-35 Lightning's built to date were also lined up in a neat row in another plowed area beside the runway. Their canopies were open with techs leaning inside on some. On others, mechanics or techs had fuselage panels open and were working to ensure readiness. Behind the F-35s were rows of F-16s with similar activities taking place on and around them. Everything must be ready for the next day. This was a modern armada preparing to do battle.

Inside the main buildings, things were also wrapping up.

"Departure runway 17, the 23rd at 1400 hours," Colonel Moorhead confirmed to the group of RPV Pilots and their Sensor Operators in the Command and Control Center, and those listening in to the 411 mission briefing from their remote locations.

While some pilots would fly the UCAVs direct from the Saglek base, others would be doing so from remote locations in the United States. The orders were simple: fly to the target, dump their smart bombs or fire their rockets where stipulated, and return to base. The success or failure of the operation depended on the target's reaction and the work of the Mission Recovery Team. Moorhead finished the briefing with: "You have your orders. Good luck, gentlemen!"

The multiple split, 80-inch display screens in the room showing the faces of dozens of UCAV pilots faded to black. In the Saglek briefing room, their own contingent of pilots gathered their notes and left.

Colonel Moorhead and Major Stone met in his office five minutes later. Everything was on the table now.

"Same MO as St. Onge," Moorhead was saying. "But this time we watched them from 15,000 feet while they went in an entrance at the base of the mountain. Late the next day, they emerged on top. Obviously they have IR suits as they later left the tent without us spotting them. They must have gone back down through the shaft last night. Where were they going? We have to assume it's to the base since they didn't emerge from the mountain. And, they plan on coming back on top."

"How so?" Stone asked.

"They left the dog tethered up there."

"Maybe he's expendable?"

"Maybe, but somehow I doubt it. If so, they wouldn't have tied him up."

"Does your GPS tracker tell you where they are now?"

"No. It was primarily backup to follow them so we could find the mountain entrance; we never expected it to work inside solid rock. When they exit, we'll pick them up again."

"If there is a shaft inside leading to the top, it still doesn't reveal the entrance to this base?" Stone said. "If there is one."

"Who knows? It may be a virtual entrance, opening when needed," Moorhead said. "Nothing would surprise me about their capabilities. But at least we nailed the mountain entrance."

"That's positive," Stone said.

"Certainly," Moorhead asserted. "As for why climb to the summit? No idea. Unless they get picked up."

"Did you figure out what the light show was all about?" Stone asked.

"They have airships that can go from solid to ethereal in a nanosecond. They have airships that can go from zero to thousands of miles an hour in a nanosecond. And, they have airships that can make right hand turns in a nanosecond. *And* we assume these gyrations still leave whoever, or *whatever* is inside, alive. Maybe the light show was about inspecting Corrigan and St. Onge. Maybe that's why they have to be up there; to be inspected for some reason."

"Speaking of which…?" Stone said, leaving the question hanging.

"As we've discussed Major, the civilians aren't our priority. If they get out, they get out. If they perish, they perish. Our objective is to get in there, salvage whatever technology our quarry has left behind and safely get out. That's why we've spent $50 million on this black ops project. So we need it to pay off. Still, if we see them we'll pick them up."

"Yes, sir," Stone answered.

"One slight modification in our plans. Your gear is quite bulky so we reconfigured the loads. Rather than four Mountaineers flying in separately, the copter will take four scientists and three Mountaineers with some gear. We'll use the ski plane to bring in the additional equipment you'll need. One of the Mountaineers will fly it and the remaining equipment in, and rendezvous with you north of the entrance we've found. And, based on timing and the days being so short, you'll likely spend the night. Appropriate gear will be aboard."

"Got it."

"Your team is ready?" Moorhead asked.

"Ready as we'll ever be."

"Good, because once we start, there's no turning back."

"One question, sir," Stone said. "What if they don't cut and run? What if they turn and fight?"

"All the Intel says they're leaving; their mission is wrapping up. So we're assuming it will be much more expedient to just leave. That's why timing is critical. And they usually fly at night. So we'll hit them in the afternoon. From what we know, their base has been a safe haven for them for decades. Of course they'll have some warning once the squadrons take off. But it won't be much. Surprise is paramount to cause panic and pandemonium. It's all more about big bangs and smoke than any wish to create real damage or hurt any…life form. We want them to flee and leave stuff behind."

"And we'll go in and look for crumbs."

"Their crumbs would be like a ten-course banquet for us."

"Yes, sir."

"Get a good sleep tonight, Paul" Moorhead advised, reverting to his informal voice. "You're going to need everything you've got for tomorrow."

* * *

Sky and Matthew had fallen asleep wrapped in each other's arms. The small cave was a good 85 degrees, so being covered with a few items of clothing was certainly enough. However, their activities had taken a toll on their grass mattress and they awoke simultaneously groaning as they rolled over on the rock shelf. Matthew looked at his watch and noticed the date had slipped to the 23rd so they had been sleeping all night. It was 10 AM.

He looked at Sky whose body was lit by a yellow glow from a rising sun filling the entire outer cavern and spilling into their stone ante chamber. She stretched, fully naked and he thought: this girl isn't merely beautiful, she's glorious.

Awakening slowly, she looked over at him, smiled sleepily and languidly stretched again. He smiled back. No wonder he felt so damned happy.

Not moving she watched Matthew as he rose and rapidly covered himself with his pants.

"The old double standard: naked women are beautiful, naked men are comedic," she said.

"Just the way it is," he replied, unsuccessfully stifling a yawn.

"Well, I don't agree," she declared with a light laugh, the sound resembling a quick tinkle on the treble keys of a piano.

She also stood and they embraced and kissed, held each other close for a few seconds, and then kissed again. "I do love you, Matthew."

"And I thank the Gods for that fact, Sky." he said sincerely. "To me this is the real thing."

"Like Coca-Cola?" Abruptly she slapped hands over her mouth. "Damn, your sense of humor is contagious."

He merely grinned as they dressed.

"I wouldn't do what I did to you, nor let you do what you did to me, unless I was damn sure this was the real thing for me too," she continued.

He grinned happily. "Good!"

"And I want everything too, Mathew," she continued. "The ring, the wedding, the house, the bassinet, family vacations, growing old together …the works. Okay?"

"Roger that!" he said.

They dressed quickly though he had no idea what was on the agenda. In fact, he really didn't care much. What had transpired between them and the resulting commitment to each other was worth all the hardships of the trip alone. The one thing he did know was that after their multiple bouts of lovemaking, he was ravenous. He wondered if she had any survival bars left.

"Matthew?"

He looked out of the small cave. Sky, now fully dressed, had moved a few yards away. She was standing on a small island at the edge of a pond amidst some tropical looking ferns. She stared across the grotto at the far opposite wall. It was where a sheet of white water plunged over a high cliff and dropped into a small lake, a natural waterfall.

When she called out, he had immediately noticed her tone was different. Gone was the playful nymph who teased and beguiled him. In fact, her entire visage was transformed back to the serious guide, the no-nonsense northern scout, most at home when standing in the snow with carbine in hand.

Back to business...again?

"What is it?" he called, pulling on his boots and lacing them up.

"I need to show you something."

"Sure. When do we meet these people?"

"A little later."

He joined her, their hands slipping together as naturally as if they were longtime lovers. Gently she began leading him across grass plots, and over rocks and small streams. Occasionally they detoured around some formidable boulders. The closer they came to the waterfall, the more nervous she appeared. Again he was impressed with the size of the grotto which really had no recognizable references on which to accurately judge its dimensions. But when he looked up, he estimated the height to the ice roof was probably 800 feet or more above them. He'd flown planes lower than that.

"This is one huge cave," he said, as the sunlight continued to grow brighter in the grotto. Birds flitted overhead. Bees buzzed by them.

Sky said nothing.

He noticed a moist glint in her eyes and thought, not unkindly: What is it? Why is she getting upset?

Sky kept her gaze averted as they moved busily along, looking up, down and around as though trying to distract herself.

"What do you want to show me?" he asked again, now becoming concerned.

Again, she didn't answer or comment. She shook her head and kept moving.

They reached the base of the waterfall which emitted a daunting roar. Its mass drowned out any attempt at conversation as it plunged into the lake sending out waves in a frothy wake.

Her grip tightened while she led him around another small stream flowing into the lake. They walked towards the right side of the waterfall. As they drew near, he could make out a side opening where they could go behind the curtain of water. They found themselves on a sandy beach of sorts. The air smelled fresh and clean.

Moving behind the falls, they entered relative darkness. They walked on sand compressed by the small waves lapping at the shore. The roar of the water was much muted. Mist permeated the air. She looked back at him and there were, indeed, a range of emotions playing across her face. Their vision soon adjusted to what light filtered through the waterfall.

He pulled himself forward, caught and embraced her. "What is it, Sky?" he asked gently. "What are we doing here?"

"We are in a sacred place, Matthew," she said, her voice breaking.

"Sacred to your people?" he asked, thinking they were on ground holding special significance for native peoples.

"No," she whispered in his ear, her face close to his.

He felt the moisture on her cheek and gently wiped it away. "Sacred to who?"

She looked steadily at him and let everything out, barely pausing for breath. "Sacred to us, Matthew. To you and me. What you will see here wasn't meant to happen. Though these other people frighten me, they are good people. They are very just people. And, they are so sorry. That is why they wished you to visit. And, that is why I brought you here."

"Sky," he said, holding on to his patience. Despite their union and his love for her, this game was severely testing him. "Visit with *who*?"

She clasped his hand tightly and pulled him ahead, carefully stepping around slabs of damp shale and cantaloupe-sized rocks glistening in the mist behind the waterfall. She turned and led him deeper into the shadows.

As his eyes further adjusted to the gloom, he finally made out a long, silver shape materializing in front of him. Next he saw a tall metal tail and wings coming out of an aluminum fuselage. The RCAF CF-101 Voodoo sat behind the falls, forever still in the ghostly glow of the ambient light. It was perfectly preserved; not an ounce of rust nor rot showed. Resting among a litter of rocks, it was tilted on a slight angle towards them.

Matthew was astonished on seeing the aircraft. He noted the RCAF blue-bordered, white circle with the red Canadian maple leaf insignia in the center, and the Canadian Air Command red pin striping. A Canadian flag was proudly displayed on the tail; it gleamed as bright and fresh as if it had been painted that very day.

The significance suddenly hit him, and he knew. In his heart, he knew exactly what he would find in the aircraft. He dropped Sky's hand and broke from her. He ran towards the silver vessel with all his might, every muscle straining to move him faster, emotions welling in his heart as he raced towards the jet.

Years dropped away as he ran…

…Again, he was a small, fair-haired boy calling out: "Daddy, Daddy…Daddy…!" and running towards his father, a tall man in uniform, only to find a stranger there instead.

…Again, his teary-eyed mother was catching up to him and apologizing to the much distressed airman who knew full well their sad story of loss.

…Again he was dissolving into tears of resentment, confusion, and screaming: "Give me back my Daddy. I want my Daddy to come home. I need him…my Mama needs him!"

As Matthew ran towards the aircraft, a confusing litany of memories flooded back: a funeral with no casket, whispers of a secret mission, the arrival of a box with a ribbon and medal in it, and finally, the officer with the letter saying they could no longer live on the air base.

And, he remembered his mother's tears, and her broken heart as, amidst the many packing boxes, she lit a candle and set the table for three…for one last time.

Of course, Captain Dave Corrigan couldn't return, even for their last night on the Goose Bay Air Base.

Despite the disappointment, despite the sorrow, and despite the little-boy anger he often felt, his mother insisted they both kneel by his bed each night and tell his Daddy in Heaven how much they both loved and missed him.

And, as he now ran forward, he remembered how hard it had been to finally accept that he would never be held by his father again. He would never laugh with his father again. He would never feel the security of his father's strong arms pushing him high in the air to play airplane.

Matthew reached the aircraft, jumped onto a rock and from there leaped onto the wing. He slipped and fell hard on the damp metal, but was back on his feet in an instant and desperately scrambled forward. He jumped from the wing to a large rock perfectly positioned in front of the engine intake, right beside the cockpit...

...and he looked inside.

He held his breath. His throat closed. And his own tears began to run unheeded down his cheeks.

The pilot looked as though he was sleeping. The man he remembered, the man he had seen in so many family photographs, the man he loved so much even though he was gone...sat at the controls of the Canadian Forces interceptor. His helmet was tilted slightly back showing a wisp of blond hair peeking out. His eyes were closed. His oxygen mask had been pulled aside by gloved hands that now rested quietly in his lap. Matthew could see the identification patch on his breast: *Corrigan*.

As he became aware of Sky joining him, he tried to turn. But she put her hands on his shoulders, pressed herself against his back, and encouraged him to continue to gaze at his father. "Grandfather says they told him the beam that hit them removed the air and sealed every opening in the plane making it instantly air tight. The vacuum has kept them as perfect today as the night they went down in 1981," she said. "No pain; they quickly went to sleep."

Matthew's eyes were as full at that moment as they had been when he was a child. "How?" he gasped, trying to control a sob.

"It was an accident, Matthew," she said, gently over his shoulder. "It never should have happened."

"H-How did the plane get here?"

"They brought it here."

"Who?" he asked.

"The other people."

He turned and looked at her, an impossible suspicion forming.

She allowed him to pull away from the side of the aircraft. But then gently guided him back to the second flier occupying the navigator's position. Matthew noticed Sky's lip trembling as she took a deep breath and looked at the second man.

The navigator was pretty much in the same position as his father, eyes closed, hands in his lap, oxygen mask pulled aside revealing features that were swarthier than Captain Corrigan. Black hair poked up from under the lip of his helmet which framed proud, chiseled facial features. He looked like a strong man. He looked like a proud man. And, he looked like a man who had no regrets. Somehow the face, one he had never seen before, tugged at Matthew's recall. But he had no idea why it was familiar.

He looked at Sky who gazed at the navigator, an enigmatic look that was half sorrow and half pride on her face. She kissed her fingers and gently pressed them against the acrylic canopy.

Matthew's glance went to the identification patch on the man's flight suit…and he froze: *St. Onge*! "How…how can that be," he stammered. "Who…?"

"My father," she said, quietly. "They called him SO for short. He served with great pride in the air force. He was one of a very few northern Innu who became an air warrior for this country. And Grandfather was so proud of his only son."

Matthew stared at her, the implications finally being driven home. "Your father and my father were fellow airmen. They were a flight crew?"

Sky smiled, wiping away the moisture on her cheeks with her fingers. "And friends. He wrote often to Grandfather of his good buddy Dave Corrigan. So you see, we are connected by more than love. We are connected by our fathers."

Matthew turned and sank down on the rock, his back against the cool aluminum skin of the aircraft. His mind was racing as childhood memories flooded to the fore. He immediately thought of a red-haired lady who used to come over to their house on the base and hug him extra tight. After his father disappeared, she and his mother would quietly cry together in the living room. He was always careful to stay in his bedroom during those times. Now he realized the visitor could only have been Sky's mother.

Sky joined him, took his hand in hers and stroked it gently. He told her of the red-haired lady hugging him as a little boy. And he said how sorry he was that she had also lost her father. She smiled and kissed him gently on the cheek.

"And these other people…exactly, who are they?" he asked.

"People from other worlds."

"Other worlds? C'mon, Sky. Really!?"

"Yes…really."

This was too much; this was too crazy. If he'd thought he might have entered some bizarro world before, now he was certain of it.

"People from other worlds?" he muttered again.

"Various races have been here following and studying our progress for eons, Matthew."

"And your grandfather *knows* them?" he asked, slowly looking over at her.

"The same night this aircraft was brought down, December 26th, 1981, Grandfather got into trouble on the ice. And, when no one else could save him, the other people chose to do so."

"Because they had killed his son?" he asked, incredulous.

"No, they had no idea who was who. It was simply an act of atonement, something they were not allowed to do by the provisions of their mission here, but they rescued him anyway. You see, Grandfather happened to be on a hunt off the coast of Labrador when our fathers' fighter was scrambled out of Goose Bay to intercept something strange over the Torngat Mountains." She paused for breath.

"Matters moved beyond anyone's control after that: the intercept, the attack, the crash, the storm, Grandfather's peril on a broken ice flow, and the fact that the other people had accidentally taken two human lives. It made them determined to save at least one person that night. And the frantic radio calls, the helicopter and aircraft looking for him, and his own attempts to transmit his position led the others directly to my Grandfather."

"This is totally unbelievable," he said, trying to come to grips with what he was being told. You're telling me there are extraterrestrials here? People from other planets?"

She nodded. "Yes, from the stars. One of the air force officers who later came to see Grandfather felt very sorry for him and explained that NORAD had ordered his son's plane to fire on another craft; this craft reacted instantly to the threat and they were brought down. He didn't give details but he swore my Grandfather to secrecy. He said he would be court-marshalled if they knew he revealed classified material. The officer had no idea Grandfather knew exactly who *they* were because *they* had saved his life.

"And, since they had initially brought him to their base to recover before taking him home, he saw where they lived. He swore he would never talk about them with the authorities. In turn, they showed him the aircraft and his son. Twice he brought me up here to visit my father. But now, as they leave us, they wish to talk to you."

Matthew found what she was saying hard to believe, but how did you get a complete RCAF Voodoo behind a waterfall in a cavern in Labrador without a dent or scrape? Or prevent two 35-year-old bodies from surrendering to nature? How do you melt a 3,000 foot plus shaft, with steps, in the middle of an ancient mountain in Labrador?

Dazed by the revelation, he elected to forego further questions. Right now, he wanted to see his father again.

He scrambled to his feet, looked once more into the cockpit at both crew positions and then moved to the forward one and whispered: "I love you, Dad. And Mama loved and missed you so much. She mourned for you till her last breath. I hope she's with you now. I'll love and miss you until the day I die. You were a wonderful father: I am so proud of you."

Sky rose beside him as he moved to the rear position. He looked solemnly at her father. "I have never met you, sir, but you keep good company. I do know your daughter, who is one of the most special people in the world. I promise you, I will love and look after her…forever."

He placed his arm around Sky's shoulders and, lost in their thoughts, the two of them spent a few more minutes with their fathers who rested peacefully together in their aircraft.

Also…

…forever.

~5~

"I want us to take them home," Matthew insisted. "I want to give them both a proper burial."

"So did Grandfather," Sky answered. "But it's not possible. They are as they are because of the other people. If we tried to move them, they'd become less than dust."

He digested her logic, knowing she was right. Their environment was totally artificial. And, as a former military flyer himself, he knew that there were worse places for airmen to rest than in their aircraft. He and Sky would return. They would visit them again.

Matthew made the sign of the cross and saw Sky follow suit. Of course, as a Montagnais and Irish girl, the odds had been good she was Catholic too. They both took one last look before jumping down onto loose sand below the rock.

"I want to meet these other people," he said, his gaze hard. "They had no right to take the lives of our fathers."

Sky nodded sympathetically. "But I can't be there when you meet, Matthew. I can't. Even though they're careful, something inside me knows they're different and I'm terrified. Unreasonably so. And I'm not exactly a shrinking violet. The first time I met one, I shook so bad I thought I was going to throw up. Instead I fainted. And had nightmares for months."

"That's okay Sky. What do I do? Where do I go?"

"You'll go to the rock where we swam and wait. But first I have to show you something else. Where the diamond came from."

"I don't care about any diamonds," he said.

"Please, Matthew. It's important. It'll only take a minute."

He nodded. She led him farther along behind the waterfall, heading for the other side. As he walked, he kept looking back at the silver aircraft. Like the ghost that it was, it gradually faded from sight, swallowed up by the mist, the gloom and the darkness.

They paralleled the falls for a few minutes. So they wouldn't fall, Sky wordlessly pointed out indentations formed by water trickling like tiny rivers through the hardened sand, as well as the many haphazardly scattered wet, slimy rocks.

Eventually they exited from behind the curtain of water onto a series of flat rocks. On one, a semi-round, six-foot high boulder rested. Matthew noted that it certainly wasn't natural to its surroundings. As he got closer he recognized its origin by its appearance.

There was little doubt that it was a meteorite as evidences by a black fusion crust covering most of it, and a telltale leather-like pattern.

But that's where any similarities to most meteorites ended. He stopped in surprise.

The sun had almost reached its pinnacle over the ice roof of the cavern and its golden rays now beat straight down. In the illumination he was shocked to see that, every eight-to-ten inches over its entire surface, a crystal-like gem was lodged. And all, regardless of color – steel grey, white, yellow, orange, red, blue, pink, purple and even black – sparkled with an unreal incandescence. In each he suspected he was looking at a polymorph of crystalline carbon, a super-hard type of diamond.

Testing, of course, would require polishing in a lab with a diamond paste to see if was indeed harder than a regular diamond. What was also incomprehensible, however, was the fact that the gems were about an inch across. How deep they went was anyone's guess. Still, Matthew estimated that by their brilliance and size, he was looking at a treasure trove of diamonds worth hundreds of millions of dollars, maybe even billions. He could actually feel his heart beating faster at the discovery.

Indeed, this could be one of the most important diamond-related events of the century, if not the millennium. The fact they were contained in a meteorite was moot.

He circled the boulder, marveling at the inherent beauty of the crystal-like gems gleaming in the shafts of sunlight. Now he saw why Sky had been hesitant every time *he* mentioned diamond mine. Apparently there was no diamond mine; these gems had arrived on earth in a totally unique fashion.

"I imagine you're going to tell me the 'other people' brought this meteorite to earth," he said, trying to contain his awe.

"Yes they did Matthew. It's their gift to you."

"Gift to me?" he said, taken aback. In fact, his mind was already on overload. He continued to study it. "I can see a fusion crust where it entered our atmosphere."

"Grandfather told me it probably entered *an* atmosphere at one time, but it wasn't ours. As he said: They recovered it from another planet and brought it here."

Despite the surprises he had absorbed over the past few days, as a geologist he couldn't contain his interest and wonder. He moved his hands over its surface: "I have never seen anything so magnificent in my entire life. And the variation of colors in such close proximity." He desperately wished he had a jeweler's loupe. "These gems would blow away everyone in the diamond industry. If this all proves out, what I'm seeing could reclassify every diamond in a $70-billion plus industry. *The Millennium Star,* the *Excelsior,* the *Star of Africa,* the *Hope Diamond*...all would be relegated to lesser status by comparison."

"It would also change your life," Sky said, not without suddenly feeling some trepidation. Would she fit in with someone who had suddenly become super rich? But the thought only remained for a second since she knew money didn't change a person; it simply magnified who they were to begin with. So any worries about Matthew were groundless.

"Change my life?" Matthew said, distantly. "Sky, it's my boss who is funding me up here. Your Grandfather approached him."

"And told him to give you that sample diamond he had. And to send you to Nain. He didn't promise anyone a diamond mine."

Matthew realized she was right. At no time, did she or her grandfather promise Jacquard a diamond field. They let the man draw his own conclusions to get him to cooperate. Somehow, though, the optics didn't sit entirely well with Matthew. It was game playing at its best or manipulation at its worst. He decided to stall to give himself time to consider everything. For certain, a decent percentage of the proceeds from this "space traveler" would give Jacquard all the finances he needed to continue his company. That was one avenue to entertain.

"We had to get you here, Matthew. To see your father and understand what happened. You would never hear the story from our own government. The other people felt they owed this to you."

"You're telling me again, that there's other life in the universe and it's landed here on earth? That's what you're saying, right? You aren't kidding?"

"No," she said, quietly. "Deception is not part of my Innu culture."

Matthew felt immediate contrition for his doubt.

Sky approached him, reached over and began to unbutton his shirt. At any other time, of course, he would have welcomed the ministrations. At the moment, however, he was preoccupied with the inherent and total strangeness of what he was being told.

"What are you doing?" he asked.

"Showing you a little extra proof. Remember the dream you told me about. The night before last when we were on the summit?" She finished with the buttons and lifted his undershirt.

"Yes."

Sky pointed to his chest. "You said some lights came into our tent and one hit you in the chest, causing some discomfort?"

Matthew felt a chill running down his spine. It had seemed real at the time but in the cold light of day he had dismissed it as a macabre dream.

She continued: "We were up on the summit for good reason: To show we were alone, and for the other people to check us out. To make sure we weren't carrying even a minor earth disease such as a cold or flu that could be lethal to them. But their scan noticed something and they did you a favor." She pointed to his chest.

Matthew looked down and, for the first time, noticed a red mark the size of a quarter under his left nipple. "What is this, Sky?" he asked, puzzled. "I've never seen it before."

"The others sometimes communicate telepathically," she explained. "That same night on the mountain they told me two things: Grandfather had been repaired…and so had you."

"Repaired? Me? What do you mean: I was repaired?"

"Lung cancer, probably from the pipe you smoked."

Matthew stood speechless, absorbing news of his brush with mortality as she buttoned up his shirt. She looked up at him without a hint of humor in her eyes.

"They neutralized the cancer and saved your life," she said. "So be nice to them. And remember, if they want, they can turn you into a pumpkin."

* * *

Operation Flashbang certainly did look like a modern day armada as the 50 UCAVs, backed up by the five F-35s and 12 F-16s behind them, lined up for takeoff at the Saglek airport. The drones were spread across the end of the runway while the aircraft were lined up in position on the taxiway, engines whistling. As two unmanned aircraft raced down the runway and lifted into the air, two more advanced to their takeoff positions, paused to receive clearance and then did likewise. In turn, as space opened up the jets advanced slowly along the taxiway. Eventually they would take their turn.

The unmanned aircraft would complete their bombing mission first, with the F-35s and the F-16s flying in a holding pattern fifteen miles away. If it appeared the drones had no effect, the manned aircraft would be called in to unload their missiles and smart bombs as well. Colonel Moorhead would be watching the entire operation at a safe altitude compliments of pilot Lieutenant Reynolds and his Sensor and Armaments Operator, Lieutenant Grenfell.

The mission was designed, not so much to inflict damage on any particular craft or facility as it was to make a heck of a lot of noise, smoke and fire. Hence its name "*Flashbang*" after the well-known stun grenade. In turn, it was supposed to create panic and hopefully a disorganized retreat which would force their quarry to leave behind some "souvenirs."

On the apron in front of the tower building were parked two cammo-painted Bell Helicopters and a Cessna 172 sporting regular paint. Neither the helicopter nor the Cessna were at all cammo strategic in a land dominated by ice and snow. The Mission Recovery Team would ride the Cessna and one helicopter in right on the heels of the first or second wave depending on the outcome of the overall battle strategy.

Major Paul Stone and his "Entourage," as they had taken to calling themselves, were checking their gear in a "Ready Room" in the Tower Building. When the last bombs were dropped and missiles fired, they had to be in position for a landing near Castle Peak.

While the morning had started off as a beautiful, clear sky day, the afternoon was ushering in light cloud cover. Meanwhile, the serious stuff gathered off the coast. Warmer air sucked up moisture into tall dark clouds which slowly made their way towards landfall. True to its prediction, the forecasts had called for light snow at first, with a 60-percent chance of everything going to hell later.

Colonel Moorhead stood over Lieutenants Reynolds and Grenfell who confirmed they were in for a major blow. "Why today?" Moorhead groused, standing over the Avenger crew who were rather glad to be flying remotely with major weather likely coming down the pipe.

"Nature of the beast, sir," Reynolds replied. He had counted and they'd had exactly 25 days in the last 30 days that featured, if not a full-fledged blizzard, blizzard-like conditions at some point during each day.

Moorhead turned to the short, rotund civilian man in the green sweater and oversized jeans beside him. "There's been no traffic in or out today, sir. It looks like we were right."

Mr. Black nodded. Without benefit of a carefully tailored suit, his shape looked more round than ever. "Good. Now all we have to do is make them think World War III has started and it's time to get the hell out of Dodge."

"We have enough fire power," Moorhead commented. He led Black out of the Radar Ops room and back to his office. There was a 42-inch LED screen set up there along with communication gear to function as a full, remote Command & Control Center during this phase of the operation.

"What's their ETA?" Black asked, taking a seat in the office while Moorhead prepared to don his earphones and mic. Directions to Black had been clear. Once Moorhead was engaged, Black would not question, or second guess anything the colonel did; he was a passive observer except for the decision to send in the manned war planes. It was a role he didn't like, but accepted. Let the military experts do their jobs.

"ETA is 1430 hours," Moorhead responded. "We'll commence the first run at 1435 hours. We have no idea what their surveillance capabilities are but we're reasonably sure they'll see us coming and have enough time to evacuate. Which is what we want. A panic-type evacuation."

"And the civilians…?" Black asked, more curious than concerned.

"No idea where they are but they probably won't have time to evacuate."

"Too bad," Black said, distantly.

"Our copter pilot has orders to pick them up if he happens to see them."

"Of course," Black said. "Then we'll decide their fate."

Moorhead looked up in surprise to see Black grinning at him. "Just kidding, Colonel. Just kidding."

But Moorhead wasn't so sure. Covert projects like *Operation Flashbang* never liked loose ends that might initiate embarrassing questions later on. He signaled to Black to look at the display on the wall as it went live; Reynolds was holding his position over Castle Peak. There was some interference from the snow but the mountains peaks were still mostly visible. Quickly he put on his communications gear. There was a second set of earphones for Black and he donned them. He noticed his earphones were missing the integrated microphone.

A master deception had also been negotiated at NORAD headquarters at the Peterson Air Base and Cheyenne Mountain Air Force station, both in Colorado Springs. In effect, software had been reprogrammed so that action in northeastern Labrador would be overlooked and ignored for this afternoon. No alarms, bells or whistles would go off because of live ordinance being used. In effect, returns would show nothing more than a sanctioned War Game.

Even though they were now broadcasting on a secure and exclusive frequency, full radio procedures would be in effect.

"Arctic Fox Leader, Bear One, do you read me, over?" Moorhead radioed.

Captain Ladd Heldenbrand responded immediately: "Bear One, Arctic Fox Leader. I estimate I'm reading you four-by-five, sir." Static! "Request a short count, over."

That meant for every five words being transmitted, he was receiving, or able to comprehend, four of them. Not an ideal situation since, unless reception improved, it would require tedious repetition and confirmation. Moorhead gave him his short count.

"Arctic Fox Leader, Bear One: One, two, three, four, five…five, four, three, two, one. How do you read now, over?"

"Bear One, Arctic Fox Leader, much better. I read you five-by-five now, over."

"Arctic Fox Leader, Bear One: Advise on commencement. Pick your time, over."

"Bear One, Arctic Fox Leader, wilco, out."

Moorhead flicked a switch on his communications gear and spoke directly to Lieutenant Reynolds. "Lieutenant, I want a visual when the flight arrives. Also, advise me immediately of any weather anomalies, over?"

"Yes, sir, out" Reynolds acknowledged.

Moorhead flicked the switch and looked at Black again. "Nothing to do except wait."

They both looked at the seemingly still picture of the deserted mountain peaks far below them. The view of the mountains shifted as

Reynolds brought his Avenger back to do a fly-over. Eventually they vanished altogether as he flew out over the Labrador Sea to make his turn.

"I've been in touch with my colleagues," Black said, leaning back in his chair. "They almost scuttled the mission."

"What?" Moorhead exclaimed. "After all this effort and cost? Why?"

"There has always been an element that argued against this initiative. Finally they made themselves heard with their latent concerns we were biting off more than we could chew. That maybe these guys are so far ahead, they'd obliterate us with some sort of death ray!"

"So what changed their mind; why proceed if they think it's so risky?"

"Because they figured that if we could get our hands on that 'death ray' or whatever…we'd continue to be King of the Castle for a very long time."

They both began to laugh at the irony.

"Go big or go home?" Moorhead said.

"In for a penny, in for a death ray," Black agreed.

Moorhead realized this was one of the few times he had ever seen Black laugh. "Maybe we should be dropping olive branches," he said, in jest.

"You subscribe to 'make love, not war'?"

"Not really," Moorhead responded. "My motto is strike first and strike hard."

More laughter. This was turning into a regular session of Laugh-In. All they needed was Goldie Hawn giggling: "Sock it to me!"

After conversing for some time, Moorhead suddenly picked up his communications gear again and popped it on his head. He nodded towards the screen. The Avenger was turning south. It paused in its turn to fixate on what looked like a large swarm of 'hornets' buzzing up the Labrador coastline. Unfortunately more snow was beginning to fly, so the picture wasn't perfect.

The *Flashbang* flight turned to starboard and 67 aircraft flew out to sea where they would assume 'finger-four' formations composed of a two-plane Lead, and a two-plane Second Element. The Lead featured a flight leader and his wingman, while the Second Element featured a second attack aircraft and his wingman. While normally the wingmen were charged with providing cover for the Flight Leader and Second Element, in this case they didn't expect any resistance. So after the Flight Leader fired and peeled off, his wingman would do likewise. The same procedure would be taken by the Second Element and his wingman. However, the piloted aircraft would only join the attack if there was no reaction after the UCAVs had their turn.

"Alright, Mr. Black," Colonel Moorhead said. "Time to poke the bear."

* * *

Sky took a deep breath and walked with Matthew towards the center of the cavern. Her heart was pounding as she readied him to meet the other people.

"So what?" Matthew asked her, starting to feel a little concern. "I'm about to meet a space alien?"

She shook her head. "I think they'll come to you in a shape that is pleasing," she said. "They can make themselves look like anyone. But it's not real. It's a mirage, or some sort of hologram they use to cover themselves so as not to alarm us. But they told Grandfather some people sense they are not human and freak out. Sort of like me, I guess."

"All right," he replied. "Pleasing shape, eh? I'm sort of partial to Victoria Secret models if I can choose."

Again with the bravado.

"Not any longer you're not," Sky said, taking a light swipe at him.

"Seriously, Sky, is this for real?"

"It's probably just a conversation, Matthew."

"Probably? I like the certainty there. It's *probably* just a conversation. Or not. Are you sure about this?"

Sky's expression was serious. "I understand how you feel. I'm a physician, grounded in science. So Grandfather didn't bother telling me what I'd see. Instead, he showed me. And, while it's strange, it's also very real."

Sky stopped walking and pointed to the rock about half way across the cavern. Gradually they made their way to it. The pond, where they had taken their first swim, still had a light, steamy mist drifting off it.

Matthew turned to her. "How do you know where I'm supposed to go? Or, what I'm supposed to do."

"They tell me somehow. I feel it in my mind. As I did that night on the summit. It's the same way they talk to Grandfather when he's here. Telepathically."

"So I'm about to become a mind reader or something?" he asked. The longer this went on, the more certain he was that he didn't want to participate.

"Relax, Matthew. No harm will come to you," she said. "Or I wouldn't let them near you."

Somehow that made him feel much better. "Fine, I'll wait. Where will you be?"

"In our little cave."

"Great! Enjoy the bomb shelter. Don't worry about me. I'll fend off the Cardassions out here. The Star Trek ones, not the soapy, annoying, forever in-your-face ones." He tried to smile. It wasn't genuine. "What if *I* freak out?"

"You're my hero. Heroes don't freak out," she said. 'Now I have to go. Sorry…but I have to go right now."

"Are you going to wish me luck or tell me to break a leg or something?" he called as Sky moved off, rapidly traversing the rocks.

She didn't look back, nor did she answer.

He looked around nervously. Nothing was happening. He inspected the ice ceiling and noted the sunlight had disappeared. More of the "roof" was being covered with white; obviously there was a snow squall in progress high above them. He thought of Atemu on the other peak, probably curled up in the tent. He wondered if he had reconciled himself to eating the survival bars yet.

Matthew took a deep breath and listened. The only sound was the waterfall cascading into the small lake on the opposite side of the cavern. Behind it were two airmen, frozen in a moment from 1981. When he began to question his own faculties, he thought of his father. But it wasn't long before his thoughts returned to his present situation. Seriously, was he really waiting for an ET in a cave in Labrador? Would ET, maybe, want to call home? Was it aware their Sat phone was busted? His attempt to calm himself with humor failed miserably.

He sighed in relief as he spotted Sky heading back to him. She looked in a hurry. Maybe they cancelled, he thought. Maybe they had forgotten an appointment at the Interstellar Hair Salon or something. Maybe they spotted the *Enterprise* off their port beam and changed course for the neutral zone.

Sky jumped onto the rock, barely keeping her balance.

"So what happened?" he asked her. "Did someone finally admit they're having fun with you?"

She looked at him blankly.

"You know? The jokes on you, the jigs up, we can't produce any ETs," Matthew said.

She reached out her hand and touched Matthew's arm. He immediately felt an electric tingle where she touched him. Goosebumps rose on his neck and spread down his shoulders and onto his arms. He could also feel them on the fronts of his thighs. "Sky?" he asked, feeling his legs go a tad rubbery.

She smiled at him. "We are happy to know you, Matthew."

"This isn't a joke is it, Sky?" he asked, every nerve in his body seemingly on alert. "Because if it is, it's not funny."

Never before had he felt the fight-or-flight syndrome so acutely.

She cocked her head. "No joke, Matthew. We chose this shape in the hope it would not alarm you. Would you like another shape?"

"Sure," he said, his fear beginning to ease. It was all BS. He could get with the joke. "Make yourself look like me."

He found himself looking at…himself.

"Jesus Christ!" he yelled, stumbling back, his heart racing and the hairs on his neck ram-rod straight. "What the hell?! What the hell?!" Right now, he knew that naked, he would resemble a plucked turkey, a mass of gooseflesh covering every inch of his body.

The person in front of him wavered, and formed back into a perfect rendition of Sky.

"This was a peripheral example of structured dematerialization and materialization," she said. "Your own scientists have already used the quantum entanglement principal to disassemble and transport light from one location to another and reassemble it. But they have a long way to go before they can disassemble and reassemble physical objects. Particularly living ones." She smiled at him again. "So, is this shape better for you?"

"Yes…yes…yes," he said, breathing fast, gulping air as though he'd run a mile. No wonder Sky was terrified of them. Maybe terrified was too mild a word. Using every bit of his inner strength, he reclaimed control of his nerves. "Exactly how did you do that?"

"Our evolutionary process is many millennia ahead of yours," she said. "We better understand the principals of matter. So it's not magic. It's nothing but science."

Abruptly she sat down on the rock, pulled her knees up and grasped them with her arms. "Can you sit too?" she asked, looking at him sideways, head cocked at a coquettish angle.

He sensed it was an act designed to calm him down, put him at ease. He was grateful for the gesture because it gave him an excuse to sit down before he fell down. He was actually feeling dizzy as he realized the significance of what was happening.

Sinking onto the rock, he worked to slow his breathing before he hyperventilated. The tightness in his head was beginning to dissipate. Passing out wasn't a good idea, he thought. "Are you really…really an extraterrestrial?" he stammered.

"We are visitors from elsewhere, Matthew, scientists on exoplanet missions who have long been studying the origin, history and structure of your plant life, human physiology and human behavior. As we do on other populated planets. In addition, we are now learning the realities of your varied cultures and your attempts to bridge your differences. We have long watched the human race develop."

Trying to keep his voice even, Matthew replied: "So you know we're all nuts?"

She smiled again but it looked more like it was "flashed on" somehow in reaction to what he said.

Joke alert!

"Humanity does have its problems," she acknowledged.

"Huh!" That was all he could manage as his mind raced. He had to accept what he was seeing and his intellect was processing, crazy as it was. Suddenly he grasped the idea there was an extraordinary opportunity here to gain some amazing knowledge. If only he could rein in his galloping mind. If only he could come up with something a little more insightful than his last comment: Huh!

"Does the government know you're here?" he asked, finally.

"Your many governments know more than they are telling." She answered. "Of course, they all fear that knowledge of our presence would somehow undermine their authority and power. They would be asked to do something about 'us' and their credibility would then suffer. Mainly because your technology is too archaic to do *anything* about us, of course."

"Are you going to tell people...I mean, reveal yourselves to the public?"

"No, we are not here to interfere with your evolution, merely observe. However, there have been mistakes. When your governments retrieved equipment from some of our crash sites, it has been used to prematurely achieve technological advances. Hence your society has advanced more in the past 60 years than it has at any other time in its history. Some advances, however, are kept hidden by various governments so their military can use them to their advantage."

As Matthew listened, he tried desperately to put aside his fear. If this was real, if he wasn't hallucinating or drunk, or drugged or having a mental meltdown, then he was having a chat with an extraterrestrial. He should try to learn as much as he could. Ask anything, he thought. Ask a big question.

"What about God?" he blurted out. "Is there a God? Do you believe in God?"

"God is to us, as God is to you. Most races look to a higher power for wisdom and guidance, each in its own form. Understand that universes and galaxies team with life in different stages of evolution. Some are planet bound while others, such as yourselves, are taking their first steps towards space exploration. All but the most basic life forms have personal belief systems that serve their current needs."

As the shock wore off, Matthew realized he needed another big question. "What is our biggest challenge now? What do we need to know? What should we fear?" He half expected an answer containing warnings of on-going wars, pollution, scourges, pestilence with the occasional nuclear apocalypse thrown in as icing on the cake. Instead he got the flashed-on grin again.

Would he have nightmares every time he saw Sky smile after this?

"What should you fear? Two things: Those who purport to serve and that which serves."

"Do you mean government?"

"Not your government but those who control your government: Your commercial leaders. Humankind used to have a say in its own fate, but those who control the many for the benefit of the few, fear the collective and have divided you on many fronts. Even in western countries, you no longer have true democracy; most live under an oligarchy. They feed you technology, not as an aid, but as a distraction. At the same time they crush individual thought and creativity through manipulation, legislation, untruths, and generating fear and paranoia. Indeed, fear is their most powerful force. These hidden influencers portray themselves as benign, but their goal is to aggressively preserve their power and enrich themselves at any cost. Your political leaders must learn to resist the sociopaths to fabricate a just society."

"Corporatism," Matthew said.

"Yes."

"What did you mean by '…that which serves'?" he said.

"Technology," she replied, "Not the technology itself but your maturity in using it. Invariably you first seek to weaponize your technology in some way. Next, to exploit its commercial value. Finally, to see how it can improve life. Great benefits have come in areas such as science. But, on a macro level there has been a price. You are now losing your individuality, your privacy, your liberty, and your decision making, all which affect your destiny. You connect more, but know each other less. You have access to more information and yet remain relatively uninformed. You have more power through connectivity to bring about change, but fail to use it. The human condition and happiness are sacrificed for convenience. And the more convenience is bestowed on you, the faster you give up personal control and freedom for that convenience.

"More and more, as we observed you, we found humankind staring down at hand devices, oblivious to the declines in the justness of its society. You are asleep on your feet.

"And this plays right into the hands of those who would rule you. You are becoming slaves to technology and giving up your power to think, to feel, to reason and to create. 'Let the machines do it; it's easier.' And, as you become more removed, those who benefit most rejoice at your distraction, and at your lack of empathy and sympathy for your fellow humans. This allows them to exploit the many, and grow richer and more powerful.

"Know this: The quest for total power is the path to self-destruction. It is a human failing spawning eons, from when humans first discovered their ability to subjugate other humans. First you used a club. Now thermonuclear weapons can destroy your entire planet. And one mistake with your biological weapons can wipe out the human race.

"Beware those too quick to sacrifice other's lives to accomplish their goals and leap at conflict as a solution. If they truly believe in war, ask them to lead with their own presence on your battlefields. Do not buy into the myth they are too *important* to risk. Ask yourself if your leader's life is more important than your child's life?"

"So you're saying that if the One Percent had to sacrifice their lives, we'd have no wars?"

"Exactly. Instead, citing patriotism, they send your youth off to die while they and their families and colleagues live safely at home and leverage your sacrifice to feed their greed. They give you medals and parades and temporary honors. Then they bury your sons or daughters and retire to their mansions to shed their concerns with their suits.

"Enlightenment only comes when the needs of many are a priority over the needs of a few, and sharing becomes preferable to acquisition."

"Yeah, that'll happen," Matthew said, sarcastically.

She looked at him steadily for a moment, her head cocked to the side again. "Another…joke?"

"Not really," he answered, sadly.

Please don't smile.

"Your greatest gifts and your greatest strengths are self-awareness, conscience, empathy and spirituality, the things that make you human. Your masters want a hive mentality of uninformed obedience and unquestioning loyalty. One where you are afraid to speak out as an individual or as a group. Whenever they achieve this, they win. Your history shows us this happened many times. But there have been revolts over time: Rome, France, and Russia. The same will happen assuredly in other western countries as greed eclipses fairness, and the few own and control everything.

"In our own social structure of multiple races, including interdimensional ones, we default to seeking greater cooperation, balance, fairness and harmony," she said. "Your native peoples inherently know this need for fairness and balance but are disregarded and shunned as ignorant and simplistic. Many of them wish to preserve your world from the excesses. But your corporate leaders, who embrace greed over wisdom, look on native peoples as fixated on the past, unable to see that they are actually looking to the future."

"Where did we all come from?" Matthew asked. "Were we created by a higher power or did we evolve from a single cell?" Matthew actually felt pretty good about this question.

Look out Diane Sawyer, here I come!

She smiled. "These theories are not mutually exclusive. But if you look for the origin of your humanness, consider that we are all governed and directed by laws given by a higher power. You are a human species largely because of genetic manipulation by our scientists, inspired by the higher power. Hence you will never find your famed "missing link" between yourselves and your animals Populating earth was an experiment that began many millennium ago that introduced transitional humans, or proto-humans, which evolved into thinking, planning, creative beings. But our experiment had to stop when you became self-aware, when you became fully sentient beings. Genetic manipulation could no longer continue, according to our laws. So we do not intentionally interfere with humanity's development any longer. To do so would be to remove your inherent right to self-determination."

She paused for a breath, squirmed uncomfortably on the rock, and then settled back down and continued on with her revelations.

"This was for good reason. We could not just appear on your evolutionary scale once you displayed logic and reason. From your own history you know that whenever a technologically superior race interacts with a technologically inferior race, the inferior race is generally destroyed. You must evolve at your own pace, learn your lessons, and, we hope, come down on the side of a just societal world. Your destiny has become your own to decide."

Matthew hoped he could remember, or at least conceptualize, what he was being told. With no idea how much time he had, he decided to find out where ET called home.

"Where do you come from?"

"We are one of many races from many star systems beyond your view, your reach or your knowledge. In truth, the universes have much and varied life in them. As you are finding out. You are now discovering planets that occupy what you call the Goldilocks Zone, and mirror the physical characteristics of your own. What you call Kepler 452B is one such planet. In reality, there are millions out of the trillions of planets in multiple universes. And understand that your deep thinkers and scientists look to colonialize other planets, not merely for scientific curiosity or knowledge, but because logic tells them that greed, pollution and overpopulation will eventually destroy your own planet. You will suffocate because of your needs. So, under the guise of exploration and scientific curiosity, they look for a new home for the human species."

"You went to a lot of trouble to bring an unknown geologist up here and give me a meteorite filled with diamonds."

"Matthew, as we said, we look for balance and harmony. To keep balance we try to make atonement for wrongs. What happened with your father and Sky's father was wrong. An accident. They fired, and our ship, that is partially organic, and thinks a trillion times faster than we do, saw we were in danger. It neutralized the threat before we could intervene. On review, we know your fathers were under orders and we know they disobeyed them to give us a warning. Our craft thought it was a 'miss' and acted. Sadly we could not undo their death."

"You couldn't help him...them?"

"No. We cannot undo death. We cannot see the future. We cannot work magic. We work within the parameters of science as we know it. Granted, our science is much more advanced than yours."

"Sky says you treated *me*?"

"Yes. Once again, atonement for your father. And since wrongs are largely redressed in your society by giving wealth, before we leave, we wished to give you what you are seeking – diamonds. And, also to tell you of our regret."

"And you saved Sky's grandfather years ago?"

"We had destroyed the lives of two humans; we saved one that night. It was what you call *coincidence* that it happened to be the father of one of the aircrew."

"Have you been...watching me?"

"When you were in danger. In the country of sand, we provided information to you in your thoughts that kept your aircraft safe."

He had flown in many danger zones and avoided disaster by following his instincts.

She continued: "And yes, one of our ships was in front of your single moon that night in the mountains. Our delegate tracked you to ensure your safety. So you would come to us."

"I-I don't know what to say. I can't believe this is even happening," Matthew said.

"We offer you one more service before we leave this night," the girl said. "Tell us where you wish the diamonds to be placed and we will transport them there."

His head spun. "Home delivery? Like Amazon? Absolutely out of this world!"

"How will you get them if we take them out of this world?" she asked, puzzled.

"No, no…I'm saying –." He stopped as she had risen to her feet and he could see alarm in her eyes. She was looking around anxiously.

"What's the matter?" he asked, quickly.

"They come!" she said.

"Who's coming?" Matthew asked.

"Your military warcraft."

"What? We didn't know…?" his voice trailed off as the reality of Saglek Harbour set in. "It's not a research base, it's an operational base. And they followed us here."

"I must go and you must seek shelter now!!" she said, beginning to move very quickly off the rock and across the cavern.

"I'm sorry," he yelled.

"It is not your doing," she called back. "Seek safety near the center shaft. Go now!"

As she jumped from rock to rock, getting farther away, Matthew saw that she was dissolving, morphing into another shape. She disappeared behind some rocks before he could fully discern her true form.

Where was Sky? Was that Sky?

His mind was now in a turmoil but the turmoil was soon replaced by dread. After what he'd seen, was there no Sky? Was there no daughter of Jerome St. Onge? Had he been travelling with an ET the whole time? Was this special love-of-his-life, in actuality, something else? Or nonexistent? As the questions whirled in his brain he became afraid. In fact, more afraid than he'd ever been. Had he lost her? Was she a mirage too? In this peculiar world, suddenly anything seemed possible.

He headed for the cave, running as fast as he could over the rocks, across the grasses and around the small ponds. He was halfway to the cave when he stopped dead. He could see inside.

It was empty.

~6~

"Arctic Fox Leader, Bear One, over." Colonel Moorhead said.

"Bear One, Arctic Fox Leader, go ahead, over," Captain Heldenbrand came back.

"Arctic Fox Leader, Bear One, status, over?"

"Bear One, Arctic Fox Leader, we commence action in 30 seconds, over."

"Roger Arctic Fox Leader. Good luck! Out." Moorhead knew it was time to get out of their way. They would concentrate on their attack now, mainly blowing up rock but hopefully enough to send their quarry packing.

Mr. Black nodded to Moorhead. "It's all coming to fruition. It's all coming to fruition," he repeated.

"Bear One, Recovery Team, we are en route, over," came Major Paul Stone's voice over the speaker and through the headsets. "ETA twenty five minutes."

"Recovery Team, Bear One, acknowledged. Good luck, out," Moorhead replied. That meant the Bell Huey copter with Stone's team and the Cessna 172 were heading north towards the theatre of operations. If their calculations were right, they should arrive as the last bomb was dropped and rocket fired.

He looked up at the office display screen and watched as, despite the snow becoming increasingly heavy, he could see the UCAVs line up in their four-finger attack modes and begin flying towards Castle Peak. Behind them, the F-35s and F-16s orbited in several holding patterns.

"Bear One, Arctic Fox Leader, over."

Moorhead answered. "Arctic Fox Leader, go ahead, over."

"We have a heat signature on top of the south summit, over."

"It's a dog, Captain."

"Roger."

"South summit is not a target, over," Moorhead reminded the pilot.

"Roger, sir, just letting you know. Fido is going to get spooked, out."

On the screen, the first volley of four Hellfire missiles streaked towards the side of the mountain peak. All four detonated before they reached the rock. Blossoms of orange fire and smoke spit sideways in midair. More missiles rushed toward their targets. Again they detonated prematurely, not reaching the wall of rock. The airwaves were suddenly full of voices.

"Attack One: What the hell happened?"

"Attack Four: They didn't reach the target."

"Attack Six: They hit something!"

"Attack One: Well it wasn't the side of that mountain."

"Break right, break right."

"Attack Eight: We're on your six. Anyone sighted any enemy, over"

"Attack Four: Enemy? It's a war game. What the bleep are we looking for?"

"Break left, break left!"

Moorhead and Black watched in surprise as the first four UCAV's peeled off to starboard to circle back behind other formations lined up over the sea ready for a second run. Four other UCAVs inbound, also having fired, their missiles in vain, now peeled off to the left.

The same thing happened as more missiles were launched. Mushrooms of orange flames and black smoke spewed out in flattened detonation patterns as though they had hit a transparent, impenetrable wall in the sky. Again the excited chatter. In the heat of battle the pilots dispensed with protocol. The Bunker Buster Bombs from the Super Eagle drones, easily distinguishable by their massive explosions, also had zero effect, detonating harmlessly in the air.

"Did you get through?"

"Hell no!"

"Okay, who put up the glass wall?"

"Don't be ridiculous!"

"It's a friggen force field."

"It's right out of Star Trek."

"Thanks, Roddenberry!"

"My smart bombs ain't so smart!"

"Arctic Fox Leader, Bear One…status…status, over?" Moorhead radioed as the screen showed more airborne smoke, fire, drones breaking left and right, and a virtual battlefield in the sky showing multiple pitches but no hits. None of the missiles or bombs were coming anywhere near their intended targets. Smoke was obscuring everything; the sky now looked like it was filled with anti-aircraft fire, black, smoke-ringed flashes everywhere.

Bear One, Arctic Fox Leader, looks like they're hitting some sort of…a sort of…I don't know what it is, sir," Heldenbrand radioed. "They can fly through it but the missiles can't penetrate it. Permission to engage, over."

Black, flushed, his lips set in a thin, pinkish line nodded quickly.

"Go," Moorhead radioed. "Engage."

"Roger, Flight Leader going in…I'm going in!" Heldenbrand answered immediately. After a moment they heard him exclaim in an aside: "Son-of-bitch that sounded so Hollywood."

Black looked at Moorhead. "What's going on?"

"Technology is what is going on, sir. Technology from far away," Moorhead responded, quietly. "Some sort of force field."

The RPA pilots were chattering away as each fired missiles with zero effect.

"Flight Leader to all UCAV personnel," Heldenbrand said, over the radio. "Cut the chatter. Disengage, I repeat, disengage!" Heldenbrand's tone was terse but professional. "Flight Leader engaging target alone. If I can fly behind that wall, or whatever it is, maybe I can launch from there. But it's gonna be close. Out."

The trick for the fighter would be to penetrate the force field and then fire and peel off before smacking into the side of the mountain.

Moorhead and Black watched from on high as the armada of UCAVs peeled off prematurely from their bombing runs. An F-35 Lightning broke off from the formation of aircraft orbiting some distance away, rapidly climbed to gain altitude, looped over the top and then dove straight down towards the side of the north summit of Castle Peak.

Suddenly he visibly slowed as he throttled back and flew through the invisible barrier. Moments later two missiles struck the side of the mountain at about 1,000 feet.

Success…!

* * *

"Sky," Matthew yelled, dismay and a tinge of panic in his voice. "Sky, where are you?" He was standing in the cavern, spinning helplessly in his frantic search to find her.

"Matthew, I'm here," she called back, making her way through some fauna and around some small palm trees from the left side of the cavern. "I saw her…I saw her looking like me, and running away. What's happened?"

"She said warcraft are coming," he said breathlessly. "She must mean fighters or bombers heading this way."

"Saglek! The Americans!"

"I guess all those hangars weren't for show."

"They knew," she said in despair. "They must have known for years. Surely they can't be attacking. Don't they understand what the other people can do to them?"

"You said they're leaving now?"

"Yes, that's why we had to be here by today."

Staring desperately at her, Matthew said: "Sky, for God's sake, it *is* you isn't it? I don't know what's real and –!"

Sky grabbed him and kissed him hard.

"O-kay…" he said, drawing out the last syllable, breathing hard. "It's you alright."

A low rumble suddenly sounded and grew in intensity and strength; the ground trembled and jerked.

"What the hell is that? Are they bombing us?" he asked.

"Oh my God…if they do, the fight will be very short." The rumble grew louder.

"She said we should take shelter near the shaft," Matthew said.

"Listen, they're already here," Sky yelled back, grabbing Matthew's hand. "Come!"

Together they ran towards the small cave still several hundred yards away. As they moved the entire cavern lit up with a yellow light. Snatching a look upwards they were in time to catch an explosion of orange fire tinged with an expanding black mushroom cloud. A massive piece of the ice roof fractured. Major chunks of ice began to fall, almost in slow motion.

"Faster!" Sky screamed.

They flew over the rough ground desperately leaping over streams and rocks. Reaching the cave, they dove into it as the huge shards of ice hit the waters of the ponds and the lake with gigantic splashes. Simultaneously, other pieces smashed into the floor of the cavern, obliterating the islands of rock, earth and sand they had run over mere seconds before. Pieces of ice shrapnel exploded off the main hunks and shattered against the cavern walls. Fragments flew into their small cave, but by the time they ricocheted off the walls, they had lost most of their force.

Matthew covered Sky with his body as they crouched together. They protected their heads with their arms and huddled against a side wall taking cover behind the lip of the cave entrance.

"We have to get to the tunnel and make it over to the chimney in the other peak," Matthew said. "We'll be in the center of the mountain and much safer."

The explosions and blasts from above kept coming. More ice fell and shattered.

"It's not getting better," he yelled. "If we wait, everything may collapse and we'll be trapped."

The words were no sooner out of his mouth when another explosion sounded and piece of granite thundered down, smashing into the lake and almost emptying it. Dirt, shattered rocks and water exploded throughout the cavern; everything was drenched. Thankfully only a few pieces of shrapnel reached their cave. He snatched a look outside.

A cold wind whistled into the cavern as it began to snow. So much for the roof.

"We have to stay to the side and circle towards the exit tunnel," Matthew shouted over another thunderous rumble. They heard the piercing whistle of a jet aircraft sweeping directly overhead. The sound of its engine entered through the broken ice roof, magnified tenfold as it echoed off the cavern walls. "Let's go before he comes back for another pass!"

"What about Atemu?" Sky cried frantically, grabbing their jackets.

"I don't know, Sky. We'll do what we can." In reality, since Atemu was fully exposed on the other summit, Matthew felt they had little hope of seeing the dog alive again.

Together they grabbed their jackets and sprinted forward, circling the edge of the cavern and trying to reach the tunnel before the aircraft returned. They could hear more explosions outside and flickers of orange and yellow light found their way into the cavern. An idyllic, green paradise was now a shattered, dirty mass of broken trees, filthy dripping water, and fractured, smoking rock mixed with huge chunks of ice. The air stunk of cordite, ozone and smoke.

They reached the mouth of the tunnel and ran inside. The sound of more explosions reached their ears but they were farther away now. Sky switched on her headlamp and pulled its harness over her toque. Matthew did likewise, shrugging into his jacket as they ran. The tunnel was wet and slippery; more than once, they slipped and crashed against a wall.

At the speed they were running, it took them only twenty minutes to travel underground from one peak to the other. They reached the chimney and looked up the shaft. It was about 800 feet to the summit where Atemu was tied. It was dark.

"I'll go up for him," Matthew said. "I want you to stay here."

"No, you're not going alone," she responded.

"I am and I don't want an argument. If he's there, if he's okay, I'll tie him to my harness and come back down." He grabbed his helmet and slipped his headlamp on it.

"Don't be foolish, Matthew, you'll fall."

They heard another explosion. Though it reverberated through the rock, there was no flickers of light from above. Matthew looked up suspiciously. "How come we aren't seeing any light from up there?"

Sky looked up. "It's a good eight hundred feet. That's why."

Matthew looked at his watch. "There should still be daylight. Look, Sky, let me go up so far. As soon as I see light, I'll yell and you can come up. I'll do a little reconnaissance to check things out. It'll be faster and we'll know the conditions up there. Please!" He grabbed a rope coil and slipped it over his shoulders.

"Alright, go, but if I haven't heard from you in fifteen minutes, I'm coming up."

"Fair enough," he answered.

"Tie yourself off as you go."

"Sure," he said, grabbing steps above him with two hands and stepping out over more than 2,000 feet of empty space. Quickly he began to climb."

"Tie yourself off," she cried again, her voice hollow in the chimney.

"I will," he yelled back, climbing a bit like a mountain goat himself. In fact, tying himself off would be too time consuming since the attacks seemed to be increasing in frequency. If Atemu was alive, he had to get there immediately. Still, he knew that one slip and he was looking at a life-ending fall with a significant number of bumps along the way. He compromised by developing a process where he first made sure that the steps he grabbed would support him if his feet slipped. By pulling himself upward as well as using his feet, he felt fairly safe.

He climbed for ten minutes, moving as fast as he could. He could barely hear Sky yelling upward and asking if he was okay. He yelled back down that he was okay.

He made himself concentrate on climbing, carefully testing each step on which he placed a foot. He knew that one wrong move and he'd never recover.

He'd gone another twenty minutes and was feeling his leg muscles starting to cramp when he heard a muffled bang. It was followed by another noise which sounded like an irregular tic-toc sound. It was getting louder. "What the hell is that?" he asked himself aloud. The volume was definitely increasing like the sound of a huge clock; it was coming from above.

Tic-toc…tic-toc…tic…tic…tic-toc…toc…toc!

Suddenly Matthew knew exactly what it was and he felt a sick chill as he realized his life expectancy was probably measured in seconds.

"Sky, get back in the tunnel!" he screamed into the black, bottomless void.

* * *

"Arctic Fox Leader, Bear One, acknowledge, over," Captain Heldenbrand radioed, his voice echoing in the earphones as well as from the speaker.

Colonel Moorhead and Mr. Black, headsets on, were scrunched forward in their seats watching the display screen and seeing the fighters successfully blasting through the artificial and transparent "wall." Though it wouldn't allow tracer shells, bombs or missiles to be fired through it, UCAVs or fighters could safely carry them beyond it and then fire. Obviously this wall, or force field, or whatever it was, was strictly defensive. The only drawback was some of the drones failed to pull up or peel off sideways before hitting the side of the mountain. So far, 13 UCAVs had kissed the rocky walls of the Torngat Mountains and turned into individual $14 million-dollar black blotches. The fighters had all survived, but Uncle Sam still wouldn't be pleased.

Those who did manage to take evasive action sometimes wound up shooting their missiles harmlessly into the air. But they lived to fight another day. The jets fired and then pointed their noses skyward, engaged afterburners and went ballistic.

The light was fading fast and the snow was growing heavier. Finally, most of their payloads had been dispensed and a few UCAVs had turned back and were massing to head south to Saglek Harbour.

"Bear One, Arctic Fox Leader, go ahead."

Arctic Fox Leader, Bear One…there is something happening on the north side of Castle Peak, sir."

"Arctic Fox Leader, what is *something*, over?" Moorhead snapped.

"Bear One, the rock is funny."

"Jesus Christ, Captain, can't you do better than that?" Moorhead screamed, dispensing with formalities or protocols. Or, control of his emotions, it seemed.

"Bear One, there is a square section of rock that must measure about 200 by 200 feet that is a different color; it looks like its undergoing a metamorphism or something. The piece is definitely geometrical in shape; this isn't nature doing this. Almost looks like a door, getting ready to open up or something. I'm heading back for another pass, over."

Black and Moorhead looked at each other.

"The way they get in," Black breathed, his mood changing from dire to almost happy.

"And how they get out," Moorhead ventured.

"Imagine what we could do with that capability," Black said.

"If they're coming out, we don't want to be in their way."
Moorhead clicked his transmit button. "Arctic Fox Leader, have the
flight stand down. Stand down! Stay well away and observe.
Acknowledge, over."

"Wilco, stand down and observe. Out."

"God in Heaven, what are we going to find in there?" Black
whispered, looking more and more like a plump kid with visions of sugar
plums dancing in his head.

"Bear One, Arctic Fox Leader. It's happening, sir." Heldenbrand
didn't bother to wait for acknowledgement. The excitement seemed
almost too much for him. He streamed out what he was seeing. "A piece
of the mountain is opening...nothing but a black hole...and...round
lights. More lights, colored light are flying out...too bright to see what
they are...wait...a huge disc approaching. I don't like this, sir,
permission to engage!"

Moorhead and Black could see the F-35 cruising past Castle Peak as
lights streamed out of the mountain below. They also saw a blue-lit disc
approaching the jet. As it drew closer, a burst of static erupted from their
radio.

"Arctic Fox Leader, do not engage, I say again, do not engage!"
Moorhead radioed frantically. He got nothing but static in return.

Heldenbrand seemed not to hear him.

"Arctic Fox Leader, I repeat, stand down." Moorhead yelled again
into the mic.

More static. The disc abruptly shot up beside Heldenbrand's jet and
cruised beside his cockpit.

"That thing must be interfering with his radio reception!" Moorhead
said.

They watched as the disc joined Heldenbrand on his starboard side.
Suddenly the jet peeled off in a tight turn away from the disc, climbing
as it did so.

"Jesus, he's going to engage!" Moorhead cried. "He clicked his
radio button repeatedly and then shouted into it: "Arctic Fox Leader, do
not engage!"

But it was no use. Reception was obviously compromised. Sure
enough, the jet dove at the blue-lit disc that had innocently maintained its
course.

"I'm locked on…Fox three, fox three!" Heldenbrand yelled, indicating he'd fired his missiles. His transmission was clear, no static.

"No!" Black screamed, though he knew it was now useless.

They watched the F-35 as it peeled off from its attack run. The blue disc simply maintained its course. Two airborne missiles, trailing exhaust, streaked forward on a deadly inbound trajectory towards the disc. Suddenly they circled, steered towards one another and collided in a cloud of smoke and fire.

"What the hell?" Black said.

"I don't know," Moorhead replied. "Malfunction?" Even as he said spoke, it was clear he didn't believe his own explanation.

"He's coming round towards that disc again," Black said, leaning in towards the monitor.

High above Castle Peak, Moorhead and Black saw there were now more than a hundred smaller lights merging into a single red one.

They watched the F-35. Rather than continue the attack, it rejoined the blue disc, flying in formation with it.

"Bear One, Arctic Fox Leader, over." The captain's voice seemed strangely calmer. "Fire control system is off line. Weapons no longer functional. Target not hostile, over."

"Whoa!" Black exclaimed. "He's changed his tune. What's going on up there?"

"Arctic Fox Leader, Bear One, what happened, over?"

Both Moorhead and Black watched in awe as the blue disc suddenly did a barrel roll over the F-35, under him, and back over him three times in less than five seconds. The disc resumed its flight beside the jet. Clearly it was demonstrating its superiority. And, perhaps delivering a warning.

Suddenly the disc slowed and dropped behind the F-35, staying on its tail for several seconds before abruptly resuming its position beside it. Heldenbrand did not take any evasive action.

"Bear One, my buddy told me he's friendly," Heldenbrand radioed.

"Arctic Fox Leader, what do you mean, told you!?" Moorhead exclaimed. "How did he tell you, over?"

"Bear One, Arctic Fox Leader, no idea, sir. No idea! I-I just know." There was a pause, then Heldenbrand continued his transmission: "I have the Mission Recovery aircraft in sight now. Majority of my flight is black on ammo, bingo fuel. Returning to base, over."

As Moorhead and Black watched, the gigantic red light hovering over Castle Peak grew brighter. It seemed to swell, then contract and then raced away towards the south.

The blue disc dropped 500 feet below the jet in a blink of an eye.

Now it was flying parallel to Heldenbrand again.

Finally it shot off to the north. The Avenger's sensor tried to follow it but it was already out of sight.

"Arctic Fox Leader, Bear One. Before you return to base, Captain, do you have enough fuel to do a fly-by of the opening, over?"

"Bear One, Arctic Fox Leader, doing so as we speak."

"Arctic Fox Leader, Bear One, what do you see, over?"

"Bear One, Arctic Fox Leader...I see nothing but a wall of rock, sir. Nothing but a wall of solid rock!"

* * *

Matthew heard the tic-toc getting ever louder. Its timbre had changed and it sounded bigger and "badder." He pressed himself against the side of the shaft as tightly as possible, his helmet scraping the rock. Balancing on one step with two feet, he extended his hands over his head and grasped another step. If he managed to live through this, it would be pure, dumb luck. The errant hunk of rock was now smashing off the steps with resounding booms. How large was it? Would it sweep him off his perch and carry him to his death below?

"Sky, get in the tunnel," he cried again, holding on to the step above with a death grip. Sweat was running off his forehead and stinging his eyes. He pressed himself as hard as he could against the chimney wall.

Gravel rattled off his jacket and small pieces of debris whizzed by him; he pressed his cheek tighter against granite, headlamp showing pieces of debris as fist-sized. So how large was the main course? It couldn't be more than three or four feet or it would have lodged in the shaft before this. But if it was anywhere near that size, it would surely take him with it on its downward journey. Tumbling down 800 feet from above, it would have built up some impressive kinetic energy.

Bam, Bam. Bam...!

"Dear God, I'm done, I love you Sky," he yelled just as the hunk of rock reached him. He felt gravel explode around his ears and…a glancing blow on his back. He hung on.

Then it was gone, continuing to bash its way downward...bam, bam, bam! And as it faded...tic toc…tic toc…toc…toc…toc….

He let out a breath; he was still alive!

Though his shoulders and upper back felt numb, he swung his right foot over in the shaft and further secured himself by getting his second boot on a second step.

"Sky!" he yelled again, desperately.

Silence.

Matthew began making his way down, carefully avoiding damaged steps. Then he stopped and focused his light upward. He must be only a few hundred feet from the top, and yet there was still no light. Add this to the fact a fairly hefty rock had dislodged and come down the shaft, and it tallied up to a blockage above.

He resumed his journey downward. His back felt soaked with sweat. In fact, it was running down his back and pooling at his belt. "Sky!" he yelled again.

"Matthew, hang on, I'm coming," she called from below.

He couldn't help feeling a great warmth towards her. Here he was scared to death for her and her only thought was to rescue *him*. He yelled for her to stay where she was. They soon met up at the tunnel entrance, her all ready for an ascent with harness on and rope coiled over her shoulder. He swung out of the shaft onto the ledge and they embraced.

"Oh Matthew, I could hear it too. I thought I was going to lose you," she said, holding him tight.

Out of breath, he finally managed: "I-I thought I was going to lose me too."

Despite everything, she laughed, light-headed with relief.

He felt the danger was almost worth it to hear her laugh. "Can't go up," he gasped. "Got to be a blockage. No light and that rock didn't fall out of the sky."

Sky stared at him and swallowed hard. The verdict doomed Atemu. "Oh God, I love him so, Matthew. He's been there for me since he was a puppy."

"Sky, we don't know that he's…gone…yet. He's resilient, he's smart and he has shelter. We'll get back to that damned base. They must have a helicopter. And, they'll either scramble that sucker to get us back here tout suite, or the Canadian Government is going to learn all about the bloody games they're playing. And so will the media!"

She looked up at him, "We'll come back," she asked, hopeful again. "Right away."

"Count on it!" he promised.

They began working their way down, this time rappelling 50 feet at a time. Without Atemu, and not working against gravity, they hit bottom in less than six hours. There was a pile of rocks and smaller rubble at the bottom. They stumbled over it and squeezed past.

Matthew felt quite weak; his back ached and he was perspiring so much he sensed even the backs of his legs were damp.

They sat on their toboggans inside the entrance to Castle Peak. With wool blankets draped around their shoulders, they talked about their coming journey the next day. The first order of business would be to find their snowmobiles.

Sky's GPS was on the summit with all their other gear, so trying to find their transportation at the moment would literally be a shot in the dark. Stepping out of their small cave, they saw, high above them, burn marks plainly visible on the granite walls of Castle Peak. Shredded metal, likely from bombs or missiles, lay everywhere in the surrounding snow. After a day of unprecedented explosions and screaming aircraft, nothing but an eerie silence now permeated the evening. Snowflakes began to gently fall in the twilight.

"Why did they attack the others, Matthew?" She led them back inside.

"No idea, Sky, but looking at the Saglek base and all the trouble they went to, it must have been planned for some time. And the stakes must have been very high."

"And we were their Judas Goats," she said.

"You talked of strange lights. And your grandfather being watched by soldiers. They must have been watching him. And the comings and goings of the others, for years. Even decades. For them to attack now, they must have known our friends were departing."

She thought for a minute and said: "I couldn't see aircraft or any other wreckage from either side. When you think of what they did to our fathers' aircraft, they could have annihilated those jets if they wanted."

"No doubt. But from what the girl said, they're scientists."

"Right. So why did Saglek attack them?"

"She told me that the world has benefited from discoveries retrieved from their crash sites. Gave us new technology. Maybe the military simply wanted their stuff."

"Disgusting," she said. "Like the land of the Innu and Inuit; they wanted it so they took it. By force. We are gaining it back by negotiation. But the others are all powerful. They wouldn't have to negotiate."

The last remnants of daylight were fading fast so there was little to do other than try to rest till morning.

"Ouch," Matthew said, stretching and guessing that his back muscles had suffered more than the last time from the climb. He must also have a bruise the size of a dinner plate on his back from being struck with the rock, he mused.

"Sore?" Sky asked.

"Yeah, right back here," he answered, putting his hand to his collar, reaching down and rubbing his upper back. He winced again. It hurt like hell. His jacket, sweater and shirt felt sodden.

Sky looked at him curiously as he brought his hand forward, sighed at the pain and rubbed his forehead. "Really smarts back there."

"Matthew!" Sky said, in alarm.

"What?"

"Blood! Let me see your back." She turned him around and using her headlamp, examined his neck and back. "Your jacket is torn." She made him take it off as well as his sweater, and finally his shirt. His inner layers were stiff with dried blood. He trembled in the cold.

"You have a six-inch laceration above your trapezius muscle and one mother of a hematoma on your back. I doubt you'd have weathered the climb down if you had any broken bones. You were hit by that rock, weren't you?"

"Grazed, anyhow," he said.

"You're bleeding. We have to fix it."

"I thought I was sweating."

"Damn, you need stitches. I have a suture kit in my pack but it's on top." She jumped up in frustration and went to the front of the cave, then exited it and started to pace.

She stared intently into the distance hoping to be able to see the yellow flag where their snowmobiles lay. Predictably, they were too far away and the light was too low. She looked over at the vertical rock face of the first tower of Castle Peak. She debated shouting up to Atemu to tell him they'd be back but knew it was useless. He'd never hear her.

She decided that all she could do for Matthew's wound, was to tear up some clothing and bind it as tightly as she could. She started to head back inside to create a makeshift dressing of some sort.

And stopped...

...and stared.

As the sun set, the snow had stopped falling and she could see much better.

"Matthew, come out here, please," she called.

In the cave, Matthew heard something in her voice. He grabbed his jacket, pulled it on and zipped it up. He joined her outside.

~7~

"What's that down there? That black shadow? It's not...?"

Matthew squinted and couldn't believe what he was seeing. About a half mile down the slope he was sure he was seeing an airplane. It was a dark lump in the snow but, as a pilot, the vague outline was very familiar to him.

"Light aircraft," he confirmed. "C'mon."

With blankets around their shoulders, they made their way down to the aircraft sitting silently in the snow. It was a Cessna 172, colored white with red accent stripping and outfitted with skis. A brown tarp was secured over the engine and prop.

"Where's the pilot?" Sky asked.

"Beats me," Matthew answered, looking around. "Wherever he is I doubt he's coming back tonight."

"So he just left his aircraft here?"

"Based on today, I'm sure there's an agenda. Besides, who's going to steal it," Matthew asked, then smiled sardonically. "Except me."

"We'll take off now, tonight?" Sky asked.

"No, I can't see well enough to take off on unfamiliar terrain. We'll wait till morning. If we tried and hit a rock or some debris, we'd probably do a ground loop and that's the end of our ride. And maybe us."

He opened the door and began to poke around inside the Cessna.

"What about keys?" Sky asked.

"Most military aircraft don't have keys…," Matthew said, "…but Cessna's usually do, so let's see. Yes, they're here." He held them up in his hand, jingled them happily and then put them into his pocket. "I can promise you one thing, Sky. No way is he going to leave without us."

He stepped to the front of the aircraft, took off the tarp and examined the prop, opened a panel in the nose and checked the oil. Then he did a walk-around. He replaced the engine tarp and motioned that they leave. "Wait a minute," Sky said. "This is a military plane, right?"

"Of course," he said, catching her drift. "Survival gear and first aid kit!"

They opened the door again, Matthew pulled himself into the back and soon found a military medic's kit, some thermo-blankets and MREs. They carried everything back to the cave. Predictably, the kit was very complete for treating wounds.

Sky irrigated Matthew's laceration with saline, injected lidocaine subcutaneously around the wound to deaden the skin, and put 15 stitches in his back. She finished dressing it and helped him on with his shirt. Then she made him half strip below where she used a sponge and alcohol to clean the blood off his butt and legs.

He thanked her profusely, got dressed again and opened the MREs. He used the chemical heater to warm up their suppers

"I'll bet Atemu wishes he could be here," Sky said, eyes glistening. Hastily she averted her face.

Matthew nodded. He loved animals too and had grown very fond of Atemu. The real question was: Had they bombed the top of the first tower of Castle Peak or just shattered the ice roof on the second peak? And what shape would he be in with bombs or missiles striking close by? Shrapnel didn't take sides. He decided that, hard as it was going to be, they'd have to fly over the summit in the morning and determine Atemu's fate.

"We'll take the aircraft up and check him out in the morning," he said, careful not to let emotion creep into his voice.

"Thank you, Matthew," she said, also trying to keep her emotions in check.

They slept fitfully with the wool and thermo blankets coverings them. They used their overturned toboggans as makeshift beds with a modest spring to them. Matthew rolled off his twice and finally ditched it for the stone floor. Sky slept on hers, seemingly without a problem.

Morning had them heating up another MRE and waiting for the sun to rise. Sky was silent and Matthew knew that she was tremendously worried about what they might find on the summit. If Atemu was alive and well, flying away from the dog was going to be doubly hard.

For his part, he had already been to the aircraft, primed it and pulled the prop through several times. The temperature was heating up as the sun rose in the east over the far off sea. It looked like it was going to be a decent day. He prayed he could get the aircraft engine started; it had been a cold night. He wished he could have drained the oil and kept it warm in the cave.

Under a blue sky they had just piled their blankets and gear into the Cessna when Matthew noted a dot in the sky. It grew in size until a Bell UH-1 Yankee utility helicopter, sporting cammo paint and a USAF insignia, landed a mere 100 yards away.

"Matthew?" Sky pleaded.

"You stay here. I'll ask him," Matthew replied and headed for the pilot as he disembarked. In fact, he wasn't going to ask him. He was going to insist the man take them to the summit.

"Hey…you the two civilians I'm supposed to keep a lookout for?" the pilot asked, with a 'way-down-south' accent and a wide grin. He was about 30-years-old, wearing a heavy wool sweater peeking out of well-worn flight coveralls sporting a shoulder patch of an American flag, an Air Mobile Command patch on his right breast, and a "wings" patch with the name McNab on his left breast. A wool scarf, baseball cap and black fur earmuffs completed his outfit. "I'm Lieutenant McNab. Just call me Don."

"Nice to meet you, Don," Matthew replied, shaking his hand. "Right now we need a ride." He jerked his thumb towards the top of Castle Peak. "Up there. Only take a minute."

"Not sure if I can do that," the pilot said. "Orders are to wait right here for those scientists to come back."

"Okay, let me put this another way," Matthew said, staring at him hard. "Either you take us to the top, or I'll be forced to try to fly this sucker myself and it's not going to be pretty."

"You a pilot?" McNab asked, looking at Matthew's six-foot height and noting his no-nonsense combat stance. Clearly an "uh-oh!" moment had just presented itself.

"Yes, I flew Hercules in the Canadian Air Force."

"Cripes, man, you can't fly this bird."

"I know…but we have to get up there. I'm serious, Don. We need your help."

The pilot looked up at the monstrous cylindrical peak. "What's up there?"

"A dog."

"A dog?"

"Yes."

"Is that sort of like…'Canadian'…for a special forces type of guy or something?"

Matthew sighed: "Yes, but this one goes woof-woof."

The pilot looked over at Sky standing by the aircraft. "Your dog or her dog?"

"Her dog."

"Well hell y'all, let's get that pretty little girl's dog down from there." He looked at Matthew and grinned: "Eh?"

"You're a riot, Alice," Matthew said, and happily waved Sky forward. Clearly, Don McNab was a good man.

She ran forward, thanked the pilot and they got in the copter. Matthew was surprised to see that all the seats had been removed except for the pilot's; the interior now maximized cargo space. He pulled the side door closed.

"Sorry about the seats but my first flight was to take back any equipment the Mission Recovery team salvaged. We also have a second whirly bird on standby just in case…!"

"So they are salvaging *equipment* in there?" Matthew asked.

The pilot reacted. "If you don't mind I'm going to shut up. Not supposed to talk about anything."

The pilot settled himself in his seat in the cockpit and started the engine. Above them the main rotor began spinning. Its initial whine built to the heavy thudding sound associated with helicopters. Static hissed from the pilot's radio. The craft trembled.

"Saglek Control, Huey One, over."

After a moment: "Huey One, Saglek Control, go ahead, over."

Saglek Control, Huey One...picked up two civilians. They forgot something up on the summit so going to hop up there. ETA on top, five-to-ten minutes, over."

"Huey One, Saglek Control, roger, let us know when you land back on station, over."

"Saglek Control, Huey One, wilco. Out."

The rotor sped faster and a metallic vibration rattled through the aircraft. Matthew and Sky sat on the floor, each with a hand grabbing cargo webbing on the wall as the copter lifted off. The pilot slowly rotated his craft until it was facing away from Castle Peak. He flew off about three miles, then curved back towards the mountain and began climbing steeply.

Suddenly McNab bent forward in his seat and looked sideways. "What the hell is that?" he yelled above the rotor sounds, turning the copter slightly to the left.

"What?" Matthew shouted, over the noise.

The craft stopped climbing. The pilot continued to look below him. Matthew estimated they were at about 1,000 feet.

"Saglek Control, Huey One, do you have traffic in my area, almost ground level, over?"

"Huey One, Saglek Control, negative on traffic. What do you have, over?"

"Saglek Control, Huey One, I see a high-speed military jet at nine o'clock low. I'm breaking angels one point two, over."

"Huey One, what are its markings, over?"

"Saglek Control, no markings...I repeat, no markings! All black. Uh oh! Bandit heading our way. Possible hostile incoming, over." There was alarm in the pilot's voice and Matthew suddenly realized something unexpected was happening."

Huey One....do you need assistance, over?"

"Jeez! He flew under us at about 100 feet, over...whoa!!"

The copter suddenly rose steeply, buffeted by the jet's backwash. Matthew and Sky hung on as the craft banked and dove. They could hear a roll of thunder, obviously the jet's engines. After a few seconds the copter steadied.

"Saglek Control, Huey One…we need assistance. I'd swear that was a Russian Flankers without markings, possible SU-27 or 30. I don't know his intentions but they can't be good, over."

"Huey One, we are scrambling two responders. Electric jets, ETA, 20 minutes max, over."

"Saglek Control, Huey One, Tango Mike, out."

Electric jets was air force slang for F-16s named so because of their fly-by-wire functionality.

"Bandit is coming back!" the pilot yelled to Matthew and Sky. "Hang on!"

The Huey suddenly jerked right and pulled up sharply. At the same time, the cabin around Matthew and Sky exploded. Pieces of fabric, stuffing, aluminum, insulation, dirt and dust and other debris filled the air as well as a cacophony of grinding, tearing and whump sounds. The helicopter jumped, slowed and began to spin round slowly.

"Any wounded?" McNab screamed.

Matthew looked at Sky, desperate to know she was alright. "I'm okay," she said, eyes as round as saucers as she lay on her back on the cabin floor, wondering what had happened. Miraculously nobody had been hit during the strafing. There were 15 to 20 jagged holes in the cabin walls letting in shafts of daylight. The stink of cordite and burnt electrics hung in the air. Dirt and dust particles floated in the many light cones. He clung to the webbing, reaching for Sky as the helicopter dropped. It spun faster. "We're good," Matthew shouted back. "Sky!"

"Saglek Control, Huey One: Mayday, Mayday, Mayday!" McNab cried. "Flanker engaged us. We're hit. Tail rotor damaged. Need the cavalry, over."

"Sky," Matthew yelled, extending his hand.

As they rotated in the air, the side door, damaged by fire, flew open. It jammed partway, torn metal holding it in place. The helicopter dropped, spinning faster, McNab yelled: "Hang on, gonna auto-rotate down."

With the door open, and the centrifugal force of the spinning, descending copter, Sky slid helplessly towards the opening.

"Matthew," she screamed. Within seconds her feet were hanging out the open door as she looked desperately around for a handhold to secure herself. There were none.

With his arm tangled in the webbing, Matthew was able to counter the centrifugal force. But in another second Sky would be flung out of the stricken copter. Behind her he could see the snow, rocks and mountains whirling by the open doorway. She twisted onto her stomach, desperately looking in vain for a handhold.

The Octopus ride spun faster, insanely out of control.

There was only one chance to save her. He took it, freed his arm from the life-saving hold on the webbing, and slid towards the doorway, on his back. To prevent resistance and increase his speed, he lifted his boots off the floor.

Dear God, please....!

In a second or two he would hit Sky and they would both plunge to their deaths out the door unless he did something. In his mind, something told him what to do. As he was about to collide with her, he opened his legs as wide as they would go. His left boot slammed into the bulkheads on one side of the open door, and his right boot slammed into the jammed door bringing him to a teeth-jarring stop. His legs bent at the knees and he leveraged the force of his collision with the bulkhead to make himself sit up, reach down between his legs and grab Sky under the arms. He shoved his legs straight and dragged her up and over to land on top of him. He prayed the door would stay jammed.

Sky found herself suddenly face-to-face with Matthew, held in an iron grip. Despite the fact she had been facing almost certain death a few moments before, at this moment, she had never felt safer. On another plain she half-expected some joke about 'meeting like this' but they were both trembling and breathless, their hearts pounding way too hard. Instead they held on to each other for their lives. Only his spread-eagled position with feet pushing against the bulkhead and the door kept them from being flung to their deaths.

The copter continued to rotate until the pilot lowered the collective and disengaged the rotor from the engine. He pulled the cyclic back to flare while pushing the pedal on the opposite side to the rotation of the blades. They had stopped rotating now and were dropping steadily in a rapid but semi-controlled descent. When they were about 50 feet off the snow, he flared the helicopter by pulling back on the cyclic. Within five seconds they pancaked into the ground sending a burst of snow through the open door to bury them in white.

Matthew let go of Sky and she rolled off him. He jumped up and threw himself at the snow packing the doorway. Dragging handfuls back into the cabin, he had the doorway cleared in less than a minute.

"Are you okay, Don?" he shouted.

"That bastard is going to get his," the pilot said, shaking himself, yanking off his earphones and scrambling back to join them as they piled out of the copter. "That son-of-a-bitch must have been Russian. His ass will be grass when our boys catch him."

The smell of avgas was all around them. Pieces had broken off the copter and littered the snow. The main rotor only had one blade left. Matthew was thinking hard as he looked around. He could see a dot fairly far off in the sky, likely over the sea. He couldn't tell immediately if it was growing larger or smaller, coming or going. There was a good a chance, more likely a certainty, that their attacker would return to check out his handiwork. The last thing he would want would be live witnesses.

Matthew looked around desperately and spotted three fair-sized boulders on the plain a mere hundred feet away. "Got a lighter, Don?" he asked.

"Sure," the pilot said. "Why?"

"We don't have any time. Listen to me and we can sort it out later. If we want to live, this wreck has to be flaming when he returns. No survivors." He looked at the boulders. "Give me your lighter now, Lieutenant."

The pilot dug in his pocket and handed it to Matthew. "You're not going to burn my bird."

"Yes I am. You know he's coming back for a confirmation. You and Sky, head for those boulders now and get between them. Make sure you're not seen. Go! Go!"

Sky grabbed the pilot's arm. They raced away awkwardly through the snow.

The lighter was an old Zippo with its wonderful wind guard. Matthew thanked God it wasn't a Bic. Flicking a Bic and throwing it would not work. Quickly he located where the smell of gas was originating. It was dripping from the bottom of the helicopter. Must have underfloor fuel tanks, he thought.

He grabbed a small panel lying on the ground and shoved it under the leaking tank. Fuel immediately puddled on it. He thumbed back the

Zippo's cover, lit it and gently lobbed it onto the panel where it lay sideways. The small yellow flame was plainly visible coming through the side of the flame guard. The fuel puddle quickly grew on the panel heading towards the lighter.

He glanced up and in the direction of the sea. He could make out the dot of the aircraft on the horizon. It was growing larger; their attacker was returning.

At that moment, there was a *whoose* sound and the gas on the panel ignited. It raced towards the main source. Matthew turned, and grabbed a piece of panel from the wreckage. Running backwards, he dragged the panel along the trail towards the boulders. He dove between them as the helicopter exploded in a ball of flame. Smoke billowed upward in a giant pillar of black. It burned fiercely. The wind caught the black smoke and rolled it towards them. Matthew thanked God for small favors; the smoke and his work with the panel would help prevent the enemy pilot from spotting their tracks leading from the copter to their hiding place.

The jet approached at a relatively low speed of approximately 250 knots and an altitude of about 500 feet. As it did, Sky, Matthew and the pilot crouched low between the boulders ensuring they were invisible as the helicopter burned. It presented a picture of no survivors and destroyed cargo.

The jet was painted all black, but as it orbited over the crash site, both Matthew and the helicopter pilot gasped. The sun, reflecting on the side, brought out the painted-over shiny reflection of a lone star insignia with bars on both sides.

"No way!" McNab exclaimed, looking at Matthew. "Did you see what I saw? It's got to be a Shenyang J-11."

"Yes, PLA insignia…a *Chinese* version of the SU-27."

Suddenly the jet straightened and began accelerating away. It dropped from its 500 foot altitude to less than 100 feet and dove behind Castle Peak. It vanished into the *Canyon of the Winds*.

"He's gone," Sky said.

They all stood quietly, lost in their own thoughts, watching the helicopter burn.

Ten minutes later, two F-16s roared out of the sky. They saw the burning helicopter, dropped extremely low and throttled back. Pulling quick 180-degree turns, they came back for another pass.

McNab was pointing towards where the Chinese jet had vanished only minutes before, waving his arms and yelling to: "Go get 'em! Go get 'em!"

Angry and frustrated at his inability to pursue the bogie who had downed his craft, he ran towards his mortally wounded bird. Again he gestured wildly towards where their attacker had fled.

Of course, since the trio had no functioning radio, the F-16 pilots understood nothing other than below them they had two apparent civilians, and one very excited comrade-in-arms. They waggled their wings, and accelerated away climbing as they did so in their hunt for the bandit. They split up as they vanished from sight. This meant their quarry was successfully evading NORAD's radar as well as their own.

Sky, Matthew and McNab trudged through the snow back towards Castle Peak and the Cessna 172 parked in the distance. Everyone wished they had on parkas.

"Are they crazy?" McNab queried, shivering. "Are they willing to start World War III by shooting down an American helicopter?"

"Apparently so," Matthew said. "Whatever they thought was on your copter, they wanted it destroyed."

"But there was nothing on my bird," McNab said.

"But they didn't know that," Matthew said. "You landed, picked up *something* and took off. Maybe that was the bandit's cue to act. The fact he acted prematurely before you had any salvaged equipment on board was purely accidental." A lot of things were falling into place for Matthew now.

"Exactly," Sky said. "We were an unintended cargo."

"And we attracted unintended consequences. So they wanted to destroy whatever the scientists are bringing back," McNab said.

"Looks that way to me," Matthew replied.

"Right, I'm not exactly what you would classify as a high-value target."

The sun was high in the sky by the time they reached the Cessna. It was still a blue-sky day, the snow brilliant white juxtaposed against the forbidding grey and black rocky peaks clawing at the sky around them. How long the weather would hold was anyone's guess.

"Can we check on Atemu?" Sky asked, staring up at the towering cylinders, still smoking in some spots.

"Yes," Matthew said. Then to McNab: "We're commandeering this aircraft. Okay with you."

"Not mine," McNab said, shrugging. "It belongs to Uncle Sam."

"We have room for one more," Matthew said, opening the door of the Cessna.

"Look, you're going to fly up there and check out the dog, right?" McNab said. "I have to stay here in case the Mission Recovery Team returns. I'm sure the boys have requested a rescue copter to follow the F-16s. So maybe when you get to altitude, you can check the ETA so I don't freeze my tail off. If it's going to be longer than two hours, come back down and get me. My 10-20 will be right here."

"Roger, and wilco that" Matthew said, throwing the pilot their two wool blankets and the thermo covers from the aircraft.

Sky rolled her eyes at his response.

Matthew did his walk-around, checking control surfaces, the oil level, and then removed the tarp and Pitot tube cover again. He ensured the fuel tank vent opening was clear.

It was a bumpy takeoff with them hitting a snow drift in the end that pretty much launched them into the air. Matthew found flying the Cessna 172 took some getting used to after handling the 76,000-pound Hercules for so many years. Though he'd cut his teeth on a Cessna 150, decades before, it felt like he'd been dropped into a kiddie car after driving a dump truck. Fortunately, old habits die hard and it wasn't long before he had the feel of the light aircraft. He flew out towards the coast for five minutes and then circled back, climbing at 500-feet-per-minute.

Matthew keyed the mic button on the transceiver: "Saglek Control, Saglek Control, come in, over."

"Unidentified caller, Saglek Control, go ahead, over."

"Saglek Control, can you give me an ETA on rescue for your man at Castle Peak, over?"

"Unidentified caller, Saglek Control, whirly bird getting small repair. ETA sixty minutes. And, identify yourself, sir. Who are you, over?"

"Wouldn't you like to know," Matthew muttered quietly to himself as he reached over and hung up the mic. He ignored the frantic radio calls from Saglek requesting his name, rank and serial number. He stayed silent and then the threats began: military equipment, interfering with a government-sanctioned operation, failing to identify himself. Seems he was under threat of almost everything.

They attained 3,500 feet before he leveled out. Approaching Castle Peak, he throttled back to 90 knots with 10 degree flap. Though the aircraft had a stall speed of just under 60 knots, he wasn't going to test it toting a set of skis, and with the crazy updrafts and downdrafts that could pick them up and dash them into the side of a mountain. Ahead he could see multiple black burn marks on the sides of the peaks and metal glinting everywhere in the snow below, signs of the attack.

As they neared the summit, they could also see the small yellow tent had collapsed. There were scorch marks near the shaft and a pile of rubble covering it; the overhang and opening had collapsed into itself. Though there were long swathes of undamaged or unaffected snow, there was no sign of Atemu. His heart sank.

Sky was silent as they flew northwest over the lifeless summit. They quickly approached the second peak which wasn't quite as high. The ice roof was now gone and smoke drifted up from inside. Cruising directly over the opening, they both peered down through their side windows. Grey rubble and large, irregular slabs of granite covered in frost and snow crowded the interior. There was no greenery left, no palm trees, grasses or water visible. They looked over at each other and instinctively knew they were sharing the same thought: Their fathers were forever entombed in the mountain. Their aircraft passed into the *Canyon of the Winds*.

Sky turned her head and Matthew could see she was fighting with her emotions as she faced the additional realization that Atemu was likely gone.

"I never should have left him up there," she said, softly.

Matthew didn't really hear her over the rattle of the engine but her lips formed the words and he knew what she was saying.

"We'll take another pass," he yelled. He turned in the canyon, brought them all the way around again and flew by the peaks at 3,500 feet. He turned the aircraft again and flew a slower approach this time, again northwest. The scene appeared to be the same...

...except he thought he caught movement near the tent. Unfortunately they were over the peak before he could zero in on what it was. Most likely, it was the wind he reasoned.

He shoved the throttle to the wall and climbed once more. They were flying into the canyon again with both sides featuring formidable rock walls. It took him a few minutes to find a good spot to turn the aircraft and fly back towards Castle Peak. On a southeast heading they now had a fresh angle and view.

He felt, rather than saw Sky's reaction as she pulled herself up from her seat and looked over the nose of the aircraft. "That's him, Matthew, he's there...he's alive! Atemu is right there!" she cried joyfully, pointing.

"Dog has seven lives," he said.

"That's a cat...and it's nine lives," she replied, her happy dolphin grin making his heart sing. "Oh Atemu...oh Atemu. Torngarsuk has spared you. I knew you were a Spirit Dog. I knew it. Good boy!"

Matthew adjusted the aircraft's trim and took a moment to look over the nose of the aircraft. He spotted Atemu through the spinning propeller blade and felt her joy. The dog was limping away from the tent, tail wagging. Now, excited, he attempted to spin about in a circle but he collapsed.

"He's hurt," she declared. "We have to see how bad it is. Can we land there?" She desperately eyed the relatively flat, snowy surface. "Is it long enough?"

They swept by the peak; he held his course. "I don't know," he said. "Need another look."

He did another fly-by on a northwest heading, this time noting a patch of snow that pretty much extended the length of the summit. Here and there were gaps but not too significant. He should be able to put the aircraft down. The problem was that there was no room for error and skis had no brakes. Whereas the landing roll for a light Cessna could be as little as 575 feet on tarmac, on skis there were no guarantees. So, if the friction didn't stop them they'd cruise right over the edge of the peak and be killed.

"It would be terribly risky, Sky," he said. "Not smart to even try."

He glanced over. Her look pleaded with him. She was afraid she was going to lose Atemu after all. He made a quick decision. "Look, I never said *I* was smart, so I'll land below and drop you with Lieutenant McNab. Then I'll return and try to land on the summit."

"No you won't," she said, through misty eyes. "We're going to get *our* dog together, hero. Hear what I said? Together."

Matthew nodded slowly.

He orbited over Castle Peak, inspecting the summit, and then rolled the aircraft out on a southeast heading again. He'd fly his approach northwest as before. While he didn't remember any wind when they were walking below, mountain flying could be treacherous, especially with the 'ghost winds' they had experienced, and the expected downdrafts on the lee sides of mountains. He continued to fly southeast so he could line up properly.

"Look, I'll do this on one condition," he said. "When we set down, if I tell you to bail, you bail! You'll open that door and jump. Got it?"

She nodded.

"Promise?"

"Why would I have to jump?"

"Because I can tell we aren't stopping in time and we'll be going over the edge."

"And you?"

"Hell, I'll be jumping right after you're out. So don't hesitate."

"I won't."

He turned the airplane and headed northwest. He was fairly far out so they could see the tiny figure of the helicopter pilot staring up from the ground as Matthew configured the aircraft for landing. He began to work a checklist taped to the instrument panel:

Carb heat on…

Mixture rich…

Flaps 40 degrees …

Wing leveler off…

Trim 10 degrees nose high….

He was set up perfectly for a long, relatively slow approach. The aircraft descended as he cut power further. He was now trading altitude for speed.

"Take your seat belt off. You can't jump with it on," he said, disengaging his own.

She complied and he had her open the door in flight and made sure she remembered the metal step on the landing gear strut where she could step to bail out. With the door partially open, the noise was a deafening rattle. Still she had to be ready to act on an instant's notice. Their airspeed had dropped to 80 knots. He decreased speed even more; the prop was wind-milling. The craft continued to sink.

Because of the skis Matthew had to land as close as possible to the edge of the summit to give himself the longest usable runway possible. If they coasted off the other side, there was a chance they'd have enough lift to make it to the second rocky tower. But all that would accomplish was for them to plunge through the newly opened 'roof' to join their parents below.

Matthew watched the summit filling the windscreen as the ride became bumpier. They were about 100 feet above the summit and 200 feet out when an updraft suddenly picked up the aircraft and they rose 50 feet or so. He immediately chopped the throttle and brought the nose down. But it was no use. It was taking them beyond his preplanned touchdown point. Below, Atemu seemed to anticipate what they were doing; he limped to the side.

The airplane descended rapidly. Matthew flared, bringing the nose back. The stall warning beeped as it should and they bumped onto the snow. He was able to make it stick but they were travelling much too fast.

"Belt back on," he yelled at Sky. Their runway was being eaten up at a voracious rate. Matthew had only a split second to make his decision. He could hope they stopped before they slipped over the edge, or attempt a TOGA, take-off-go-around. .

He didn't hesitate. He cut the carb heat, eased in the throttle and began retracting his flaps as they suddenly accelerated towards the edge of the cliff. The engine roared. Their groundspeed built, agonizingly slow: 55...65...75...85! They ran over the edge and dropped about 50 feet before they felt the welcome push upwards on their seats; the airplane began flying again. They droned over the second summit with a mere 50 feet to spare.

Sky looked over at Matthew. There was a sheen of perspiration on his brow. "Are you okay?" she called, her own heart pounding wildly. It had been a very close call.

In fact, Sky also knew that a second attempt to land was likely a tragedy waiting to happen. "If we can't get to him, what do I do?" she asked, her eyes brimming. "I won't let him starve to death, Matthew. I can't! And I can't let him freeze to death wondering where I am.

Wondering why I would abandon him. He's been my best friend and I love that dog like a child. What do we do?" Her voice choked off a sob as tears flowed down her cheeks. She refused to look back at her .30-30 tucked in the back of the plane. But the implications were clear. The choices were limited.

Matthew knew three things for certain: Her heart was breaking; there wasn't going to be any Old Yeller moment with him around; and, he was going to find a way to jam his damn plane onto the mountain top even if he had to break off the landing gear to do it.

Grimly he turned the aircraft in the canyon and flew back towards the summit searching for a new approach. He needed a "runway" that would expose them to just the right amount of bare rock in the snow to slow them down. Too little, it wouldn't do the trick. Too much and they would stop too abruptly, do a ground loop and possibly kill themselves.

"Okay, we're going to try again!" he yelled over the engine racket.

She looked over at him, saying nothing, her face still wet with tears.

"So, the drill is: Open the door and jump if I say so! Right?"

"Yes," she said as she wiped her face dry with both hands.

"No hesitation. Sky?"

"No."

"Okay, because the bumps and scrapes we suffer hitting the snow and rock will be nothing compared to plunging 3,000 feet straight down and becoming strawberry jam in an airplane wreck that resembles a three-foot-high, metal accordion."

Sky stared at him and then spoke loudly over the engine noise: "Matthew without the help of the Spirits, we'll never be able to land."

"I'll take any help I can get," he called back.

Sky pointed out: "We are trying to save a Spirit Dog. Torngarsuk will see this." Even as she said it, she wondered at how, despite her solid grounding in science, she was reverting back to her spiritual training in a moment of crisis? Probably not that different from any of the thousands of families she had seen praying in hospital waiting rooms while waiting for news of injured loved ones, she decided. No atheists in foxholes. Quietly she asked Torngarsuk for help.

They were approaching the summit again. With the ride getting bumpier, he hunched forward looking for a better landing site. He could see Atemu still standing off to the side. Finally, he found one run that might do it. There were two small, exposed sections of rock. The problem was that the second bare spot was so far in, he wasn't sure he'd have enough speed to get airborne again if it failed to stop them.

He looked over the nose of the aircraft, and pointed through the whirling propeller blade towards their new approach. "We'll try it this way," he yelled, making a motion with his hand. "Approach heading 310 degrees."

Sky nodded. She also leaned forward but her reason for doing so was to see Atemu one last time, just in case. "What we don't do for you, mutt," she said, knowing in her heart he was the equivalent of her child. Some people might say he was just a dog, but to her, he was her companion, her charge and even, at times, her confessor. And though he wasn't much of a conversationalist, she knew he loved her. And, she sure loved him.

Matthew began his second approach; he kept an eye on his touchdown point. Using the checklist again, he configured the airplane for landing:

Mixture rich…

Mags – both…

Flaps 40 degrees…

Carb heat on…

Wing Leveler off…

Elevator trim adjusted….

Slow and easy, he said to himself. A litany of thoughts ran through his mind: Get rid of the altitude as a tradeoff for staying above stall speed; pop it over the lip of the cliff; get those skis on the snow; pray there's no ice; and, hope it stops in time. Piece of cake, right?

Only in the funny papers, Sky King.

"Matthew….I thought of something!" Sky called over the engine noise.

"Not now," he yelled back, working the control column with his left hand and the throttle with his right. He needed every bit of concentration at the moment.

"It's important," she called.

"Later!" he yelled back, pushing the throttle in to lift them ten feet and then gradually backing off power. If he undershot, they were going to both die on the side of the peak.

"But –!"

He ignored her and concentrated on the landing. She made a decision and pressed her lips firmly closed.

The windscreen was filled with the summit once again. He took in the flattened tent, the snowy runway and Atemu limping away off to the side.

They were about five feet up as they swept in over the edge. He cut the throttle and flared. The airplane settled rapidly, the stall warning wailing. They felt a bump as their skis hit the snow. But the aircraft lifted back into the air, sailed a few more feet before coming down again. This time Matthew jammed the control column forward and was able to hold it down.

"Ready to jump," he yelled.

They skimmed along the snow heading for the first piece of bare rock. Travelling at 60 mph, Matthew saw with dismay their speed was not bleeding off fast enough. And, there was a barely noticeable downward slope that wasn't helping.

Finally they slowed to about 30 mph. He extended his flaps fully to 50 degrees for additional braking power. They hit the first section of rock which was about 12 feet across. A squeal erupted as the metal ground into the granite. A shower of sparks would be erupting under their skis at this point. They slowed a bit but were still moving fairly fast.

The sun glinted off the snow in front.

Ice!

The airplane continued to slide, now barely slowing as it hit the ice. He pumped his rudder pedals left and right slewing the aircraft to leverage whatever small amount of braking resistance the rudder maneuver would provide. They were committed to the landing now, past the point of a successful take off and go around.

Sky was sitting forward and peering over the nose. They hit the second stretch of bare rock, this one slightly longer than the first. Again the screech of metal and the aircraft slowed appreciably.

But it was still heading towards the edge.

"Door open," Matthew hollered, unlatching his own door and sticking his left leg in it to hold it open.

To open her door, Sky rotated her handle upward and pushed it wide.

"Get your foot out on the step, face backwards!" he yelled.

The airplane was only travelling about 20 mph now, but the edge of the cliff was looming way too fast. In effect, Matthew was now an aircraft passenger; he no longer had any control.

Sky's heart was pounding like a jackhammer as she poised, ready to jump.

Matthew watched them approach the edge. The 172 was slowing, slowing…but probably not enough. With their combined weight they might stop. But that was risking Sky's life.

"Jump, Sky…jump!" he cried, as they swept towards the edge of the cliff.

Sky disappeared out the door and hit the snow, rolling end-over-end.

Once he was sure she was out, Matthew kicked his door wide, rotated, stuck his left foot on the metal step and prepared to jump. The edge of the cliff was mere 10 yards away when he tried to launch himself.

Rather than diving out, he was pulled back into his seat.

His jacket was caught on something…

Sky was screaming his name in terror…

The aircraft was feet away from the lip of the cliff…

He tugged desperately, trying to free himself…

He needed to get out…

He was still held fast….

"Matthew!" came another terrified scream from Sky.

Tearing at his coat, he fought to the last, though he knew it was too late. He knew he was going to die. Perched sideways on the edge of his seat, he thought how lucky he was to be loved by Sky, even for a short time. He tensed, waiting for the sickening drop…

…and then the unexpected, the improbable and the impossible all happened at once!

Out of the northwest swept a hurricane force headwind that slammed into his aircraft like a giant sledgehammer rattling the very airframe and jamming the door painfully hard on his leg. It was if he'd hit a brick wall. The force was so strong that, not only did the aircraft instantly stop dead, it miraculously retreated a few inches backwards.

Just as quickly the wind gust died away.

All was still.

"What the hell just happened?" Matthew said, unable to believe he was still alive. He looked out the front windscreen. All he saw was open air and mountain peaks across the aptly named *Canyon of the Winds*.

He let out a sigh of relief, listening to the wind whistling shrilly in the gorge. Peeking through the half-open doorway, he looked forward and found himself staring down at the tip of the Cessna's aluminum nose ski, mostly sticking out into thin air over the 3,000 foot sheer drop. It vibrated and rattled from a minor wind gust that also pulled hunks of snow off the wall of the butte and sent them in small cyclones thousands of feet down into the cold abyss.

In the distance he could hear barking; it was coming closer by the second. He didn't dare move just yet since it already seemed a miracle that the nose-heavy aircraft had not tipped and plunged to its demise, taking him with it.

He killed the master switch and checked on what had prevented him from jumping. He found that when he had turned to exit, the door handle – upright when it was open – had slipped into his open jacket and up the sleeve. In essence, he had hung up on the handle.

Running footsteps, crunching through the snow, arrived with a fury.

"What were you doing?" Sky cried, face florid, voice livid. She reached in, snatched his arm and yanked him out of his seat to where he was safe on the edge of the cliff. "What's the matter with you? Why didn't you jump?"

"That wind! That gust! Where did it come from?" he asked. "Did you see it? Did you feel it? It had to be more than a hundred knots. It stopped the aircraft dead! It saved my life…I was hung up on the door."

Sky calmed down somewhat. She searched his eyes, the fear in her own just beginning to fade. She let out a long breath and, with it, the tension of a moment.

He merely stared at her, still in a degree of shock over his own survival.

"The Spirits always listen," she said, slowly. "Sometimes they say no and sometimes they say yes. Today we got a yes…and a Ghost Wind." Then she pulled him back further from the edge to ensure he was well out of danger. They were hugging tightly when they were hit with 60 pounds of fur and slobber. Atemu was in a frenzy. He whined and licked each of them, his tail waving in a mad circle. A chewed, broken rope trailed from his collar. Though obviously happy, he favored his right front leg where dried blood matted his fur just down from his shoulder.

"He's got a nasty gash but I'll stitch it up in a minute," she said. She checked out the wound a little more closely. Matthew did likewise and received a big slobbering lick right on the mouth for his trouble.

He then insisted they seize the aircraft by the tail and drag it back far enough from the cliff edge to where they could turn it round manually. It took some effort but thanks to the ice they were successful. He started the engine and taxied up and down slowly on the snow while Sky led Atemu back to the collapsed tent to retrieve her med kit and treat his wound. Matthew finally shut the engine down and joined her. "Be a lot easier taking off than landing."

"Why did you do that?" she asked, prying pitons from the crevices where they had secured the tent. "Taxi around, I mean?"

"Cause when you land in the winter on skis, friction heats them up," he explained. "If you leave the airplane sit, the warm skis melt the snow and then it freezes. When you go to take off, you find your skis stuck in ice. By slowly taxiing around, I let them cool gradually."

"Oh," she said, continuing to pack their gear. "At least *that's* a smart move."

He threw his arms around Atemu and, avoiding his repaired wound, gave him a hug. The dog wagged his tail in return. "By the way, what was so urgent you kept at me during our landing?"

"Oh, nothing," she said, making herself more busy.

"It must have been something important. C'mon, fess up!"

A thudding noise began echoing in the mountains.

"Well, it's just...," She stopped, trying to find the right words.

He looked at her curiously.

"Matthew, I know this sounds crazy after that amazing landing you pulled off...but didn't Saglek say there was another helicopter heading up here to pick up the pilot and the others? Maybe we could have asked them –?" She didn't finish."

The thudding noise grew stronger as the rescue copter from Saglek drew closer, the sound of its rotors echoing off the mountain sides.

Matthew merely stared at her.

She held his gaze, raising her eyebrows. "I only thought of it as the last moment too…sorry."

He finally looked away, stared into the distance for a few moments and then looked back at her, embarrassment on his face.

"It's called 'Target Fixation'," he said, sheepishly. "When a pilot is so taken with the task at hand, he can't absorb anything else at the moment. Sorry about that, Chief." When he realized what he'd just said, he started to backtrack but Sky only smiled at him.

"It's okay, Matthew. I've seen *Get Smart*," she conceded kindly, a delighted grin lighting up her features. "See? I told you that by the time we got back you'd be so politically correct you'd be afraid to open your mouth. Anyhow, Kemo Sabe saved the day."

Gotcha, hero!

~8~

"I have the final analysis with me," Major Paul Stone said, carrying the envelope into Colonel Robert Moorhead's office in Saglek, holding it up as he sat down. "Original went to Black. This copy is for you."

There were boxes everywhere except for the single seat in front of the Colonel's desk. The display screen was off the wall and sat leaning against it, wires taped to its back. The corkboard, desk lamp and other sundry items were either packed, or in the process of being packed.

Outside, the entire base bustled with activity as all personnel made ready to vacate what had been home to some for close to a year now.

"Read the salient parts to me," Moorhead said, cleaning out a bottom drawer. Not that he was disinterested, far from it. He was intensely curious, however, he'd put off dismantling his office. Now it was deadline time. The enlisted men were busy with their own wares.

"Right," Stone said. "Shouldn't we have champagne or something to celebrate our discovery?" He was intensely happy to be going home.

"If there's something good to celebrate," Moorhead said, grumpily. He looked at Stone suspiciously and waited for an answer to his question.

Stone nodded. "*I* think so. On the other hand, you may not feel the same way."

It had been three weeks since Stone and his scientist colleagues had emerged from the twin buttes of Castle Peak with a single item left behind by their visitors. It had been transported to Saglek Harbour base, and then taken on a direct transport to the Jet Propulsion Laboratory in Pasadena, California. Managed by the California Institute of Technology, and having state of the art testing equipment, it was decided by Mr. Black that JPL should be the one to secretly evaluate and analyze the recovered material.

Stone and his party had discovered two large caverns in the northern Castle Peak butte. The first had an opening to the sky but was partially filled with ice and rock. Though no bombs had been dropped directly inside, the peripheral concussions had splintered ice and rock alike.

Climbing down from the broken grotto, they followed what seemed like a pedestrian tunnel farther into the butte where they found a second huge cave. This was believed to have been a hangar/base of sorts.

Multiple rock shelves, hundreds of feet across in some cases, and apparent living quarters, had been carved out of the rock beneath the cylindrical peak. But, all that had been left behind was a single piece of very strange metal placed strategically in the middle of the untouched cavern where it was sure to be discovered. About 10 by 24 inches, and less than one inch thick, it was a metallic bronze color, with a rough raised surface that appeared to have been machined.

Stone had personally accompanied the metal sample to California and so hadn't been in touch with Moorhead in weeks. Now he'd returned on a transport carrier and was eager to share the results of extensive testing on the material.

But first Stone was curious. "What about the hostile who took down Huey One?" He knew Moorhead would be impatient to hear what the analysis had revealed, so he'd spill the beans pretty fast.

"Lieutenant McNab reported it had Chinese markings, People's Liberation Army, under its black paint," Moorhead said, continuing to stuff materials into his box. "Unfortunately, it escaped."

"So the Chinese *and* the Russians were both keeping a close eye on us? Jointly or independently?"

"No idea, but obviously they figured we were on the hunt for new technology up here and there could only be one source," Moorhead said. "They were also detecting strange craft defying the laws of physics, just as we were. They couldn't come in here without starting a shooting war but they sure as hell could send in a single, anonymous bandit to destroy what we found. Keep the playing field level."

"They jumped the gun and shot down Lieutenant McNab and the civilians?"

"Yes," Moorhead answered, throwing some wires and old newspapers into a waste basket. "By the way, that week '*The Liaoning*' just happened to be doing exercises in the Atlantic off the Labrador coast."

"China's first aircraft carrier," Stone mused. "What a coincidence!"

Moorhead motioned towards the envelope. Stone tore it open; he was already familiar with the contents. "First of all, it's an "*In-Process*" report on the object. So far they haven't been able to cut, burn or blow it up. It's a metal harder than Tungsten, Chromium or even some of the strongest steel alloys, like Micro-Melt® 10. JPL is continuing to analyze its composition via a scanning, tunneling microscope. This metal is not evident on the periodic table so it's definitely not of this earth. In other words, stay tuned."

"Great," Moorhead said, sarcastically.

"But they found something else when they looked at it on a molecular level."

"What's that?"

"There was a message."

"A message? Were they able to decipher it? Understand it?"

"Yes," Stone said. "It was written in English."

"English?" Moorhead said, in surprise.

"Yes…and French, German, Russian, Mandarin, Japanese and more than 3500 other languages. Letters are microscopic. According to JPL, the latest estimate is that there are 7,105 languages in the world, but only 3,570 have ever developed writing systems. They're all represented on this piece of metal."

"All of them?" Moorhead asked. "What the hell does it say?"

"It says: 'For defensive purposes only'."

"Defensive purposes? They deliberately gave us a metal sample for *defence*?"

"Apparently. To keep us safe. To keep anyone safe."

"Safe from who?"

"The best guess I heard was: Safe from each other."

"Marvelous," Moorhead said, again with a measure of disappointment.

"There's more here. Interspersed between each phrase, in its own language is the word *Peace*. In that particular language."

Moorhead held up his hand and thought for a moment. Outside there was the whistle of an airplane taking off to head south, perhaps for the last time. The battery-driven clock on the wall continued to tick away the seconds.

"Look," Moorhead said, finally. "This exercise might not have been a bust, after all. Maybe we didn't find any light sabers or death stars but if this metal can be replicated, we can weaponize the hell out of it. Tip our missiles, bombs and bullets with it for maximum penetration. Imagine the quality of shrapnel we could make with this stuff, tear the living shit out of anything that moves, and even stuff that doesn't."

Stone looked at the Colonel, half in disbelief, half hoping he was joking. There was no smile on the man's face.

Stone shook his head slowly. "So let me get this straight, sir. Some highly advanced, off-world group leaves us a gift for our defense, tells us in so many words to make peace with each other, and we want to take that gift, and smash our global neighbors over the head with it until their brains are mush and they bleed out?"

"That's the general idea," Moorhead replied, not sheepishly. "Just like they'd do to us."

Stone said, dryly: "And here I was thinking there was something inherently wrong with the human race."

"Really? Why would you think that?" Moorhead asked, puzzled.
Sadly, he was sincere.

* * *

Three weeks after flying the Cessna to Nain, Sky and Matthew had been summoned to the local RCMP Detachment where they found two civilian-clad officers from the United States Air Force waiting for them in a private office. They introduced themselves as Major Paul Stone and Colonel Bob Moorhead. Nor was that all. Also joining them was an RCAF officer, who gave his name as Major Finley Hipwell, and a member of the Canadian Security Intelligence Service, who wouldn't give any name at all. Sky and Matthew were told they were now to be interviewed regarding their journey to Castle Peak. Having already discussed the possibility, they told their potential inquisitors that it would be fine as long as a selection of newspaper reporters were in attendance. Of course, it would take some days for them to arrive.

The officials did not like this at all. They unsuccessfully tried to cast it as a national security issue. And, Major Hipwell reminded Matthew that, as a former RCAF officer, he was still bound by Canada's Official Secrets Act. Matthew shrugged and replied that neither he nor Sky intended to breathe a word of their journey to anyone. As far as they were concerned, a quest for a diamond mine in Labrador had not panned out. End of story. No debriefing, no discussions and no further contact. If they were harassed in any way, they'd go to the media. After an hour of demands, threats and warnings, the officials gave up. Matthew and Sky generously signed some wide-ranging non-disclosure agreements and the military officials tucked their papers in their briefcases, their tails between their legs, and left. When RCMP Constable Davignon asked what the meeting had been about, Matthew replied that it was simply a misunderstanding over the Cessna aircraft he had 'borrowed'.

Three days later, after visiting Chantal's grave and telling her all about his adventure, he got off the elevator and walked down the corridor towards the *Labrador and Ungava Diamond Explorations'* offices in Montreal. While it felt good to be back in "civilization" once more, he dreaded telling Andre Jacquard that there was no diamond site in Labrador. Of course, he could never tell the man the truth. The trick would be to tell him just enough to lend authenticity to his tale.

Approaching the door to the reception area, he saw that it was open and a man in coveralls was kneeling in front of it. Beside him was a plastic sheet; on it rested an array of paints, paint thinners and brushes.

The man had mostly removed the *Labrador and Ungava Diamond Explorations* letters as well as the artistic rendering of a diamond from the door. He was preparing to stick up a paper template for a new sign. Matthew wondered if he was going to paint: "Going out of Business."

With a heavy feeling, Matthew excused himself and stepped around the man doubting Jacquard was even in the office any longer. He hadn't bothered to call ahead; he felt bad news should be delivered personally.

Indeed, Matthew was surprised to see Mary at her desk, a big smile on her face.

"Mr. Corrigan, why didn't you call?" she asked, brightly. Strangely there didn't seem to be an air of inevitable tragedy in the offing.

"Hi Mary. I figured a personal visit was in order," he said. "Is he in?"

"Who the hell is out there?" a voice bellowed from the inner office. "Is that Corrigan?"

Matthew stepped into Jacquard's office. The man himself rose from behind his desk, came round and warmly clasped his hand. "Great to see you again, Matthew. Why didn't you call?"

"I thought I should see you personally, sir, to say what I have to say."

"That you didn't find oodles of diamonds dripping from stalactites in Labrador?"

"Afraid not," Matthew said, in surprise. "How did you know?"

"Talked to a guy named Bob Crummy up in Nain. He gave me all the dirt. Cost me a few bucks but he's a great source. Heard your Sat Phone broke too."

Matthew was taken back by two things: he already knew there were no diamonds up there; *and,* he didn't seem to care.

Jacquard continued: "And, you found a lady friend?" He wiggled his eyebrows up and down suggestively.

Bob Crummy! He remembered that Diane Underwood, the Outpost Nurse, had said he sold information but he had no idea of the level of detail the man collected. Even though Matthew hadn't said much to him, other than a hello, Sky had spoken to several people and firmly put to bed the notion they'd found any sort of diamond field in Labrador.

Her grandfather, convalescing at home in Nain, rightly claimed he'd never said there was a diamond field in Labrador. Merely that he had found a diamond. Where did he find it? Time after time he told well-wishers he couldn't remember because of his stroke. His statement was often accompanied by the wisp of a smile and a fatalistic shrug.

Jacquard said: "You're to thank for this, Matthew." He swept his arm around the office.

Matthew wasn't sure if Jacquard was being sarcastic. But there was no resentment or anger in his voice. Rather, he seemed in an ebullient mood. Puzzled, Matthew nodded as though he was in on the secret. Finally the mystery was cleared up.

"Gold," Jacquard said, shaking his head. "We're looking all over Cain's creation for a legacy of diamonds and we're tripping over gold."

"Right," Matthew said, wondering if what he suspected was true. It was.

"Matthew's Rock Collection!" Jacquard said, shaking his head. "Stan Peck brought those samples you gathered back to base camp. Weeks later they opened it and he noticed a few gold flakes and a tiny nugget in the gravel. Brian Hawkins called me right away. We couldn't get hold of you because of that damn phone. Why didn't you say something?"

"I wasn't sure if I had much of anything," Matthew said, remembering his trip to the old creek bed on the ATV. "The gravel and rock samples were left in camp when I came out. I needed to have it assayed before I said anything."

"Well, we went back to where you dug, took a larger sampling, and had it assayed," Jacquard said, happily. "It came in pretty rich. Pretty rich, indeed. Get this: 0.2 ounces per ton. Dear God, the richest mines in South Africa are coming in at 0.3 ounces of gold per ton! Labrador is one mixed up place, eh? They go looking for diamonds in Voisey Bay and find nickel. We go looking for diamonds and we find gold."

"At least we've *found* gold in Labrador," Matthew said. "Finding diamonds may take a little longer."

"Well, we're out of the diamond exploration business for now," Jacquard said, grinning. "We've secured our gold claim and we're moving in a crew, as we speak."

"Investors?" Matthew queried.

Jacquard laughed: "When I shopped these results around, they went crazy. Practically begging to throw money at me. IPO coming too."

Matthew smiled.

Sometimes things did work out.

He turned and looked out the office doorway to where the sign painter was already back-painting gold leaf lettering and a huge gold nugget on the glass doorway. He could see the rough outline of the new name: *Labrador & Ungava Gold Explorations Limited*. He turned back to see Jacquard nodding while holding the St. Onge diamond in his hand.

"Did you find out where this came from?" he asked, putting it down on the desk and rooting around in his drawer for his pipe and tobacco.

"It came from the Torngat Mountains, alright," Matthew said. "Sky took me to exactly where he found it but there was no indications of kimberlitic pipes or anything else saying: 'Dig here'."

"Not surprising," Jacquard commented. "I had it examined. Near as we can tell, it originated in outer space."

"Outer space?" Matthew said, doing his best to feign shock. As he was certainly surprised at Jacquard's discovery, it wasn't all that hard to fake an appropriate reaction.

"Yep. But the experts said it didn't arrive in a meteorite." He grinned. "Some bug-eyed monster from Mars must have dropped it off, eh?" He broke into a full laugh.

Tempted as he was to say: "They're not bug-eyed and that's not where they're from," Matthew left the matter alone. Inwardly he smiled; indeed, Jacquard didn't know how close he was to the truth.

"Anyhow, my friend," the CEO of *Labrador & Ungava Gold Explorations Limited* said, "I want to make you Chief Geologist in this little venture. And give you points in the company. After all, you found the site. And there'll be a good bonus for you in the offing."

"That's very kind of you, sir," Matthew replied. "I have some settling up to do back in Nain. Do you mind if I take a few weeks off and let you know after that?"

"Take all the time you want," Jacquard said. "With pay."

"Again, that's very kind of you. Thanks."

Matthew turned to leave.

"Hey!"

He turned back just in time to catch the diamond Jacquard threw to him. "Don't forget your diamond. Who knows? Maybe that Martian will come back for it."

* * *

"She called two nights ago," Sky said, as they trudged through the snow along the shore of Nain's Unity Bay in the dark. They turned from the ice and mounted a small hill. "We spoke for about a half hour."

"You spoke to Helene for thirty minutes?" Matthew said,

incredulously. "What did you talk about? And don't say *me*."

Matthew didn't bother to press for an answer to his last question; they both needed their breath for climbing.

It was a clear night, no moon, just the usual million or so stars visible in the Labrador sky. Their exhales formed clouds in the air in the freezing cold. Luckily the starlight enabled them to safely navigate to wherever they were going.

Sky stopped, looked around and then turned right.

They both started moving up another rise. Their boots crunched through a thin crust of ice that had formed on top of the snow after a full day of sunshine. Fortunately the snow wasn't deep; the hillside was continually cleaned up by the ever-present winds of the Labrador coast.

"What do you want to show me?" he called again, as they crested the hill. He groaned when he saw another larger hill directly behind it.

"A couple of rocks," Sky answered.

"More rocks?" he exclaimed. "Rocks, rocks, rocks. Labrador is a geologist's dream, isn't it? Rocks with gold. Rocks with diamonds. Rocks with nickel. Rocks with iron ore. Rocks underfoot. Rocks overhead. Rocks everywhere. And, what have you dragged me out in the middle of the night to see? More rocks."

Sky turned, hands on hips: "You finished?"

"Yeah, I guess so," he replied, catching his breath. "I should have studied botany."

"Then we'd never have met."

"There is that," he replied with a grin. "Okay, let's rock on."

They continued up the second hill and far below them Matthew could see the lights of Nain shimmering like multicolored jewels nestled on the periphery of the frozen bay. He reckoned they were about four or five miles north of the town. He heard footsteps receding.

He turned and caught up to Sky. "So what's up? Did she say?"

"She asked for you but when I told her you weren't here, she seemed reluctant to get off the line. She knew we'd spent weeks together in a tent and wanted to know how you fared."

"Really? Why would she care?"

Sky ignored him and continued. "She talked about the loss of your daughter and how it had damaged your relationship so badly."

"Substitute the word 'annihilated' for 'damaged' and I'd agree."

"Don't be bitter," Sky said, trudging on.

"It's not a matter of being bitter," he replied. "I tried to have us work through it for almost three years and she was having none of it."

"Well, I think she's reconsidering."

He grabbed Sky's arm bringing her to a stop: "What!?"

"It wasn't a complicated sentence, Matthew."

"She divorced me. So is this a case of wanting something you can't have."

"She doesn't know anything about...us."

"Well, she will, very soon."

Sky turned and moved on. They happened to walk into a depression between two hills. She took a flashlight from her pocket and shone it towards two square-looking, dark rocks. Each was about three-feet high and arranged on a north-south axis. Strangely there was no snow on them and no snow beneath them yet. Instead a six-foot, semi-circle of clean dirt showed. She pointed the light at the boulders, then pulled out a compass, shone her light on it, and checked a bearing. Then she pointed the light back at the boulders.

"It's under here," she said.

"What's under here?" he asked.

"The meteorite. Down about three feet."

"They got it out of the cavern? And they buried it here?"

"Just like a pirate's treasure. But worth so much more."

"My god," he breathed. "A legacy from another, distant world."

"Distant but apparently not unreachable," she said, with a gentle smile. "Look at our worlds, Matthew. They've come together. In fact, they've come together more than a few times since the cavern. Anyhow, they said their gift of atonement is there when you want it."

"Are *they* still here?"

"I've no idea where they are. Somehow they talked to grandfather and gave him the location. He asked me to take you to it. By the way, it's not on town property and it's not a Labrador mineral, so no mineral rights' issues; finders keepers." Sky entered coordinates in her GPS and handed it to Matthew. "Record these for posterity," she said.

They trekked back to the Menihek Lodge in Nain and Sky came to his room where he used the Tassimo he'd bought to make them each a cup of warm cocoa. She sat on the desk chair, he sat on the bed. With only the desk lamp on, the room was filled with yellow, suffused light making it warm and cozy.

With her grandfather back in his house, and young Joe Lightfoot living there to help care for him during his home rehab program, it was decided that Matthew should stay at the Menihek Lodge.

He had finally met Sky's grandfather; they had liked each other immediately and spent many hours in conversation covering subjects as diverse as climate change, the state of mining in Canada, and their respective family losses. The only subject St. Onge did not want to discuss was 'the others.' At least not now.

Matthew had arrived back from Montreal that day, and was pleased to tell Sky of the gold find and how his company wasn't going up in smoke. He also told of his visit with Chantal and that he'd told her all about Sky. He also told her of Jacquard's new job offer.

"Matthew, if you dig up that meteorite, you'll be a millionaire many times over," she said. "You don't have to work."

"As you said, it's there if we need it," he answered. "I tend to think we'll never need it. Then, sometime in the future, with wear and tear and erosion, some little Innu kid is going to stub his or her toe on a nasty boulder up here and be one very happy kid."

They both smiled and then Sky put down her cocoa on the desk. She moved over to sit beside him on the bed. She took one of his hands in hers. "I want you to go back to Montreal and see Helene," she said, her tone brooking no argument.

"Not going to happen," he answered.

"She may want to have another go at your marriage, Matthew."

"There is no marriage," he answered. "It was dissolved. At her insistence."

"Nevertheless, don't you think she deserves one more chance?"

"You mean because I killed our daughter?" He refused to look at her, his lips compressed in a thin, angry line.

"You didn't kill your daughter, Matthew.

"Also, I promised I'd never hurt you, Sky. And I meant it. My life is with you."

"But I don't want to go through our lives, never knowing if you're wondering about a second chance with Helene."

"I'm not," he said, firmly. "We both agreed that there was no way forward for us. That we both had to leave the bad…and the good…behind us. New beginnings. New horizons. Clean slate. All that fresh start stuff."

"Would you go and see her. For me? To set my mind at rest?"

"I want to build a life with you, Sky. I love you to death. And I want to start over."

"I understand that but I want *all* of you, Matthew. In 20 years I don't want you pondering in some far off corner of your brain if you should have seen her one more time."

"I'll see her after we're married. We can both drop in for a visit. Tea, cookies and old times."

"Are you worried about seeing her? Afraid your feelings for her will come back?"

He looked at Sky. How was he going to make her understand that he had already made a major choice in life, and there was nothing that was going to change his mind?

"There are no feelings left," he reiterated. "They were bashed, punched, whacked, kicked, trampled, discarded and eventually buried with a shovel on the side of a hill with no grave marker. And for good measure, she buried the damn shovel."

"Then you shouldn't be nervous over one last visit. For my peace of mind? I just can't invest in another relationship unless it's bulletproof."

* * *

It was a bitterly cold morning on the Nain airport ramp with the breaths of four individuals competing with Bob Crummy's running truck to see which could produce the most water vapor in the air. It was 9:30 AM and dawn was barely breaking, heralded once again only by a few golden slivers in the sky over the frozen bay. The sun would rise soon. Beside them, the Beaver's propeller sputtered and wind-milled as it warmed up after a layover the night before.

Buzz Neil had stowed Matthew's gear in the rear of the aircraft; he was then busy doing his walk-around to make sure the wing and control surfaces were free of ice or other impediments and the craft was shipshape. Two wooden chocks sat in front of the skis to ensure the airplane didn't leave without him.

Crummy stood off to one side as Sky and Matthew said good-bye. While Crummy pretended to be fascinated by something out on the bay, his exceptional ears never missed a note. By the side of the airport building, Atemu and Solomon – Crummy's White Shepherd – chased each other in fun. Atemu's leg had healed well.

"This is plain silly, Sky," Matthew said, holding her about the waist, both their parka hoods down for an anticipated good-bye kiss.

"Not to me," she countered. "I don't like loose ends. She wanted the divorce, not you."

"So I'm travelling almost a thousand miles to have coffee with my ex-wife who hates the sight of me."

"She doesn't hate you and she doesn't blame you, Matthew. She told me so."

"Fine. Good. Done. We're all guilt free."

"You have to see your boss anyhow."

"I can phone him and say I accept the job on two conditions: two weeks off for our honeymoon and a nice house in George River for my new wife after we're married."

"Married?" she said, without making further comment. She did, however, smile.

"And believe me, George River would welcome a doctor in the village."

The Beaver engine suddenly coughed several times and shot flame and black smoke through the engine exhaust. Buzz froze and looked over at it. The engine resumed its run.

"Backfire," Buzz called, still looking suspiciously at the engine.

Sky looked alarmed.

"It's nothing," Matthew said. "Long as it doesn't quit on us during takeoff."

Sky looked back at him. "That's not funny, Matthew," she said.

"Hey, you wanted me to go."

He could see the wheels turning in her head and realized she was truly nervous. He put his fingers under her chin and raised her face to his. "I'm kidding. I'm sorry, I shouldn't have joked about it. It's a radial engine. They're famous for not liking the cold."

Still, it had been well warmed up, he thought to himself.

"Alright," she said, worriedly.

The engine coughed again, sputtered and then resumed its normal sound. A puzzled Buzz climbed into the cockpit, examined his instruments, gave it a little throttle and then backed off. Everything seemed normal. He shrugged.

Atemu arrived, jumped up on Matthew once, and then sat in the snow, tail wagging. Matthew leaned forward and he and Sky kissed, long and slow."

She broke away. "When you're with Helene, I want you to look at how you're feeling, Matthew. Don't treat this lightly."

"Sky, I'm not going to do to you what that Van Horne idiot did years ago."

"I know that, Matthew," she said, her eyes starting to moisten.

"Hey, I don't have to go," he reminded her gently.

"Yes you do. You do have to go," she replied, swallowing hard, her confused emotions welling up inside her.

"Sky, why are you torturing yourself?"

"Because this is the way it has to be. She called you. It's plain, she wants to see you again. Maybe she's sorry she wasn't more forgiving. Maybe she's rethinking everything."

"*Now* she wants to talk."

Sitting in the snow, Atemu whined softly, tail wagging hopefully. He looked from one to the other, an almost puzzled expression on his furry face.

Matthew pulled her close and she held him equally tight. Crummy looked off, still obsessed with the sunrise. They were both thankful for his discretion. Buzz was also making himself overly busy with nothing. They continued to hold each other, the aircraft waiting.

"Shades of Casablanca," Matthew muttered. "Of all the gin joints...."

"Stop it," Sky said, blinking swiftly and taking a swipe at him.

"You're asking me to choose between you and Helene? You know I've already done that."

"No, I'm asking you to make sure you're going to be happy with me for the remainder of your life. If that's what you really want."

Matthew sighed heavily. He knew a losing battle when he saw one. "I'll call you."

They kissed again and Matthew and the pilot boarded the airplane.

Buzz waved to Crummy who ran forward and pulled the chocks away from the skis. The engine grew louder and the airplane began to taxi out from the ramp towards the runway. Unlike the Cessna equipped with straight skis that Matthew had flown back to Nain, the Beaver had "wheel penetration skis' that allowed the wheels to poke through and enabled the airplane to land on both tarmac and snow. It also allowed for some turning capability by applying brakes to either wheel.

Crummy came over to Sky who watched the airplane taxing to the end of the runway.

The engine backfired again.

"Why is it doing that?" she asked Crummy.

"Cold," Crummy said.

"Damn," she said, unable to stop a few tears rolling down her cheeks.

"He's a good guy, so why are you sending him back to his ex-wife?" Crummy asked. Crummy knew Sky's story. In fact, Crummy seemed to know everything.

"I read somewhere that if you truly love someone, let them go. If they come back, they're yours forever."

Crummy snorted: "Yeah. And, if they don't come back, then what? Stalk 'em!"

"Not funny."

"Nor is taking life's directions off a bloody cereal box," he snorted. He reached in in his pocket, pulled out a dog biscuit and gave it to Atemu. Then he dug out another and gave it to Solomon. Finishing the biscuit, Atemu crossed to Sky and sat beside her.

Sky wondered if she'd made a mistake after all. She was betting Matthew's love for her would outweigh almost a decade of marriage, common memories, a shared history, and a laundry list of complicated emotions ranging from hurt to guilt to love, and finally, to perceived obligation. Especially on his part.

As for the two of them, all they had personally shared were some weeks in an unreal environment that would certainly never occur again. They hadn't experienced a birthday, celebrated a Christmas, taken a vacation, or lived for any appreciable time in the real world. So why would he come back? Maybe she had blown her chance at happiness, she thought. Maybe she really was screwed up. Thoughts of a Dear John email or a somber phone call saying he needed to spend more time in Montreal, ran through her mind.

The airplane engine began its final run up on the runway. Sky couldn't help herself; tears spilled over onto her cheeks. Would this be the last time she saw him?

Atemu looked at her, looked at the airplane and barked. She turned away from Crummy hoping he wouldn't see her shoulders shaking uncontrollably.

On the runway the aircraft had begun to move forward and Sky wished nothing more than to be able to stop it. To tell him not to go.

Atemu came round, looked at her teary-eyed face, and seemed to make up his mind.

He suddenly dashed off towards the runway. The aircraft was slowly building speed on its take-off run. Flat out, doing at least twenty-five miles an hour, Atemu crossed the ramp and raced on an angle to intercept the aircraft.

Inside the Beaver, the tail hadn't lifted yet and so Matthew and Buzz were both looking out the sides of the runway for guidance. As the aircraft's tail lifted, Buzz spotted Atemu. They were now able to see their surroundings out the windscreen. Matthew also saw the black dot growing ever larger as the dog aimed to reach a point farther down the runway before they did.

"What the hell is he doing?" he shouted to Buzz. "Do you see him?"

The Beaver was at 60 knots now and getting faster by the second. Atemu was most certainly on an angled collision course and he had the speed to make it happen.

"Stop, Buzz!" Matthew yelled, though he knew they couldn't stop in time to avoid a collision if the dog didn't slow.

"Can't," Buzz said, through gritted teeth. "Committed!"

Matthew knew that meant that they were past the point of aborting the takeoff. If they tried, they'd likely go off the end of the runway and crash. In fact, with skis on, it was almost a certainty. As their speed allowed their rudder to become active, Buzz tried to slew them away from Atemu.

Out the opposite side window, Matthew could see Sky running towards the runway. At about the same time, Atemu disappeared under the nose, reaching the skis as they swept past. Matthew was sure he felt a bump as the aircraft lifted into the air.

"We missed him, we missed him!" Buzz shouted.

Matthew twisted in his seat as the aircraft made a climbing left turn. His heart sank on seeing the motionless figure of Atemu lying in the snow on the runway.

"No, we hit him…oh Jesus…we hit him!" Matthew yelled.

"I'm sure we missed him," Buzz asserted. "I know we missed him!"

"He's lying on the runway."

"You serious?" Buzz cried. "Damn it to hell!"

"We have to go back," Matthew said.

But Buzz was already turning onto his downwind leg. Within a minute he was into his base leg in the circuit.

The pilot muttered GUMPS to himself as a quick landing checklist. It was a pre-landing acronym used by fixed wing pilots to check gas, undercarriage, mixture, propeller, seat belts & switches.

As they descended on their final approach, Matthew could see over the aircraft nose that they were going to beat Sky to the fallen dog who was much farther down the runway.

Buzz throttled back, now perfectly lined up. Abruptly the engine died. "What the heck?" he exclaimed. He'd lost all power. Quickly he tried to restart it.

Nothing happened. The engine was dead.

Matthew eyed the ASI and altimeter and helped out: "Air speed 75 knots, altimeter 300 feet, Buzz. Can we make the strip?"

"I don't know," the pilot responded, abandoning any further attempt to get his power back. He had no choice other than to attempt a dead stick landing. "Can't undershoot; nothing but friggen rocks down there."

Their airspeed bled off further; the aircraft began to sink faster. "Damn!" He worked the control column, keeping the wings level, and dropping the nose, and trading precious altitude to stay above stall speed.

They settled lower. "C'mon, c'mon!" he said through gritted teeth, mentally willing the aircraft to stay aloft. "Gonna be so close!"

However, thanks to the skill of the seasoned bush pilot, Buzz Neil managed to touch down at the extreme edge of the runway; they shot past Sky with Buzz already braking as best he could in the snow. He applied full brakes on the port side and slewed the airplane round, possibly a trifle too hard. They skidded to a stop within 25 feet of Atemu.

Breathing a sigh of relief, Matthew said: "Great job, Buzz!" He jumped out, hearing Sky crying Atemu's name from down the runway. He ran to the dog, dropped to his knees and was relieved to see he was panting. His eyes were closed, however, and he wasn't moving. Matthew bent close: "Atemu, boy…Atemu?"

He waited for a reaction but there was none. Recalling his RCAF first aid training he began exploring the dog's body for cuts or blood as Sky ran up and threw herself down beside him.

"Is he breathing," she rasped.

"Yes," Matthew said, shortly.

"Let me," Sky said, gently easing Matthew away, her concern and fear replaced by her professionalism.

She pulled up an eyelid, checked his pupils. Next she lifted his leg and took his pulse high on his inner thigh, looking at her watch as she did so.

"Good," she muttered.

Leaning close, she expertly probed Atemu's body searching for obvious broken bones. Up and down she went, fingering his ribs, exploring each limb and palpitating his belly region. She paid particular attention to his head and neck, feeling his skull and then, one-by-one, his vertebrae down to his tail. Atemu's eyes remained closed.

Bob Crummy's truck skidded to a stop beside them. He jumped out and grabbed two blankets from a wooden box in its bed. Solomon sat obediently in the back, watching the action.

Carefully they eased Atemu onto the blankets. With Crummy's and Matthew's help, Sky cradled his neck and head; they turned him over. She checked him on the opposite side too and then stood up.

"I can't find anything," she said, still out of breath from her run. "Have to transport him to the clinic so I can use the ultrasound and see if he's bleeding internally. Diane has a blood pressure cuff for dogs as well."

Matthew raised his eyebrows in surprise and Sky caught his gesture.

"Any outpost nurse or doctor that doesn't know the anatomy and most of the physiology of a dog within a few weeks of getting here isn't planning on staying," she said, a worried look on her face.

Matthew nodded his head towards the pilot. Sky looked over to see a dejected Buzz standing by the plane, guilt written all over him. "It wasn't your fault, Buzz," Sky called, standing with Matthew.

"I didn't think I hit him," Buzz said, walking over to join the three of them. "Anyhow, we owe him a debt of gratitude because of our engine trouble. If we'd turned south instead of coming back in to land, we might have been further down the coast where Matthew and I probably would have plowed into a mountainside or wound up in the drink."

"Well, don't that beat all?" Crummy said suddenly, a grin lighting up his face. He was looking over their shoulders; he pointed.

The three of them spun around and stared in amazement at Atemu. He was sitting on the blankets, his tail waving slowly. Then he stood up, shook himself and bounded around them as frisky as an eight-week-old puppy.

"What the hell?" Matthew said. "Was he knocked out?"

"I doubt that," Crummy said. "I was going to side with Buzz because I thought he missed him by six feet or so. But he was lying in the snow when I got here, so who am I to argue?"

"What did you see, Bob?" Matthew asked.

"I saw the airplane go by Atemu and then he seemed to drop for no reason."

"Sky?" Matthew asked.

"I thought he was going to collide with the airplane and I looked away at the last second. I didn't see what happened."

Sky got down on her haunches and Atemu came to her, licked her face and then went to Matthew who also leaned down and scratched him behind an ear."

"That's one smart dog," Crummy said. "Right Sky?" He gave her a knowing look and an imperceptible wink.

Sky looked at Atemu and then back to Crummy. Now she understood what had just happened. She smiled and nodded. "You're right, Bob. Maybe smarter than me!"

Crummy grinned and Matthew looked questioningly at her.

"It's nothing, Matthew," she said. "Look at him. Obviously he's in good health. So, how about taking your flight bag off that damn airplane?"

"Roger!" he said, with a grin and a nod to Buzz.

But then he gently he took Sky's arm and led her some feet away from the others. "So I guess it's safe to give you this now?" He handed her a small, navy-blue, velvet-covered box.

Sky stared at it, her lower lip trembling. "What is it, Matthew?" she asked, though she knew full well.

"The diamond your grandfather gave to me."

"The one seated in the rock? It's too light."

"Well, I may have had some modifications made to it."

"This is a ring, isn't it?"

"Maybe."

"Aren't you supposed to ask a girl if she'll marry you before you give her the ring?"

"I'm presumptuous."

"What if I say no?"

"I'll ask you again."

"What if I say no, again?"

"I'll keep asking you until you say yes. I can be really annoying when I put my mind to it. Eventually, you'll cave, just to get some peace. Open the box, Sky.

She opened the small case to reveal a magnificent 18-karat yellow gold ring as a setting for a sizeable diamond cut in the shape of a four-pointed star. Surrounding and outlining the star were sixteen sparkling blue sapphires set into the gold.

"One sapphire for every day we spent on our Labrador odyssey," he said. "The center diamond is cut to signify the North Star. So you'll never lose your direction in life, of course."

He took the ring and knelt in the snow. "Sky St. Onge, will you marry me? Will you make me the happiest guy on this runway?"

Back at the plane, Buzz Neal and Bob Crummy were watching them curiously. When Matthew went down on one knee, they looked at each other and grinned.

"He's got a ring, alright," Buzz said.

"Better be a nose ring cause that's an alpha gal he's hooking up with," Crummy responded.

Sky was nodding at Matthew now and she extended her left hand toward him.

"Mind taking off the mitt?" he asked, drolly.

With a laugh and a tear in her eye, she yanked it off. He slipped the ring on her finger and she raised it high above her head where it caught the first rays of the morning sun rising over the Labrador Sea; it shone on her finger like white hot fire.

Beat that, Rocky...

"Oh my God, it's stunning," she breathed.

"The diamond is okay, but it's actually you who are stunning," he said, standing up.

They went into each other's arms and kissed until both needed to come up for air.

At the plane, Crummy shook his head with a grin and Buzz unloaded the flight bag. Atemu immediately seized the leather handle with his teeth and growled fiercely as he wrestled it across the snow and away from the aircraft. Crummy advanced to save the bag in case the dog started chewing holes in it.

Matthew turned and watched the tussle for a moment as the tug-of war began. "Looks like one individual doesn't want me to leave," he said, laughing.

"Actually, there are two," Sky replied, pulling him close. Placing her arm securely in his, she led him back towards the airfield ramp leaving Bob Crummy and Atemu to complete their tug of war over the flight bag. "And now, we can wed and live happily ever after."

"Like in the fairy tales?" he asked.

"Yes, my every wish will be your command," she replied.

"Er...okay," he answered.

Sky looked up at him with that beautiful, happy, dolphin-like grin slowly emerging: "You train so easily, hero. I'm going to like this arrangement."

"Me too," Matthew replied. "I think...."

***

If you enjoyed J. Richard Wright's **Torngat,** you may wish to order J. Richard Wright's first novel *The Plan,* also available on Amazon. And please remember to write an Amazon review for either book. The option is on the web site where you ordered it. Now please read on for a description and an excerpt.

THE PLAN

After U.S. Army Lieutenant Clay Montague is attacked by a sentient evil in the jungles of Panama, it follows him into civilian life. Recovering in a VA hospital, his nightly terrified ramblings are heard by a chaplain undergoing a personal crisis of faith. Believing something supernatural is involved, Father Gallo contacts Cardinal Malachi in the Vatican awakening a covert group of demon trackers.

Released from hospital, Clay's life is good until he begins to lose people he loves to savage and mysterious attacks. Under suspicion of murder, he spirals into depression and poverty until the Roman Catholic Church rescues him. He soon finds there is a price. Paired with a beautiful young nun with a reputed gift of second sight, he is asked to track down an evil as old as Creation. From Panama to a small town in Vermont, and then to New York, Rome, London and Scotland, the momentum of the chase builds, heading for a resolution the pursuers could never have planned for, nor desired.

And, as the hunters become the hunted, forbidden love, betrayal and murder challenge their beliefs and reality forcing Clay and Sister Maria Lapierre to battle for their love, their lives and their souls.

Available now on Amazon.com or Amazon.ca, or through my web site: www.jrichardwright.com
Or, you may simply go to Google and type in: *The Plan* **by J. Richard Wright, and it should take you directly to a page where you may order it. The following pages contain a brief excerpt from** *The Plan.*

THE PLAN

Tonight, Clay Montague knew he might die.

But as a U.S. Lieutenant with the 3rd Ranger Battalion of the 75th Ranger Regiment out of Fort Benning, Georgia, he also admitted to himself that this feeling wasn't particularly unusual when in-country.

From his crouched position by a scrub palm somewhere deep in the jungle near the Atlantic side of the Panama Canal, Clay straightened his six-foot frame. He wiped sweat from the corners of a wide, handsome mouth. Flint-grey eyes peered from his grease-darkened face and raked the darkened jungle. He brushed a large beetle off his battle dress. Not a leaf stirred, not a bush moved.

Operation *Just Cause* was in full swing as U.S. forces poured into the small Central American country to oust and capture dictator and strongmen Manuel Noriega. Panama City had already fallen to American forces as well as the airport, areas near the Panama Canal and Rio Hato. But though the majority of the 16,000 member Panamanian Defense Force (PDFs) had been defeated, there were still pockets scattered throughout the countryside in small garrisons called *cuartels*.

To avoid needless killings, U.S. Forces had created "capitulation missions" and sent Special Forces' elements with Spanish-speaking liaison officers, to arrange and coordinate the PDF surrender. While most garrisons quickly laid down their arms, contingents of hard core resistance fighters had also fled and night missions had become extremely dangerous. With the PDFs showing unexpected resilience and their Hunter Platoons not to be trifled with on their own turf, Clay's orders were to find them, coordinate their surrender or neutralize them.

Removing his M-1 steel helmet, he ran fingers through his thick brown hair now soaked with sweat and the stench of a nearby swamp. He waited a moment longer before finally shouldering the M249 Squad Automatic Weapon, a SAW light machine gun capable of delivering a devastating volume of 5.56 mm slugs at the rate of 725 rounds per minute. He signaled his ten men to get ready to move out from the protective cover of the Mangrove thicket.

SOMETHING ISN'T RIGHT!

A small inner voice nagged him, challenging his professional confidence. He ignored it. After all, they merely had to cross a small, unprotected clearing. No big deal...maybe.

He looked up.

The silvery disc of a bloated full moon slipped silently behind a thick cloud and a grey shroud settled over the jungle like a huge, humid blanket. He waved his arm and one-by-one his men moved like phantoms in the night, shadowy, furtive, hunched-over gnomes scurrying frantically for fresh cover in a jungle ripe with hidden peril. Quickly he followed them. Reaching the other side of the clearing, they again concealed themselves amongst the ferns, sedge, and mangrove forest; all motion ceased and they turned to hushed figures of stone.

Silently they waited.

He scanned the area.

Nothing moved.

Grinning inwardly at his own angst, he tried to shrug off the unsettled feeling gnawing at him. His point men were out, the jungle was alive with sounds and there were no fresh traces of the enemy. Every sign indicated they were secure for the moment.

Still the feeling refused to leave. It whispered that somehow, tonight, tragedy was poised to strike. Perhaps in the form of a stray enemy patrol, the deadly bite of a bushmaster or copperhead, or a bunch of coarsely-woven, grass-mat-covered punji pits housing upright, sharpened stakes ready to impale some poor soldier like a hapless butterfly crucified by an entomologist's straight pin.

Clay was grateful for one advantage. As a prior Panamanian ally, their U.S. unit had availed itself of American jungle warfare training facilities at Fort Sherman Military Reservation and the Pina Range Complex right in Panama. They had trained throughout 2,300 acres of both single and double canopy jungle, now enabling them to read their surroundings like natives.

WATCH OUT!

Damn, he was being as careful as he could. He shrugged off the inner voice and glanced down the barely visible overgrown pathway stretching into the night mist.

The motionless air steamed with moisture. Beads of sweat ran down Clay's face. The moon finally slipped from behind the cloud and bathed the area in a blue-white wash casting deep, fragmented shadows along the jungle trail.

The sounds of feeders seeking their prey suddenly exploded in death screams as the hunted squirmed helplessly in the jaws of a predator. Its life was quickly snuffed out in a squealing, savage tearing of flesh and crunching of bone. Clay felt a momentary sympathy as the screams gurgled shrilly in mid-note and went silent. The hush uttered a finality that only death could bring.

The night scene was beautiful, Clay thought. More alluring, however, if every patch of black didn't have the potential to hide death. He glanced up at a break in the leafy forest canopy at the mass of stars winking silently in the black sky; the jungle had become silent again.

Time to move out.

Clay lifted his hand. The patrol rose as one and made ready to resume their march. Cursing the heat, and nervously swinging their weapons to the left and right to cover the shadows, the men made their way cautiously down the trail. Adrenaline levels surged at the slightest noise or the barest glimmer of movement; restless eyes probed every leafy nook and cranny of the jungle. Silently, they bore the stress of knowing that at any moment an enemy ambush could send a withering hail of fire into their ranks and cut them to pieces.

Ahead, Clay held up a hand.

The gesture was repeated down the line of ten men, bone weary in their heavy battle gear. Warily they came to a halt, teeth and eyes shining like beacons amidst the camouflage grease.

Looking back Clay whispered: "We look like a damn traveling minstrel show." His half-hearted attempt to ease the tension caused a few men to grin; others made no sign they'd heard. Edgy, Clay thought.

His disquiet lingered.

SOMETHING IS TERRIBLY WRONG....

A quick burst of machine gun fire echoed in the distance. *What the hell...?*

The jungle immediately grew silent again but his suspicions were confirmed. The enemy was obviously on the move. A few more distant shots rang out. Time to trust those instincts alright, to pay heed to the tiny, visceral voice from his gut that loyally warned of subliminal changes in jungle and animal patterns.

The hair on Clay's neck prickled upward....

The jungle maintained its deadly quiet! *How close were they?*

Not a bird, not a cricket, not an animal stirred in a jungle that, minutes before, had pulsed with a cacophony of life.

Breathlessly the patrol waited, listened, aching, straining to penetrate the sudden hush, to pick up the slightest snap of a branch whipping back on a uniform, the rustle of leaves, or the careful tread of a combat boot in the dirt.

The hairs on the back of Clay's neck were at attention now.

SOMETHING IS NEAR....

The ten men tensed; uneasy and sweating, they waited....

After five minutes of remaining motionless Clay could feel the strain in every muscle and bone. Nerves were strung as taunt as bow strings. They waited another two minutes.

Still nothing, not a whisper.

The resumption of the jungle sounds began almost as abruptly as they had ceased. The incessant babble of night predators running, slithering, or winging their way through the moist air mixed with the squawk of prey being run to the ground. Insects buzzed madly. A few howler monkeys screamed their rage at being awakened by the distant shooting and their personal instinct for danger; a sudden, heavenly cool breeze wafted through the trees.

Clay breathed a sigh of relief and slapped at an insect whining around his ear. The jungle was telling him there was nothing nearby. Perhaps the fire came from a nervous sentry at a jungle outpost. He checked his map; they were heading for a valley.

He dismissed the persistent little voice warning of doom and gloom.

Still, it nattered on.

***

FOR THOSE READERS WHO ARE INTERESTED, HERE ARE A FEW FACTS ABOUT THE TORNGAT MOUNTAINS OF LABRADOR...

CANADA'S TORNGAT MOUNTAIN

The Torngat Mountains of Labrador run up Canada's eastern coast from Saglek Bay to the northern tip of Labrador with the range almost evenly split between the province of Quebec and the province of Newfoundland and Labrador. The entire range covers about 30,000 square kilometers of space, including lowland areas.

Torngat National Park is composed of 9,700 square kilometers of some of the most remote and beautiful scenery in the world, a natural, unspoiled wilderness of sweeping valleys, deep fiords, unending plains and reach-for-the-sky peaks. It is populated by relatively few people but many animals including: caribou, polar bears, barren-ground black bears, wolves, foxes, Arctic hares, rock ptarmigan and peregrine falcons. Along the coast, seals and whales regularly make their presence known.

Specifically, the park extends from Saglek Fjord in the south, (including all islands in the fiord) to the very northern tip of Labrador; and, from the provincial boundary with Québec in the west, to the iceberg-choked waters of the Labrador Sea in the east.

Along the Quebec border of the park are the highest mainland peaks in Canada, east of the Canadian Rocky Mountains. The valleys feature almost 200 glaciers throughout the park.

Over the past 3.9 billion years, scientists have determined that there have been five major events in the Torngat Mountains: Three happened in the Archean Eon, one in the Proterozoic Eon and one in the Jurassic Period.

Only two places in the world can claim rocks older than those in the Torngats; they are in the Northwest Territories, also in Canada, and parts of Australia.

Deep within Nachvak and Saglek fiords, cliffs rise dramatically and abruptly out of the sea, sheer, forbidding walls of rock, some more than 2,700 feet high.

One Canadian explorer, C. R. Tuttle, in 1885, recorded his impressions of entering Nachvak Fiord of the Torngat Mountains in his report in "Our North Land: A full account of the Canadian North-west and Hudson's Bay Route."

"The scene is beyond the possibility of my pen, and I shall not attempt it. The rocks were entirely barren, except here and there, on the lower ranges, where the slopes were gradual, and patches of heather, or bog, or stunted vegetation of some kind, relieved the dullness of their uniform colour. Higher up near the clouds, on the giant precipices, we could see, here and there, a rough broken garment of moss, the growth, probably, of a thousand years. The summits were capped with perpetual snow in many places that sparkled and glowed in the morning sun, as its rays broke through the parting clouds like crowns of glory. The prospect was strange and wild - strange in the angularity of the steep declivities, bold, rugged, barren and desolate, yet altogether, as one passes within the entrance, continuing to inspire a sense of security."

In fact, Parks Canada has made it possible for tourists to visit the Torngat Mountains National Park. Should you wish to do so, check out the Parks Canada and Torngat Mountains web sites for information on how to plan a visit.